'Gloriously r
brave and br
Rachel Lucas

'An absolute triumph...'
Jill Mansell

'an emotional, intelligent,
beautifully structured novel'
Alex Marwood

'a beautiful and heart-wrenching
ory of a daughter's love for her mother.'
Julie Cohen

'Coleman is a
brilliant storyteller'
Eve Chase

'one of those captivating novels
that puts you under a spell as a reader'
Lucy Dillon

Powerfully mov
glowing with lo

'Glorious.'
Sarah Hilary

The Summer of Impossible Things

The Summer of Impossible Things

ROWAN COLEMAN

EBURY
PRESS

3 5 7 9 10 8 6 4 2

Ebury Press, an imprint of Ebury Publishing
20 Vauxhall Bridge Road,
London SW1V 2SA

Penguin
Random House
UK

Ebury Press is part of the Penguin Random House group of
companies whose addresses can be found at
global.penguinrandomhouse.com

First published in the UK in 2017 by Ebury Press

www.penguin.co.uk

A CIP catalogue record for this book is available from the British
Library

Hardback ISBN: 9781785032417
Trade Paperback ISBN: 9781785032424

Printed and bound in Great Britain by Clays Ltd, St Ives PLC

Penguin Random House is committed to a sustainable future for
our business, our readers and our planet. This book is made from
Forest Stewardship Council® certified paper.

MIX
Paper from
responsible sources
FSC® C018179

*To Lily, who is so clever, kind
and courageous, and has the
whole universe at her feet.*

'Why, sometimes I've believed as many as six impossible things before breakfast.'
Through the Looking Glass, *Lewis Carroll*

PROLOGUE

* *

OXFORDSHIRE,
6 JUNE 2007

Watching my mother's face for the first time since the night she died, I am altered. I am unravelled and undone – in one instant becoming a stranger in my own skin.

There is a theory that just by looking at something you can transform the way it behaves; change the universe and how it works at quantum level, simply by seeing. The observer effect, we call it in physics, or the uncertainty principle. Of course the universe will do what the universe always does, whether we are watching or not, but these are the thoughts I can't shake out of my head as I watch my mother's fragile image, flickering as it's projected on the wall. That just by looking at this film of her, I have changed the fabric of everything I thought I knew.

Just seconds ago my mother told me and my sister that my dad – the man I grew up with, and whom I love – is not my biological father. Yes, the universe around me shifted and reformed for ever; and yet the second she said it I understood that I have always known it to be true, always felt my incongruity, in every beat of my heart, tilt of my head. In my outsider's blue eyes.

There is no choice now but to watch on: the course is set and I am travelling it. I have to see, no matter what, although looking will change everything. It's simple physics, the mystery of the universe encapsulated in these intimate, pivotal moments.

But there is no equation to express how I feel, looking at the face of the woman I have missed every second for the last eight months.

She sits in the Oxfordshire country garden of the house I grew up in. The same garden is in full and glorious bloom outside the creaking barn door now, the roses still bear the scars from her pruning, the azaleas she planted are still in bud. But the garden I am watching her sit in may as well be on Mars, so far away from me does she seem. She is so far away now, out of reach for good. A light-grey, cotton dress blows against her bare brown legs, her hair is streaked with silver, her eyes full of light. There's an old chair from the kitchen, its legs sinking slightly into the soft grass. This must have been recorded in late summer because the rose bushes are in bloom, their dark glossy leaves reflecting the sun. It was probably last summer, just after Dad got the all clear, after a few terrifying weeks in which we thought he might have bowel cancer. That means that as long ago as last summer, months and months before she died, she knew already what she was going to do. I experience this realisation as a physical pain in my chest, searing and hot.

'Although the watch keeps ticking on my wrist,' her captured image is saying, the breeze lifting the hair off her face. 'I am still trapped back there, at least part of me is. I'm pinned like a butterfly to one single minute, in one single hour, on the day that changed my life.'

There are tears in her eyes.

'To everyone around me it might have seemed that I kept walking and talking, appearing to be travelling through time at the allotted sixty seconds per minute, but actually I was static, caught in suspended animation, thinking, always thinking about that one act ... that one ... choice.'

Her fingers cover her face for a moment, perhaps trying to cover the threat of more tears; her throat moves, her chest stills. When her hands fall back down to her lap she is smiling. It's a smile I know well: it's her brave smile.

'I love you, my beautiful daughters.'

It's a phrase that she had said to us almost every day of our lives, and to hear her say it again, even over the thrum of the projector, is something like magic, and I want to catch it, hold it in the palm of my hand.

Leaning forward in her chair, her eyes search the lens, searching me out, and I find myself edging away from her, as if she might try to reach out and touch me.

'I made this film as my goodbye, because I don't know when – or if – I will have the courage to say it in person. It's my goodbye, and something else. It's a message for you, Luna.'

When she says my name, I can feel her breath on my neck as she speaks.

'The truth is, I don't know if I ever want to you to see it, to see any of this. Perhaps you never will. Perhaps here, in this moment, in this way, is the only time I can tell you and Pia about my other life, the life I live alongside the one I have with you girls and your father, the life I live in a parallel universe, where the clock's second hand never moves forward. Yes, I think ... I think this is the only place I'm brave enough to tell you.' She shakes her head, tears glisten, whilst behind her head the ghosts of long-dead bees drone in and out of the foxgloves, collecting pollen over the brickwork of a derelict building.

'You see, once, a long time ago, something really, really bad happened to me, and I did something terrible in return. And ever since that moment, there has been a ghost at my shoulder, following me everywhere I go, waiting everywhere I look, stalking me. And I know, I know that one day I won't be able to outrun him any more. One day he will catch up with me. One day he will have his revenge. One day soon. If you are watching this –' her voice hooks into me '— then he already has me ...'

She draws so close to the lens that we can only see one unfocused quarter of her face; she lowers her voice to a whisper. 'Listen, if you look very hard and very carefully you'll find me in Brooklyn, in the place and the moment I never truly left. At our building, the place I grew up in, that's where you will find me, and the other films I made for you. Luna, if you look hard enough – if you want to look after you know what I did ... He wouldn't let me go, you see. Find me ... please.'

7 JULY 2007

'This distinction between past, present and future
is only an illusion.'

—Albert Einstein

CHAPTER ONE

We travel in a kind of bubble, my little sister Pia and I, sheltered in the quiet, cool interior of an air-conditioned cab, while outside the searing summer streets of an unfamiliar landscape unfold ever outwards as we make each turn. We slip past bridges and buildings that are a kind of second-hand familiar, the relics of the tales that we grew up listening to; a constantly increasing map of a world neither of us have ever visited before, but which is written into our DNA.

Bay Ridge, Brooklyn, is nothing like I imagined it would be after a lifetime of watching movies set in New York State. It's a low, two-storey landscape of wide avenues and neat, wooden-clad houses; small-town America, on the edge of a huge borough that lives right next door, the greatest city on earth. New York seems to peer at Bay Ridge over the expanse of the Hudson with an uninterested shrug.

There is an air of quiet certainty unfurling in the searing July sunshine. Even the people meandering down the sidewalks have an innately serene look about them, as if this place is made only for them, a safe place, a place where the rest of the world never looks, a place where secrets might never be discovered if you know where to hide them. This is where life and love and death can quietly play out, without barely making a ripple of the surface of the planet. It's almost as if when you cross the Brooklyn Bridge times slows down just a little, right at its zenith.

This is the world where our mother grew up, the world she ran away from, never to return. It never occurred to us that one day it would be us travelling back here, all the way back to her starting point. Officially we are here to finally settle her estate, and begin the sale of the long derelict, boarded-up building she co-owned with her sister, a woman she hadn't spoken to in thirty years. The building had once been her home, the centre of her universe. Unofficially, secretly, we came because she told us to. To look for her, and to look for clues about my biological father, whose existence still seems like a mangled dream to me.

'She could have just got it wrong,' Pea had said after the film ended, disturbed dust still settling in the light of Dad's projector that we'd had to borrow in secret. 'I mean, in her darkest moment, she had delusions. She had fantasies. She could have just been living a nightmare out loud, that could be it.'

'Yes,' I said, slowly, uncertainly, letting her words seeps into me through every pore. 'Yes, it could be that ... but ...'

I looked at my sister, and I knew she was beginning to see what I already knew. My bright-blue eyes, the only blue eyes for generations on either side of the family, as far back as anyone can remember.

'But you have to find out if it might be true,' Pea finished for me. 'They loved each other so much, especially back then, when she left Brooklyn, left her family to be with him. It just doesn't make sense that there would be another man … But even if there was, it doesn't change anything. You're still you. You're still our Luna.'

She couldn't know that I had always felt a little bit like a stranger in my own family, a little bit out of step with them. That, somehow, what Mum said was strangely comforting.

Dad had wanted to come on this trip, but we'd persuaded him to stay at home. Even now, months later, he was so fragile after losing her, his blood pressure still high, and the doctor didn't recommend flying. We didn't tell him about the film, even though we could have. We could have asked him outright if it was true, and taken him at his word, but we didn't. It seemed too cruel for him to lose a wife and a daughter in the space of a few months, even if we loved each other in just the same way as we always have. I think him knowing that I knew would hurt him. So we begged him to stay at home, be taken care of by his friends, and let us sort out the paperwork. And maybe uncover secrets, and part of me. The part of me that was most like my mother truly believed she might be waiting there for us.

Her sister, Stephanie, had wanted to sell the minute their father, our grandfather, had died in 1982. Lawyers' letters came in the post thick and fast and, although I didn't really know what they were about, I could see how just the sight of the distinctive airmail envelope would make my mother's hands tremble. Mum had refused to sell, she wouldn't budge. She had her reasons; we never knew them, but whatever they were, perhaps she had planned it this way, because she had left her half of her family home to Pea and me. And now – just when we need it – there is money waiting to be accessed. One trip to Bay Ridge, put the building on the market, and there should be enough from the proceeds to get my sister back on her feet, this time for good. And perhaps I can find answers to questions I've always had, even if I haven't quite known what they were.

Pea – I've called her that since she was born – sits nervously; her fingers twitch in her lap, her nails are broken and bitten down, knuckles pinks and grazed, with combat, but not a fist fight. These are the scars of her daily battle not to reach for a drink or a pill. Twenty-four years old and eight weeks clean this time. Last time she stayed sober for eighteen months, and I thought maybe she had cracked it, but then Mum died, suddenly and shockingly. I fought so hard to hold on to her, against the tsunami of grief and chaos that we could both see was coming to sweep her away, but I wasn't strong enough.

This time I won't let my sister down.

This time, I will keep her safe. If I can just hold on to what matters, what is *real*, then I will be able to save her.

Resting the weight of my camera on my thigh, I reach out and take her hand, stilling it. She looks at me from behind the pink, heart-shaped sunglasses she bought at the airport.

'What did you bring that old thing for, anyway?' she asks me, nodding at the camera, my dad's old Pentax, the one he was looking through the very first time he set eyes on Mum. 'You couldn't even get fifty quid for it on eBay. I know, because I tried once. It's all digital now, you know.'

'I know, but this is more than just a camera, it's a ... relic. It's a little piece of Mum and Dad's story, and besides, I like looking at things through a lens. I thought I could shoot the places that Dad shot, recreate the images for him. He might not have been up to making the trip but his camera could, I thought he'd like it.'

'He will like it.' Pea nods. 'You should have been a photographer, not a scientist; you're too artistic to be a scientist.'

'I'm a physicist,' I remind her. 'And actually a lot of what I do is art. How are you feeling?'

'Like I'd really like a drink, a hit or both,' she says. 'But then again, I'm awake, so nothing new there.'

We let the road slip under us in silence for a few moments.

'But how are you?' she asks finally. 'I mean *really*.'

I hesitate; if I were to answer that question accurately I'd say full of rage and grief, terrified and lost, unsure and unable to find a sure-footed place to stand. But I don't. Our beloved mother died from an overdose, and, even after a lifetime of a family that revolved around her depression, we didn't see it coming in time to save her, and I can't forgive myself for that. And more than that, there's a stranger inside me, a stranger who *is* me, a crucial part of me I don't have any reference for, and that unnerves me.

'I think it will be a challenging few days, being here without her,' I say instead, choosing my words carefully. 'I'd always thought we'd come back here one day all together, you, me, Mum and Dad. I always thought there would be an end, like a resolution, and she'd be better, be happy. I never thought the ending would be that she'd—'

'Kill herself,' Pea finishes.

'Christ.' I bow my head, and the now-familiar surge of sickening guilt rises in my throat over the fact that I didn't see what she was about to do. 'How can it be real? How can that be what's really happened? I didn't see it coming. I should have seen it coming. I should have ... but she seemed, better, brighter. Free. I relaxed, I shouldn't have relaxed.'

'Maybe it's better that you didn't,' Pea says. 'That *we* didn't.'

'Pia, how can you say that?'

'Because. Because it wore her out, all that effort at being happy. For our whole childhood, painting on smiles just for us and Dad. She was exhausted by it, but she saw it through, because she loved us. I'd been clean for more than a year, you'd got your doctorate, and were going to move in with Brian. Dad was through the cancer scare. Don't you think she finally thought that now we were all OK, she could just go? Just stop feeling the pain, and go. Don't you think that's why she seemed happier? The end was in sight.'

I don't know how to answer, so I don't speak.

'Seen Brian?' With ease Pea changes the subject from one thing I can't bear to talk about to another.

'No.' I shake my head. 'I'm glad I haven't seen him. He isn't the sort of person you want to see when you're ... conflicted.'

Pea snorts. 'Conflicted. Yep, our mum tops herself and we're "conflicted". I take it back, you are the perfect scientist – analytical to the last.' The spasm of hurt her words cause must show on my face, because she takes off her glasses, and leans into me. 'You know I don't mean it,' she says. 'And, anyway, it was a good job you found out what a flake Brian was before you ended up marrying him. It's good to know if someone will be willing to stick by you in a crisis. And he, well ... you know.'

I do know I'd discovered Brian was on a minibreak in the Lake District with another woman on the day of Mum's funeral. It should hurt me more than it does; after all, we'd been together for two years and talked about making it official. But somehow I am numb to that petty betrayal. It took me leaving Brian to realise that, as much as I liked him, and respected him, I was never in love with him, and he knew that. When I think back, I doubt that he was ever in love with me either; it was more that I fascinated him, I was atypical, an anomaly, and, as a neuroscientist, he liked that about me. I was a woman immersed in the most rational of sciences, determined that my sex wasn't going to hold me back, even though most of the rest of the world I moved in tried to.

I can see, now, the reason I was drawn to him was because I thought he understood me. I thought he was like me, but that was a mistake. It wasn't our similarities that he enjoyed about me; it was our differences that he liked to study.

It probably didn't help that I told him my secret. I shouldn't have told him. That just after Mum died something started happening to me that hadn't happened since I was a little girl. That sometimes, more and more just recently, I see things; people, places … things.

Impossible things. Things that are not there.

CHAPTER TWO

* *

You don't have time to go mad, is what I tell myself. Too many people need you. So just don't go mad. Just don't. It's an inelegant solution, but it's the only one I have. To seek help would be impossible. The news that I had a psychiatric problem would spread through the research community in a matter of hours, and it's hard enough to do the work I do as a woman, a young woman not yet thirty, without there being another reason to call my judgement into question. The mad woman in the attic, that's what they'd called me behind my back. And even if I did get a diagnosis of some kind of psychosis, Brian had already told me the sorts of drugs I might be prescribed and what they'd do to me. They'd stop me thinking.

And if it isn't madness, if it's the side effect of some physical disease, then ... well, I don't have time to be sick either. Best not to think about it, best to put my faith in mind over matter, or anti-matter. That's a physicist's joke.

No, everything is fine. These moments when they happen come and go quickly. They're nothing more than flashes of reflected sunlight on glass. If things get worse, then I'll think again, but for now everything is fine; it's not like there are voices in my head. It's some kind of epilepsy, Brian thought, although I wouldn't let him put me in an MRI machine because I didn't want to know any facts that would have to be acted on. He told me the story of a young French man who'd suffered so many tiny but relentless brain seizures that he lived in a constant state of déjà vu, as if he'd experienced every moment that he lived before. The universe inside our heads hold more mysteries and secrets than the one I've spent my life trying to understand, and yet I know that at its most basic level they are one and the same thing. I won't be partitioned from what matters by medication.

Focus, that's what I have to do. Focus on each single second as it happens; keep hold of what is real. Focus on Pea, and being here, and everything we need to get done. I will try and spend as much time as I can looking through the lens of Dad's camera, because – and I don't have a theory as to why – the ... episodes ... don't seem to happen when I'm looking through the camera, almost as if the lens filters out delusion.

So focus on now, focus.

Because I really don't have time to go mad, we have arrived at our destination.

Our cab slows down and comes to a rest outside our lodging house, the only place we could possibly stay when we decided to make this trip, a set from the love story of my parents. It's in this very house that my dad stayed when he first came to Bay Ridge, on his first major freelance-photography project, embedding himself in with the film crew and shooting behinds the scenes of the first movie he was ever involved with: *Saturday Night Fever*. A film my little sister and I have watched at least a thousand times since we were kids and, in actual fact, far too young to see it.

'Mum and Dad must have walked up and down these streets a million times,' Pea says as we climb out of the cab, stretching our tired and travel-cramped bodies hard against the sky. 'They probably kissed right there, on that piece of sidewalk, under that tree – hey, is that *the* tree?'

'No, wrong street,' I tell her. I know the exact location of the famous tree, because it's at the top of my list of locations to find, to see if it's still standing, and to take a photo of Mum and Dad's names carved into its bark.

As Pea pays the fare, I lift the camera to my eye, searching for the same frame as one of the photos I've pored over so often in Dad's albums. Then this decaying building was neat, pretty, full of pride and house rules, even in the way the geraniums grew so neatly in the window boxes. Now Mrs Finkle's lodging house looks fatigued, slouching into the ground. The once-pristine blue-and-white paint is peeling and cracked, the blue turning grey, the white yellowing like smoker's teeth. Even so, it is a house that someone still loves; you can feel that radiating out of it. I lower the camera when I see something that wasn't in Dad's original photo. A statue of the Virgin

Mary greets us. She is about two feet high, balanced on the window sill nearest the door, inclining slightly downwards, towards a considerable drop. She has clearly been in exactly that perilous position for some time, her paint faded away almost to nothing, her benevolent hands chipped and broken, her eyes white and unseeing. With the lens, without the lens; yes, she is definitely there.

'Luna and Pia, right?' A woman, who can only be Mrs Finkle, opens the front door and stands on the top step. I'd expected a housecoat and maybe rollers, but I am wrong. Mrs Finkle is truly elegant. Her hair, which might once have been blonde, is still glossy but now silver and pinned behind one ear. Wearing a cool white shirt over light denim capri pants, she looks more like a Lauren Bacall than a Mrs Finkle, which makes me smile. I like being wrong; being wrong always leads to something more interesting than being right.

'Yes, hello,' I greet her. 'We're Luna and Pia Sinclair.'

'You're here!' She briefly clasps her hands together in obvious delight as she trots down the steps and hugs me so tightly I can feel the Pentax press into my ribcage. 'Let me look at you!' She takes a step back, her hands on my shoulders, her hazel eyes scanning my face.

'Oh, but I see her in you, I do. I see her in your nose and your ears, and this hair. You know, when your mom left I never thought I'd see her again, but here she is, in you, oh, and you too!' She leaves me to embrace Pea with equal warmth, and I know that I instantly love her. I love her for not noticing my blue eyes or wondering aloud who I take after, and best of all for saying that I look like my beautiful mother.

'You've got your father's crazy hair,' Mrs Finkle says, smiling fondly at Pea's cloud of curls and frizz, which should be as dark as mine, but which she insists on bleaching to oblivion every chance she gets. 'But I see her in you, too. Marissa Lupo lived her life with her chin lifted just a little bit higher than anyone else. You've got that.'

'I have?' Pea's hand rises to her chin, and she smiles too. 'Cool.'

'So, what are we doing standing out here? Come in, come in out of the heat.' Grabbing her bag, Pea follows Mrs Finkle up the neatly swept steps and past the Virgin Mary. 'It's been unbearable this year, I haven't known it so bad since ... Well, I suppose since the year your dad and the rest of the film crew guys came to stay here. The heatwave of nineteen seventy-seven ... Now *that* was a year.'

It's like a little power surge to my brain; that's always the first sign that something is about to happen. Then I sense someone watching me, eyes grazing my skin. I could look away, go inside and ignore the buzzing in my brain, but that doesn't work. Only looking right at an anomaly makes it stop.

As Pea follows Mrs Finkle inside, I turn and make myself see. Searching down to the end of the not-quite-empty street. At its end, in something like a halo of yellow sunlight, there is a young woman watching me. The light dances and dazzles, so that she is out of focus, almost not there. I see her for a split second before she is gone, a cool, blue shadow filling the space where she stood. My head swims as I close my eyes and I feel my knees weaken. Someone walks over my grave. That's what my mother always used to say. Lifting the camera, I look again. The street is empty.

Focus. I need to focus on the here and now.

'Luna, what are you doing?' Pea asks me impatiently from the doorway, which is code for 'please come in here and help me make small talk with this woman'. With one final glance at the empty sidewalk, I follow her up the stairs.

Our apartment is at the top of the house, the border between Mrs Finkle's territory and her guests' clearly marked by where her procession of framed photographs ends, and a clean, white-painted staircase begins. It's bright and light, one small bedroom, bathroom, and an all-purpose living area with a sofa bed and a functional kitchenette.

'Your father will have told you I used to have rooms,' she says. 'All rooms, one bathroom; that was amusing at times.' She smiles fondly. 'These days people want more though. I don't normally have tourists in here. Tourists don't come to Bay Ridge. Normally it's young people looking for a cheap place to stay that's not much of a commute to work. I was so pleased when you called. My last girl just moved in with her boyfriend and I was about to advertise. It was kind of like fate, to have Marissa and Henry's girls here with me. I loved them both, you know.'

'Dad speaks so fondly of you,' Pea says, and she means it, although she doesn't mention Dad's colourful tales of how Mrs Finkle fell for one of the younger men staying with her, and seduced him with the skills of a noir femme fatale. 'He's only sorry not to see you. I think after a life travelling around the world, taking photos of the world's most famous and beautiful, he's finally glad to be at home in his garden, talking to the bumble bees.'

'I was so sorry to hear about your mom. And I'm sorry not to see Henry again,' Mrs Finkle says, her smile enigmatic. 'Those were fun times, the crew, the actors, the filming. Yes, Bay Ridge sure got a little stardust sprinkled over it that year! I loved being a small part of it. You know, Travolta nearly came to my house once.'

'Did he?' Pea grins from ear to ear, her love of the subject of Dad's first major photographic assignment knows no bounds. Once she had had a framed copy of every one of the photos he took on the set of *Saturday Night Fever* adorning the walls of her flat. When we were girls she watched it at least once a week. 'Did he stay here?'

'Probably a good job he didn't.' Mrs Finkle covers her heart with her hands. 'I wouldn't have been responsible for my actions; that man, so handsome. Like a Michelangelo in blue jeans. Well, get settled in. You can see me as much you want, or as little. I'd prefer the former, but I guess you have a lot you want to do and see, and you'll finally get the Lupo building sold?'

'That's the plan,' I tell her. 'It's seems like the right time at last.'

'I think it is.' Mrs Finkle nods. 'That place, it's been boarded up and crumbling away for so long, it's like that little corner of the avenue is stuck right there, the day your mother left. Though, now that I think of it, your grandfather lived there a couple more years after she left. But every time I've looked up at it in the past thirty years, I could almost see her there, leaning on the fire escape, smoking and waiting. Waiting and smoking. I'm glad she won't be waiting anymore.'

CHAPTER THREE

* *

'Can you imagine her, walking these streets?' Pea asks me as we trail back along 4th Avenue, after a late dinner of burger and fries. 'Young and sexy, like in those photos Dad took of her in hot-pants and wedged heels. She was quite something back in the day.'

'I can,' I say, thinking of one particular photograph, the first photograph of her that Dad ever took, one that is carefully tucked into the back pocket of my jeans right now. In it, Mum is twenty years old; the light of a sunny Brooklyn spring evening dapples her tanned skin, her slim arms shielding her eyes. Half of her face is in shade, revealing slightly parted glossed lips. She is wearing a striped singlet, no bra underneath; her throat is bare, effortlessly sexy in a way that seems out of reach to me. I'd first found the photo when I was twelve years old, awkward and plump. I'd been so beguiled, so envious of the ease with which she had inhabited her skin, that I'd stolen it from between the pages of a rarely-looked-at album and kept it ever since. After Mum died I'd remembered it with a start, fearful that I hadn't taken enough care of this precious image of her, that it would be lost. But I'd found it, at the bottom of a shoebox of old photos and drawings that I'd collected over the years. From that moment on I never went anywhere without it. And, as the night sets in, I'll be content to simply look at it until I fall asleep, hoping to dream of her here, in the very place the photograph was taken.

'She always wore the most beautiful clothes,' I say. 'Always turned heads.'

'Like you would if you stopped dressing like a teenager,' Pea says pulling at the hem of my habitual white T-shirt, which was paired with my usual faded jeans and one of three pairs of Converse I own. 'And looking like one; it's embarrassing that my older sister looks younger than me. You should drink more, smoke … I don't know, do something to look your age!'

'I dress how I dress because in my job the less men notice you're a woman the better. I can't help the fact that I look younger than I am, it's no fun getting asked for ID when you're twenty-nine!'

Pea stops in the street.

'I can't believe that she's dead, Luna. How can it be true that she left us like that? I can't believe it. How can it be true that she wanted to die and we didn't notice?

'Do you know what frightens me the most? That one day it will me, it will me who can't fight life anymore, and who feels that pain so deeply that it's easier to die than live for the people that love you. You, you're more like Dad, everyone always says so – and I don't care if he's not your biological dad, he raised you and you're just like him. But me, I'm just like her. Luna, what if one day that's me?'

'It won't ever be you,' I promise her. 'I won't lose you too, just know that. I'll do whatever it takes to keep you safe.' I don't tell her that I worry that one day it might be me who can't fight anymore.

The moment of doubt seems to pass like the clouds over the moon; my mercurial sister has her second wind. She sprints up the steps that lead to Mrs Finkle's front door, and down again.

'We should just go, let's just go there, now.'

'Go where?' I am moments behind her as she accelerates through her own thoughts at light speed.

'Mum's place, the building, it's nearby, right? Let's just go and see it and explore! Come on, I can't sleep now, I need to do something, we could just go and see it now'

The buzzing starts, the surge rising up through my feet, and I turn away from her, somehow managing to keep my feet on the ground.

'I don't want to there right now,' I say.

'But why, just for a little walk?'

'Because ...' Even if I wanted to explain this feeling that has suddenly gripped me, I couldn't; it's like a kind of fear mingled with the certainty that something awful is about to happen. I don't know why the building terrifies me, but it does.

In my mind's eye it's a desolate place, blackened and decaying. And somehow this terrible, ridiculous idea has gripped me hard; this feeling of certainty that Mum is still there, trapped inside. Lost, looking for a way out, rattling frantically at window latches and door handles. And if I go there now, I'm afraid I will see her, peering out from between the boarded-up windows.

Taking a breath, I push my heels into the asphalt. Focus on now.

'Maybe I could make you some tea?' Mrs Finkle says as she opens her door, and I'm grateful to focus on her, her long, silk negligee, and her elegant hands adorned with rings that catch the streetlight.

'Mrs Finkle!' Pea grins at me, raising her eyebrows.

'I'm not spying on you,' Mrs Finkle assures us. 'I just heard your voices outside and I can't sleep either. I have some camomile somewhere. Come in and have tea, and I'll bore you with stories of your mom and dad until you'll be begging for sleep.'

'Cool, come on, Luna, tea!' Pea takes the lifeline with both hands and bounds up the steps.

'I'm just going to …' I don't know what to say. 'I just need a minute.'

'OK, I'll leave the key with the Virgin here,' Pea says, and Mrs Finkle steps back to let her in.

'Your sister will be OK with me,' she tells me. 'You take your time, dear.'

The city is quiet at last, just me and the half-moon, the same moon that Dad used to walk Mum home under. The same moon, watching everything unfold and never altering itself.

I thought the electric charge in my head had subsided, but suddenly it flares, lighting me up from the inside, and I know there's something out there. Something small, registering in the very periphery of my vision. Something so minor I would normally pay no attention to it, hoping it would go away. This time, though, there is no ignoring it; I can't because it's a call, a beckoning.

Something impossible is about to happen.

CHAPTER FOUR

I notice how the halo around the street lights suddenly flares, with a vicious ripping sound, and, when I look up, I can see the stars spinning overhead, see them burning, brighter than the city they cover.

I'm moving, I'm torn away from where I was, and I don't know how it's happening, only that it is. Reaching out for an iron railing, my fingers seem to pass right through it, and I no longer know what is real and what is imagined. I'm moving, but I don't know the why or the how. Then I see – no, I *feel* – the where. I feel it like a punch in the gut.

Mum's building, her home. Its crenellated outline cuts into the night sky, windows blank and expressionless, covered with boards, a chain-link fence with security warnings skirting it. It's nothing like I imagined it before, a dark and ruined castle full of ghosts. It feels like a haven.

A narrow alleyway dissects the property from the others in the row so that it stands slightly apart – a lone sentinel on the corner. Forcing my mind to focus on it, as I will my distant body to move towards it, I discover that I can almost taste the bricks and mortar on my tongue. It takes just a few seconds to reach, but in my head each second seems to pull me slowly further apart, as if I'm leaving a trail of crumbs of my consciousness in my wake.

The links of the security fence dance around me, and I fall into it, so heavily that I feel like my weight could tunnel right through it, through the asphalt and into the mud and clay below. Feverishly, I hope some weakness in the fence will give and let me in and, amazingly, as soon as I think it, it happens, because I am tumbling through, stumbling down the narrow alleyway, careering into walls that scrape and bruise my shoulders and elbows. The ground disappears from beneath my feet and I half tumble, half stagger, into the narrow crevice between the buildings, where I find a tiny square of concrete paving outside a side door. After a moment that could have been a million years, my knees buckle beneath me as I fold heavily onto the floor. Looking up between the buildings I see narrow strip of sky. I'm not sure if it's real or imagined, but I watch it opening inwards, upwards, fire pouring out of it. I taste burnt black ashes on my tongue just before the flames consume me.

CHAPTER FIVE

* *

It's the same moon. That thought writes itself out behind my closed lids.

I don't know how long I have been unconscious or what's happened, but I'm relieved that I'm not dead. Pressing my hand to my chest, I can feel my heart beating, fast and irregular, but definitely beating.

Lying there for a moment longer, I feel the cooling concrete register under my shoulder blades and buttocks. I must have been out for a while. As the fog gradually clears, I feel the tendons in my neck scream in protest against the way they have been twisted. It hurts to realign my vertebrae, but I don't have much choice. Pea will be wondering where I am. I'm wondering where I am.

Is this the episode that means I finally have to go and see a doctor?

Cautiously, I slowly open my eyes, peeling back my heavy lids with some effort, searching for that thin strip of night sky, half expecting that instead of looking up at it, it will have claimed me, and I'll be looking down on a network of

Brooklyn streets instead. I breathe a sigh of relief when I see the sky is still where it should be.

Easing myself into a sitting position, my back against the side door, I wait for the blood to stop rolling in my ears and temples. If I dare to be honest, I know that I've felt like I might break ever since I got the news that Mum had died. That moment, that awful phone call with Dad, his own grief thickening the words he spoke, making them seem too impossible to be real. That moment was a kind of axis, a lever on which the rest of my life has been balanced ever since. Maybe now – after the film – I'm no longer bending under the pressure of her loss; maybe now I'm breaking.

'We apologise for the break in transmission, normal Luna will shortly be resumed,' I whisper, and the sound of my own voice comforts me. I'm still real at least.

Resting for a moment, I hear two kids walking by at street level, accents so thick I'm not sure what they're saying, perhaps they're speaking ... Spanish? Slowly, as my eyes begin to focus, I realise small but definite differences from what I thought I saw, just before whatever this is that felled me. The huge dumpsters, that I could have sworn I careered into on my way down, are gone. Instead a pair of old-fashioned metal garbage cans stand just to my left, stuffed full of rotting matter and trash, the acrid stink filling my nostrils. Whoever filled these bins doesn't keep up with their recycling. Turning my head away from the stench, it dawns on me that the pounding isn't coming from inside my head, but from *inside* my mother's building.

Yes, the slow steady beat of a bass drum is vibrating on the other side of the vivid-green basement door. As my dizziness passes, I see the fence I thought surrounded the building is not here at all, and the alleyway, filled to the brim with oppressive dark, is wide open. I peer down its length as a car rolls past. It looks old – vintage even – like something you'd see cresting over hilltops in a *Starsky & Hutch* car chase. Its loose exhaust clatters along the road. The windows are rolled right down and young men spill out of every gap shouting, catcalling some poor woman I can't see.

Turning back to the building I try to pin down the location of the noise. The first floor. Anger glues me to the spot. This isn't their place, it's *hers*.

There is no choice, I have to go in. My limbs still feel both weak and full of lead as I go to the door. It has a bizarre, lion's-head brass knocker on it, and a handle that looks like it used to be on an internal door. It's unlocked – whatever Aunt Stephanie pays the security company that looks after this place it is too much.

Two bright strips of flickering fluorescent lighting obliterate any shadows in what I guess used to be the workshop. I'm surprised that the interlopers have managed to connect the power. A wave of emotion sweeps through me as I stand looking around this room; I feel as if I know it. Mum often told us tales of growing up in this place, and how, when she was very small, her mother taught her how to use a sewing machine, just as Mum taught me at the same age.

Amazingly, as I look around the room, I can see several bolts of material – burnt orange, deep purple, patterns and stripes that sing – still stored on specially-built shelving units. Two sewing machines are sat on a long table, reflecting the glare of the light. They look so shiny; I wonder if they might still work. When Aunt Stephanie moved out in the early eighties, she must have left the building exactly as it was right then, a time capsule, a monument … maybe a memorial.

I find my way to the foot of the stairs, where 'Hotel California' gets louder.

Adrenalin propels me up the stairs, and I fling open the door to the room where the music is coming from, and the six or so people in there turn and look at me. In that moment I get it, and I laugh out loud, with relief more than anything. These aren't hardened drug dealers with a fondness for progressive rock; they are young, younger than me, students maybe, and this is a 1970s costume party – everyone here is dressed to perfection. Everything that meets my eye shines out in bold and bright colours, like I'm looking at them through the lens of my camera.

'Who the hell are you?' A short, thick-set blondish guy asks me, half grin, half attitude.

For a moment I am not sure how to answer, I charged in here full of fury, but now ... this whole thing, it's kind of charming.

'I was passing, I heard the music,' I say, smiling, playing up my English accent. 'The door was open so I just came up.'

Everyone watches me, curious but unconcerned that they might have been caught out. I count a group of seven. A few young men, drinking beers out of bottles, girls sipping something out white paper cups, divided by gender. This must be a pretty serious hobby for them. Looking around I see a sideboard cluttered with ornaments, a standard lamp that casts a warm, orange glow, a sofa with bright-yellow cushions, and, in the corner, a wood-effect veneered TV, its bulbous screen reflecting the room, takes pride of place. Tacked to a wall over it an Elvis calendar, opened to July 1977; the King is sweating and bejewelled, singing into a microphone. There's a folded copy of the *Daily News* on the coffee table, proclaiming, 'F.B.I. STEPS UP SEARCH FOR SAM'.

Every detail is correct; there's even a circle around today's date, with the words 'Pops away' scrawled inside the box in a scrawling hand.

'That was an accent.' A tall, young man, with dark, wavy hair and muscular shoulders, grins as he approaches me. 'Right? You're not from round here?'

'No, I'm from London,' I say, a little disarmed by his green eyes and thick, black lashes. I take two steps back, avoiding his curious gaze, which doesn't seem deterred by my loose white T-shirt. Men, scientific men, I am very good at talking to. I've learnt the precise language they understand fluently, and when I impress them, attract them, it's always by default, a by-product of me knowing what I'm talking about and also having breasts. Boys – men – who are simply hot, I'm not very good at talking to at all. The only reason I was good at talking to Brian was because for a very long time it didn't occur to me that he was one. This one, though, he is definitely hot. And now so am I.

'Well, I should be going, really,' I begin, feeling my cheeks flush. 'It's just that, this building, it belongs to my family so ... if, when you leave, you wouldn't mind ...'

'It don't.' A girl with short hair, cut into the nape of her neck, leaving it to curl on top, takes two swift steps towards me, clearing my view of the other young women in the group. 'This building don't belong to your family. It's my dad's – he owns it, every brick of it.'

'And don't we know it,' the blond guy says, digging the green-eyed hunk in the ribs.

The short-haired girl is standing very close to me, her brown eyes fixed on mine.

'Look, I don't mean to intrude,' I tell the girl, wondering where I recognise that soft snub nose from, but knowing that I do, because it seems a little out of place in such an angular face. 'I can tell you've really made an effort. It's just that I'd really appreciate it if you could leave the place the same way that you found it.'

'Can you believe this chick?' The girl jerks her thumb in my direction as she steps aside and addresses someone sitting behind her.

Then I feel it again, the siren call, singing its way to me and through me. And finally I focus on the figure behind the snub-nosed girl. Another young woman sits on the back of a brown sofa, her bare feet digging into the seat cushions, toes clenched.

It feels as if all the breath is sucked from my body in one second, the same second as my heart stands still and I stare at the young woman. Her long, slim legs are crossed at the knee, her long, dark hair is like a sheet of black ice, collapsing over her shoulders.

And then tears spring into my eyes, which I hastily blink away.

Because the woman I am looking at is my mother. Not as I last knew her, but younger than I have ever known her. This is the woman my father first photographed back in 1977.

Remembering the camera around my neck I lift it to my eyes and search for her through the lens. She's still there.

And she sees *me*.

CHAPTER SIX

⋆ ⋆

I'm dying, that must be it. It must be that, what has seemed like several minutes to me, has really taken less than a nanosecond to unravel. A dream world conjured up by endorphins and neurotoxins, death's last gift to me. Maybe the 'visions' I'm seeing are a symptom, perhaps an embolism or an undiagnosed tumour, and, suddenly, something has given way in my head. That has to be it. It's the only explanation. But I can't die now. I can't leave Pea and Dad now; they need me too much. And yet, and yet, look at her. I look at my mother, and she's smiling. I want to be with her so badly.

All the fear that's coursing through my body burns away in one bright flare, and I can almost see it floating away in slowly cooling, greying embers. There's no need to be afraid. Just be here in this moment, I tell myself, silently, for as long as you're able to be. Just be close to her, in all her fierce, unfamiliar glory. Whatever this is, if it's a dream ... even if it's death, welcome it. It's worth it to see her like this, so saturated with colour, so vivid, so unlike the colours from the old, faded photo albums and movies at home, she seems to inhabit that world that I've only ever seen trapped behind clear plastic or projected onto a screen.

Everything here is brighter and more intense. Edges defined, shadows deeper, with the clearest resolution I have ever seen.

My brain must have created this image of her from a thousand forgotten fragments, because even though I clearly never knew her at twenty years old, I know that this version of her is exactly right, down to the bump on her slightly asymmetrical nose, the little crescent scar at the top of her shoulder, which she said she got when she fell off her bike, aged eight. The mole beneath her ear, the tilt of her head as she registers my gaze on her and challenges me with a returning stare. Even the Catholic medal, a gift from her late mother for her confirmation, that she'd told me she had worn every day for years until the day she lost it, glints on a chain around her neck. All these things I know about her, all these things I might have dragged from the furthest corners of my memories, all accessible to me now, but this is so much more than just a patchwork of old thoughts stitched together in haphazard squares. Here she is, as I have never known her – Marissa Lupo; confident, strong, jaw set with determination, holding court while sucking a Pepsi through a red-and-white straw, about to pass judgement on this strange gawking older woman in her midst.

'Who are you?' the first girl asks me, and now I recognise her. She's Stephanie, the older sister. Aunt Stephanie, who didn't even come to the funeral.

'No one,' I say. 'I mean, my name is Luna. I just arrived today, I'm staying nearby at Mrs Finkle's ...'

'Mrs Finkle's?'

She speaks – my mother speaks to me – and the sound of her voice, young and unpolluted, fills me with elation. An idiot's grin spreads out across my face. I feel my cheeks stretching tight; to hear the sound of her voice again, to see her sharp dark looks, her uncanny perception. 'Can't be, her place is full up, I know because—'

'Oh yes, that's right, not her,' I scramble for words, fearing that if I let my cover drop, I'll do something to dissipate this vision. 'Yes, I'm actually staying with someone else she recommended because her place is full.'

'The Obermans', on ninety-first?' the good-looking guy with the shoulders nods encouragingly at me.

'Yes, that's right.' I grab the lifeline, wondering why it's been thrown my way; maybe my mind created him too, maybe just for this reason.

'Yeah, her and Finkle tip each other off all the time,' he says, backing me up, and I am grateful to him, this strange handsome creation I have made up for myself. 'And we all know Finkle's got her hands full keeping all those men happy.'

'Oh, shut up, Michael, you're disgusting,' Marissa Lupo says, dismissing his comment with a wave of her hand. Leaning forward she looks at me long and hard.

'I seen you before?' she asks. 'I know you from somewhere.'

'I don't think so,' I say, because if I say what I want to say, if I say, yes, yes, I'm your daughter, your little girl, the one you left behind when you died, all of this will vanish. The other girls watch her, waiting, their faces turned to hers, and I see she is the northern star in this group, the compass that sets their direction. Marissa Lupo is the leader here, the alpha girl. This is a version of my mother than I must have conjured up from the photo in my pocket, a fantasy version I never met in reality. Stephanie is the only one who resists, walking away from the girls to the boys and taking the hand of the fair-haired man, as soon as she sees that Marissa is in charge now.

'You're from London? I know someone from London.' My mother's glossed lips curl into a smile. 'He's my boyfriend actually. He was on assignment photographing the movie, and then, after it wrapped, he stayed behind to be with me. We've been going together three months already. His name is Henry Sinclair, would you know him?'

'I don't.' I sound apologetic, and I feel it too. With a sudden pang of sharp sadness, I think of Dad sitting at home, abandoned by his daughters, probably sitting in his old chair, opposite the one where Mum would sit and sew and talk, while he read and wrote. Probably looking out into the garden where the flowers she planted will be cramming the border with colours and scents. Henry Sinclair, the man that Marissa Lupo smiled about so sweetly just now, sitting all alone, lost in the glory of an English summer thirty years and an eternity away.

This must be what it's like, the final unravelling of a mind, a kind of beautiful chaos, no order, no rules, anything is possible. I'd love to tell Brian about this; it would make him smile and crinkle up his eyes, while he worked out what it all means.

'Hey, Riss.' The good-looking boy winks at me as he addresses Mum with a nickname that either I didn't know I knew or I must have invented for myself. Riss. I like it; it suits her. 'Let me get our guest a drink. How often do we get any visitors round here, right? Let's show her we're good hosts.'

'Yeah, sure.' She turns back to her friends. I sense Stephanie bristling at my side. No one asked her for her opinion.

'Is that OK with you?' I ask my aunt, politely. 'It would be so nice to meet some people, I'm going to be around for a while.'

I don't know why I said that, a vain hope I guess, a wish to spend more time lost in this fantasy.

'Makes no difference to me,' she says, turning her back on me. 'Do whatever you want.'

Hanging back, I watch as Riss laughs, sharing a private joke with the other girl, whose bottle blonde hair is tight with curls. They are whispering secrets to each other behind cupped hands. As Riss leans in closer, her bangles slide down her arm, and the other girl says something that makes her laugh out loud, throwing her head back. I've seen that laugh a million times, but never like this, not without that trace of sadness that always seemed to linger in Mum's eyes, the promise of the fall that always came after the high.

'So what do beautiful English girls drink?' the handsome man – I soon learn is called Michael – asks, and I force myself to look at him. Beautiful, that's not a word anyone uses to describe me, except in a fantasy of my own construct; some part of my subconscious must have always secretly longed with it. The other guys are watching us, their interested naked, and he takes a step between us, his back shielding me from their view.

'Don't mind them,' he says, his smile dimpling. 'They got no idea how to talk to a woman, only how to look at one.'

'We know what you want to do to her,' the blond one calls over. 'And it ain't talking.'

Michael sighs and shakes his head.

'I'd love a beer,' I tell him. It interests me that I am still hot and thirsty in my fantasy world, my mouth dry, my heart pounding. My eyes return to Riss. I want just to be near her. How to go over there and talk to her? How to find a reason just to stare at her, a reason to ask her not to go, not to leave me behind?

'Come with me?' Michael asks. 'If I leave you here, those guys will be all over you like bees on honey.'

'I can look after myself,' I tell him.

'I bet you can,' he says. 'I just want to talk to you some more, that's all. Come with me, Luna. Luna, like the moon.' He sees my look of surprise and laughs. 'What, you think we don't go to school round here, or something? I like space, as it happens. You know in a couple of months' time NASA will launch its probe, *Challenger*, and it's going to take photos of everything it floats by and send it back to earth. Isn't that something?'

Lord, I really did create my dream man: green eyes, muscular shoulders and an interest in astronomy.

'Imagine if it keeps on sending back data,' I say, 'even when it's left the solar system and is travelling into deep space.'

He laughs as if I'm a little foolish. 'I doubt it will keep going that long; it would take it, like, twenty years or something to get to Uranus.'

More like forty, actually, I think, but I don't say it out loud.

I follow him into a small kitchen, crammed with free-standing units, packets and tins visible behind frosted-glass sliding doors. There's also an ancient-looking cooker and a huge refrigerator that looks as if it could withstand a nuclear blast. Michael inches around a central table with a wipe-downable table cloth of green-and-white gingham, where it looks like intimate family dinners take place, to get to the giant, purring appliance.

'You sure you want beer?' he asks over his shoulder. 'We got rum and Pepsi if you'd rather? The girls, their pop is staying over at his mother's house; she lives in Queens. Otherwise there'd be no rum. He don't like his girls to drink, don't think it's ladylike. Don't think he knows his daughters at all.'

'Really?' I say, sounding more interested than I should. I knew that my mum lost her own mother young, but I didn't know that I knew anything at all about her grandmother – my great-grandmother. Certainly not that she'd lived in Queens, or maybe I made that up too. 'Beer, please.'

'One thing you should know about Leo Lupo.' Michael lowers his voice leaning into me, and I smell the sweet, sharp, pungent scent of his aftershave, and I realise with a rush of recognition that it's Old Spice. 'He acts like he's a small-time businessman, but there's nothing small about him, word is he . . .'

'Bellamo!' A voice shouts out from down the hall. 'What you doing in there? Is it legal?'

'Mind your own,' Michael shouts back. 'So, English Luna. Tell me about yourself.' He takes a bottle, clipping open the lip on the table top in one practised move. 'You got any Italian in you?'

I wait for the rest of the crass chat-up line, but it doesn't come. He is actually asking me a question.

'My mother's family,' I say, leaning my head out of the door, so that I can watch Riss in the other room, my heart pulling towards her. How many precious seconds have passed in the real world, while I've been making small talk with a figment of my imagination. I need to get back to her, before this all blows away, taking me with it. Riss is on her feet now, acting out some incident, perhaps from earlier in the day. Just by watching her I can tell it's the story of some stuck-up customer who thinks she's all that. The whole group is watching her now, howling with laughter as she skips from part to part, her can of Pepsi still in her hand. Even Stephanie is smiling.

Could it be one of these boys? The thought strikes me swiftly, and sets me spinning. Could one of these young men be my biological father? The fair-haired one, he has blue eyes; could it be him?

'Hey, Luna – look at me for a moment, would you? You're giving me a complex,' Michael speaks.

'It's just that ... shall we go back in there?' I suggest, and he shrugs.

'Sure.' He seems a little disappointed. 'Whatever you want, Luna-like-the-moon.'

In another world, in another universe, where this is the only reality, I'd like to lean against the door frame and look into his green eyes for hours on end, but now, every stretched-out dream-second I have, I want to spend with her, with my mother. I want to know what happened to her to make me.

CHAPTER SEVEN

* *

'Bellamo struck out, there's a woman who can resist his charms after all!' The fair-haired guy smacks Michael hard on the shoulder.

'Ah, can it, Curtis,' Michael says, blushing across the bridge of the nose. 'We were just talking about outer space, actually.'

'The space between your ears, you mean.' Curtis laughs, and Michael takes it in good humour.

All the same, he stays in the doorway as Riss finishes her tale.

'So I said to her, lady, if you think you are a size six then you need to see a psychiatrist and a math teacher.'

Turning, she catches me watching her.

'Hey you, what's your name again?'

'Luna,' I say, suddenly shy, right back in the shoes of eight-year-old me, pinned into the corner of the playground by one of the cool kids, who didn't bully me so much as simply didn't get me. Unlike my gregarious sister, I was a curious specimen to be prodded, poked and peered at.

'You always dress like a guy?' She looks me up and down. 'Don't you want men to notice you?'

'I ... er ... no, not really.' I shrug, and suddenly Riss is simply that, a beautiful young woman who is baffled by my unbrushed hair and make-up-free face. 'My job means that ... well, the men I work with are so easily distracted by ... bits and bobs.' She laughs and I blush.

'What *is* your job?' she asks me.

'I'm a research scientist,' I tell her proudly. 'Quantum physics, the study of neutrinos, to be precise. They're like these subatomic particles that are everywhere, but you can't see them; we only know they exist from the way they interact with other particles ... actually, a lot of the time they don't exist, they sort of pop into existence when ...'

I trail off into silence as the girls just stare at me, and eventually my gaze drops to the scuffed toes of my shoes. I'm not enjoying my delusion anymore, not since it made me feel like that little girl who had to hide her brains to get through each day at school – alive, anyway. 'It's a pretty boring job, to be honest,' I say at last, 'mostly typing.'

'I'm a secretary too,' the girl with the bottle-blonde hair tells me brightly, and I don't correct her. 'I can do ninety words a minute. What about you?'

'Nowhere near,' I assure her.

'Linda's big plan is to marry her boss,' Riss tells me. 'That's why she's dyed her hair blonde, because she afraid Son of Sam will kill her before he proposes otherwise!' She grins at my blank expression. 'You know who Son of Sam is, right?' She doesn't wait for me to answer. 'But he only kills brunettes, so you'd better watch out. Half of Brooklyn's gone blonde.'

'Not you, though,' I say, nodding at her dark hair.

'I don't scare easy,' she assures me, and I wonder where it went, that courage, the fire I see in her brown eyes. The woman that raised me always seemed to be scared of something.

'Oh well ... I'm sure they'll catch him soon,' I say. It's fascinating, the vast ephemera of information my seizing brain is throwing into the max. I didn't know I knew anything about Son of Sam, and yet here we are discussing this obscure detail of a serial killer case I've barely heard of.

'So what are you doing in Bay Ridge?' Riss asks me. 'If you ain't with the movie, what are you doing here? There's nothing to see here, nothing to do.'

'I ...' I don't have an answer, and my mind scrambles to find one. 'I'm just travelling for the summer. I wanted to see New York, but couldn't afford to stay there, so ...'

'You came to Bay Ridge on purpose?' Riss laughs. 'No one ever does that. You're kind of a freak. I like you.'

I'm bathed in the sudden warmth of her smile, and it's my mum's smile, the one that could make everything all right again in an instant; the one I spent my whole childhood on tenterhooks for, dying to catch a glimpse of.

'Come with me.' She hooks her arm through mine, and I can feel the warmth of her skin against mine, even the beat of her pulse. It's the strangest sensation as I walk hip to hip with her through the hallway and up another flight of stairs, to another tiny corridor that mirrors the floor below. I feel safe, and at home.

Riss guides me through an open door into a tiny bedroom dominated by a huge, dark-wood wardrobe; the only furniture apart from a narrow single bed. A pretty, white, chiffon dress, off the shoulder with a cape-like neckline, hangs from the wardrobe's ornate carvings that jut sharply out from its corners. I stop and look at the wardrobe, gothic and dark, like it should have gargoyles carved into it. Like you should be able to open it and a flock of bats might fly out, or you might also be able to walk right through it and into a wintery wonderland.

'Crazy wardrobe,' I say and she laughs.

'It came over on the boat from Italy,' she says. 'I have no idea how, or why, but I'm the one stuck with it for some reason. Do you like it?' she says, and I know she's not talking about the wardrobe but the dress, which she carefully lifts down to show me.

'Dad always lets Stephanie and me use off-cuts and remnants to make stuff for ourselves, but I saved up for this especially. It's rayon chiffon – I paid for a whole bolt myself – with satin-look lining. It's a copy of the dress that Karen Lynn Gorney wears in the movie. You've heard about the movie, right? *Saturday Night Fever*? She plays this girl that John Travolta chooses to enter a dancing completion with. She wears a dress like this on the big night! They shot it here. You won't have seen it is yet, but it's gonna be great and her dress is beautiful. Henry says they'll have a premier, right here in Bay Ridge, at the 2001 Odyssey, the club where we go to, where they filmed a lot of the movie. If I'm still here, I'm going to wear it.'

Henry; she's talking about Dad. This is my mother in the summer she met my father, just before she ran away to London with him. It seems right, that this is the world my brain has created for me, this perfect time, this dream romance my mother would tell us about sometimes, where love was enough to save the day just before something terrible happened.

'If?' I prompt her.

'I don't know when it will be released,' she says. 'Henry says maybe not until next year and I'm not sure if I'll still be here then. Come on.'

Riss beckons for me to follow her as she climbs out of the narrow, open sash window at the end of her room and onto the fire escape. The metal creaks and sways as I ease my weight onto it, and I find myself gripping onto the window frame. Even now, as late as it is, the air is still thick with heat and exhaust fumes. A few streets away someone is shouting; a car engine revs at the stop light on the corner. Riss perches on the edge of the railing, oblivious to the three-storey drop below, and lights a cigarette. Smoking and waiting, that's what Mrs Finkle had said.

Everything here seems so real, if this rusty old fire escape gave way I feel like I'd plummet to the ground along with it. I grip the corroded iron railing even tighter, and try to look cool. I remember with sudden clarity how Mum used to look at me sometimes. When I turned my back on endless reruns of *Scooby Doo* to read a book about how the planets move around each other, her brow would furrow, her lips compress, as if she were trying to work out where she knew me from. That's the feeling I am having now; it seems as if I've always wanted my mum to think I am cool.

'Henry wants me to go back to England with him.' Riss gestures at me with her cigarette. 'Do you think I should?'

'Yes,' I say, without hesitation and Riss's eyes widen.

'That's the first time anyone's said that. Everyone else is all "you should take your time, talk to your pops, don't rush into anything". Not you. I bet you're real spontaneous, aren't you?'

'Um, yeah, sure,' I say, although exactly the opposite is true. 'So, is Henry the one? Or are there other guys you like?'

Anger flashes across Riss's face, like summer lightning.

'I'm no slut,' she says. 'There's never been anyone before Henry, not like him. Not even him yet; we'll wait until we're married.' She makes the declaration with fierce pride, and it takes me my surprise.

'You mean you've never—'

'No!' Riss shakes her head. 'No, girls that give it up like that, they get used, they get hurt, passed around from boy to boy, you know that. That's not me; it matters to me what people think of me. I'm not that girl, and Henry respects that about me. He's happy to wait. It's one of the reasons I love him. What about you? Is it different in England? Have you been with a lot of guys?'

I wonder about how to answer that question, what constitutes a lot of guys? Does she mean fifty, fifteen or five, which is the actual answer, four of them as an undergraduate, when I was still reeling from the novelty that boys wanted to sleep with me, before I realised that boys want to sleep with anyone. Those four and Brian, who was kind and sweet in bed, and always made me tea afterwards, just how I like it.

'I've had one serious boyfriend,' I say, which is something like the truth.

'You broke up?' Riss looks appalled for me when I nod.

'It's OK,' I tell her. 'I wasn't in love with him, not the way you love Henry. It wouldn't have worked out.'

'That's what Stephanie keeps saying about me and Henry. Before she died, Mom used to take us to church three times a week,' Riss tells me. 'I still go, on Sundays anyway, because when I'm there, talking to Him, I feel ... right inside, you know?' She tugs gently at the medallion around her neck. 'Which is why I wish I'd fallen for a Catholic boy. And why Pops doesn't know that Henry and I are so serious. And why I don't know what he'd do if I told him I was leaving for England. Get real angry, that's for sure. God, this is such a mess.'

Riss looks up at the half-moon, her face edged with silver, and I sense she is offering a silent prayer. In all of my life, I have rarely set foot inside a church except at other people's weddings and christenings. Mum brought us up to think, to question, to wonder about everything, but she never brought us up believing in anything. I can't help wonder, where did it go, that faith?

'I seem to like English people,' she says, regarding me through lowered lids. 'I bet I'm going to like you. I don't know why, but I can tell, there's something about you that just says I am.'

'I know that I am going to like you too,' I say, offering my hand, and she smiles as she gives me a formal handshake.

'Before the movie, nothing ever happened here. No one ever came here, we just lived. Doing what we do, being us, and it was like it was the whole world, you know? And then for a little while the whole world came here. I liked it. Now I'd like to see the rest of the world. Wait there a second.'

She hands me her cigarette and disappears back inside. I can feel the heat of the ash, smell the smoke. I graze the lit end of the cigarette against the heel of my palm and my hand recoils from the burning heat. It's so real, it's all so real, but of course it isn't. It's a wonderful dream; it would be so easy to just stay here, forever. And perhaps I won't have a choice about that, but if I can, I have to fight my way back to consciousness. Pea won't manage without me right now, and Dad, he can't take losing anyone else.

'Here.' She hands me something I recognise, something I know. My mum's Super 8 camera, the one she seemed to document every second of our lives on, ending each year with an epic, highlights-of-our-family montage, played after Christmas lunch. The same camera she made her last ever film on. I can feel the weight of it, run my fingers over the smooth plastic and metal – it looks brand new – all created out of thin air. Brian was right, the brain really is remarkable. 'Henry gave it to me.' She grins, hugging the camera to her. 'He makes life seem exciting.'

Dad exciting – I repress a chuckle. 'So are you using it, making films?'

'Sure.' Her dark eyes are luminous. 'I took it out with us on Saturday night; we were dancing. I don't know how it will turn out; I've got to wait to get it developed. Let me film you now.'

'Oh no.' I turn my face away and offer her back her cigarette. I never enjoyed the edited version of my life that Mum spent so much of my childhood documenting and then presenting annually as a time of perfect happiness. Lots of that life was perfect, lots of it was happy, but it was never as happy and as perfect at the home movies. They always seemed like someone else's memories. As soon as I was old enough to say no, I did.

'You're shy,' she says.

'I guess I am.' I shrug. 'Are you happy here?'

'Am I happy?' Her nose wrinkles as she considers the strangeness of the question. 'I've never been this happy before. It finally feels like I'm alive. I'm starting to see there's so much more I can do with my life. Well, like you, look at you. You aren't sitting at home waiting for life to find you, are you?'

'I suppose I'm not,' I say. 'And your friends, those guys, none of them were ever special, more like a boyfriend?'

'No.' She looks appalled at the suggestion, the corners of her mouth tugging downwards. 'Gian, he's in love with Michelle. Curtis, he likes to think he's Stephanie's boyfriend, but she only wants him when there's nothing better around. Poor guy hasn't been the same since he came back from Vietnam, all jumpy and nervous, running with the wrong types, if you know what I mean.'

I don't know, but it doesn't matter; just listening to the rhythmic rise and fall of her words, the wonderful music of her voice, is enough. Her Brooklyn accent is more pronounced than it ever was when she was my mother. She is glorious.

'And you've met Michael. He's been pretending to be John Travolta ever since they wrapped on the film but he's a good guy, sweet, once you get past all the tough guy stuff. I've known him so long he's like a brother to me. All the guys, even Curtis, they look out for us on a Saturday night; there are guys in the clubs who take liberties. I don't need them so much now I got Henry, because everyone knows I'm taken.'

Her expression as she says his name again is so very sweet, so very hopeful, proud and sure.

'Jeez, it's still so hot.' Riss tips her chin back to blow smoke into the hair, fanning her face with flat hand. 'Sun's been down more than an hour and it's like I can't breathe.'

'It is. I'm not used to this much heat. In England it rains every other day and we wear gloves all year round, seriously, and hats too, with bobbles.' I joke.

Riss laughs as she shakes her head.

'You're nuts.' She tilts her head. 'You should come over again, hang out with us.'

A current of friendship flows between us, and it feels acutely real, even though I know I am creating, or recreating, these moments, filling this artificial version of my mother with all sort of hopes and dreams, building whole universes and then collapsing them again in the blink of an eye. Right down to the stink of rotting garbage that rises from below.

'I got to go,' she says, checking her watch suddenly as if she is late for someone. 'But you'll come over again, OK? Just come round the side; it's always open.'

Before I know it she is leaving, heading down the ladder of the fire escape so fast in the dark I'm afraid she will stumble. As I try to track her descent I see something glimmer on the metal steps, just for a moment, caught in the headlights of a passing car.

Without a tenth of Riss's certainty, I make my way down the metal ladder, searching the now-grilled platform for what I thought I saw, running my fingertips over it until they touch a fine chain. I pick it up: the medallion her mother gave her.

'Wait, you've lost your necklace!' I call out to her as she hits the sidewalk on the opposite side of the crossroads.

Riss stops, her hand flying to her slender neck.

'Shit!' she swears, waiting impatiently as I hurry to bring her treasured necklace back to her.

She watches me, her arms crossed, left hip jutting, as I make the awkward final leap off the ladder, which springs back up behind me with a rusty creak.

'Henry said you don't have fire escapes like ours back in England,' she says.

'Nope.' I laugh, and I put the medal in her hand.

'Oh my goodness, thank you,' she says, putting it back around her neck. 'Mama gave it to me when I was thirteen for my confirmation. It's Maria Goretti, patron saint of young women, to keep me virtuous. It's real silver, you know. Would you check the clasp for me?' She turns her back to me, and sweeps her hair to one side, as I refasten the necklace, pressing the slightly loosened link that holds the clasp back together as hard as I can.

'Are you meeting Henry?' I ask her.

'Maybe.' She dips her chin and smiles. 'Are you going back inside? Don't tell them I've left, say I was tired. I've only got a little while so ... We'll catch up, I'll introduce you around, yeah? Gotta go, I'm already late.' She gestures in the direction that she was running in and takes a few backwards steps, giving me one final wave, before she turns and disappears into the dark.

Someone is waiting for her in the dense absence of light between buildings; I can sense him, sense his longing. I watch her figure disappear into the dark, every line of her body, every angle, every movement is defined by undiluted joy, and I wonder who is waiting for her, Henry or my biological father. I want to follow her, but I can't; my feet are glued to spot by one thought.

If this is what my mother was really like in the summer of 1977, what happened to her to break her heart, her mind and spirit, when she should have had everything she needed for a happy ever after?

Standing alone, goosebumps rise on my forearms and I shudder. The darkness seems to close around me, and I am suddenly afraid. I don't want this to be it, I don't want it to be over. I want to wake up, I want to live.

I want to know.

CHAPTER EIGHT

The only thing I can think of to do is to keep moving. Perhaps if I take my mind back around to the side of the building where I must have collapsed, that might prompt it to reboot back to consciousness.

A siren screeches a couple of blocks away, and I can make out a couple of guys on the corner in the shadows, the flicker of a lighter briefly illuminating the spaces between them. It's late – past midnight – and the streets are empty but not quiet. It feels like, in every dark hiding spot, all of my secrets are having whispered conversations about me.

Then everything shifts, freezes and jumps. There's a cooler breeze cutting through the thick air, a modern car cruises by and there's a different atmosphere as another world, my world, reveals itself just fleetingly before it's gone. I'm coming round, that must be it.

I just need to focus. Focus on not being dead.

'Hey, Luna.'

I start, even though I recognise the voice at once. Brain, I tell myself, this is no time for handsome diversions.

'Michael,' I say, turning to look at him. If my subconscious has gone to the trouble to imagine him, I might as well appreciate him.

He has hooded eyes, a straight nose and full lips. His body, under his jeans and T-shirt, is lean with narrow hips. His Adidas trainers are white with yellow-and-blue stripes, old and well worn, but kept carefully clean.

He shifts a little under my gaze, embarrassed by my scrutiny.

'I saw you leaving through the window. Thought you might like me to walk you home. A girl shouldn't be out here on her own, not while there's a killer on the loose.'

'I'm a bit lost,' I say truthfully, more than a little wan. 'I'm not really sure how to get home.'

'OK, so I'll walk you.' He smiles, jerking his head in one direction. With no other option, I simply follow him.

'So what are you really doing here?' Michael asks me, and I look sharply at him.

'I said ...'

'I know what you said, and I may be just some punk from Bay Ridge, but I know a story when I see one.'

'Honestly?' I slow down. 'I don't really know what I'm doing here. I don't even really know how it happened. And I don't know how to get back to the people I love, but I really, really want to.' I find myself looking up, looking around, as if I'd just clicked my ruby slippers together three times and might find myself at home any moment.

'You OK?' Michael frowns at me. 'Something bad happen to you?'

'Would it sound really crazy if I said I have no idea what's happening to me, right at this moment?' I ask him. 'No idea where I am ...'

'Well, that's easy, you're on ninety-second and third.' He takes my hand without prompting, and I let him. His touch feels warm and solid, so real. 'You need to go about another two blocks and you're there.'

He begins to walk but I don't move. He tugs at my hand gently and I take a couple of steps closer to him.

'You're lost, but you don't want to go home?' he asks me, frowning.

'I ... the thing is ...' I stare at him, wondering how to explain this situation to a man who doesn't exist, whose presence in my brain meltdown doesn't make any sense at all. What's he for?

'The thing is, I've just got to go now,' I say. 'You're ...' I run my palm down the length of his torso without actually touching him. 'You're very ... very, very ...' I had no idea I had an imagination *this* vivid. 'But I can't. So I just have to go. I have to find my own way back. Thank you.'

Except I don't move; there is something about his bemused smile that keeps me pinned to the spot.

'Very, very, huh?' His grin ignites mine. 'I'll take that. I won't make a big thing of it, or anything, but I'll take it. The English chick thinks I'm hot.'

'I didn't say hot, and anyway ... Well ... goodbye.' I walk on, knowing that I don't want to walk into that strange night of whispers and hidden glances.

'Wait up!' Michael falls into step beside me. 'I ain't letting you walk on your own, and that's that. My ma would kill me. I promise not to dazzle you with my good looks, or seduce you with this handsome physique, not unless you ask me to, OK? You're safe with me, I've been raised right.'

He bows a little, gesturing the direction with his hand and we walk on in silence. The hot and heavy air seems to press into my pores, the sidewalk feels hard under the soles of my feet, and I hear traffic, though the street we turn into is quiet and dark.

We turn a corner and Michael stops dead, stretching his arm in front of me to block my path. Just down the street, in the shadows, there is some kind of scuffle, a fight. Three men surround around another lying on the ground. Kicks and punches are being targeted at the balled figure on the floor in industrious silence. Michael takes my hand and we are about to leave, go another way, when a sharp cry cuts through the dark.

'Please, let me go.' The voice is high. And very young.

'Shit,' Michael swears under his breath, turning to me. 'Stay there, don't move.'

I stand still as I watch him approaching the group.

'Guys, what's going on?' he says, spreading his arms, his voice is full of bonhomie, like he's simply shooting the breeze. The beating stops as he approaches, and the boy, because I see now it is a skinny boy of perhaps no more than twelve, scrambles to his feet. He makes a break for it, but one of his attackers grabs his ripped and bloody shirt and holds him still. My feet are charging towards the scene before I know it.

'What the hell are you doing?' I shout. 'Let him go at once!'

I don't know if it's my accent or just my sudden appearance that shocks the man into releasing his prey. I put my arm around the bony shoulders of the boy shepherding him away. His skin is slick with sweat and blood; he's trembling. He shrugs off my embrace as soon as he can, his whole body tense and alert, looking for his moment to run.

'Jesus.' Michael steps in front of me, blocking a lunge from the man I liberated the kid from. 'OK, step back now.'

'You need to keep your bitch on a leash,' the biggest of the three men says, nodding at me, but talking to Michael.

'You need to watch your mouth.' Michael's shoulder square. 'You don't talk to her like that. And what the fuck you doing, anyway, three grown men beating on a kid?'

'He shouldn't be round here.' The big man squares up to Michael. 'One of his kind round here, he ain't up to no good. There's no place for them in this neighbourhood, you should know that. We're sending a message, teaching him a lesson.'

It's then I realise that it's not the boy they hate, it's the colour of his skin. He's black and that's enough of a reason for them. I feel sick with shock.

'You racist bastard ...'

'Jesus, he's just a kid,' Michael speaks across me, sending me a warning look, and I bite my tongue. 'Kid, what you doing out so late, anyways?'

The boy shrugs, searching the streets, looking for his escape.

'Shouldn't you be at home?' Michael asks him.

The boy looks at him, and shrugs again. 'Nothing there for me.'

'His mama's probably on her back, making a living,' one of the guys says, and his friends guffaw with laughter.

Michael presses his lips together and I watch as he makes a concerted effort to repress his fury.

'Well, you've had your fun. He's gonna leave now.' Michael nods at the boy. 'Kid, go home.'

The boy doesn't even look at me before he half runs, half hobbles, into the night, his arms wrapped around his body.

'Fuck, now what are we going to do for fun?' One of the guys steps closer to Michael. 'We could do your girlfriend, I guess.'

'Go home, fellas,' Michael says. 'Go see your old lady, tell her how you beat the shit out of a little kid and see if it makes her hot for you.'

'You little—'

'Run!' Michael grabs my hand and before I know it we are flying through the dark streets, until my lungs are gasping for air. We turn corner after corner, and my ribs hurt. We career to a stop, almost colliding with a wall, and Michael laughs, bending over double to catch his breath.

'That was risky!' I tell him, pushing him in the shoulder.

'No, they were drunk and fat. I knew we could outrun them. Well, I knew I could. What was risky was you marching in there, grabbing the kid. Girls don't act like that round here.'

'They do where I come from.' I lean back against the wall, wondering why, in my own hallucination, I am required to catch my breath.

'I get that about you,' Michael says eventually, his voice echoing in the silence. And somehow I know he is choosing his words carefully, trying to tone down his accent to impress me. 'You're real interesting. Crazy, but interesting.'

'Interesting?' I repeat the word, because I'd love to hear him say it again.

'Interesting,' he obliges, after a moment.

'What's interesting about you is that you stuck up for that boy against those racists thugs.'

'Round here you stick to your kind, you know.' Michael shrugs. 'They didn't think they were doing anything wrong.'

'But you did,' I say.

'I don't care whether you're black, pink or yellow, I won't stand by and see a kid beaten on by grown men. My mama ...'

'Raised you right,' I finish for him. 'I think I like your mum.'

'What about me?' Michael's smile pulls at something in my chest. 'You like me?

'I'm not sure yet,' I say. 'What else is interesting about you?'

'I don't know.' Michael's bravado melts a little at the question. 'I like to read, you know? Read and sometimes I make up stories. I wouldn't ever tell that to the guys. They'd think I was a pussy. But I can say it to you somehow, I don't know why. Maybe because you talk like Mary Poppins.'

'Do you want to be a writer?' I ask him.

'Nah.' He shakes his head. 'That's just a thing I like doing; it's not a job, not for someone like me. At the moment I work in my dad's bakery. He wants me to take it over one day.'

'Do you want to?' I keep talking as we walk further into the dark, and the further we walk, the louder our footsteps sound, the more it feels as if the world beyond what little I can see with my own eyes has crumbled away to dust.

He doesn't answer, just shrugs, and says at last, 'Anyway, you're here. The Obermans'. Second house on the left.'

He nods vaguely towards a terrace of brownstones. I hesitate. What now? What happens now when he's gone?

'OK, night then,' I say.

Perhaps I could just keep walking around every corner and my mind would make up a backdrop to meet each turn, or maybe it would be like those video games Pea and I used to play when we were kids, and you come up against an invisible wall, your legs still pumping but never getting anywhere.

'Hey,' he says, as I start to walk away. 'I hope I see you again, Luna. I mean that, though next time, if you can avoid getting in a fight with a bunch of hoodlums, I'd appreciate it.'

As he speaks the world warps and rearranges itself around me; it feels like my chest plunges into my guts, knocking the air out of my lungs.

I can't reply. I just keep going, as far away from him as I can.

Everything shifts, just a little, everything I see, the buildings, the cars, trees, people, fade in and out. I start to feel the hard cool of concrete pressing against my thighs, even as I am standing. I reach out for a railing to steady myself and at the same moment as I feel cold metal in my hand, I also feel it flail through thin air.

'Luna?' He follows me a few steps as I hurry away. 'Goodnight!'

I see the world exploding into the air. A million tiny atoms collide and ricochet away; one picture fades in, another fades out, and just as I sink to the ground, rolling onto my side, clutching at the cracks in the sidewalk trying to keep myself anchored to the planet, I see him turn around and walk away. He doesn't look back.

My mind tilts, my stomach lurches, I close my eyes and feel the stars swing like a million bright pendulums on the other side of my lids. Finally, finally I am still. Opening my eyes, the first thing I see is the waning moon.

It's still the same moon, I find myself thinking.

CHAPTER NINE

* *

'Hey, lady, you OK?' a young woman, still holding her boyfriend's hand, bends to peer at me as she asks.

'I'm fine, I just fell, but I'm OK.' I drag myself to my feet. The street around me swirls and spirals, and I want them to leave so I can find something solid to hold on to.

'You sure?' She looks uncertainly at her boyfriend, who pulls her away, eager to be gone. I nod, and feel fluid rush around my head. As I watch them walk away, I realise that I am not in the same place where this all began, by the side entrance of the Lupo building. Somehow I have moved, and moved quite far. Slowly, very slowly, feeling as if lead weights are rolling to and fro in my head, I sit up wincing with every iron clank. The thought that I might have been wandering around caught up in some sort of hallucination terrifies me, but my wallet is still in my back pocket, at least, and so is my photo of Mum.

Taking great care, I trace my way back along 3rd Avenue to 93rd Street. It's only a couple of blocks but I walk very slowly, gaining a little confidence and energy with every step I take that is met with a hard surface, that doesn't fall away into nothing. As I finally climb the steps up to Mrs Finkle's place, my face is beaded with sweat and my hands are trembling. The front door key is just where Pea left it, behind the statue of Mary.

Well, I'm here. I am not dead. Whatever happened, it was … it was substantial. I need to call Brian, see a doctor as soon as I can. I can't hide from this anymore.

Pausing for a moment, I compose myself, taking a seat on the top step. This isn't something that I want to share with Pea, or anyone, quite yet. Whatever it is, it is mine alone. And as much as everything that happened tonight was impossible and terrifying, it was fascinating and beautiful too. I'd been afraid that by not falling to pieces when Mum died it somehow meant that I hadn't loved her enough. And then when I found out about my parentage, I'd been caught up in my own guilt, the awful certainty that I'd missed something, some hidden detail that could have saved her. But she was there, right at the centre of this catastrophe my brain was going through, like a beacon. A light I could home in on. There is something very wrong with me, something I can't ignore for very much longer. Whether it's psychological or medical, I don't know; all I know is that, whatever it is, it's bound to change my life. But for this moment, I am grateful for whatever is happening in my head. Grateful to experience just a few moments where I didn't have to miss my mother, to fear for her and mourn her.

Mrs Finkle opens the door behind me, startling me. 'You've been out very late all by yourself.'

'You're up very late,' I reply. Mrs Finkle winces as she takes a seat on the step next to me.

'I don't sleep so good anymore,' she says. 'Night comes and I watch it pass by following the shadows on the wall. It's very dull, getting old. Comes a time when you find a young woman weeping on your doorstep and you punch the air a little. Something to do, you know?'

She smiles as I smile, and leans into me.

'Your sister made her excuses after barely twenty minutes. I figured you'd be home a good while before now. You OK?'

I nod. No words will come.

'Nothing good ever came from bottling stuff up, you know,' Mrs Finkle tells me. 'It festers, spreads like an infection. Better out than in. You can tell me anything, I'll be dead soon anyhow.'

'You won't!' I say. 'I'm fine, really. I think being here, everything is catching up with me, that's all. No work to keep my mind focused away from everything that has happened. That's how I cope. I work, or deal with other people's problems. Pea's usually. And then suddenly we're here, and it's all about my mum. Everywhere I look, I miss her.'

'Where did you go anyway? You look like you been gone a real long time.'

It seems like a strange thing to say, but I suppose she is talking about my rumpled and dirt-smudged T-shirt and tangled hair. The sheen of feverish sweat that I can feel pricking my skin can't look so good either.

'Just walking around the neighbourhood,' I say.

'Would you like to have a drink with me? I know a lot of stories about your mom.'

'I would,' I say. 'I really would, but right now I'm dead on my feet, do you mind?'

'I don't mind. I wish I'd known, when I was younger, how falling asleep easy wasn't something you got to hold on to forever. You rest, sweetheart; seems like you lived a whole lifetime tonight.'

The apartment is cool, dark and quiet. I walk to Pea's bedroom and push the door open a little. She's sleeping on top of the covers, on her back, her arms flung out as if she is about to break into song. There is a glass of water by her bed. Just water.

Daybreak can't be too far away now; it would be nice to sleep before I wake up again, perhaps a sleep full of dreams and people that I love. In the morning I'll phone Brian; he'll help me, I know he will. He'll tell me what to do. And I'll talk to Pea, make sure she's got the support she needs before I begin the long process of finding out what is wrong with me, and watching my life change forever.

Now, though – oh, I am so tired – I simply want to sleep.

Tiredness sweeps over me in shuddering waves, and I'm grateful that Pea has already pulled out the sofa bed for me and made it up. Mustering the last of my energy, I wriggle out of my jeans, leaving them in a pool on the floor, finding a vest to sleep in. I search for my toothbrush in my luggage, and with my eyes half closed stumble into the bathroom, turning on the tap and waiting for the water to run cold. As I brush my teeth, I look in the mirror, studying my reflection that is studying me right back, and something is different. Something is unfamiliar. Prickles of disquiet punctuate my spine as I lean in closer, searching my blue eyes for some sign of what's going on behind them, and then as I put my brush down, about to shake away the uncertainty, I see it: the glimmer of silver on my throat.

In an instant I am wide awake, adrenalin racing through me.

I touch a quivering finger to my neck, and feel the object, real and solid. I'm sure it is. Resting just below the hollow at the base of my throat – my mother's medallion, the one I gave back to her in my ... *dream?* My mother's Saint Maria Goretti medallion is hanging around my neck.

And yet, until tonight, I barely remembered it had existed.

Is it really there?

'Pea!' I turn the light on in her room and she rolls over, covering her head with a pillow. 'Pea, wake up! I need you to look at me, look at me!'

'What Looney Tunes, what?' Pea sits up pushing her hair out of her face blinking at me. 'What the hell?'

'Is there something around my neck? Can you see something around my neck?' I keep my hands at my side, very still.

'Did you score crack or something when you went out?' Pea asks.

'So ... so there's nothing there?' My fingers fly to my throat, stopping short of actually touching my skin, too afraid of what I might feel.

'Only your necklace, you nutter,' Pea says. 'Did you think you'd lost it?'

'My necklace?' As I ask the question an answer seems to hover just out of reach, something that I almost know.

'Yes, Luna, seriously! The only thing around your neck is the medallion Dad found when we were clearing out Mum's things. He said it was her confirmation necklace. You're the one who's been wearing it ever since her funeral! Can I please go back to sleep now?'

'Yes,' I say, slowly, turning off the light and closing the door behind her. It's there, it's really there, the necklace that Mum almost lost, but I gave it back to her. It's there around my neck, where it wasn't before.

That's not possible. And yet it's true all the same.

CHAPTER TEN

I find my jeans in a tangle on the floor, my hands fumbling
as I try to shake them out, coins falling to the floor, a lipstick
rolling under the sofa. Hesitantly I reach into the back pocket
and touch the edges of Mum's photo, of Riss's photo.

As I draw it out, I see the familiar and now meaningful
words written in pencil on the back, 'July 12th, 1977'. A
few days from now, one day before she left Brooklyn with
my father.

The photo trembles in my hands as I turn it over, and I
hold it under the light.

Mum is wearing the medallion. And I know she has
always been wearing it in this photo and yet, at the same
time, I *know*, I am *certain*, that until just now, in this photo
that I have loved and treasured, pored over and looked at
almost every day of my life, there was no necklace. I know
both these things at once. Something happened, something
impossible, inexplicable, happened; something that makes
it seem that, in picking up my mother's dropped necklace,
in something like a dream, I changed the past, I changed
reality. I changed it enough to alter the present.

That can't be true.

That can't be possible.

It's just crazy talk.

And yet, I can't escape the thought that forms in my head so clearly that I can see it written large in my vision. If that *was* possible, if I had somehow stepped from one time into another and back again, then everything I thought I knew about space and time, everything *the world* thought it knew, would be wrong. But it hasn't happened, it couldn't have happened; this all has to be another symptom, that has something to do with my brain, it has to be. Because, imagine, just imagine for a moment if I had really visited the past and changed the future in this one small way. Imagine what that could mean. I'm not thinking of discovering who my real father is – it doesn't matter – as far as I care it's the man who raised me. The man I call Dad. No, I'm thinking of something better than answers.

If I could change the past and alter the present, I could do anything. Change the course of history, just enough to stop her from doing something unthinkable; something that scarred her forever.

I could alter my mother's life. I could save her.

I could bring her back from the dead.

CHAPTER ELEVEN

The necklace is there, around my neck. I feel it. And it's in the photo; I see it.

And I remember the day Dad gave it to me, the day of Mum's funeral.

I'd found him sitting in his study, staring out at the garden, his face hollow, empty, his dark suit hanging off of him as if, when she died, she had taken a physical part of him with her.

'The car's here,' I'd said. Pea was already in it, behind the tinted glass, sitting screwed up into a knot, and, although I didn't know it then, washing down painkillers with vodka from a hipflask.

'I knew she got sad sometimes,' Dad said, his eyes focused on the window, a riot of flowers and blue sky reflected in his glasses. 'Really sad, sometimes it was bad ... you know that.' Typical Dad, not mentioning directly the weeks she spent in bed, the long dark times when she didn't smile or look at us, just locked herself away in her summer house, working on projects we never saw, waiting for her smile to come back again. 'She had her problems. Moving here, away from everything she knew, and –' he'd paused and looked me '– she had stuff to deal with. But I always thought I'd helped her, made her better. I thought, eventually she'd see what we have and she'd be happy. I didn't see this coming.'

'None of us did, Dad,' I'd said, kneeling down at his feet. 'This wasn't your fault. None of us saw this, not after so long. She fought it for so long, I guess she was just tired of fighting.'

Dad had reached into his pocket, and brought out the medallion. And I remember how my heart leapt when I saw it, this achingly familiar object that I had seen resting against the skin of my mother's throat every day of my life, how I'd played with it as she'd rocked me to sleep as a baby, how I'd sweep back her long, midnight hair, and undo the clasp, on those times when she'd let me look at it, and tell me stories about her mother and her life as a little girl, running free on the street of Brooklyn. And as I close my eyes, I feel the same pain, the same pressure of tears, behind my eyes, and the rise of pride and love in my chest as Dad said: 'I was going to put this in with her, but then I thought, she would want you to have it. She knew how much you loved it, and I'd like to see you wearing it.'

After he'd fastened it around my neck, we'd hugged, and I cried until Dad's friend, Jack, had coughed politely outside the door, and we'd made our way to the funeral car.

That happened. I know it did, I remember it in every little detail.

But I also remember, less clearly as the minutes tick by, a whole other life where there was never a necklace. Where there was no moment in Dad's study, when it was Mum's hair that I played with when I fell asleep in her arms, and a story, she once told of a half-forgotten Catholic medallion she had worn, but lost long ago, one night just before she ran away from home.

Which one is real, which one is ... some kind of hallucination, I don't know. I don't know. And it's terrifying.

'Luna?' Brian's voice is muddled and confused as if I've just woken him, although it's gone eight in the morning there. Of course he's not expecting me to call him; we broke up. We haven't talked since, not because there is anger left, really. Just because it was done, and yet, if you asked me what he meant to me, I would still call him my friend. I'm about to find out if he feels the same way.

'Brian, it's Luna. I need to talk to you, I'm sorry. Is it OK?'

'Of course, what's wrong?' I hear him moving, closing doors. His voice is warm; he sounds pleased to hear my voice, and that makes me a little braver.

'I been having ... experiences?' I tell him.

'Experiences?' Brian asks.

'Yes. And I think ... I think there's something very wrong with me ...'

After I finish talking, Brian is very quiet for what seems like a long time.

'You're dealing with a lot,' he says. 'The death of your mum, and now finding out that you may have a different father from the man you grew up with.'

'I don't care about that.'

'You care about it more than you realise,' Brian tells me. 'That man, whoever he was, his medical history, is part of you. This might be something you inherited from him.'

'My mum was the one with mental health problems,' I remind him.

'Yes, but what you're describing isn't a mental health problem. It sounds physiological to me ...'

'Brian, what's happening?' I prompt him.

'Luna, I wish you weren't so far away.' He's upset, worried. I can tell he's collecting himself before he speaks. And that frightens me.

'What should I do?'

'You need a CT scan at once,' he says. 'You need blood tests, to look for biomarkers ... From what you're telling me, it's not psychosis, it could be stress related, exhaustion ... It might be some kind of chemical stimulant possibly, but you're not on drugs and this isn't the first time you've experienced this kind of thing ... I thought epilepsy before, but now ... Why didn't you let me get you checked out before?'

'You tried,' I reassure him. 'This isn't on you. What aren't you saying?'

'That it's more likely to be a physical anomaly.'

'A tumour.' I say the word out loud, because he won't.

'Visual hallucinations, like the one you describe, confusion, memory loss ...'

'It's not memory *loss*, it's memory *gain*,' I interrupt him. 'I have two sets of memories, two different versions of my life. What does that mean?'

'Sometimes a trauma can repress certain memories, and other cataclysmic events, like your mother's death, recent revelations, can throw up, muddled, even false memories that seem real and ...'

'This isn't false-memory syndrome,' I tell him.

'Well ... I can't say, but it's possible you have something going on in your temporal lobe, interfering with the optic nerve, that could cause hallucinations, although I've never heard of anything as vivid as you describe ... Jesus, Luna, I'm three thousand miles away, I don't know how to help you – speculation is pointless. You need to see a doctor, *today*. Get a CT scan, get bloods. I can find the name of a good specialist in New York and get you an appointment right away.'

I wait for a feeling of terror to grip me, but none does.

'Brian,' I say slowly. 'Remember how I used to tell you about my imaginary friends, the ones I had when I was little? The old woman in my bedroom, the kids in the playground that only I could see? For a lot of my childhood, right up until I was about twelve, and then I just decided not to see them anymore?'

'Yes, I remember, but I don't really see what that's got to do with this?'

'What if I am not ill, what if I just … stepped through time? What if I've been doing that all my life, what if we can all do it, but some of us are better at it than others. After all, people feel things, think they see things, all the time, and blame it on ghosts or the supernatural. What about déjà vu? What if it's just that sometimes the constructs of what we think of as time break down, just enough for us to get a glimpse of all the other moments happening around us?'

'Luna, you're a physicist.' Brian is anxious, I can hear it. 'Time travel is impossible, you know that. So you had imaginary friends as a kid, like thousands of other kids. There isn't a portal to an alternative reality in your brain, and if you are seriously considering just for moment that there is, then, well, you really are ill. And I am worried about you.'

'In less than a year from now they will switch on the Large Hadron Collider at CERN,' I tell him. 'And maybe, just maybe, they'll discover the God particle, maybe even the secrets of dark matter, ideas that once seemed like fantasy could become fact. Incredible discoveries happen all the time. The only thing that is impossible is the thing that no one imagines.'

Brian sighs, his frustration and anxiety audible. That he cares enough to be cross with me, touches me. We are still friends.

'Are you quoting Einstein?' he asks. 'Luna, this isn't funny. This isn't you, this person who isn't seeing the facts, the reality of what is happening. Please get some help. I'll find numbers; I'll get them to you. You never wanted me to take care of you when we were together, let me take care of you now.'

'Thank you, you're a good friend. Thank you for your help. I'll get to the bottom of this, I promise.'

'Good,' Brian hesitates. 'Whatever this is, once you know what you're dealing with, you can face it, fight it. As long as you know.'

Going to the window, I see the darkness of the night already giving way to another fierce summer day. I should be afraid, frightened for my health, my sanity and my life, but I'm not. Instead, as the sun burns a path into the sky, I am filled with a curiosity that is just as hot and intense.

Brian is right about one thing – I'm a scientist. I have to know the truth, whatever it may be. I have to know what happened to my mother, and what she did that she could never recover from. And the most wonderful discoveries that have ever been made by mankind always happen when someone decides to believe in the impossible.

8 JULY

'The long unmeasured pulse of time moves everything.
There is nothing hidden that it cannot bring to
light, nothing once known that may not
become unknown.'

—Sophocles

CHAPTER TWELVE

'Are you sure this is a lawyer's office?' Pea says as we stand outside the strange, store-fronted practice, after a few hours of fitful sleep. It had felt like I'd be up for a whole day by the time she emerged from her room, but it was only just nine. I'd been waiting for her to wake up, sitting on the edge of the unmade sofa bed, working out ways to explain to her that I probably had a brain tumour, but just before I got that checked out I wanted to test the theory that I might be able to travel through time.

The minute she had finally appeared though, in an outsized T-shirt, lost behind a cloud of hair, her legs covered in the bruises that she gets so easily, I had changed my mind. Every scientific experiment needs a control. Something that isn't influenced by external factors. I can't tell Pea what's happening to me, I have to show her. She can be my control.

'What?' She looks at me now over the frames of her sunglasses.

'What do you mean "what"?' I shrug.

'You're looking at me as if was *me* who wandered off last night and didn't come back for hours, and then burst into my room raving about a necklace, but it wasn't. It was you, madam. Are you OK? You seem a bit ... off. And I know I mostly make everything all about me, but you know, you can talk to me if you're having a breakdown about Mum or what she told us. Or if you're thinking of scoring crack or something. I know all the best spots.'

'Nothing so exciting,' I say. 'Just sleep deprived, and emotional, being here. It's driving me a little bit nuts but, yes, this is the lawyer who is handling the sale's office.'

'Really? Because frankly, if it is, then I'm worried for our safety.'

'That's his name on the sign,' I say, pointing up at the hand-painted, peeling signage. 'WATKINS GILLESPIE, ATTORNEY AT LAW'.

'So you're not worried that it looks like a junk shop that's gone out of business?' Pea says, and she has a point. The display unit behind the grimy plate glass is painted black. A thick film of dust dulls its surface, and a sizeable dead spider lies huddled against the glass.

'Well, he's the lawyer who's been appointed to sell the property; Aunt Stephanie chose him, I suppose. If we want a sale to go through, there's nothing else for it; we have to go in.'

Inside, the shop is dusty and still, except for a woman behind a rickety-looking desk, sitting at a very old-looking PC, her lips pursed in concentration as she types.

'You gonna just stand there all day?' she says eventually. 'Or you gonna tell me why you're here?' She raises a perfectly shaped eyebrow at us over her monitor.

'Oh, sorry,' I say, 'I thought you were busy ... We have an appointment with Mr Gillespie?'

'You're the Sinclairs,' she tells us. 'Here about the sale of a property jointly owned with one Stephanie Coulson née Lupo.'

'That's us – ta-dah!' Pea says, waggling jazz hands, and I stare at her. She shrugs. 'Just injecting a spot of levity.'

The woman's stern countenance melts into a warm smile, and she chuckles as she extends her hand over the desk.

'And they tell me you Brits are always so uptight,' she says. 'Pleased to meet you. I'm Lucy Cortez. I'm Mr Watkin's paralegal. You go right on through. And don't mind him. He may come over like he's drunk or mad, but he's still the best lawyer there is in Bay Ridge. Well, on Third Avenue anyway, unless you count Cynthia Curzon, which I guess you better.'

Pea smiles at me as we go through and knock on an office door with smoked glass; Mr Gillespie's name is etched on it in gold lettering.

'Ah, you must be Luna and Pia Sinclair,' he says, standing up with some effort in order to greet us. White shirt, grey suit, well made, if a little worn and shiny at the seams. He is older than I expected – in his seventies, I am guessing – but he carries himself as if he's not, making a noticeable effort to square his shoulders and straighten his back. Something about him speaks to me at once; I know that at the very least I want to like him. 'Via Scotland, I do not doubt, but before that sons of Normandy and the St Clair dynasty, who came over to your fine country with William the Conqueror.'

'Um. Via Oxfordshire, actually,' Pea says, pushing her shades into her hair.

'Recently, perhaps,' Watkins Gillespie says, gesturing at the two plastic garden chairs that he seems to have arranged for us to sit on, opposite his desk. 'But everyone is via somewhere else much more ancient that we remember. All of us via the plains of Africa if we travel far enough back in time. Imagine that, you and I, we share a common ancestor.'

'You're right, of course,' Pea says, smiling, 'and I read somewhere that about one in two hundred of all men are directly related to Genghis Khan.'

'The cranky ones, I imagine.' Mr Gillespie chuckles. 'So, you're here to sign some papers, to allow the sale of the property known as three zero two one, Ninety-Third and Third, also known as Lupo's Tailoring and Alterations, that your late mother jointly owned with her sister, my client, after their father's death in nineteen eighty-three. Is that correct?'

'Yes, but we want to see the building too,' Pea adds. 'As you know, we lost Mum recently, that's why we are here. We want to see the place she grew up, find out more about her life before she left America.'

Mr Gillespie pauses, his blue eyes rising to meet mine. 'I knew her, your mother, Marissa. I knew the whole family; they made my suits, you know. But I had a soft spot for Marissa, so beautiful, so full of light. She had always seemed to me like one of those people who were born on fire, you know what I mean? Burning for something more. I wasn't at all surprised that she left Bay Ridge, but I think maybe I was the only one that wasn't. I was sorry to hear of her passing.'

'Thank you,' I say, and Mr Watkins nods.

'We're keen to see inside the place that she grew up,' I tell him. 'Afterwards, we want to get the building on the market as soon as possible.'

'Do you know why your mother never agreed to sell while she was alive?' Watkins asks me.

'We don't know, only that she wouldn't even talk about it. Maybe she hoped she'd come back here one day,' I tell him. 'So, how do we get things moving?'

Watkins smiles. 'We simply take a stroll.'

'I don't know why, but I feel like Mum will be there, waiting for us,' I say, more to myself than the room.

'Ms Sinclair ... May I call you, Luna?' Gillespie asks. I nod. 'I lost my darling wife, Serena, a whole lifetime ago. Every day since I've felt like she's in the next room, or waiting for me on the corner, every day for so long that I could only reach one logical conclusion.'

'And what's that?' Pea asks. Mr Gillespie beams at her.

'Quite simply, that she is,' he says. 'You see, our physical bodies, they break down, eventually returning to dust, but *energy*, energy is never destroyed. And what is love, if it isn't the most powerful energy we know of?'

'Yes, the first law of thermodynamics.' I smile. 'Although I'm not sure you could technically describe love as a form of energy ...'

'Of course you can.' Mr Gillespie grins at me. 'Love is life, and life is the very definition of energy.'

'Well, that's poetic but ...'

'It's so amazing to meet people who knew our mum then,' Pea interrupts me before I can start a scientific argument. 'Every time we do we're building up this picture of her, of this girl, this woman, that we never really knew.'

'If you have any questions at all while you are here, or need any help, come by. No need to call first, my door is always open to you. I'd enjoy talking about the old days, and about Marissa and the Lupo family again.'

'Thank you. Mr Gillespie, would you mind if I asked you a question about Stephanie?' It's Pea that asks.

Mr Gillespie nods his assent.

'Have you been in touch with her all of these years?'

'On and off,' Gillespie says. 'I've known her and her husband for a long time. I guess that's why she asked me to handle this sale.'

'Well, maybe you don't know – but was Stephanie sorry to hear of my mum's death?' Pea's dark eyes become still and serious.

Watkins Gillespie observes us both for a moment.

'Well now, young lady,' he says. 'I think your aunt never wanted your mother to leave Brooklyn, maybe never forgave her for going. And I guess she's made a lot of difficult choices in her life, choices she might regret and, what I know is, she's angry and … well, to tell the truth, an unhappy person. And angry and unhappy people are always sorry about something. But if it helps, I happen to know that she bitterly missed your mother every day of her life.'

'Then why did she never get in touch again?' Pea asked. 'Why did Mum never hear from her, except via a lawyer every time she wanted to try and sell?'

'That I don't know.' Gillespie looks thoughtful. 'What I will say is, from what I know of Stephanie, she wasn't ever the sort of person to admit she was in the wrong, no matter how much it cost her. Maybe that was it. But anyway, once the sale is completed, you won't ever have to think about her or Bay Ridge again if you don't want to.'

'Oh, I don't know,' I say. 'I think we've only just started our journey of discovery.'

CHAPTER THIRTEEN

Watkins Gillespie regales us with tales of local villains, felons and their many misdemeanours, as we take the short walk to the corner where Lupo's Tailoring and Alterations is situated. With every step I take, I find I have to check myself, slowing down to match his more leisurely gait, trying not to show that I already know the way there.

'Of course, round here, you paid your respects to the people that mattered,' he tells us, as we finally cross the road towards our destination. I stare at the building, halted in my tracks by what I can see of it above the fences that imprison it. Under the glare of the noonday sun it seems to squint, blinded and boarded up, the brickwork crumbling and collapsing into itself, so fragile-looking that it might only be held together by the roots of stubborn weeds that grow from the cracks in the mortar.

'You look like you've seen a ghost,' Pea says.

'It looks so different.'

'Different from what?' Pea asks me, turning her face to the near ruin.

'Er … from what I expected,' I say. The building I thought I'd visited was old, but was cared for, maintained. I couldn't have mistaken that home, full of life and people, for this shadow of a building.

'I don't know why, but I feel nervous.' Pea takes my hand. 'Seeing the place that Mum grew up in, we're expecting it to mean something, but what if it doesn't?' Her eyes track back across the street, searching out a noodle bar, a health food shop and finally drawing her gaze with its siren call, a dark and narrow bar. 'I'd kill for a beer now, anything to take the edge off how I'm feeling.'

'I'll take the edge off,' I say, dragging my eyes away from the crumbling bricks and mortar and onto her. 'You and me, together. There is nothing to be afraid of in there, whatever we feel or find, even if it's nothing, we came here together, we leave here together. Just coming here – it's enough.'

Pea studies my face, trying to interpret my new certainty, and I know she senses it, the optimism I am feeling, the expectation; she just can't figure out where it has come from Pia knows it was here, or somewhere near here, that Mum did something she thought of as a terrible sin, something that ruined her life. And if Pia knew what Brian thought, if she knew what I'm risking just to test something that cannot possibly be, to try and find out, she'd probably want to kill me.

Mr Gillespie is still talking, seemingly unaware of our whole exchange, as we come to a standstill by the security fencing. 'No, you never wanted to get on the wrong side of the guys who ran things, nobody wanted to pay a visit to The Gemini Lounge. That never ended well. Me, I stayed out of it as much as could, paid my dues, kept my head down. They thought I was small fry. I was, and happy to be, flying under the radar. Well, ladies, we have arrived. This is your inheritance, or half of it is, at least.'

A chain-link security fence, topped with spirals of razor wire, stretches around the circumference of the building, and behind that a plyboard wall has been erected, some time ago by the looks it. It's weathered and worn, and covered in many layers of graffiti. Every window we can see is covered with solid, steel shutters, screwed to the bricks, preventing any hope of breaking in. Around the corner, as we walk down the alleyway, we find a heavily padlocked gate set into the external defences, and beyond that, another steel door covering the side entrance that I thought I walked through last night.

Well, I certainly didn't wander through that in the grip of a delusion or an hallucination. I'd have been caught and cut up by the wire, stopped by the door.

'Ah, here's Mr Green, from Ridge Security Solutions.' Mr Gillespie greets a heavily set man in a dark suit; a thick metal ring bristling with keys jangles against his hip. He's carrying a tool box in one hand and has a large box tucked under his arm. As he approaches my eyes are drawn to the box. It is open and full of smaller packages. Even with the label partially obscured by the bend of his arm, I recognise the handwriting on the top one. It belongs to Mum.

'Mr Green, are you a Reservoir Dog?' Pea asks, and Mr Green smiles wearily; that's not the first time he's heard that joke.

'Watkins.' Mr Green nods at Mr Gillespie. 'Are these the relatives?'

'Yes, Mr Green.' Gillespie nods back.

'Well, then, I guess this belongs to you.' Mr Green offers us the large box, and it's Pea who takes it.

'It's heavy,' she says, steadying it with one knee, seeing what I've already realised. 'It's Mum's writing on the label.'

Pea and I look at each other, and I take the box from her.

'When?' I can't seem to find the rest of a sentence, and fortunately Mr Green doesn't seem to need one.

'It arrived months ago. I didn't feel like I could pass it on to Mrs Coulson. It's not addressed to her.'

That was certainly true; the recipients written large, on this label at least, read, 'My Daughters'.

'I just held on to it. Figured that maybe one day the lady that sent it might come and collect. I never opened it, I don't know what's inside. When Gillespie got in touch and told me the other lady that owned the building had died, and that her daughters were coming out, it kind of made sense. So I brought it over.'

Seven months ago, around the time that Mum died. Does that mean this box contains the answers to everything we don't know? Might it contain his name?

'Thank you for keeping it,' I say, because someone has to say something, and Mr Green smiles, satisfied that he's done the right thing.

'I could take that back to the office for you, if you like?' Mr Gillespie offers. 'You don't want to be hauling that around.'

'Thank you, but no.' I shake my head. 'Seems like this package has been finding its way to us for a while, I don't want to let it go now. I suppose we'd better get on with this.'

As we wait, I wonder what we will discover inside, if anything. What frightens me the most is the prospect of finding nothing here, no answers, Just empty rooms.

We stand back as Mr Green opens the gate, and then, taking an electric screwdriver out of his toolkit, he begins to unbolt the steel shutter that covers the door.

'Would you mind?' It's Pea who steps in and braces her slight form against the metal door as he takes the last bolts out, until, taking the weight of the door off her, he slides it to one side with some difficulty, the metal screeching as he drags it along the rough brick work, finally laying it to rest on the floor.

A fizz of adrenalin charges through me from my chest to my fingertips, like lightening, as the side door is revealed. The vivid-green side door, although now faded and peeling, is exactly as I saw it last night, including the strange lion's-head door knocker and the out-of-place handle. Hefting the weight of the package on to my hip, I reach out, closing my fingers around it; it's real.

Is there a photo somewhere of this doorway, forgotten in one of Dad's stacks of albums? Did Mum tell me stories of the lion's-head door knocker when I was a little girl, and the colour of the door? Logic says this information had to have come from some dark corner of my memory, but what is logical isn't always what is correct. My heart has just found a reason to start beating again.

'When was the last time anyone was in there?' Pea asks, gently removing my hand from the door.

'Early nineteen eighties,' Mr Gillespie tells us. 'Stephanie and her husband moved your grandfather down to Florida. I think that was eighty-one ... Yes, I'm sure of it.'

'But we make routine inspections of it, every couple of months,' Mr Green adds. 'Last time in the log book just a couple of week ago, when Stephanie told us you were coming. She wanted an inventory.'

'So, no big secrets or surprises in there then?' Pea asks.

'Not unless you count spiders, and maybe some rats.'

'Jesus!' Pea's laugh flashes like a burst of light in the shaded alley.

'Here's the keys and a couple of flashlights, you'll need them.' Mr Green holds out the items in the palms of his hands, almost like offerings, and Pea takes them.

'You have access now for the duration of your visit,' Mr Gillespie says. 'You know where to find me if you need assistance of any kind. Are you sure don't want me to keep hold of that box for you, until you're done?'

'No, but thank you.' We exchange nods and wait for what seems like an age as the two men reach the end of the alleyway and turn the corner at last.

'Luna . . .' Pea looks at me. 'A box of packages from Mum, what the hell?'

'I know,' I say. 'Let's deal with one thing at a time. Shall we go in?'

Pea looks long and hard at the door, and nods.

'There's no turning back now.'

CHAPTER FOURTEEN

As soon as we step inside, the door swinging to a close with a soft thud, darkness engulfs us. Standing perfectly still, I let the spaces around me slowly reveal themselves. Mixed in with the smell of dust and mildew there is just a little syrupy drizzle of light filtering in, from under the door and around the edges of one tiny boarded up window. Despite what Mr Green told us, Pea tries the light switches.

'Torches,' I remind her, edging my way to where the pattern-cutting table was, a spike of adrenalin sends a fizz of energy to the tips of my fingers. I knew exactly where the table would be. I stand still, searching for that tell-tale surge of electricity that seems to proceed these mysterious events, certain my sense of déjà vu is a trick of the brain, but there is nothing. Just a dark and dusty room.

Easing the box down onto the surface, I slide it through a thick carpet of dust and fine debris.

'Oh yeah.' Pea passes me a flashlight and two haphazard beams bounce around the room, dazzling me before skipping away again.

'Point your torch somewhere sensible!' I complain, shielding my eyes as she points it right at my face again.

'Like where?' Pea asks, demurely.

'At things, not me!' I say. 'Come and stand by me, we can operate a sweep system.'

'You're hilarious.' Pea's grin is exaggerated by the shadows the torches cast. 'Everything has to be orderly. Everything must be scientific.'

'Not everything, just important things, and anyway just do as you are told for once.'

'Or what, you'll terminate the experiment?'

Nevertheless, Pea picks her way over an accumulation of trash and bits of fallen ceiling to come and stand by my side. We start a sweep left to right, tracking our torches over the room inch by inch. As every beam of yellow light passes over the dirt and decay, I see glimpses of what I somehow already know is there, and each discovery fills me with more fear and something else; something like excitement, something like hope.

What if?

An image of Riss as I saw her last night, laughing and talking, fades into one of Mum, testing the water with her fingers as she runs the bath that she doesn't plan to ever emerge from, and I wonder what *she* saw when she thought about this place. When she was writing out those labels, sending missives to an empty building. I've always believed that nothing on earth, not even the burden of the pain and secrets she carried, would have let her leave us unless she thought we would be OK. As the bath filled with warm water, as she topped up a glass of red wine, and unscrewed the cap on her antidepressants, she must have been picturing our lives without her, and she must have thought that we would manage, that perhaps we might even do better without her. But we aren't doing better, not really. Dad wanders around from room to room, like a lost dog. Pea is on the brink of disaster every second of the day, and I ... I want Mum back so badly that it feels as if I'm turning the universe all around me to dust, just to be near her again.

'Funny how a room becomes something else completely when there have been no people in it for a very long time.' Pea breaks my train of thought, her voice amplified in the dense quiet. 'Like a negative of a print, full of the absences. Take some photos, Luna – we should record every moment of this.'

'It will be tricky in this light,' I tell her. 'I don't have a flash, the right speed of film or lens – most likely nothing will come out, but I'll try.'

Lifting the Pentax to my eye, I adjust the aperture to let in as much of the light as possible, shooting into dark corners and deep shadows, uncertain of what I am taking an image of: perhaps nothing; maybe everything.

'I guess the shop must be through there,' Pea says, stepping over a broken and rotting floorboard to pull open a door, forcing it a little, ploughing a path through crumbling plasterboard and rotting wood that has built up behind it. She vanishes into another room, and all I can see of her is the light zig-zagging beyond the crack in the door.

'Luna, get in here, there are still a couple of mannequins standing in the window! It's really creepy.'

I don't reply, every detail I take in, even by torchlight, confirms something that simply cannot be. As old, empty and broken as it is, this is the same room that I walked into last night, exactly the same physical space. Brian would say the world and people and places are not nearly as different or unique as we think they are; Brian would say it's not so much an extraordinary coincidence as much as life being intrinsically quite samey, and my injured brain turning that into something that seems magical. But that's not what I see. I see a thousand impossibilities that are somehow now within my reach.

'Luna?' Pea's head appears round the door that leads into the store. 'Aren't you coming?'

'No.' I shake my head, turning off the torch, double-folding the dark in an instant. 'Whatever's in the box, it's a message from her; it's answers. Maybe a reason why she did what she did? Maybe about who my father is? I mean my biological father. We need to open it, and I think we should do it here, in her room, now.'

'How do we know which room is hers?' Pea's tone is reluctant. She'd much rather play at *Scooby-Doo* and delay opening the box for as long as possible and I don't blame her, but the number of seconds between now and peeling back the tape that holds it shut are irrelevant. Sooner or later it has to be done.

'Mrs Finkle told me how she used to sit out at the top of the fire escape and smoke,' I say, thinking of the girl I met last night and how she leant on the slender iron railings without the slightest fear of the drop below. 'Whichever room leads out onto that will be her room.'

Pea shrugs, lighting the way for me as I pick up the box and test the bottom stair. It groans under my weight but seems sound.

'I'm scared all of a sudden,' Pea says, just as I reach the second step, her voice sounding very small and very young.

'Of a spooky old building?' I try to sound teasing, patronising.

'No,' she says. 'Of what's in the box. Of knowing the truth.'

CHAPTER FIFTEEN

* *

The first-floor rooms feel as if they haven't been occupied for a hundred years. The windows are brutally secured, as on the floor below, but unlike the workshop, a fair amount of daylight makes its way through the iron cladding, casting narrow bolts of sun across the room, each one revealing a universe of dust particles. Somewhere I hear faint music playing. I turn to look at Pea.

'Where's that coming from?'

Lost in her own thoughts, she wanders into the space where at some point last night I saw my mother as a young woman, sitting on the back of a sofa, digging her bare toes between the cushions. She was here, as real as the weight of my camera in my hand, she was here.

In quantum physics, two atoms can exist in more than one place at once, changing their behaviour depending on the way that we look at them. Two particles can interact instantaneously, even if they are a million light years apart. There's a theory called the quantum multiverse, where an infinite number of universes coexist in exactly the same place. What if this is something like that? A universe where all moments of time exist at the same time, for all time? And while we've been arguing over the paradox of time travel since H.G. Wells, what if it isn't a machine we need to travel through time? What if the apparatus already exists in our minds? My heart rate picks up at the possibilities I'm allowing myself to consider, and the distant music grows louder.

'Pea?' I prompt her. 'Where's that coming from?'

'Where's what coming from?' Her tone is vague, her eyes sweeping over the mouldering decay, tracing the darker patches on the walls and floor where once pictures and furniture stopped the sun in its tracks. I match one dark patch to a 1977 Elvis calendar, in the corner where I somehow know a TV used to stand.

'I ... I don't know, must be a car radio or something.'

Shrugging, she listens for a moment, shakes her head and moves on.

'Kitchen's through here,' Pea calls, as she explores the other two rooms that radiate off the small landing. The music fades as I follow her into the small space, replaced by the more natural sound of creaking floorboards and passing traffic. There's a damp gap, filled with thick, black mould, where the sink used to be, and brutal scars left by long-gone shelves on the wall. Hard and rotting lino bubbles and cracks under our feet.

At the bottom of the second flight of stairs the music breaks through again, this time loud enough for me to be able to pick out phrases of melody, a bass line. I listen hard trying to make sense of it; it doesn't seem to be a song I know.

'You don't hear that?' Pea doesn't even register my question.

'My arms are getting tired, carrying this box around. I'm going up,' I say, stumbling up the second flight of stairs. The air feels charged, electrified, as if a storm is about to break. The music grows in intensity with each step I take, until suddenly it fills every corner so loudly that it deafens me, boring into my eardrums, enough to cause me pain. I catch my foot on some fallen debris and trip, staggering past the door that I know leads to Riss's room, thudding into the one opposite. Putting the box down, I place my palms against the rough surface of that door, where the music is coming from. Peeling paint crumbles away from my fingers, and the rotten wood vibrates in time to the bass line.

And yet, the moment I touch the handle, the music stops. No, not stops; it jumps like a stuck needle on scratched vinyl, repeating the same five words over and over again, 'The year of the cat, the year of the cat', so loud I can't hear the sound of my own short, panicked breaths. Every single moment that has ever happened, or ever will, feels like it's all existing in this one space.

'Who's there?' I shout, pushing the door open hard enough to make it bounce off the wall, leaving a puff of plaster dust in its wake.

For a fraction of a second I see a young woman sitting there, as clear as the daylight streaming in through a clean glass window. It's Stephanie, I realise, sitting at a little ornate, cream, dressing table, its drawers and edges gilded with gold, carefully applying lipstick, her mouth an open 'O', a frown of concentration reflected in an oval vanity mirror. A heady, heavy perfume mists the air, maybe from the bottle of Charlie that has rolled onto its side. In the very fraction of a second that I see her, our eyes lock as she catches my reflection in her mirror and screams.

And then there is silence, darkness and dust. The room is empty, nothing of what I just saw remains, except a single broken drawer, probably from a dressing table. A drawer that I know, if I took it to the light and wiped it clean, I would find was edged with gold.

A tidal wave of nausea doubles me over, my eyes filling with water as I struggle not to retch. Heat flushes through me, a droplet of sweat hesitates at the end of my nose, before smashing on the dusty floor. Everything hurts.

'Were you shouting?' Pea makes me start as she calls up the stairs. Forcing myself straight I take a couple of deep breaths, wiping the perspiration from my face with my palms in the seconds before she arrives. But when she enters it isn't me she is looking at. Her eyes scan the empty room.

'Who were you shouting at?' She turns to me.

'Not me,' I say. 'Outside, maybe.'

'This place is so strange and quiet, I forget there's an outside ...' She hesitates, grabbing me by the wrist and pulling me into what little light there is. 'Luna, your nose is bleeding.'

'Is it?' I touch the back of my hand to my face and a drop of blood balances there. 'Oh, it's nothing, just one of those things.'

'Here.' Pea passes me a tissue. 'Sure you're OK?'

'I'm fine.' I don't think she sees the way my hands are trembling, or how I am having to fight to stand up straight. A nosebleed. Is this a physical side effect of some kind of growth in my head, or is stepping between dimensions taking its toll on my fragile flesh? With some effort, I gesture to the other room. 'That must have been Mum's room.'

Pea shudders and grabs my hand, pulling me into the hallway.

'What if we just leave the box here?' she says. 'Dad doesn't know about it, about any of this, and we don't have to tell him, *we* don't have to know. We can just leave it here, where it belongs. Maybe she never meant us to see this stuff, maybe we shouldn't look.'

'It's too late now,' I say. 'We know it exists now, everything has already changed. There's no going back.'

Very slowly she shakes her head.

'Then let's get it over with.'

The heat seems to be pressing into every crevice and crack, thickening with dust so that I can almost taste it, like burnt air on my tongue. We push open the door to Riss's room.

'Oh!' Pea's hand flies to her mouth. 'I didn't expect there to still be stuff in here. Her stuff, Luna. The place where she slept!'

I take in the single bed and its sunken, stained mattress; the same heavy, dark wood, gothic wardrobe that I saw last night, staggers against the wall opposite the bed. I'm half expecting to see the dress she had made still hanging off one corner, covered in cobwebs, like a sort of updated Miss Havisham, but it isn't there, and I'm relieved.

'OK,' I say, retrieving the box from the hallway and placing it on the bed.

'Ready?' Pea asks.

'I'm ready,' I say. Of course, that's a lie.

No one is ever ready for the world they thought they knew to burn down all around them.

CHAPTER SIXTEEN

* *

Pea holds the torch, training it on the box.

It's padded with the crunched up sheets of our local newspaper. News of local fairs, and school choirs making regional finals seems so alien and out of place here. Pushing it aside with my fingertips, I search for the box's contents. It doesn't take me very long to find the first object.

'Shit,' I say, my finger resting on it, delaying the moment when I have to take it out.

'What?' Pea is insistent.

Reaching in with both hands I carefully lift the first object out.

'Mum's old projector,' I say. 'I hadn't realised that it wasn't at home, I don't know why I didn't notice. She must have sent this here, knowing . . .'

'Jesus.' Pea stares at it as I set it on the bed. 'What else?'

Next something heavy and unfamiliar, but as soon as I see what it is, my heart breaks a little more. The forethought and the planning that went into this package. The intention.

'It's a power source, a battery, the one Dad bought for that disastrous camping trip we went on, the one where we all ended up in a hotel – something to run the projector from.'

'She thought of everything.' Pea's voice is very small, very quiet.

Finally I take out a tin, a biscuit tin, aged and dented; it must be one that Mum had had for a long time. Inside there are four numbered reels of Super 8 film.

'So what do we do?' Pea asks me.

'Watch them,' I say. 'That's obviously what she wanted us to do. This is why we didn't find a note at home. A throwaway note; that was never going to be Mum's style. She made us more films, and sent them here.'

'Luna, I'm not sure if I can . . .'

I look up sharply at my sister.

'Pea, you can. I need you to be able to do this with me. I need you to be strong, because I know one thing, I can't do this alone.'

'Right.' Pea nods. 'OK.'

'I guess we start with number one,' I say. 'The far wall is pretty good for projection. I think I saw a chair downstairs; we need something better to set this up on.

'I'll get it.' Pea's tone is flat, quiet, as she heads downstairs.

When she returns she holds the torch and I work to set the projector up, taking the task moment by moment, not thinking about what will happen when we finally start it running.

'I don't know how much juice is in this battery pack,' I say. 'Depends if Mum thought to charge it before she . . .'

'Well, she thought of everything else,' Pea says. 'Luna, this whole thing. The building, the projector – shit, even the trip. None of it seems real, does it? It's all a bit like it's some kind of dream, don't you think? Like we might wake up at any minute.'

And she only knows the half of it.

'But am I in your dream, or are you in mine?' I ask her, plugging the projector into the power pack. I hold out a hand to her. 'Ready?'

Taking it she nods. 'Ready.'

The room that was virtually pitch-black seconds before is now filled with dazzling light, a rainbow of colours flickering and flashing as the film feeds through the reels: scratches, hairline flaws, for an instant nothing at all, and then her.

Like the film we watched at home, she's in her beloved garden on a warm summer's day. Hollyhocks and lupins stand tall and beautiful behind her, superimposed on the lumps and cracks of the wall behind, the peeling wallpaper and mould-ridden damp patches. It takes Mum moment to settle into her carefully positioned chair, a moment more as she stares into the distance, deep in thought. Then she turns, and looks into the camera. She looks at us.

'What I'm about to tell you is going to be very hard for me. I've lived all my life with this story and it has never gotten any easier. But for you, too, it's going to be very hard for you.'

Pea's fingers tighten around mine; we are utterly silent and still.

CHAPTER SEVENTEEN

* *

'Jesus.' I clasp my hands over my mouth, as if I am trying to stuff the last few seconds of time down my throat and swallow them whole. '*Jesus.*'

The air around me fills with heat, and exhaust, pushing its way into my lungs, but still I suck it in, grateful for any oxygen that has seen sunlight. Glad to be out of that building filled with ... with words I cannot allow to be true. My knees buckle, and I see the sky fall away from me, as I stagger out onto the street, before the vibrant pain of my head crashing against the sidewalk is lost in darkness.

Feet, brightly coloured, block heels, yellow flares, red sandals step over me.

The hems of pleated summer skirts flare in my face as busy people rush by, and, as I watch them, I see the street, empty and composed, except for an elderly lady, trailing a trolley bag behind her. At exactly the same time, a group of women talking loudly about some guy called Paulie and what a dirt bag he is. They walk where the old woman walks, at exactly the same moment, like a double exposure, they occupy the same space, the same moment. I am not here.

No one sees me. Feet don't step *over* me, they step through me. I don't them feel moving through my core, because I am both here and not here. I am then and not then. In this moment, I am nowhere.

I understand the peace that Mum was so desperate for; I get just a glimpse of what it must be like to be a ghost, feeling that if I could find a way to raise my hands to my eyes, I could watch myself fly away into the air, one particle at a time.

I remember what she'd said in her film, her reasons why, and a sob rips through me. It can't be true, it just can't be true.

We sat there, the two us, hand in hand in that dark and dirty room, as she told us, once again, so close to the camera that we could only see part of her face, that she had been stalked all of her life by a ghost that never let her go.

And then she looked at me.

'Luna, I was never going to tell you,' she says. 'But I have to, I see that now.' Mum stopped, looking at the camera, and somehow, even before she said it, I almost knew what was coming next. 'I was raped, at home, in my bedroom. By someone I knew and liked, someone I thought I could trust.' She closed her eyes, and I saw that all-too-familiar crease deepen as she fights back a memory. 'It was bad, and I was hurt. I was unconscious for a little while, and as I was coming round I realised he had his hands on my throat. The pain, the pressure, the desperate need to breathe. I knew that if I blacked out that would be it, I'd never make it out alive. I thought of Henry, and my sister – and somehow I even thought of you, my children, and the future that I wanted so badly – and I didn't want to die, I refused to die for him.

'I don't remember much, I don't know where the strength or fury came from, only that I wasn't going to die, and it was clear that if it wasn't going to be me, then it would have to be him. I kneed him hard, between the legs. It winded him, and in his fury he hit me, but he lost his grip, lost his balance. He fell, slipped in blood, my blood. I heard this crack as the back of his head hit the corner of my wardrobe. He was dazed, lying there, jammed between my bed and the wardrobe. And I ... I knelt on his chest, grabbed his hair again. I took hold of his head and I smashed it as hard as I could against the wardrobe, and I did it again and again, until most of the blood on the floor was his. Until he was silent and still. I was twenty years old and I'd just killed a man, a man I knew everyone liked and respected. But I didn't die, I didn't let him have that.'

The summer sky over her head had rippled against the dirty wall, pocked with mould.

As we watched, she took a deep breath, and I saw the tension, the weight of what she has lived with, drain away from her. 'I couldn't go to the police. Besides, back then it wasn't the cops we went to if we were in trouble. But, in any case, it didn't matter, because I knew I wouldn't be believed. He was a pillar of the community, beloved not only by me, but the whole neighbourhood. My father respected him. Thought he was a good man. So I knew that it would be my fault, it would be because of what I wore, that I'd invited him into my home. They'd say that I set out to seduce him. I knew it would be like that, because that's what it was like then. A girl like me, who liked short skirts and strappy tops, well, a girl like me was asking for it. God knows, before it happened to me, I felt that way too.

'So I ran away. July thirteenth, nineteen seventy-seven, the night of the blackout. The city was dark, except for the fires from the looting. It was chaos, no cops anywhere, the only people out on the street were the people who were up to no good. It was the perfect night to get away with a crime and I was lucky I had a sister who knew how to do it. If it had been Dad that had come looking for me instead of Stephanie, it would have been a very different story.'

Her gaze shifts past the camera, and it's as if she's looking into the room, into the corner, as if she can see where it happened. Mum returns her focus down the lens. 'Stephanie was dating a guy who was a foot soldier for the Mob; he knew people, I guess. People who cleaned up this sort of mess. And he'd do anything for Stephanie. My sister didn't even blink an eye, she just took over. There was no question of cops or telling anyone. She ran a bath, scalding hot, on a boiling hot night. She had to cut my clothes off of me, there had been such a lot of blood. Some mine. I remember her hands on my shoulders, guiding me into the bath, and how it scalded because it so hot it was nearly unbearable, turning my skin red raw. I sat in that bath until the red water became cold and I started to shiver.

'Eventually Stephanie came for me. She told me everything was taken care of, I was to never say a word about what had happened to anyone. I was going to leave with Henry as planned. I was in shock, I guess, but so was she, I think. It was only when I was ready to go, ready to find Henry, that I realised that the remnants of the dress I'd been wearing were still in the bathroom. I picked them up, and stuffed them behind the wardrobe in my room. I poured bleach onto the floor and left it there in a pool. It wasn't until I was on the plane to England that I started to shake, and I couldn't stop. Henry thought I was frightened of living somewhere new, but I was frightened of what I'd left behind, and the secret I took with me.'

Mum's hands, so fine and delicate, replicate that tremble as she reaches for the cigarette that had been sitting, waiting in the ashtray on the garden table. 'I knew about you a couple of weeks after we arrived in London. I knew you had to be from him. I thought I would hate you, I thought that Henry would hate me. When I told him I was pregnant, even though he knew that you couldn't be his, he didn't ask any questions, and I couldn't tell him how it happened. I couldn't allow myself to even think about it. Maybe he knew, maybe he sensed what had happened, but if he did, he also knew that I couldn't talk about it, not then, not ever. I realised just how lucky I was when he held me and told me he'd loved us both. I thought, maybe I can just walk away from this, maybe if Henry loves me enough I can find a kind of peace. And I loved you, Luna. I think if it hadn't have been for you, when I'd woken up from the nightmare, I'd have ended it then. But you gave me thirty more years of life, and love and joy, and then Pia too. I'm so grateful to have the most wonderful two daughters in the world, and thirty more years of almost happiness that I didn't deserve. Thirty more years that I cherish, and I'm so grateful for that.'

She turned her face into the afternoon sun, light edging her profile.

Film fluttered round and round the projector, tick, tick, tick. Then nothing, but the blank light of the bulb against the rotting wall.

And that was when I scrambled to my feet and ran.

Something hard, and painful, jerks at my neck, and everything comes into sharp focus. A boy, hardly more than ten, has grabbed my camera and he's trying to rip it from my neck.

'Give it back, you little prick!' I yell, grabbing at the strap, which strains and pulls tighter.

'Fuck you, lady.' He pulls so hard that the strap burns my neck and I see him racing off; the few people who pay any attention at all simply watch him go.

'Stop him!' Shouting as I get to my feet, I taste blood on my tongue, the skin around my neck stings and I want to cry. 'Please stop him, it's my dad's camera! I can't lose that too!'

As the boy reaches the end of the street, and I'm about to lose all hope, he comes to a crashing stop, running into the stomach of a tall man, dressed in a suit and tie, despite the heat. The man grabs him by the scruff of his torn shirt, and whispers something in the boy's ear, something that stops the boy struggling at once. Boiling tears scorch their way down my cheeks as I watch him being dragged him back along the sidewalk, his feet barely touching the ground as he is marshalled into line by his captor.

Still in the man's clutches he holds out the camera to me, and I take it, cradling it close.

'What do you say, Ricky?' The man's voice is familiar, but not the tone, authoritarian and utterly confident. 'What. Do. You. Say?'

'I'm sorry, ma'am,' the boy mumbles, scrambling away the instant that he is released.

'Thank you so much, I don't know what I would have done if I'd lost it.' I look into his light-blue eyes, framed with auburn lashes, and it isn't until he smiles back that I realise who he is, the wonder if it suspending everything else for a beat. It's clearly him, even if the last time I saw Watkins Gillespie he was thirty years older.

'Miss, are you quite well?' He sees my tear-streaked face, and his hand supports me at my elbow. Gratefully I lean against it.

'Mr Gillespie?'

'Yes, I apologise, have we met?'

After the film finished, I didn't know what else to do but tear myself out of that space, out of that moment, and run. I had to get away, far way. I didn't think about Pea, or anything, I just needed to be away from the place where it happened and where I had discovered the truth about my birth. My head pounded, my stomach lurched, and I felt sick and full of bile as I exploded out of the building. Somewhere during those moments did I pass out, or pass through? If I'm out cold on some hot sidewalk, Pea will find me soon enough. If not, if somehow I am here again in 1977, then there is only one reason, one purpose I have to be here.

I need to save my mother's life.

'We haven't met,' I say, collecting myself. 'Not yet, anyway. I've heard of you.'

Gillespie's face is kind and concerned. It gives me a little strength.

'Well, then, Watkins Gillespie, pleased to meet you.' He offers me his hand, and I take it; it's firm and strong.

'How did you get that kid to just hand my camera back?'

'I've helped half his family stay out of jail, or get out,' he says. 'He's a good kid, just a hungry one. I told him to come by my office later and I'd feed him.'

'That's kind,' I say.

'I can't help noticing that you're in some distress. Is there anything I can do?'

I shake my head, fighting the threat of tears once again.

'I've recently had some bad news, but there's nothing you can do. Thank you for asking.'

Reaching into his top pocket, Gillespie produces a business card.

'You'll be amazed, there is *always* something a lawyer can do. Call me if you change your mind.' His smile is charming. 'I'll give you the best rate just for being so beguiling. Good day ... ?'

'Luna,' I say.

'Luna, as luminous as the full moon,' he muses. 'Well, now, I have an appointment with some gentlemen who do not like to be kept waiting. I wish you good day.'

'Mr Gillespie, before you go... ?'

He hesitates.

'Could you tell me the date and time please? I'm on my way to a very important appointment too.'

'Certainly. July eighth, and it's a little after one in the afternoon.'

'Thank you,' I say. 'Goodbye.'

Just before it happens again the air vibrates. Holding the camera, I cradle it close to my chest and I brace myself for the next shock wave. A cacophony of colour and pain explodes outside and within, and when I come to the camera is still in my arms, my cheek jammed hard against the sidewalk.

'Luna?' Pea's voice cuts through the chaos, and I cling on to it, my north star, the one fixed point that I can navigate towards. 'Luna, it's OK, It's OK. I'm here with you. It's going to be alright.'

'What happened? What did you see?' My tongue is thick and dry, but somehow I form the words, unable to move while my legs still feel so heavy, like gravity has doubled and trebled just for me.

'Nothing, I just came out a second ago and you were on the floor.' Pea rests a cool palm on my forehead. 'Just for a minute, maybe less. Maybe I should call an ambulance? You might be in shock. Christ, your neck is bright red, like a burn or something? I'd better call someone.'

'No, don't, I'm fine.' As I struggle to sit up, the sidewalk tilts dangerously; I reach for Pea, clinging on to her to keep tethered to this world. 'Just need a minute. It's the eighth of July right? What's the time?'

'It's just turned one.' Pea frowns. 'Luna, Christ. I mean ... I just don't know what to say.'

'You heard what she said,' I say. 'She really said it, didn't she? It's not in my head?'

'It's not in your head,' Pea says. 'I just ... I mean, she was ill, much more ill that we knew; we can see that just looking at that film. She hid so much from us, it's possible. It's possible that she was muddled ... mistaken.'

'No, she wasn't.' I sit still, letting my body settle into the sidewalk, the truth settle into me. 'She was telling the truth. I think ... I think maybe I've always known it. On some level. But now I know for sure. There's a reason I'm the only person in my family with blue eyes.'

I look at my sister.

'Dad isn't my dad.'

'That's what she said on the first film.' Pea takes my hands in hers. 'We knew that.'

'My real dad is the man that raped her, Pea, the night she ran away from New York.'

'Yes.' Pea nods, her voice catching. 'Mum was raped.'

'By the man she killed.' I say the words because I have to. Because saying them might make them seem real.

'Yes, she killed the bastard that did it. She said she did that. And that Aunt Stephanie helped her clean up the mess and somehow got rid of the body, that's what she said. She said that happened, and she left for London with Dad and found out about you later. That's what she said happened.'

And there it is in a few words. The truth that Mum had run from all of her life, the truth she couldn't hide from anymore. The ghost that had stalked her and would not let her rest, the reason that she wanted to die.

I need what's happening to me to be real. I need it to be some miracle of the universe, a secret portal unlocked just for me, just at this time and not the structures of my brain collapsing inside my skull.

I need to know, to prove that I can move through time and change it.

I need to know I can save her.

CHAPTER EIGHTEEN

. . . .

'Luna, people are looking at us,' Pea whispers, pulling me back into the moment. 'Let's try to look a bit less like a pair of crazy people.'

Getting to her feet, she offers me her hand, and I clamber up, dusting myself down.

'Look, there's a bench under that tree, let's sit there.' Pea guides me over and we take a seat, watching the passing traffic. Pea puts an ancient-looking brown paper bag on the length of bench between us.

'I found it,' she says. 'I thought maybe … I don't know. Mum liked telling stories, and not all of them were strictly accurate, like that one she told us about fairies that lived in the woods and you went off and came back with a moth in a jar …'

'There's no way she'd make this up,' I say, staring at the bag.

'I know, but I also know she lived some her stories, she lived them like they were real, so I just … I looked and I found it.'

The fragile bag sits between us. It's creased and stuck to itself, by something dark enough to turn the paper black.

'It was where she said it was, behind the wardrobe.' Pea carefully peels open the bag, tearing it a little. Our hair tangles, dark and bottle blonde, as we put our heads together and peer inside.

Reaching in I pull out a mass of shredded georgette, gently tugging at it to work it loose from the plastic it has bonded to over the years since it was abandoned. Carefully I shake loose the once-white fabric, now yellowed with aged and blotted with black stains that mesh and glue the layers of material together. A few black flakes flutter away to dust in the breeze. As tattered and as torn as it is, I know it's the dress I saw hanging on Riss's wardrobe when I visited her room last night.

Time trickles slowly, like the final few raindrops after a storm, and I see it, moment by moment, fall into the palm of my hand, and as the final drop falls, I understand it all with horrifying clarity.

The man whose blood is turning to dust on the wind. The man who raped my mother, the man she killed. They are my mother and father.

The man that made me. And the woman that made me who I am.

And I don't understand anything of what is happening to me. Except that, perhaps I have stumbled on a way to change everything, put everything back the way it should have been, before the events that forced my creation set in motion a thirty-year-long row of dominos, each one pushing the other towards this moment when the truth came out.

For although I don't know the how or why of time, I just know, deep in my heart, that the time is now.

CHAPTER NINETEEN

* *

'Some people might think it's too hot for stew,' Mrs Finkle calls from the kitchen, as Pea and I set out three mismatched plates and glasses on her table. Growing up, we were always short of grandparents; we never met Mum's dad, and her mum died when she was a child. My dad's parents ... well, they would turn up on birthdays and holidays, with carefully selected gifts, but they never really understood why their son had brought home a blue-collar Italian-American girl, when he could have had any woman he wanted in Bedfordshire; and somehow by extension, they never really understood the two barefoot girls, who would rather go down to the bottom of the garden to catch butterflies than talk about what happened at school. There's something comforting about Mrs Finkle ordering us around, waving us here and there with one of her long bejewelled fingers. This must be something of what it would have been like if I'd ever met my Grandma Rosa, this feeling of calm that being around her brings.

'My late husband, he always said the best way to cool down in a heatwave was to heat up. That's what they do in India, he said. I bought wine from the liquor store, red, because of the meat, but then I remembered Luna telling me that you don't drink, Pia, so I hid it.'

'Somewhere I won't find it, I hope!' Pea calls back cheerfully, before whispering to me, 'I'm worried that she is so very non-specific about the meat. What if this week's stew is last week's tenants?'

'I don't care,' I whisper back. 'I need this. I need some time to think. To not think about it all.'

Mrs Finkle had opened her front door as we had approached it earlier with her usual preternatural intuition, and had handed me a small, amber-coloured drink, which I had downed at once without stopping to enquire what it was, then or after she refilled it, although now I can see a bottle of bourbon standing on the dresser. Pea had been handed a freezing-cold can of Coke, which was the third drink given to me, and I'd taken it gratefully, pressing it to my forehead and the back of my neck.

'Figured you might have had an emotional morning.' Mrs Finkle was clearly pleased that she had guessed right. 'So get some rest, no matter what happened, you need it, and tonight I will cook for you. No arguments,' she cut Pea off before she could get out a word of protest. 'I promised Henry I'd take good care of you, and that is what I am going to do.'

And so we are here, after an afternoon sheltering in the cool of our apartment, Pea in her room, me on the sofa, not talking, not really even thinking. Just waiting for the sun to go down. A little before we were due to go downstairs, I heard Pea go out while I was in the shower, and every one of my sore and battered muscles had tensed, wondering if she would come back drunk or sober, or perhaps even at all. She had returned before I was even dry, carrying the box we'd opened at Mum's building.

'What happened?' I'd never seen her look so white, not simply pale, but as if the blood had drained away from beneath her tanned skin.

'We'd left it, so I went back to get it,' Pea told me, with a shudder, lowering her eyes. 'It just didn't feel right, leaving her in that place … Look, I know you'll want to watch the other films, but we don't have to do it there, where it's dark. Where it happened. Anyway, it's all locked up again now. We never have to go back in there if we don't want to, we can just leave it to its own devices.' A moment passed before she lifted her head and looked at me questioningly. 'I suppose we just need to think about what's next?'

'Thank you for going to get this.' I'd taken the box from her, and set it down in the corner. 'And as for what's next? Dinner with Mrs Finkle is what's next.'

Mrs Finkle's dining room is cool and comforting, her thick, lace curtains cutting out half of the blazing evening light. Wandering away from the table, I find myself drawn to the walls of photographs that seem to line every surface, both vertical and horizontal.

'Are there any photos of Dad?' I ask Mrs Finkle as she comes into the room, carrying a streaming terrine.

'I'm sure there are, although I haven't really looked at them for a long time. I don't like to look at them too closely. Don't like to notice all the people that aren't around anymore, I guess. Now I just need the potatoes ...'

Pea comes to stand at my shoulder as we scan the photographs, face after face fixed in timeless grins, celebrating some moment whose meaning has long since been lost, a gallery of forgotten happy days.

'Oh god!' The words burst out as I come across a photo of Mum with Dad, and a group of six other people standing outside of Mrs Finkle's house. 'It's her, it's Mum! Look, Pea, it's Mum!'

Reaching up I take the photo down carefully, a little shower of dust coming with it, and I bring it over to the window, dragging back some of the heavy lace curtains to let in a little more light.

'So it is.' Mrs Finkle comes over to look, smiling fondly at the photo. 'There she is; she was right here all along.'

'Mum, and Dad, and whoever this lot are – some more of the crew?'

'Yes, that'd be right ... Harvey, Jim ... that one, quiet but sexy, you know ...' A tiny secret smile tells us everything else we might need to know about Jim. 'And this one, now what he was called? ... Oh, it will come back to me. Sometime I don't need it, like when I'm at the ATM trying to remember my number or in the middle of the night, but eventually it will come back. Ladies, shall we eat while it's hot?'

The hardest thing about losing Mum, harder than anything else, has been the feeling of always having to leave her behind. In a grave in Oxfordshire, in a box in a derelict property or captured in a photograph. Before, wherever I went, whatever I did, I took her with me somehow. And now, she's not there. She isn't anywhere, except perhaps somehow through a tear or a loop in time that I don't understand and I can't control. And even if I do find a way back, whatever happens I will still have to leave her there.

'Luna?'

'I'm sorry, I don't mean to be rude.' I reluctantly rehang the photo and take a seat.

'No need to apologise.' Mrs Finkle smiles. 'Coming across a photo of her like that, when you didn't expect it, must be like running into her on a street corner. A shock.'

'Did you know her very well?' I ask. 'I mean, before Dad met her?'

'I did. I knew all the kids from Third Avenue well; this end anyways. Back then, we were a real community, you see; we stuck together, we were all in the same boat. All trying to make ends meet, all helping each other out, the best we could. And, of course, you'd see your neighbours at church, maybe three times a week. Your mother, she went every Sunday. Her mother was religious and she kept going after she passed and never stopped. She found a lot of comfort there, and support – and everyone loved her. I mean everyone. She was just one of those people, well, you girls will know; folks were just drawn to her. Her smile, the way she joked and laughed, she could make anyone feel like the centre of the universe.'

Pea and I glance at each other, at home Mum never went near a church if she could help it. She never spoke about religion, never tolerated more than the typical British habit of being religious only when there were gifts of chocolate eggs involved. And although she was our sun, the centre of our world, for the most part she kept herself to herself, certainly after we moved out to the house in the Cotswolds. She loved her garden, the high wall of honey-coloured stone that enclosed it and the feet-thick ancient walls of the house. She loved her world, making her films, Dad and us, and, as for anyone else, we always got the impression they scarcely mattered to her. I know that Pea is wondering the same thing: did she make the mistake of making the man that attacked her feel like the centre of the universe? And, afterwards, of course she would want to hide away, of course she would want people to stop seeing her.

'What were her friends like? Who did she hang out with?' I ask, tentatively searching for clues I wasn't sure I wanted.

'Well, Stephanie, of course. They were close; even though most of time they were fighting on the outside, you could tell those two would always stick together, through whatever. Had to, I guess, after dear Rosa passed. That's why I was surprised that they lost touch the way they did. Stephanie would never talk about what happened between them, and she left a few years after Luna did. I always figured she was angry at your sister for leaving her behind. Their father, your grandfather, Leopold, he was a good man, but he wasn't equipped to bring up two young women, and he had a temper. Never hit those girls, but oftentimes I used to see the kid from the hardware store going over there to patch up another hole in the wall. Funny thing is, the worse his temper got the more defiant those girls got; he never did understand them. But Leo was an important man round here, people treated him with respect ...'

'Was Grandpa in the Mafia?' Pea asks, and Mrs Finkle presses her finger to her lips, as if Pea has just taken some deity's name in vain.

'Back then, you weren't in it, or out of it. Bay Ridge *was* it, and the rest of Brooklyn and a lot of New York. Those guys took care of their own, and we were their own. There were protection rackets, sure, and things could get out of hand, but if there was trouble on the street, you knew who would get it sorted it, and it wouldn't be the cops.'

'What about Curtis? He was one of the regular gang, wasn't he?' I remember the young man from that night with Riss, slightly older than the rest of them, standing out from all the Italian-Americans with his Irish colouring, fair hair and pale lashes that fringed blue eyes, eyes like mine? I test a name from that reality on this one.

'How do you know about Curtis?' Mrs Finkle looks surprised. 'I haven't thought of him in years.'

'Mum talked about the old days sometimes,' I say, glancing at Pea. 'I remembered that name.'

'I guess Curtis was part of that gang. Well, hardly surprising he and Stephanie got closer and closer, especially after Riss left.' Mrs Finkle looks at me a little too closely, and I drop my gaze. She knew his name, which meant he existed, in real life, not just in my head. It was possible, just, that I picked something up from Mum, something I'd overheard and forgotten, and that scenario was still more plausible than the idea that I travelled back through time, but still, Curtis was real.

'I always thought Marissa might end up with Michael Bellamo,' Mrs Finkle says, and my heart stops. Michael. 'The way they used to argue, that sort of arguing when you know the people doing the shouting really care about each other, and he was so good-looking, film-star good-looking that boy was, eyes as green as grass. Travolta had nothing on him.'

'Did they date?' An awful thought that Michael could be my father? Except Mum said he was older, a pillar of the community. If anything, Michael was a little younger than Riss, and the realisation is a relief. I remember Michael walking me through the darkness, with neither of us having an idea of where I was going, or where I was from, the heat from his body, the feeling of his hand in mine. It doesn't feel imaginary.

'I don't think so.' Mrs Finkle ladles yet another spoonful of stew onto my plate, so that gravy brims on the very edge, putting her white tablecloth at serious risk. 'Marissa always said he was like a brother to her.'

I want to ask more about Michael, find out what happened to him, but Pea interrupts me.

'Who else did Mum date before she met Dad?' Pea asks.

'No one seriously, that I recall,' Mrs Finkle says. 'She loved dancing, they all did, all the kids, get up in their best and go to the 2001 Odyssey club on a Saturday night, no need to cross the bridge and queue with the rest of the wannabes outside Studio 54; they had it all here. As I recall, Marissa loved dressing up and looking pretty; she liked the boys to notice her. But she was a good girl, your mother. And that was important back then, not like these days when you can sleep around and no one cares about it.' She laughs. 'What it is to be young in the twenty-first century; we never really left our neighbourhood, and you've got the whole world at your feet.'

Mrs Finkle's stew is surprisingly good, and I hadn't realised how hungry I was. As we eat she talks, selecting tales at random and spinning them out as large as life for us, as she were projecting it over the table. This food, this evening, these stories, they are everything that I need right now. The evening ebbs away around us gently, a little oasis of space to feel and think. What next and how?

Pea must be having the same idea, because she's the first to push her bowl of ice cream and tinned fruit away.

'Well, I'm exhausted. Shall we go up?'

My sister wants to talk. I can see it in her face, her love and her determination to be there for me for once, to repay me for all the times that I've been there for her. I can see that, and the way her eyes keeps wandering back to that bottle of bourbon on the side, and the strain in her face, and the fact that she's been crying too. She wants me to go upstairs and for us to talk it through, and for her to be there for me.

I just don't think I can face that yet.

'You go,' I tell her gently. 'I'll help clear up.'

'Quite a day you had,' Mrs Finkle tells me, as I sink my hands into the warm washing-up water. She lowers her voice. 'Maybe now I'll pull the cork on that red, what do you say?'

'I say do it.' I pause, my hands still covered in suds, to take a drink from the glass she gives me. As soon as I put it down she tops it up; I get the strong impression that it makes a nice change for her to have someone to share a glass of wine with.

'Strange to be in that place, was it?' She takes a plate from me, drying it meticulously.

'Strange isn't a strong enough word,' I say. 'The Marissa you know, when you talk about her, she seems like a different person to our mother. Your Marissa was bold and carefree and cool; our mum was quiet and sad and she struggled a lot, all of her life, with depression. It's hard to understand that she wasn't always like that.'

'A lot happened that summer,' Mrs Finkle says, folding her tea towel and picking up her wine. 'Something dangerous was in the air, across the whole city. You knew about it, the crime, the violence, the poverty, the drugs … you knew about it, but it was always a couple of blocks away, always happening to someone else, that's what you always thought, anyway. But that year, the danger came here, too. Came in with the heatwave and Son of Sam, and stayed. Though I missed him with all my heart, I was glad my darling Norm never lived to see the neighbourhood like that.

'The night Marissa left, the night of the blackout, bad stuff went down around here, across Brooklyn, the Bronx, Queens and Manhattan. If you were ever going to do something bad, that was the night to do it. You're going to think I'm some crazy old woman, but there was evil in the dark that night. I felt it, sticky and thick. In some ways I think she got out just in time. Whatever it was that made her decide to run away that night saved her life, because it got a lot worse after that, shootings, rapes, murders. One time Brooklyn was the murder capital of New York State. You know, the cops printed out these leaflets to give to tourists when they arrived at JFK telling them how not to get mugged or killed? It stopped being around the corner that all the bad stuff was happening, stopped being a couple of blocks over. Started being right outside the front door.'

'And yet you stayed,' I say. 'You and Mr Gillespie. Lots of people stayed.'

'Sure, lots of people stayed, but that's because lots of people didn't have no place else to go.' Mrs Finkle shrugs, and then something occurs to her. 'You know, your mum wasn't the only person to vanish that night.'

'No?' I feel a shiver rush down my spine. A man who vanished the night Mum left Brooklyn, that could be him. That could be the man. 'Who?'

'Thomas Delaney.' Her smile is fond. 'Now there was a man; I would say he kept the hearts of at least half of Third Avenue's ladies in his pocket. He must have had secrets, though, because he just walked away from everything he had here on the night of the blackout, not a word, not a note, nothing. There were rumours he might have tried to challenge the wrong people, you know? Tried to stand up to "powers that be". And some people thought he'd been caught getting a little too close to someone else's wife … There'll be a photo of him on my walls somewhere, more than one most likely, I always used to get a picture of the church summer social, every year, best night of the year …'

I follow her as she goes into the hallway, peering at the procession of photos, gradually taking one stair and then another.

'Bingo!' she shouts when she is halfway. 'There he is. Thomas Delaney. This was … yes, seventy-seven. Look at him, he was such a fine-looking man. And this was the night of the blackout; this must be the last photo taken of him, round here anyway.'

Holding my breath, I make myself look at the photo. There is Mrs Finkle flanked by two smiling men, head and shoulders shorter than both of them. I stare at one man, light-brown, wavy hair, dark-maroon suit and tie. I feel nothing.

'I must admit,' I say, 'he doesn't look like the neighbourhood heartthrob.'

'Oh, well, that because that's Robbie O Connor,' says Mrs Finkle. 'No, that's Thomas Delaney on my left. Father Thomas Delaney, the priest that broke a thousand hearts the day he took the vow.'

My heart stops as I peer closer and look into those smiling blue eyes and I'm drenched in cold.

It's him, I just know that it is. The pillar of the community. A priest. Older, respected. Disappeared on 13 July 1977. It has to be him. The man who raped my mother. My father.

9 JULY

'Time passes, and little by little everything that
we have spoken in falsehood becomes true.'

—Marcel Proust

CHAPTER TWENTY

When I wake up, I know what I should do. I should make arrangements to see a neurologist, I should get examined, have a CT scan. But if I do, and there is something there, something physical, then all this is over. I could go and get a scan, and that would provide me with one kind of proof. But I don't want that kind of proof. I have plenty of circumstantial evidence; the necklace, the friction burn on my neck, the names of the people I met in 1977 that Mrs Finkle knew. What I need, though, what I want, is the definitive proof that I am travelling through time. And today I am going to find it.

Young Mr Gillespie told me it was exactly the same day of the month, exactly the same time of day when I found him. And it was exactly the same date, exactly the same time when I first stumbled into Riss's home, like taking a sideways step that spans thirty years. And both times it happened, it happened close to the building; maybe that's the key. Perhaps the building is a kind of portal, a door through to another thread of time; maybe all days happen, side by side, moment by moment, stretching out from the beginning of time. Time is just a river, one of my professors told me once, flowing everywhere, everything happening all at once. You only see it as linear because humans are linear; you're born, you live and you die, in a straight and ordered line. And anyway, it doesn't matter how it happens, there will be time to understand that later. For now, it only matters that it happens, and that I can prove it.

Somewhere, through the finest of veils, Riss is waiting for me to go back, and if I can find a way to her, I can protect her, I can save my mother from the horror she couldn't live with any longer. I can give her back her life the way it was meant to be, create a whole set of new memories, just like the ones I have for the necklace, new memories that are getting stronger every day, the old one fading away, harder to hold on to, more and more like a dream I might have had, and will soon forget.

The question is whether or not to tell my sister.

Pea says we should go out for a walk.

'That's what I do when I feel like I am losing it, and I want a drink or a hit, or whatever. I walk, it doesn't matter where or when, I just keep moving until the worst of it is over.'

'I don't want to walk,' I tell her. 'This isn't the same thing, I need to talk to Dad, I need to tell him about all of this ... figure out what to do next, formulate a plan.'

'That is the last thing you need to do!' Pea had actually shouted, picking my bag up and throwing it at me as she'd headed for the door. 'Dad can't hear this over the phone! It would kill him. No, we don't tell him anything, not yet. Not until we've talked about it properly, worked it through ...'

'Pea, I don't need a support group,' I say, bending to pick up my scattered loose change before following her down the stairs. 'And I don't need a walk, I've got things I want to do ...'

She stops me in Mrs Finkle's hallway. 'You're in denial.' The house was full of cool shadows and quiet, and I guess that Mrs Finkle must have gone out before the heat of the day set in. 'Trust me, I know what it's like, I'm more familiar with this shit than you are. And I want to go there too – the nice safe, booze sodden place where you don't have to think about anything – I really do. But you can't, we can't. I know how to get you through this, and the best way is to walk and talk it out. Talk about how it makes you feel, and things that happened in our past that make sense, and what it means for the future and—'

'I don't want to talk about it, I don't want to go for a walk,' I try to tell her. 'I need some time on my own. I need to figure this thing out.'

'Bloody hell, Luna, are you made of ice?' Pea snaps, bringing up me up short and sharp. 'Why aren't you tearing your hair out, crying and wailing, going to the bar and ordering a line-up of shots? So much heart-breaking stuff has happened that I think you have to let your heart break. This isn't something you can fix, Luna. It isn't some equation you can solve. This is something you have to learn to live with, and you have to start doing that *now*!'

'You keeping forgetting one very important thing,' I say quietly. 'I'm not you.'

It hurts her, and for the briefest fraction of time I mean it to. I want her, I need her, to back off and leave me alone. But as I watch her storm off, her head down, her chin set against showing any emotion, I regret it at once.

'Pea!' I catch up with her by a bakery. The sign over the doorway read 'Sam's'. 'I didn't mean I'm handling it better than you, I just mean that what works for you doesn't work for me. I need to understand it in my own way. And ... well, I think there is more to understand than you know, yet.'

'What do you mean?' she asks me, crossing her arms. 'You know you talk to me like I'm an idiot, but I've got A levels. I've got half a degree; I'm not stupid.'

'I didn't say you were; in fact, you are probably going to think I am when I tell you what I mean.'

'I'm hungry,' Pea says, looking into the bakery. 'You can buy me a doughnut to make up for being a bitch.'

We stand in line in the bakery, not talking, Pea tapping her foot and checking her watch every three minutes as if we have somewhere to be, and me trying to find the best way to phrase the revelation that I believe that I can somehow travel through time to save our mother. There doesn't seem to be a good way of doing it.

'Yeah?' an older heavy-set man behind the counter asks me, without looking at me.

'Two doughnuts, please,' I say.

'Four, four doughnuts,' Pea says, over my shoulder. 'Jam.'

'Jam?' He looks up at me, and I catch my breath. He's older, much heavier, his skin is ruddy and his face is set in an expression of frustration, but I recognise the eyes; they are a little faded, more seagrass than bottle-green, but they sparkle, and when he smiles I feel a little tug in the pit of my stomach. It's him, it's Michael.

He stares at me for the longest moment, and I feel myself leaning, just a little, towards him.

'Jelly, she means, jelly,' I say, feeling a blush creep across my nose; this time it's me who lowers my gaze. Why is this overweight guy in his fifties making my heart beat faster? Do I talk to him about Mum? Do I ask him about Delaney? They should be the first questions that come to my mind, but they aren't. The first thing I think is, does he remember me?

'You remind me of someone,' he says when I look back up. 'A girl I met once, long time ago.' He smiles faintly and I see a glimpse of the boy I ran down the dark streets of Bay Ridge with, just yesterday and thirty years ago.

'Do I?' I ask him. 'What happened to her?'

'Met her once, never saw her again,' he says. 'Never forgot her though; something about her got to me. Always had a thing for British accents and Converse shoes ever since.'

Time freezes for a moment as we look at each other, and I know, I know that he has seen me before, and I have seen him, in his glory days. And I know that if I can find a way to master it, then I can make time mine.

'Lady, are you leaving or setting up home there?' a voice asks me from behind, and I pick up the doughnuts and go.

'So what was that about?' Pea asks me as soon as we are outside in the glaring sun again. 'I haven't seen you look at a man that way since ... I don't think I've ever seen you look at a man that way, especially not one that looked a bit like Homer Simpson.'

'I wasn't looking at him, I was looking at the doughnuts,' I say, looking back through the window where Michael's head is down again.

'Fine, now we are going to go for a walk,' Pea says. 'And whether you like it or not I am going to talk this thing out with you.'

And she talks; she talks and talks, and I hear most of it, listen to some of it even, but all the while I'm thinking of ways I can get back there. Get back to Riss, warn her, save her, change everything just for her. And as Pea talks, about coping strategies, and grief counselling and mindfulness, I do not allow myself to consider for one moment more that perhaps all of this, everything I see as evidence to support my theory, is really just another symptom of a disintegrating brain. I can't, you see. Because if I do, then everything Pea says is true. Everything I fear is true. If this is some reality-altering disease eating away at the architecture of my mind, then I stand to lose everything that I love, my work, my life as I know it. And everything that happened to Mum, every horrific thing she told us in her films is true, and, more than that, it has to stay true. It has to stay true in every moment of time for all of time. It will always be her life, and mine.

And I can't allow that to happen.

I won't let that be real.

CHAPTER TWENTY-ONE

'I'm going out for a bit,' I say, picking up the camera. After we'd got back from Pea's walk, I'd fixed the strap as best I could and it felt good, having the familiar weight hanging around my neck again. A little bit like having Dad's hand on my shoulder. It hadn't escaped me that, although Pea had called him, I hadn't spoken to Dad since we left. I didn't know how to talk to him without telling him everything that had happened, and it wasn't the right time for that, not yet. Pea was right: this wasn't something we could talk about for the first time over the phone.

'Wait, I'll come.' Pea makes a half-hearted effort to get up from the sofa, and I silently thank the universe for those strappy sandals that she chose to wear all day; they have rubbed her heels raw.

'I just need a bit of space,' I say tentatively. 'A bit of time. Alone.'

She doesn't know I already have the keys to Mum's building in my back pocket.

'Right, OK.' She makes a visible effort not to mind. 'So ... ?'

'We'll have dinner when I get back. We can check out that little Italian place up the road, it looked really good.'

'And ... should we watch another one of Mum's films?'

'I think we have to,' I say. 'The more we watch, the more we really know about her.'

'Luna.' Pea twists on the sofa bed, reaching for my hand. 'If there was any chance you might be about to go to that massive bridge up the road and throw yourself off it, you'd tell me, wouldn't you?'

'Only vehicles allowed on the Verrazano–Narrows Bridge,' I tell her. 'And no, there is no chance of that. I promise you.'

'Good, because I can't do life without you, OK. Forget all that bullshit I said about being there for you earlier; I need you to be there for me, at all times, on a twenty-four-hours-a-day, seven-days-a-week basis.'

'As long as I am alive,' I tell her, 'I'll be at your beck and call.'

'A tad dramatic, but hey, I'll take it.' Pea releases my fingers and goes back to her sketchbook, filling it with drawings of the snapshots she has taken in her head all day long.

I watch her for a moment more, before I close the apartment door behind me.

And I go out to throw a brick into time's river, and see how much the ripples might change the world.

CHAPTER TWENTY-TWO

I stand across the street from the building that used to be Lupo's Tailoring and Alterations and stare at it. It watches me back, dark and covered by its own system of shadows, even in the early evening sun. People on their way home from work, kids with balls tucked under their arms on the way to the park, an old man drinking beer for a bottle, all pass it by. They don't even give it a second glance. They've gotten so used to the place, as it crumbles and decays behind the boards and the barbwire, that they've ceased to see it. But it still sees them. It still sees me.

Half of me is hoping to feel that quiver that sends tremors through my body, to feel the earth tip and slide away from me, and everything else that has happened to me before, but currently Bay Ridge stands solid and sedate around me, determinedly real.

It takes me a few moments to fumble with the keys on the fence gate, and another as I stand outside the exposed green door, its paint blistered and flaking. Deep terror drenches me as I look up at the mass of the building. It's not her I'm afraid of, not Riss; it's her I long to see. And it's not even how every time I find myself in 1977 it feels as if it leaves something like a little scar somewhere on my body ... tears a significant chunk of me away. It's that other day that happened here, that darkest hour that occurs four days from now, and thirty years ago. The hour, the event, that turned this home into this dark and crumbling ruin. All moments of time may run simultaneously side-by-side, but that moment feels like a fixed point to me, a dark star or a black hole, sucking everything that dares to come near into it, crushing everything it encounters. I can feel it, the same moment, repeating again and again, and each time it does, the dark mould creeps a little higher up the wall, the shadows get a little deeper, the cracks a little wider.

Without realising, I've retreated. I find myself backed up against the board fence, my heels jammed hard against it, the rough surface biting through my T-shirt. I don't want to go back in there as it is now; I'm afraid to. It's that happy place – that place full of family and laughter, music and Elvis calendars, before the pernicious darkness got in – that I want to go back to. Somehow I need to find a way to make the shift happen.

Staring at the door doesn't work.

Simply being here clearly isn't enough. There has to be a way to cast a line out through time, to hook on to that other summer and reel it back onto this one.

Thoughtlessly, I begin to hum to myself. Tuneless at first, but gradually it begins to take form. 'Love Train', that's it, it's one of Mum's favourite songs, one of the few that could be guaranteed to get her off her seat or from behind her camera and dancing, usually with Pea and me trailing in her wake. Closing my eyes, I listen very hard to a moment, a memory, long ago, that wasn't even mine, and yet if I am very still and very quiet I can hear it. I tap my foot, thinking of her in those special, bright moments when something she loved would take her out of herself, almost literally. Of how Pea and I would orbit around her, basking in the heat of her joy. As I sing, as I see her, a band strikes up, more voices join in, a great weight seems to descend on me, pushing its way down through the top of my head, and it feels like I am certain to crumble away under the pressure. Staggering forwards, I feel my body thrown hard back towards the fence that will surely break my fall, but the fence is not there.

Landing hard in the road, a car swerves, the sound of its horn screeching as it narrowly avoids me. Scrambling onto the sidewalk, I stand, waiting for a moment for the world to steady around me. I can taste blood.

'That was close, you OK?' It's the curly-haired girl I met at Riss's party. Michelle, young and fresh faced. This is then. 'You OK?'

'Yeah, I don't know what happened. Tripped, I guess,' I say. The sound of The O'Jays drifts down the alleyway and I turn my head towards it.

'Come on.' Michelle links her arm through mine. 'Mr Lupo is out, and we're gonna turn the radio up loud and have some fun while we can, just us girls.'

'If you're sure I'm not intruding.' I don't know why I say that; what would I do now if she suddenly decided I was imposing and changed her mind?

'Nah, come on. Riss was hoping we'd see you again.'

Nerves contract my stomach muscles; it feels like the first day of school. Will she still like me?

There's a little cheer as Michelle enters through the green door, propped open with a brick to let a little sunlight and fresh air in.

'Look who I found on the street.' Michelle propels me forwards. Shyness overcomes me, and there's a beat before I can bring myself to look at her. How strange it is, how much I miss her, my mother, this stranger, this woman I barely know and would do anything to protect.

'Luna, you're back!' Riss jumps up from her seat at the sewing machine, and hugs me briefly. 'I've been thinking about you since the other night. I couldn't figure out what it was about you, but something was driving me crazy and then, at two o'clock this morning, I got it! Now where is it . . .'

What is she looking for, I wonder? A time traveller's handbook and a photo of her mother that looks just like me?

'Want a Seven-Up?' Stephanie offers me a bottle and I take it gratefully. I see now that making the transition for there to here, or now to then, drains you like power from a battery. I crave the sugar, and it tastes better than anything I've drunk before.

'She's like a dog with a bone when she gets an idea in her head,' Stephanie tells me, leaning against me, tilting her head towards mine. 'She likes you. And when she likes someone, she's all in. She doesn't wait to see what they're like.'

'I like her,' I say. 'I like you all.'

'I don't know you.' As she speaks, she watches Riss shifting through a pile of fashion magazines, throwing them at Michelle and Linda, who pick them up and thumb through the pages. 'I don't make friends as easily as Riss. I take my time.'

'That's a good policy,' I say, and I can tell my choice of words has irritated her. 'But look, I just like her, I like you. All of you guys. I just want to hang for a while. I mean, seriously, what harm can I do you?'

'Not much, I guess.' Stephanie looks me up and down. 'I guess you're OK.'

'Here it is!' Riss holds up a magazine, a copy of *Vogue*. 'This is the April issue, but I've been dying to find someone to make this for, and it's you. With your fair skin and dark hair you'd look a knockout in it, like a sexy Snow White.'

Taking the magazine, I look at the spread: Farrah Fawcett, her skin golden and glowing, her blonde hair perfectly curled, wearing an Yves Saint Laurent gown, fitted top, loosely laced down the front, to reveal a glimpse of brown, bare skin, offset with a necklace of gold coins.

'She looks great, but me . . .'

'No, wait.' Riss stops me. 'I wouldn't just copy it – I'd make it for you. So you could wear it, so, you know, a skirt you can dance in, maybe match a georgette to go over the silk, silk-look anyways. I'd shape it over your tits, so it'd look real good, get you out of those T-shirts, get you into something that will make guys crazy for you.'

'What about one of these girls?' I gesture at the others.

'Nah, Stephanie is too short, Michelle is too shy, Linda's too much of a pain in the ass.'

'Hey!' Linda complains, but shrugs at the same time.

'You got to let me make it for you. I've been dying to, and I even got this nice bit of fabric left over from some little princess's prom dress that will do just fine.'

'Well, why not make it for you?' I say, smiling at her enthusiasm. 'I mean, it's not that I'm not grateful, it's just that I don't really do dresses.'

'Why not?' Riss stamps her foot in exasperation, making me laugh; it's a classic Pea move. 'I've got a wardrobe full of clothes already, and, besides, you're going to need something else to wear if you're coming dancing with us.'

'I'm coming dancing with you?' I laugh, the idea of me dancing is so preposterous.

'Sure you are,' Linda says. 'We like you, but more importantly, Michael Bellamo likes you, and I saw him this morning and he was all starry eyed, so yeah, you're coming dancing with us and you can torture that bastard like he tortured me.'

'I told you not to mess with him.' Riss wags a finger at her friend. 'Michael's one of the good guys.'

'And I wouldn't have if he didn't look so damn good in those tight jeans ...' The girls laugh, and I laugh with them.

'You really think Michael likes me?' I ask, before I can stop myself.

'Oh, look at that, Luna's blushing!' Linda crows.

'Shut up a minute.' Riss stops stock-still as she hears something on the radio. 'Oh God, I love this song. Turn it up!'

'I Feel Love' fills the workshop, spilling out of the building, onto the street, the layered, repetitive rhythm of the electronic keyboards, Donna Summer's pure, high voice, full of yearning, lust and need. Just at that moment each note, each nuance, reflects exactly how each one of us feels, looped up in the swirl and beat of the track. They dance, they sing out, voices high and thready, blotted out by the volume, each one of them perfect pitch.

Riss throws her tape measure around her neck as if it's a feather boa, grabs a stapler and sings into it. Without thinking of what I'm doing, I take the camera and begin to shoot them, walking around them as they throw themselves into the song, and for its duration I feel part of them, part of their group, as the base line vibrates against my ribcage and Donna Summer's voice soars up from through the tips of my toes. Will they be in this moment that I'm photographing, or will it be empty shelves and dark dusty corners? I don't know, and for now I don't care, this is the only time there is, this very second with her. As the track fades away the girls slow down to a standstill, looking at each other, laughing as they catch their breath, and the moment is gone.

'I love that song,' Riss repeats, picking up the magazine and pulling her tape measure from around her neck, beckoning me to her with a crook of her finger. 'Come here, I'm going to make you look amazing.'

It would be so easy to forget why I am here, so easy to forget who I am, as the girls laugh and dance and gossip around me. Whatever danger I expected to feel, whatever sense of purpose I had, hasn't materialised; instead I feel safe, at home, like I belong here, and I might never need to go back. And then Riss brings up Henry and my heart stops dead. And I am a woman out of time once again.

'Henry is the best kisser there is,' Riss tells Linda, who has been regaling us with her dance-floor antics with some guy called Sonny.

'Well, you oughta know.' Linda's smile is wide and sharp. 'You've kissed half of Brooklyn.'

'The male half,' Stephanie adds.

'Kissing doesn't count.' Riss smiles. 'And anyway, now I've got Henry, I don't want to kiss anybody else ever again. You don't get it, Stephanie, none of you do; none of you have ever truly been in love.'

The howls of derision drown out the radio.

'So you're really going to go and live in England and wear a hat and drink tea?' Michelle asks.

'I don't think you have to wear a hat,' Riss says, as she pins in darts around my waist. 'Luna, do you have to wear a hat?'

'Yes, it's compulsory, all of the time,' I tease her. It's hard to be this close to her and remember that this girl, one day, will be my mother, though she isn't now. She has the same smell, of course, a sweet coconut and warm skin. And the look of concentration she has as she works on her garment is one I know so well. I miss her; even though she is standing within inches of me, I miss her. The woman who would always stop to talk to Pea and me, to listen, no matter what she was doing. She would always make time for us, except for those long days and weeks when she just stopped completely, stopped talking, stopped seeing us. Those days when we'd hover outside her closed bedroom door and whisper to each other about what we thought had made Mummy so sad and so sleepy.

'Well, anyway, I don't know.' Riss shrugs in exasperation. 'I mean, I don't know what to do. I don't really want to leave home, Stephanie, you guys. But he's got to go on the fourteenth, he's got another job lined up. He's stayed as long as he can. And I love him, I really do. And he loves me, I know he does.'

'You could be pen pals,' Stephanie suggests, lighting a cigarette and blowing smoke towards the open door. 'I bet he writes a nice letter.'

'It's not his letter-writing skills she's into,' Michelle adds, with a sly grin. 'Jesus, Riss, if you go, your dad will have a fit. The Pope will excommunicate you.'

'Maybe not.' Riss's smile is secretive. She takes a step back from me to examine her handy work. 'I'm going to meet with Father Delaney, see if there's any way he can help smooth things over. If the Church is OK with me and Henry, then Dad will have to be. I mean, sure, Henry's not Catholic ...'

'He's not anything,' Michelle reminds her. 'Apart from a hippy.'

'But, you know, does that really matter nowadays?' Riss counters. 'If we marry in a Catholic church, in *our* church, and all our children are raised Catholic, and if Father Thomas is on my side, he'll get Dad to come round too, I know he will ...'

Even his name on her lips makes me feel so angry and sick. It's all I can do not to scream at her to stay away from him, not to tell her what I know. The sense of serenity I'd had is gone, and I struggle, desperate to find a way to stop this awful thing in its tracks.

'When are you seeing him, Father Thomas?' I ask and Riss gives me a puzzled look.

'Why do you care? Do you want to come?'

'Most women do when they get a look at Father Thomas,' Linda quips, and Riss laughs and crosses herself at the same time. 'May God forgive you and, anyway, what is he, forty-five or something? He's really old.'

'He's mature. I like my men to be mature,' says Riss.

'You like your men to be alive,' Michelle says.

'I'm just saying, that man is too good to waste on God, amen.' Linda puts her hands together in mock prayer, and Riss turns her back on her.

'Father Thomas is good to me; he's really looked out for me since Mom passed.'

'Like *Thorn Birds* good to you?' Michelle winks at me. 'I've heard about that book.'

'Like a good priest should be,' Riss tells her primly. 'He cares about me.'

'Haven't you ever noticed that he seems to care about his pretty parishioners just a little bit more?' Stephanie asks, working on something of her own. 'Look, see Father Thomas, maybe he will help, but Riss, you really going to go and leave me here alone with Pops?'

'You won't be alone, you'll have these guys.' Riss sees how unimpressed Stephanie is. 'And Curtis. Curtis would do anything for you.'

'Christ, Curtis.' Stephanie lights another cigarette. 'He's like a stray dog, show him one bit of kindness and he'll follow you anywhere, forever. Sometimes I feel like I can't shake him loose.'

'He's OK. He's nice-looking at least.' Michelle sighs. 'I'd like a guy I can't shake loose.'

'Curtis ain't bad-looking, but he's running with a dangerous crowd,' Linda points out.

'So what?' Michelle says. 'It's not like Mr Lupo ain't pretty tight with that crowd himself.'

Stephanie shoots Michelle a warning look, and she shrugs.

'You know it's the truth. It ain't no secret that your dad got this building through doing a few favours for the right people.'

'Maybe.' Stephanie shrugs. 'But that don't make it something you can gossip about. Anyway, Pops grew up with those guys, they're like brothers, they take care of each other. It's different with Curtis. Curtis wants in all the way, and he's got to fight hard to get there. I don't want that, that danger, that not knowing if my fella will come home at night, you know?'

'You seen the cars they drive?' Linda asks. 'The clothes their wives wear? I'd put up with a little danger for that.'

The conversation has already moved on from Father Delaney, like he's a nothing, an afterthought.

Riss takes the dress fabric off of me and, seeing a chance to catch my breath, I walk to the open door. As much as these girls have taken me under their wing, I'm still feel a stranger, an outsider. What possible reason can I come up with to stop Riss from spending any time with Father Delaney?

'Riss.' Michelle lowers her voice. 'You made it with Henry yet?'

'No!' Riss's eyes widen. 'I mean we done a lot of stuff, stuff I never done before.'

'Like what stuff—'

'When are we going dancing?' I interrupt.

Time travel I can take, family skeletons and secrets too, even meeting my own mother as a young woman, and dark and frightening buildings, but I can't take listening to details of my parents' sex life, and, besides, I have no idea how long this visit will last, or when I will be ripped out of here. The more I am here, the more I can influence what happens, find another key moment to fix on to, to have a chance of doing something to prevent her being alone with that man.

'I don't know, but it's got to be soon. Henry's flying back on the fourteenth. I got to talk to Father Thomas before then, too. Maybe get everything sorted out with Pops before Henry leaves, and that way I know that he'll come back for me, and we'll be together, everyone happy.'

'Riss, you're a fool if you think that's going to happen,' Stephanie warns her. 'Pops doesn't even know about Henry, and suddenly you want to spring the news that you're going to marry him. You've got to give it time, break it to him in little bits. So he can take it in without that vein on his forehead exploding, or calling in a few favours and putting a price on Henry's head.'

'Pop's wouldn't do that!' Riss exclaims. Stephanie raises an eyebrow.

'Well, even so, I don't want to wait,' Riss says. 'I don't want to wait to be with Henry and for my life to begin. You don't get it, none of you have—'

'*Ever been in love*,' the other girls chorus, erupting into laughter.

It overwhelms me suddenly, to see her so happy, so at home wearing her heart on her sleeve, despite the flak she is getting for it. The thought that this sunny, optimistic girl becomes so consumed with what's about to happen to her, and with what she did, hurts. Once again I return to the open door, looking for answers in the long, late-afternoon shadows. The sun has sunk low enough to edge the skyline with burnt copper, even burnishing the edges of the alley.

Riss appears in the doorway. 'You don't really mind, do you? Me making you a dress?'

'Of course I don't.' The metallic light burnishes her skin, setting her aglow. 'I think it's lovely. I guess I'm just a little overwhelmed.'

'I just feel like we've been friends for a really long time,' she says. 'And when I live in England, I hope you will still be my friend, my first friend over there.'

'You sound so certain about what you want,' I say. 'I'm nearly thirty and I've never been certain about anything really.'

'Wow! Are you really that old?' Riss looks horrified, and I laugh.

'I am, is that bad?'

'You don't look it . . . It's just that I've never been friends with anyone that old before, well, not unless you count Father Thomas. Come on, there must be something in your life you feel totally sure about.'

'I used to think it was my work, my research. But now . . . now I think the only things I am sure about are my family, and how much they matter – it's my mum that taught me that.'

'Well, your mom is right, family is important, but we all only have one life to live, right?' She nods back inside. 'They think I'm crazy to even consider leaving the country to be with a man I've only known four months, but it doesn't feel crazy, it feels right. Like the future is full of opportunities, and none of them can be bad. I just think ... I think, if I can make Pops see how much I love Henry, and how much he loves me – I think everything will work out. I kind of feel like it will, you know?'

I see a narrow chance and take it.

'Do you need to see the priest? Maybe it would be better to just go with Henry, and let it all sort itself out afterwards?' I bite my lip hard, hoping that it might just be that easy.

'I can't.' Riss dips her chin. 'If I disrespect my father, his faith, my faith like that, he'll never forgive me. Having respect, especially from your daughters, means a lot around here. If I hurt him like that, I'll never see him again. And sure, he plays at being a tough guy and a gangster, but deep down he ain't none of those things. He's just my pops, who took care of me and Stephanie when Mom died, even though he barely knew how to stay alive himself. I can't lose him. I need to have both, Luna. I need to be with Henry and I need to know my family are OK.'

She wraps her bare arms around herself, and her bravado slips away just a little; I see how scared she is.

'I just need for it to be all right. I need for everything to be OK, and then I can be happy. I know I can.'

'Then it will be,' I tell her tenderly, as if she is my daughter. 'I promise you.'

'How can you?' She looks up at me, seeking reassurance.

'I just can,' I say, holding her gaze until she breaks away.

'Riss, we need to clear up, Pops will be back any minute.' Stephanie puts an arm around her sister, instinctively sensing she needs a hug.

'Come by tomorrow?' Riss asks me. 'I'll have your dress ready.'

'That quickly?'

'I'm very good.'

'I'll try.'

'My mom always used to say, don't try, do.'

'That's funny,' I say. 'So did mine.'

She returns inside and I wait for a moment before heading into the sunset that is blazing down the avenue, trusting that sooner or later I will find a way back.

If I'd ever been in doubt before about what I needed to do for my mother, for Dad and Pea, now there is none. I need to find Delaney and stop him from attacking my mother. Stop him from changing that wonderful, hopeful girl who loves to dance into nothing but a shadow, a ghost of herself.

And if I succeed? There is one outcome that I haven't allowed myself to contemplate yet, but I suppose it's one I can't avoid for much longer. If I succeed in stopping the awful act that created me, then what becomes of me?

The chances are I will simply cease to exist.

CHAPTER TWENTY-THREE

'You're very quiet,' Pea tells me as she unpacks the box, setting tins of film carefully on the coffee table. 'You hardly said anything at dinner, you hardly ate and you look like shit. It's bound to get to you, Luna. I know what you said before, about being brave for Mum, but you don't have to be, not about this. Not right now, at least. Look, I spoke to Dad while you were out, and he misses us. Don't worry, I didn't tell him anything, I couldn't bring myself to, he sounded so low. And so lonely. There's no real reason for us to stay here now. Shall we just go home?'

'I can't,' I say, drawing the curtains, and moving the print from the wall where Pea is training the projector. 'Not yet. A few more days and I know I can get my head round it. Here, I feel like we're close to her; I don't know why.'

'Neither do I,' Pea says a little testily, plugging the projector into an adaptor. 'We didn't know her here. The person Mrs Finkle and Gillespie talks about is someone we never met. We knew Mum at home, bare feet, secretly chain-smoking, creating her own little universe for us to live in. That's where our mum is, that's where our memories of her are. Not here. I really want to go home, Luna. At least right after we've visited the sight of 2001 Odyssey.'

'You can go,' I say, although the thought fills me with dread. 'I just need to stay here a little while longer.'

'I'm not going to leave you,' Pea says at once. 'What kind of a cow would that make me? Which film are we going to watch?'

'Well, these last ones, the ones that came with the projector, seem to be the ones that she wanted us to watch. I guess we watch them in order. Number two.'

'Do you think she'll tell us who he is? Your ... that man.'

'Doesn't matter,' I say, taking a seat on the floor. 'Play the film.'

A blur of brown and blue are the first images we see, and then next, incredibly, it's Henry, our father, his face coming into focus as he backs away from the camera. Young features that he hasn't quite grown into yet, thick-framed glasses, and his dark hair long on his shoulders. He adjusts the angle of the camera a little, by propping something underneath it, and backs away, disappearing out of frame, probably to the window to adjust the curtains, as suddenly the light flares and the room brightens. There are pink balloons, tied with bits of string to light fittings, and on the table in the near-distance a dessert bowl full of crisps – potato chips, Mum always called them.

'Ready?' Dad asks to someone off camera, and as I see his smile, his dark eyes crinkling behind his glasses, I realise he's talking to me. Five years old, wearing my sun-yellow maxi dress, waiting for my baby sister to come home.

'Yes!' I skip in front of the lens, hopping bouncing.

It's still the London flat where we lived for the first four months of Pea's life. I remember the paisley-patterned wallpaper, and the swirls on the carpet in which I used to sometimes spend ages looking for monstrous faces. A buzzer sounds, and I bounce up and down on my bare feet as Dad goes to answer the door.

'It's you,' I tell Pea, as I watch myself, finger clasped together, balancing on one leg as I peer around the door. I hear footsteps on the stairs and run back to my position by the side of the camera.

'Here she is, here's baby Pia.' Dad grins as Mum walks in, and I gasp at the sight of her. I have never remembered her this way, thin and grey-looking, as if the pregnancy drained away half of her life.

'Oh my God, she looks awful,' Pia says. 'She looks so sad.'

'Luna!' Mum sits down, with my newborn sister in one arm, beckoning me to her side with the other. Up until this moment, if you'd asked me what my earliest memory was, I would have said this. Mum bringing Pea home from hospital, but this is nothing like what I remember. I remember Mum, soft and full of light and love, her gentle voice in my ear as she encouraged me to hold the tiny, crimson little person that I quite unexpectedly fell in love with at first sight. Not this, not the brittle stiffness in the arm that encircles me, or the tension and anxiety in my dad's shoulders.

Grandma Pat enters, bringing with her a tray of three small glasses of sherry and the bottle of Harvey's Bristol Cream, which she sets down on the coffee table.

'Got to wet the baby's head,' she says, and she and Dad each take a sip, toasting my baby sister.

'Would you like a cup of tea, love?' Dad asks Mum, who shakes her head.

'I need a minute,' she says. 'To feed her.'

'She isn't crying,' Grandma Pat says indignantly. 'You know, nobody breastfeeds these days. Formula has got all the nutrients you need.'

'Would you like Grandma to read you a bedtime story?' Dad asks me.

'I want to stay with Mummy,' I plead. 'I want to help her feed baby Pea.'

'Just go with Daddy,' Mum snaps, and I watch, as the girl I once was recoils as if she's been hit.

'I'll come in a minute and kiss you goodnight.'

'Come on, sweetheart.' Dad and Grandma Pat lead me out of the room.

The camera rolls. For several seconds Mum stares over Pea's head, her fist clenched in a fist and then, slowly, she unbuttons her blouse. It takes a moment for the baby to latch on and begin to feed. As she does, Mum fumbles in her bag with her free hand, puts a cigarette in her mouth and lights it, inhaling deeply, tipping her head back to blow the smoke away from the baby, and then after a moment she drains one glass of sherry and then the other, fills one glass again, drains it again, and again, and again, until eventually, as the baby falls asleep on her breast, she leans back into the cushions and closes her eyes, the ash from her cigarette growing longer and longer. And the film keeps rolling. Pea and I keep watching until Dad comes back in, takes the butt out of her hand, stubs it out, and turns off the camera.

'Why is she showing us that,' Pea asks, her voice trembling. 'Do you think ... do you think she thought it was her fault, my addiction? Do you think the fact that she didn't care enough to stop smoking or drinking when I was born, or maybe even while she was pregnant with me, is the reason that I'm the way I am?'

'We've only seen this one moment,' I say.

'But it's a film she chose.' Pea turns to look at me, hugging her knees tight to her chest. 'It has to mean something. It has to be that she's showing us something. She thought it was her fault, the drinking, the drugs, the failed degree ... and ... and maybe she was right, Luna, because that look on her face, when she closes her eyes after she's drunk enough to numb the pain? I know that look. I feel it; every second of every day I long for it.' Pea springs up, pacing to the wall and back. 'Christ, I want a drink.'

'You don't,' I say. 'Look … OK, maybe Mum did think it was her fault …'

'So is that one of the things she couldn't live with? Am I one of the reasons she killed herself?'

As she paces, Pea's voice becomes more tightly stretched, her fingers knotted and tangled. 'It was me, I did it to her. I made her feel so guilty, it was me.'

'No, Pea.' I grab her by the shoulders, stopping her.

'I ruined my life and it ruined hers, stopped her from being able to move on …' She shakes her head in slow horror, her black eyes filling with tears.

'No. No.' I pull her into me and hold her tightly. 'No. Mum isn't blaming you, she'd never blame you. She's showing us how her ghosts dragged her down. Do you ever remember her being cruel or unkind?'

'Just then she—'

'Yes, but I don't remember that. I remember her and I singing you to sleep, I remember lit candles in the woodland, and turning our dolls' games into motion pictures. I knew she smoked, she smoked all of our lives, but I don't remember her smoking around us, do you?'

Pea shakes her head.

'And she drank sometimes, those times when the depression got really bad, when Dad couldn't get her out of bed, when we had sandwiches for tea. But I don't ever remember her being drunk around us, do you?'

'No, but …'

'Don't you see?' I say, feeling her body slowly relax into mine. 'Mum was a brilliant mum, a loving mum, the best and funniest and kindest mum, despite what happened to her, what it drove her to do. And she was that way because of us. She fought that ghost for us, to be with us. She didn't put this film in the box to blame you; she put it in the box to say sorry.'

'She never had to be sorry,' Pea says. 'I never wanted her to feel sorry about the choices I made.'

'I don't think we could have changed how she felt, the demons she fought,' I say. 'Once that had happened to her, once she'd ... done what she did, and run. I don't think there was ever a way back for her, a way back to who she used to be.'

'Luna, let's just go. Let's just go home, and leave the box here and be with Dad, who loves us more than anything, and forget that any of this week happened, because until we watched that first film, none of it did.'

'We can't, not yet,' I say.

'But why?' she pleads. She's almost begging; she is so afraid of not being strong enough.

'Because ...' It's almost there, the reason why. I almost tell her, but I don't have the courage, not just yet. 'Will you trust me, please? Just a little bit longer and I think ... I think I can make everything better for you.'

'Just a few days,' she says. 'Will that be enough?'

'It will have to be,' I tell her. 'It's all the time we have left.'

10 JULY

'We all have our time machines, don't we? Those that
take us back are memories ... And those that
carry us forward are dreams.'

—H.G. Wells

CHAPTER TWENTY-FOUR

* *

Pea is sitting on Mrs Finkle's steps, contemplating the Virgin Mary as she drinks coffee from an oversized mug. We talked a lot last night, or rather she did, about almost everything, everything that has ever happened to her. She told me about the first time she drank wine in the park when she was eleven years old. And when, at nineteen, she did something called an eight ball with the bass player from a college band. He's a lawyer now, she never finished her degree.

She wanted me to talk, too, about how it feels to know what Mum went through. To know that the man that raped her makes up 50 per cent of me. She wants me to tell her what it makes me feel like knowing that after Mum was brutalised she caved the man's head in on the corner of the wardrobe. But I didn't talk. I didn't tell her of the grief that threatens to overwhelm me whenever I think about the fact that I am not part of the good, kind man I love so much who is waiting for both his daughters to come home. Or that the idea that this other man lives on in me, makes me want to claw my own veins out of my body. I don't say that I am proud of my mother for doing what she did, and if I had known I would have done my best to absolve her of any sense of guilt a long time ago, and that I hate myself for feeling that way. I wouldn't say any of that, not out loud. Because I believe, I have to believe, that I can erase all of that pain, all of that anguish, perhaps even my sister's addictions and disease, if I am right about what is happening. If I can go back to 1977, and stop the attack from happening at all. And if I do that, then this miracle that I'm living will be worth it, even if it means I erase myself in the process.

'Mrs Finkle says there's a photography studio on Eighty-First and Fourth,' I tell her. 'She doesn't know if they have a darkroom, but I thought if it's on the way to your next pilgrimage sight, we could drop in. I'd love to see if I can develop the film I've taken so far.' Of course, I don't mention this theory I have that I might have captured moments played out thirty years before I was born. That I'm looking for tangible proof to the single greatest scientific breakthrough of all time, or my own mental-health issues, one or the other. Or that, either way, I'm looking for something, anything, that might give me an easier way back to where I need to be and a less rough ride home, because I do want to come home again. I want to come back to the people I'm doing this for.

Leaving 1977 last night had been harder than I wanted it be; I'd walked for almost an hour, weaving my way in and out of strangers long gone, stepping over the garbage that collected in the gutters, remnants of a summer of strikes and an almost-bankrupt city on the verge of ceasing to function at all, avoiding the drunks as the sun went down, and the lights came on. Then the streets had filled with a different sort of person, and as the last of the day faded away, I wondered if maybe I would ever make it back to my own time, and I was filled with such a painful longing to see my sister, at least once more, that I cried out loud, a half-moan, half-shriek. It was enough to make a group of guys turn and look at me; one minute they were peeling themselves off a wall to check me out, the next they were gone and I was back, my skin feeling as if it were on fire, as if a layer had been burnt away in an instant. I'd thrown up into the gutter, my eyes filling with tears, but at least this time I was still standing.

'Everything is on the way to 2001 Odyssey,' Pea says. 'It's miles away, why are there no cabs in Brooklyn? You know, we've been a subway ride away from Manhattan for a few days now. Why don't we just get on one, and go and see what all the fuss is about. Have breakfast at Tiffany's or dance on that giant piano from *Big*.'

'You'd really rather do actual sightseeing than go and stand in an abandoned car lot that used to be a night club from the movie that you have watched eleven thousand times ... this year?' I ask her. 'Do I know you?'

'Fuck it, you're right, let's get going to that abandoned car lot. Who knows what other magical things we might see on the way.' Pea leaves her mug on the windowsill next to Mary, giving a cheery wave to Mrs Finkle, who we both know is watching us from behind the curtains.

'I got a darkroom, kinda.' The woman who owns the studio studies us from behind the counter; she's fair and tanned, with skin that looks like she spent a good deal of her life outside. It suits her, though; laughter lines are etched around her face, giving her an air of permanent happiness. She gestures at the portraits that line the walls, girls in prom dresses, couples in wedding attire, misty-eyed-looking dogs. 'But I don't usually let people walk in off the street and use it. Anyway, I don't really use it myself anymore. It's all digital now; I'm thinking of converting it to an office. I'm not even sure if I have any developer or fixing agent ...'

'Can we look? Please?' I give her my best smile. 'I'll pay you for your time, of course.'

'Well, it's nice to see someone who is still interested in film, I guess ...' She purses her lips as makes up her mind. 'I'm Christie Collins. Come through, see what you can find. I'll be out here giving a beautiful bride the perfect smile, if you need me, but hopefully you'll find what you need in there.'

The darkroom is very small, scarcely bigger than a cupboard, but after a few minutes of searching I find everything I need: developing tanks, fluids – although probably only just enough – and agents. There are even pegs on a line that stretch about the darkroom. Taking the Pentax, I manually rewind the film, and opening the camera I take out the roll of film. Switching the lights off, I work by the glow of the red light, winding the film on to a developing roll, and placing it into the tank. As I pour in the sharp-scented chemical, I'm careful to avoid air bubbles, trying to remember everything Dad has taught me over the years.

'How long?' Pea asks me.

'I'm not sure,' I say. 'Dad always says about six minutes. Can you see your watch in here?'

'No,' Pea says. 'I'll count to sixty, six times.'

It's the best that either of us can come up with, and we wait, Pea tapping her finger against the counter as we count in our heads.

'About now,' she says.

Carefully, I pour in the stop agent and shake the film again, before adding the fixer.

'OK, so we need to dry this,' I say, hanging the film from the line. 'I have no idea what we are going to get.'

A few minutes later, I switch the lights on, and Pea and I stand side by side as we examine the film. The shots that stand out at once are the ones I took on the journey from the airport, houses and streets framed by the cab window. And Pea, posing in the various locations she has taken us to. One of the Virgin, white-eyed and blind, and Mrs Finkle standing in her doorway.

Jangling with nerves, I take a magnifying glass to more closely study the shots of the building, afraid of seeing a face peering through one of the gaps in the shutters, but there is nothing out of the ordinary. On film the building looks sedentary, sedate. Simply an empty ruin, hollow of secrets and mystery.

And then five almost-black-shots in a row, the ones I took in the workshop on our first visit. As I suspected at the time, hardly anything recognisable appears, a blur of torchlight, nothing in focus, nothing that makes sense. I trace my way down to the end of the reel, feeding it through my fingers, holding my breath as I come to the shots I took with Riss and her friends. Nothing. No, not nothing; in the first and the second shots there are colours, a myriad of colours, blurred and out of focus, like a rainbow bled into the paper. I am stunned, because I shot *something* with enough light to make these coloured patterns where there should have only been dark.

And the very last shot slips through my fingers and I gasp.

'God!' Pea gasps, covering her mouth with her hands. 'Oh my god!'

I stare at the photo: clear, crisp, perfect. It's the smile that Riss gave me before she told me she was going to make me beautiful. It's her face, that light in her eyes, the last of the day's sun edging her cheek. That moment that should be impossible has somehow imprinted perfectly onto this film.

'How did you do that?' Pea asks me, and I turn to her, my mouth working, but no words emerging. I hardly know how to begin, let alone where.

'Did you take a picture of a photograph of her, is that it?'

'I ... yes, that's it,' I say, my fingers trembling. 'I found it on Mrs Finkle's wall ... I'm sorry, I forgot about it. I didn't mean to shock you.'

'For a moment I thought you'd photographed a ghost.' Pea presses her fingers to her chest, her laugh brittle. 'Christ, Luna, please don't do that to me again.'

'I won't, I promise. Come on, let's ask Christie to make some prints for us.'

'Even of the ones that didn't come out?'

'Even those.'

I needed proof: proof for myself; proof for my sister. And now I have it the relief that floods through me almost brings me to tears. It's some kind of impossible miracle that I'm living, not dying, through. It's no disease, nor tumour, no mundane arbitrary death that awaits me, and I want to laugh out loud because until I saw that photo I didn't want to admit how scared I was of dying. I can stop avoiding Brian's calls, phoning to check up on me, to see that I've followed up with the specialist he sent me. I'm not dying, I'm living, through some kind of life-changing discovery that could alter everything if only I could tell the world, but I can't, of course. And perhaps there have been others, before and since, who have discovered exactly what I have, but who will forever remain hidden from history. Because if I succeed in altering the past and saving Mum, then no one, except perhaps me, will ever know anything of what I've done. And I might not even be here to whisper the tale to myself.

It's a special kind of pain, the kind you get when you realise exactly how much you value life, just when you plan to obliterate it.

CHAPTER TWENTY-FIVE

Searching for the respite of shade, Pea stops outside a dark little shop, its front painted black and over-the-top gold letter proclaiming 'THE BROOKLYN RARE ARTEFACTS GALLERY'. The contents of the window are restrained behind a metal grid that doesn't quite tally with the grand name of the store. Pea and I stare dumbly at a strange collection of jewellery, clunky sovereign rings, bejewelled brooches and curious pendants sitting in little black boxes in three uneven rows at the front of the window. Behind that a collection of books, comics and old toys mixed in with ancient-looking electrical appliances.

'Sometimes I think this whole experience is one great big trip,' Pea says, as we peer into the window, then reads a faded handwritten sign out loud. '"Dealing in Gold and Silver. Old Toys. Collectibles. Rare and Precious items." Huh, since when was a Magimix rare and precious? Luna?'

I hear her, but it's as if she is muffled behind some sort of fog. Staring through the tiny squares of the grid, I'm looking into the shop and I see it morph and flex beyond the glass, the crammed, dark shop reforming into something lighter, brighter; people come and go, in and out of my field of vision. My knees buckle; I slide against the glass.

No, not now, I'm not ready now. I thought this could only happen at my mother's building, not anywhere, not at any time. What if Pea sees me go? Not now.

'Luna, Luna? What's going on?' I can hear Pea, feel the grip of her hands around my wrist pulling me back into the moment she is standing in. I feel her and it hurts, like I'm being ripped in two.

'I don't know,' I gasp, as I lean into her, clinging on to her, determined to stay. 'Let's go in here, they might have air con. I just need to cool down.'

The more people who see me, the more fixed I will be in this time; at least that's what I hope, inventing rules to comfort myself with when I don't even know what game I'm playing.

'OK, come on.' Pea opens the door and guides me in, and I hear her talking to someone.

'Do you have a place where my sister could sit down and have a glass of water?' Behind my closed lids, the room swims as they sit me down on a stool and a glass of water is pressed into my hand. I can still feel it, that other moment, that other time, tugging at my edges with a fierce, magnetic force, but I try to will it away. With Pea here, with the other person who has given up his stool for me, I hope I can't just disappear, that my existence in this time is confirmed and locked in. Taking a chance, I open my eyes and sip the cool water.

'Thank you,' I say after a few mouthfuls. 'I'm feeling better now. We probably should have stayed out of the midday heat.'

'Nose bleeds, dizzy spells,' Pea says. 'You aren't pregnant, are you? I'm taking you to a doctor when we get back.'

There is a moment when the strange man we are with looks from Pea to me and back, and then he shrugs and grins.

'Well, they do say only mad dogs and Englishmen,' the storeowner says, and Pea smiles at him. Tall, lanky, long hair and goatee beard, he is exactly Pea's type, which would normally worry me, except he doesn't have that sheen of a night spent drinking, or the smell that somehow comes out of your pores. His arms are free of track marks; he seems safe for now.

'You stay there as long as you need,' he tells me. 'I'm not exactly rushed off my feet here.'

'I'm Pia. This is my sister, Luna.' Pea offers him a hand, adding a flick of her curls as a flourish.

'Milo,' he says, nodding his head as he takes her hand; they maintain contact a second longer than is necessary.

'So tell me,' Pea asks, 'do you make any money from this crap?'

Milo laughs, and shakes his head. 'Sometimes,' he says. 'If the right piece of vinyl or sought-after coin or rare first-edition comes in, yeah, I make enough. In the meantime, I think of myself as a kind of curator for lost things, you know? All these things in here, all the crap. It meant something to someone once. And I'm not really a storeowner, I'm really a writer.'

'Oh yeah.' Pea grins. 'Isn't that what all failures say? Like, I'm not really a recovering addict/art-school dropout, I'm really the next Damien Hurst. If he was a very attractive woman.'

She's testing him, and he passes when he replies, 'Cool, do you have a sketchbook I can look at? I can show you my poetry if you like.'

'Have you got anything from nineteen seventy-seven?' I ask him on impulse. Something in this store reached out for me as we passed, perhaps something here is important, another part of the puzzle, another signpost.

Pea rolls her eyes as she fishes her latest sketchbook out of her bag. Milo looks at me with mild surprise, as if he didn't expect me to be able to talk whole sentences.

'Almost certainly,' he says. 'What exactly, I can't think off just off the bat … Wait, there's a first edition of *The Shining* right at the back of the shop in the books section, and I might have some old currency around somewhere, in here … want me to show you? Although, you know, it looks pretty much the same as new currency.'

'Are you OK to wander around, Luna?' Pea passes Milo her sketchbook. 'Because I'm sure Milo wouldn't try the hard sell on someone who was just nearly passed out.'

'I'm fine, and Milo was answering my question. I'll go and look for the book; you stay here and talk about art and writing.'

It's not a suggestion she is opposed to, but she hesitates, worrying about me.

'Honestly,' I say, 'if something terrible happens you'll know because I'll crash into one of his shelving units and it will be like tipping dominoes in here.'

'Please don't do that,' Milo says, low and sardonic. 'It took me ages to alphabetise this crap.'

Pea is instantly charmed.

The way to the back of the shop is dark and narrow, though thankfully cool. Milo really has crammed as much as he possibly can into it, on tall shelving units stacked very close together, forming a kind of maze, and I'm pretty sure that none of the strange and curious things he has on display are organised alphabetically. Right at the back, though, it's another story. There is a step down to a smaller back room, square and empty except for the bookshelves that line the walls floor to ceiling, carefully arranged by author. Honing in on a handwritten 'K' taped to one shelf, I run my thumb along the shelf, past many volumes of Stephen King, until I find one hardback of *The Shining*. Holding my breath, I take it off the shelf and open it to the title page. The smell of dust and words peels off of the paper and I inhale its heady mixture.

'You like that book?' A voice speaks in my ear, and I turn expecting to see Michael, but the room is empty. The past is still here, seeping through, trying to reach at me, and I'm scared. I don't want to go.

Black chasms open up in my mind and I fall into them, sinking slowly to the floor, dispersing into dust; I can see myself fade away and reform. I can feel it too. It hurts.

'I said, you like that book too?' Michael is leaning against the shelf and it's the same shelf, but different. Looking around behind me I can see that now this is a sort of book-cum-record store, and it's busy for the middle of a weekday. A group of guys around Michael's age are talking in the other part of the shop, but this part is for books, new books like this now-pristine copy of *The Shining* that I'm holding in my hands.

'Are you OK?' he asks, concerned. 'You look ... like you got a fever or something.'

'It's hot in here,' I say, smiling weakly. He is the one familiar thing here. I don't want him to leave me so that I spend hours alone again, not sure what will happen to me next.

'I do like *The Shining*,' I say. 'It's one of my favourites.'

'First time I read it, I stayed up all night.' Michael's smile is sweetly enthusiastic. 'Man, I couldn't put it down. My dad was so mad at me next day at work, I kept napping on the job. You should try *Carrie*, if you like that.'

'I will,' I say, looking past him again, searching for Pea or Riss, or both.

'So, what are the odds that I bump into you here on my lunch break, huh?'

Michael bends a little at the knee so that he makes eye contact with me, and bobs from side to side until I look at him. He is very wonderful to look at, somehow cooling and reassuring. In daylight I can see the deep glade-green of his eyes, fringed with black lashes, and the longer I look into them the calmer I feel; in fact, I look into them for so long that he blushes and breaks away.

'I mean, that's fate, right? You and me, running into each other again ... that's a sign right there.'

'Is Riss here?' I ask him. Why am I here? There has to be a reason that I'm here now. In this place, something called me.

'Nah.' He looks a little hurt. 'Riss is just my friend, you know, more of a sister. There's nothing going on between us, if that's what you think?'

'I haven't thought about you at all,' I lie, unable to resist teasing him. He leans a little closer to me. The first time I met him, I thought he was a dream, a fantasy I'd created, but now I know he is flesh and blood it becomes very hard to stand close to him and breathe sensibly. What happens to this vibrant young man, so full of the power of life and lust, that wears him down to that exhausted-looking man in the bakery? If it's simply life, then it doesn't seem fair. It doesn't seem right that just living can do much damage. But then again, that's entropy. That's what it's all about: the inevitability of decay. Unless it isn't inevitable, unless nothing is.

'I can tell you're warming to me. You're thinking: look at this stud; he's built like Superman, got the brains of Clark Kent. Am I right?'

Laughing, I turn a little away from him, enjoying this moment and instantly regretting it. The last thing I should do is start to care about more people, when I know I'll have to say goodbye to all the ones I love already.

'You look sad,' Michael says. 'What did I say?'

'Nothing,' I tell him. 'I suppose I'm just sad that things aren't ... they aren't the way I want them to be. I've lost a lot recently, and I think ... I think to put it right I have to lose a lot more. I don't want to care about anyone else at the moment; I don't want anyone else to lose.'

He studies my face for a moment, before breaking in to a playful smile.

'Well, you can't lose someone who won't go away. Let me take you out tonight, take your mind off it? I know this place we can go, it's real romantic. I've been saving it for the right girl.'

'No, I can't,' I say. 'I have plans.' His confidence falters a little, and his smile retracts, just a fraction.

'Fine, well, you can't have plans for the rest of time, Luna,' he says. 'Let me buy that book for you, and I'll put my number in it.'

'No, honestly, I already have a copy,' I say.

'Yes, but that copy doesn't have my number in it. Wait there, I'll be right back.'

He goes; I see him laughing and joking with some of the other guys on his way to the counter, and I hear Pea's voice calling me from almost exactly where he is standing. A dark painted interior blots him out, and I'm wrenched backwards, forwards, torn out of one moment, and thrust into the other. The pain in my head is excruciating.

'Shit, I knew I shouldn't have left you.' Pea finds me with my head in my hands. The book I was holding has vanished; maybe I dropped it on the floor. I blink, trying to steady myself, hoping that my vision will return from the blaze of white light it has become lost in. 'We should go home. 2001 Odyssey can wait.'

'I'm so sorry, Pea. I think maybe we should,' I say.

My strange encounter with Michael, in this random place that has nothing to do with Riss or my plan to save her, unsettles me. I want to be somewhere safe, somewhere lockable, where I can curl up under a crisp, white sheet and be reasonably sure I'll wake up in the same place.

'A long walk in this heat is a terrible idea, isn't it?' Pea says. 'We'll get you back as soon as you feel up to it.'

'I'll close up for ten minutes and drop you back,' Milo says. 'My car's out back.'

'OK.' I nod. 'Thank you.'

'Oh, you didn't find it yet.' Walking over to where I am standing, Milo lifts a hardback copy of *The Shining* off of the shelf just behind me. 'You know I inherited this one; it was here when I took over the lease of the shop, in a bunch of boxes in the storage unit at the back. It's practically mint condition. Or at least it would be if some dude hadn't vandalised it, trying to get laid by writing his phone number in it.'

He opens the front cover and shows it to me.

'If you let yourself be found, you can't ever be lost, Mx'

'I'll take it,' I say, grabbing the book and holding it close to my heart.

CHAPTER TWENTY-SIX

'Let's find Mum and Dad's tree, you know, the one Dad reminded us about when we decided to come here. We promised we'd try.'

It's evening, it's late, the sun has gone down at last, and a soft breeze that runs from one open window to another has cooled the room, cooled my fever. I spent the afternoon alone, under that crisp, white sheet, exactly as I had planned, and I thought hard.

If I can't control what happening to me, if I can't use it to save Mum, then it's meaningless, and I can't allow something so miraculous to be arbitrary.

This is what I know:

The date and time there is exactly the same as it is here. All that's different is the year. Which means I don't have long, only a couple of days, to change the course of my mother's life before this loophole closes and it's too late.

The things that happen around me in the past, stick. They stay.

The pendant, the ripped camera strap, a dedication in a novel. They stick. Perhaps every time I alter something, a new universe is created, a new version of reality, although not even the more radical physicists believe that anymore. And neither do I, and, as of about forty-eight hours ago, I'm the wackiest physicist of them all. No, I believe there is just one past, one present, one future, but each is a movable feast, full of possibility.

I also know that making the transition hurts, whether I want it, or – like outside the Brooklyn gallery – it wants me, it hurts. After every experience I have been weakened, been bruised, almost bloodless. I think that, one way or another, embracing this incredible gift means accepting there is a price to pay, and that, in all probability, the price will be me. That even if I had infinite time to go back and try and fix things, I don't think I would survive long enough.

There are so many variables as to what makes a person a personality. Certainly I am part my mother and part the man that raised me, but of course I am part him too, the man that ruined her life. That makes me part Italian, part American, part scientist, part photographer, devoted to my family, loyal and true. Those things I know came from my mum and from Henry; I know because I can see it, it's obvious. And maybe my courage too, because I know how far I would go to save my mother from committing a sin she couldn't bear, and maybe I'd commit the same sin to save her, and maybe I would bear it. Perhaps I get that from him. That, and my single mindedness, my determination to succeed, my ability to detach from anything that isn't relevant right then, to switch feelings off. From my blue eyes to my sense of isolation in the midst of a family I adore, that comes from him too and I can't regret that. I can't hate that, because that's me. I'm not perfect, not at all, but I am *me*. If I alter the future, there will be no me left, not in my current configuration. Unless I've been wrong all my life, and there is such a thing as a soul.

If I make a better future for my mother, and my sister, it's me that will vanish. It's me that will go missing from history. And it's me that has to pay that price, because it's me and me alone that can erase the harm my true father did. I was never meant to be, and there is only one way to correct that.

'Yeah, the tree Dad carved their names into.' Pea sits up. 'Are you sure you're up to it? You still look really pale.' Pea had gone back to the store with Milo and spent the afternoon there, and there's a little glow about her that I haven't seen in a long time; she's even twirling her curls around her fingers like she used to when she was a little girl. I wish I didn't have to throw her into the middle of this, but I need her.

'The thing is I have to tell you something,' I say, bracing myself. Pea leans forward, her brow creasing at once. 'And I am going to need you to believe me, right off the bat. And you're going to find that hard, and I wish I didn't have to tell you, but ... I can't do it on my own.'

'Luna, you're scaring me.' She sits on the edge of the folded out sofa bed. 'Are you ill? Is it ... cancer?'

'No, I'm not ill.' When I see the relief that floods through her face I feel sick with guilt. Sitting up, I reach for my jeans. 'I know the address of the tree,' I say, calmly. 'I wrote it down. Let's go and see if we can find it, and when we do, I'll tell you everything.'

'Tell me again,' Pea says, standing under the fourth plain tree on the right-hand side of 83rd Street, her fingertips pressed into the carved 'R + H', enclosed by a roughly hewn love heart. It had been the one thing that Dad has asked of us when we came out here to get the building sold: check if it was still there and take a photograph of their history.

'Tell me again,' Pea repeats as I take another picture of the tree.

'I've told you twice already,' I say, I reach for her hand but she pulls it away. 'Look, I know it sound—'

'Tell me the fuck again.'

Her expression isn't one of derision or disbelief; it's something else. Fear, maybe.

'The first time it happened was on our first night here,' I tell her. 'Although … do you remember when I was small, I had a vivid imagination? I thought for a while it was that, or that maybe I was sick. That first time, I thought I'd passed out, or I was having a dream or something, but it wasn't a dream. I woke and I was wearing the medallion.'

'The medallion that Dad gave to you the day we buried Mum.'

'Yes, you remember that,' I said, 'because it's true now. But, before I picked it up and gave it back to Riss in nineteen seventy-seven, it wasn't true. The second time, I nearly lost the camera. I had the friction marks around my neck; they're still there. The third time, I took that photo. The photo of Mum. It's not a picture of a photograph. It's her. I was there with her in nineteen seventy-seven.'

Pea covers her mouth with her hands, walking away from me.

'Look, I don't know how it happens. It shouldn't happen; it defies every single one of the laws of physics. Pea, don't you see, if I can stop her from meeting with the man that attacks her, I can change the rest of her life: no more sadness, no more pills, no more fear or guilt. No reason to kill herself. If I can save her from what he did. I know it's hard for you to believe, but—'

'Oh, I do believe you,' Pea says, as she turns her face towards the tree.

'You do?' The noise of the surrounding city seems to hush in an instant, as if the world around us is holding its breath. Waiting.

'I saw her too.' Pea says with a shrug, and whatever I expected her response to be, it was never that. 'The evening I went back to get the projector? I was in her room, packing away the stuff, and I heard voices downstairs. At first I thought that some kids had followed me in or something, so I went running down there, ready for a fight. But there was no one there, it was quiet. Not just quiet, but silent. Like the world outside wasn't there anymore. And I felt cold, freezing, even though it was boiling hot outside. I wanted to get the box and get out, but as I was going back to her room, just for a moment, just a second, there was this shadow in the doorway.' Pea swallows, moistening her lips, and when she speaks again her voice is strained. 'I didn't see a face, it didn't speak, I certainly couldn't touch it, but it was her, I know it was her, I felt it. I felt her, and she felt so *sad*. If I'd known, there's no way I would have been crazy enough to go back up the stairs and get the box. I thought it was her telling me not to leave her there alone.'

'Why didn't you tell me?' I put my hand on her bare arm; it's rough with goosebumps.

'Because ... I thought you'd think I'd been drinking or taken something. I swear to you, I hadn't, Luna. It's been hard, but I haven't.'

'I know,' I tell her. 'What did you do?'

'I grabbed the box and ran out of there as fast as I could. Didn't matter if I thought it was Mum's ghost, I was still frightened, and that's why when I saw that photo you had the other day ...' Her eyes widen. 'That *was* her, wasn't it?'

'Yes. I have no idea how it worked or why, but, yes, that's her.'

We rest our hands flat against the tree, against the carving, our feet occupying the spaces where her feet would once have stood. Riss and Henry's.

'You said you always had a vivid imagination!' Pea says, suddenly, and I'm afraid for a moment she's going to do what I should want to do, to rationalise this whole thing away. 'Remember you used to tell Mum that you'd been talking to the old lady in rocking chair in your room again, and Mum said she always thought the lady was your imaginary friend, a sort of replacement granny. And then one day, you and her had been sorting out stuff in the barn, ready for Dad to make it into his studio, and she'd found a box of these old Edwardian photos, mostly eaten away by mice and damp, and all stuck together, but you'd found this one image of this old lady with a pipe, and you'd said, "Oh, there's my friend Ellen." You'd recognised her.'

'Are you saying I'm seeing ghosts?' I shake my head. 'They don't feel like ghosts. I touched her, she was warm, she smoked! She was flesh and blood.'

'No.' Pea shakes her head. 'I'm saying that maybe every moment of time does take place at the same instant, like you said. And maybe, sometimes, some people catch little glimpses of it, déjà vu, or a chill up the spine, or even see a shadow, like I did. Glimpses of a million other moments that are happening at exactly the same time. And maybe you see more than other people. Maybe you can step through into other moments, moments that mean *something*. Like the last week Mum was truly happy, the last few days before she killed the man that raped her. That makes perfect sense to me. So yeah, I believe you.'

I don't expect the hot tears that flood my eyes, or the sense of relief not to be alone in this anymore, whatever this is.

'I do,' Pea says. 'But Luna ... I want Mum alive and happy, I want to save her. I don't want to lose you. You know that if you do this ... well, what will happen to you?'

'I don't know.' I walk away from the tree to the curb. A little way down the street there is a group of people, laughing and talking outside a bar. In less than a minute Pea and I could be amongst them, connecting to now, connecting to life, talking, maybe even flirting at a push. Life, going on as it should do without Mum, is just a few feet away. Life, which, after a few weeks, would become less painful, after months and years, full and happy and sad, in all sort of ways that have nothing to do with one brutal night thirty years ago. We could just walk away; we could just live that life and perhaps everything would be all right. Maybe. But Riss would still be there, huddled in a scalding bath, washing away the blood of the man she killed. She would still be there, in the moments before and afterwards, forever, and I can't leave her. I just can't leave her, but I have to be sure Pea is with me. 'What should I do? Should I try to save her?'

Pea raises her dark eyes to mine, and finally she takes my hand.

'Do it,' she says. 'Because, unlike you, I believe. In God and fairy tales and unicorns, and I believe that at the end of all of this there will still be you.'

CHAPTER TWENTY-SEVEN

Darkness creeps up on us as we unlock the security gate to gain access to the building once again. Neither one of us wants to be here, but we need to test what's possible, and, short of waiting for something to happen, the only place I have been able to influence the movement of time around me is here.

'It feels like we're breaking the law,' Pia whispers, as I unlock the door that leads into the workshop.

'We've got keys – and it's half ours …'

'Then why are we whispering?'

'I don't know,' I whisper, and then testing my full voice against the dark. 'I don't know'

As I speak the atmosphere seems to shift, moving from a passive collection of dust particles and gasses into something watchful, knowing. Pea falls silent, and I know she senses it too. The building sees us here, and it's waiting to see what we do next.

'I think it's going to happen,' I say, as the ground seems to drop several inches, leaving me feeling as if I am suspended in mid-air. 'I think being here is enough to trigger it. Let's go to her bedroom.'

Pea follows behind as I race up the narrow stairs, inhaling a thousand footsteps worth of disturbed dust, reality melting around me as I stumble into Riss's room.

'We should go.' I hear Pea as if she is at the end of very bad telephone line. 'Luna, I've changed my mind, I'm frightened.'

'It's fine, let me try,' I say, or at least I think I say it. I see the words in the air, but not as words, as pictographs that shimmer and disappear.

'So what do I do?' she asks.

Sitting carefully on the edge of the bed, feeling for its edge to reassure myself that I am not about to sit back into thin air, remnants of the vivid-orange wallpaper pattern of abstract birds and plants clamour to be seen.

'Go outside. Go away and wait. In a few minutes come back and see what's happening.'

'But, Luna ...'

Perhaps my eyes roll up in my head as I tip back into a river of shadows, because I hear her gasp, and she grabs my arm.

'I don't like this, Luna.'

'Go,' I think I say, but even if I don't, suddenly I know I am alone.

It's black, total darkness presses against my open eyes, and then gradually it draws back a little to reveal a slash of electric light under the bedroom door.

A skein of heat trickles through me; I watch it threading its silent way, a scarlet, silk snake, reaching into every nerve ending, and I sit up and look around the room. The white dress is hanging on the wardrobe, a little chiffon frill trim added to the skirt and neckline. My phone buzzes in my jeans' pocket, making me jump – I'd forgotten I even had it. Has it just received a text?

Taking it out, impossibly I see it is still showing a signal. I turn it off and tuck it inside the mattress cover. As I lift it, I find a worn-out and much-thumbed copy of *Fear of Flying* by Erica Jong. I open the front cover. 'Be brave', it says in my mother's handwriting. It's almost as if she left this message here just for me.

'I will be brave,' I whisper, carefully replacing the book. 'I won't let you down.'

Outside on the landing it's quiet, the house asleep. As I open the door, something rushes in, the scent of white lilies. I know that scent anywhere; it's Pea's favourite perfume, here now, in this room, in this space that I am standing in, only it is some other now. Creeping out onto the landing, I only realise I am holding my breath when my lungs begin to hurt. Second guessing each floorboard as I make my way down the stairs, flight by flight, I wonder what I would do or say if I am caught, and realise there is nothing I can say or do. One thing I know, Riss isn't home. I know where she is, or I would never have risked this. She's with my dad, and they are about to carve their initials into the bark of a tree.

Once I'm outside, in the alley, the air thick with rotting garbage, I allow myself to breathe again, sucking in the tainted air as if it were nectar.

'Hey, baby, let me take you for a ride.' A car slows down and a group of guys leer out of the window at me.

'Come on, honey, we can show you a real good time.'

Keeping my eyes down I hurry on, trying to get my bearings. Left and then first right, back to where the tree was.

'You giving it away for free then, baby?' Another voice, slightly younger. Lighter.

'You got fine pair of titties on you, sweetheart.'

I keep walking, trying not to let discomfort and fear alter my purpose. Trying not to imagine them dragging me into a car, and then, what? I know that rape and murder were regular occurrences in the late 1970s, that within five years Brooklyn and the wider city of New York would be the crime capital of the world. I know that Son of Sam is stalking the streets nearby, that drug dealers and street gangs shot each other to death almost every day. Even in Bay Ridge's blue-collar community of church-going families, you didn't have to look very hard to find genuine danger, and it didn't have to look at all to find you. I am not immortal here, far from it. If anything, I feel more fragile, more vulnerable, as if each time I push my way through the veil I leave a layer of skin clinging to its barbs. After all that it's already cost me, there is no turning back, I lift my chin and square my shoulders. I will have to face much worse than some guys on the make if I am to save Riss. A few seconds more and the car shifts gear and accelerates away, with a squeal of rubber on asphalt, leaving a trail of insults in its wake.

The risen half-moon looks beautiful and benign, perfectly clear as it sails low in the sky. Looking up at it, I feel the gravitational pull of its dark side, the half lost in shadow. I can't see it, but I know it's still there, and that's what I need. I need a little faith. I can't see Pea, or my own time, but I know that they are still there.

No sooner have I turned a corner than another battered-looking car, riding low to the ground, with a clattering back bumper tied on with string, crawls along next to me. I steel myself.

'You want a ride, baby?'

Pivoting on my heel, I shout, 'No, I don't want a ride, you lecherous ... Michael?'

The guys he is with in the car fall about laughing, actually hooting, and if it wasn't so dark I think I might be able to see him blush.

'Shut your holes, already,' he says to his friends, climbing out of the passenger side, stumbling a little as his sneakers hit the sidewalk. 'Where did you go before, and what you doing on the street at this hour?' His expression is part concern, part a desperate attempt not to lose face in front of his friends.

'What are *you* doing on the street at this hour?' I retort, hurrying on, keen not to miss my appointment, and the car explodes into laughter and jeers again, and he edges me away from the curb, lowering his voice.

'You can't be out here on your own, it's not safe, and, anyways, you'll get a reputation.' In every angle of his stance, it's clear how important it is to not lose face in front of his tribe, almost as if he's asking me not to shame him.

'Why you again?' I say thoughtfully. 'I mean, what are the chances I'd run into you now, again?'

Michael's brow furrows into a frown; he sees my question as a challenge.

'Well, that's my dad's car, and those are my guys, and see that over there?' He points over to a house, lost in shadow, with one light burning in an upstairs window. 'That's my house. My folks' house, anyways.'

I study him for a moment in the streetlight, allowing the emotions in my chest to settle. It's not disquiet I feel seeing him again, it's pleasure. It's butterflies, bona fide thrilling butterflies, and that is simply ridiculous.

'Look, thank you for worrying about me, but I've got somewhere to be …' I try to walk on but he blocks me.

'You meeting someone?' he asks.

'What's it to you?' I am a little sharper than I mean to be.

'Nothing, I guess.' His voice softens as he glances back at the car, three grinning faces watching his every move. 'I just, I feel responsible for you, kind of. You don't know what it's like round here. You got to be careful.'

'Thank you.' I find my hand reaching for his as if it's the most natural thing in the world. When our fingers touch a kind of recognition and expectation fizzes through me. 'But I'm fine, really. You go and drive around with your friends and do whatever it is four guys in a car do and, I swear, I'll be fine.'

'Is it a guy you're meeting?' Michael's regret at asking shows on his face at once. 'I'm not trying to be ... Look, it's just that ... well, I like you, Luna. I'd like a chance to get to know you. I thought you might have got that by now?'

There's something about the way he stands there, the slight drop in his shoulders, the dip of his chin. Artifice, posturing, falls away for just a second and I see him, just him, and he's sweet and kind, and worried about me.

'It's not a guy, it's a friend,' I say gently. 'And I'm late.'

'OK.' He nods, and on impulse I lean forward and kiss him briefly on the cheek. As I turn and hurry away I can hear the cheers coming from the car. The feel of his cheek lingers on my lips.

The story of the tree carving is legendary in our family, one that has been told and retold to us all our lives long; it's the story that Dad chose to tell at Mum's funeral. For the night that Dad carved their names into a plain tree on 83rd Street was the night they admitted out loud to each other and to the universe that they never wanted to be apart again.

'I was walking Marissa home, just past midnight,' Dad had said in the watery grey light of the church on that March morning. 'It was a quiet night, no one around very much and we were just dawdling down this street, a street like any other in Bay Ridge, nothing special about it, nothing magical. Just houses and trees, and cars on the street and the half-moon in the sky, and it was all so ordinary, so commonplace, and yet with her hand in mine I felt like I was walking on stardust. I felt – we felt – invincible. Which was how I knew that I loved her. I mean, I'd fallen in love with her the instant I had seen her, but on that street, under that moon, I realised it was much more than that. I realised I'd do anything for her, for all of my life. That there was nothing she could say, nothing she could do, that would change how I felt. And when we stopped and she looked into my eyes, I knew she felt the same. And it seems foolish now, seems like we were a couple of kids in love, but at the time, when I took out my pocket knife and put our initials in the wood, it felt like we were making vows. I don't know if that tree is still there or not, but I like to think it is. I like to think that no matter what else has happened in life, the vows we made to each other that night still stand, and always will, even after we are both gone.'

Before that day, the day Dad last told the story in church, this was the part where Mum would always add, 'Yes, it was just then by the tree on Eighty-Third that I knew for sure it wasn't a fling or a summer romance, I knew that whatever it took I had to be with Henry, no matter what it cost me. That something that special was worth fighting for. When I was with him, for the first time in my life I knew who I was.

Not a daughter, not a sister, not a girl in a pretty dress, but who *I* was, and what I was capable of. Loving Henry made me stronger than I ever knew I could be.'

On that day, Pea and I had sat holding hands, remembering the hundred other times we'd heard that story, saying Mum's part in our heads. Now, looking back, I can see what it meant, that flint-hard glint in her eye when she said that being with Henry was worth fighting for; what she meant was that it was worth fighting to stay alive for. Worth killing for.

Somewhere a church bell tolls the midnight hour. My heart quickens as I hurry on, fearing that I am lost. I'd been keeping an eye on the streets that I passed, counting them down, but after Michael, in the few seconds I was thinking about him, I lost track and perhaps I have come too far. Turning one corner and then another, the right street, but am I too late? ... A long sigh of relief escapes as I see them, two figures in the shadows as they embrace beneath a tree. Riss and Henry. Mum and Dad.

'Riss!' I'm so relieved I call out her name when I don't mean to.

'Luna?' Riss steps into the streetlight. 'What the hell are you doing here?'

Faltering, I shrug, staring at her in her sunflower-yellow halter-neck shirt pulled on over some faded and very short jean shorts. Riss is beautiful in a way that I never recognised in Marissa my mother. Beautiful in a way that Pea and I never have been, carrying that youthful belief in herself that is untouched by life and loss. My sister and I have never had that shine, not even for a little while. We were born touched with sadness and the certainty of loss, our DNA imprinted with what our mother had lived through, my DNA infested with it. To see her like this, utterly unaware of how vulnerable she is, is wonderful and heartbreaking in equal measure. God, how I miss her, this woman I never knew, I miss her so much that it takes all my strength not to blurt it all out, who I am, who she is to me, and to beg her to never change.

Instead I say, 'Couldn't sleep, so thought I'd go for a walk.'

'Are you crazy?' Riss is cross with me. 'Anything could happen to you.'

'I'm fine, really, I know karate.' I chop through the air in Miss Piggy-style to emphasise my point. 'Who's taking care of you?'

It's such an absurd thing to say it makes them both laugh.

'Don't worry, I'm taking care of her.' The voice is gentle, reserved, uncertain of me. Henry is in the shadows, as am I. Riss stands alone in a little halo of light. Should he see me? Does it matter if he sees me?

'Hello,' I say, a little too warmly.

'You're English.' Polite, wary – there is something about me that makes him nervous. Perhaps he senses our back-to-front connection.

'Yes, my name is Luna.'

'Henry Sinclair.' Still in shadow, he extends his hand, and mine moves to meet his. As our hands briefly connect and I smile at him from the safety of the dark, and he peers at me through his glasses, round, wire frames whose style has rarely changed in thirty years.

'Where are you from, Luna?' he asks and Riss laughs.

'Is this what English people do, make small talk, even on the mean streets of Brooklyn in the middle of the night? You'll be suggesting high tea next! Luna, why are you out here? It's dangerous. You shouldn't be alone at this time of night, karate or no karate.'

'I know, I suppose I forgot,' I say. 'I went for a walk and now I wish I hadn't. But I'm going back soon, now I mean. What are you two up to?'

They exchange a look, a smile.

'Nothing much,' Riss says, in a way that actually means 'everything, ever'.

The longer I am near them, the more I find myself falling in love with their love, the more the thought comes, faintly at first, and then stronger and stronger, that this is what love looks like.

'Won't your father kill you if he catches you,' I say, but I'm grinning to see them like this, their fingers intertwined, hips touching. It makes my heart sing.

'Which is why I have to go back soon.' Riss looks longingly at my father and I see him instinctively step towards her. They want to be alone; I want to never leave them. Awkward.

'Let us walk you home,' Henry says eventually, although he is gazing at Riss.

'It's fine,' I say. 'It's just down the block ...'

'The Obermans?' Riss looks puzzled, and I have forgotten my back story.

'I moved, another place. I can see it from here. You stay there.'

I go to say goodbye before she can ask me any more questions.

'It's been really nice to meet you.' I inch a little closer to Henry and he steps out of the shadows. I almost expect some level of recognition on his face, but of course there is none. Putting one hand on my father's back, I lean in, kissing him on the cheek, at the same moment slipping the knife from his pocket and concealing it in my hand.

'We'll watch you go in,' Riss calls after me.

'There's no need,' I say. But I know they are watching me as I pocket the knife and walk on down the road. I stop outside a house that's as good as any, acutely aware that she probably knows the people that live there. Offering them a final wave, I trot up the steps, hoping the stoop will hide my presence. When I look again they are gone.

I run down the street to the tree and unsheaf the blade, which is dull and difficult. My heart racing, I carve my own name into the wood, just below their initials. It's rough and awkward, angry looking almost, but I do it as deeply and as certainly as I can.

And here, standing alone in the same small pool of light that Riss occupied just minutes before, I make my own promise, swear my own vow to them, to Riss.

No matter what it costs, I will save you.

CHAPTER TWENTY-EIGHT

Somewhere, thirty years from now, Pea is waiting for me in the building. It feels important that I get there before Riss does – to avoid meeting her – and try and get home. After all, I could hardly explain to her what I'm doing hiding in her home if she happened to run into me on the landing. Breaking into a run, I wish that running here, in this time I am not meant to be in, was like flying in dreams, effortless and magical. Instead, I am sweating and gasping for breath in the hot, thick night. Pausing for a second as I slam against the wall of the building, I catch my breath before letting myself in.

My mouth is full of the fear of discovery as I edge ever so slowly up first one flight of stairs and then the next. Her bedroom door is shut, and I don't remember shutting it. Hesitating outside, I feel as if I am glued to the floorboards by adrenalin. Did she beat me back, climbing in through the window via the fire escape? I can't risk opening the door.

Uncertain of what to do now, of how to try, I stand in the darkness of the landing and listen. A faint humming coming from Riss's room, and a masculine cough from downstairs;

it must be my grandfather. Then I catch the scent of white lilies, and I sense my sister is near me again; the veil is thinning. Following her trail back down the stairs, treading as light and carefully as I can, I walk into the kitchen where her scent seems to be the strongest, and close the door. Feeling the hard edge of the knife press against my hip, I take it out, looking around for a place to hide it. There's an air vent in the wall, and it doesn't take much effort to pull up one corner and slide the knife behind it.

As I imagine Pea waiting for me, I try to will myself back to her.

'It's time to go back,' I say as purposefully as I can, as loudly as I can, trying not to be afraid of waking anyone up. 'Go back, go back! GO BACK NOW!'

There is a creak in the floorboards up ahead, and I hear footsteps.

'NOW!' I make myself shout, the words filling the corners of the room.

All that is solid blows apart in one great explosion at incredible speed, before somehow rewinding and coming together again; the same but different, older. I come to in the present with a panicked start, leaning up against a door, my legs heavy as lead, lost inside my own body. It feels as if every drop of life has been wrung out of me.

Opening the door, I'm disorientated. Nothing is where I thought it would be. I thought my sister would be on the other side of it.

'Pea?'

She appears out of the shadows in the living room, pointing a torch right at me, forcing me to twist my head away to avoid the glare.

'FUCK.' Pea presses her hand to her mouth. 'Fuck, fuck, fuck, fuck!'

'What?' I ask her. 'What happened, what did you see?'

'I opened the door to Mum's room, just like you told me to and you weren't there. You'd vanished.'

'Really?' Until that moment, I still half believed it might some sort of delusion, or a kind of illness – a seizure that brought me to a physical standstill while my mind travelled on. But Pea says I vanish; I actually disappear into another time. 'Fuck.'

'Luna,' Pia repeats my name as if she wants to make sure I am real. She points over my shoulder. 'You just came out of the kitchen. And I have been standing here, freaking the hell out, the whole time. There is no way you walked past me. Pea stares at me. 'Luna, you vanished in the bedroom and came out of the kitchen.'

Pushing past her I race back up the stairs and into Riss's room. 'Quick, shine the light on the mattress.' My fingers fumbling, I finally grasp the zipper and pull hard. It is stuck and rusty, and I pull hard again, this time ripping the mouldering material. Reaching inside I feel decaying sponge give way beneath my fingers and, yes, a small hard object, one that is so familiar to my fingers. I pull my phone out and stare at it in the torchlight; the plastic casing has collapsed on itself, there is a crack across the screen. I hand it to Pea and reaching again under the mattress find the book, yellow and thick with dust, the inside pages now glued together with mould. I can't open the title page, but I don't need to. I know what's written on the inside.

'Be brave.'

Pia and I hold hands as we run back to the tree; the sound of our soft shoes impacting on the sidewalk seems unnaturally loud. Pia shines the torch onto the tree and we scan the bark, our fingers running over every groove.

'Crazy bitches,' a couple of teenagers say as they walk by, out way too late for boys their age. 'Feeling up a tree, dude.'

'You should both be in bed!' Pia snaps at them.

'You offering?' They punch each other in the shoulder, pleased with their wit, as they turn the corner.

'Fuck.' Pea breathes the words out, long and hard. 'Fuck.'

The torch is shining on Mum and Dad's initials and beneath them is the crude carving of my name, faded, mottled with moss, that I made about twenty minutes and thirty years ago.

'Shit,' I say, staring at it. 'Shit.'

'Understatement of the year, years, all of time, whatever.' Pia is blinking fast, walking away from the tree and then back again. Away and then back.

'We did it,' I say, because with Pea by my side it feels like it's both of us that are making this happen. Without warning the adrenalin that has kept me on my feet depletes, and I sit down hard on the curb before I fall down. 'I went through when I wanted to and came back, too. And I changed the past again. That means we can do this, we can really do this.'

'Save her?' Pia sits down next to me, resting her head on my shoulder. I wind my arms around her and suddenly we are ten and five again, sitting on a felled log in the moonlight, pretending that we are running away, although we both know we'll sneak back in to bed before the clock strikes one.

'I've already changed two things,' I say. 'I've changed the history of Mum's medallion. I've changed the carving on the tree. I can save her. If I can change what happens, what she does, then I can stop her being attacked, raped, and I can stop her from killing him. If I stop her life from being ruined, if I do that, everything will be different, she'll be different, she'll be happy. She'll be alive.'

Pea's huge, dark eyes widen in the darkness, her pupils dilated so that her irises are almost invisible.

'Luna, I'm scared. I'm not as brave as I thought, now I've seen this … now it's so real. I'm afraid of being lost to chance. I want to save Mum, but I want my life too. I've been shitty and a fuck-up and stupid for most of it, but it's still mine, and I love it.'

'I know,' I say, taking her hand. 'Look, I don't know how to explain it, or how to reassure you, but somehow I just know that you'll be a part of an altered future, I feel it. In just the same way that I can feel the past just a few millimetres away, I can feel the future too, all of them, all of the variables. And I just know you're there in every version, Pea. I know what I said before, but the truth is, if I wasn't sure of that, I couldn't do this. I couldn't sacrifice you. You're their child, Mum and Dad's. You'll always be their child. You're a constant, something, someone, who is meant to be.'

Pea's fingers tighten around mine, and for the first time today I feel the chill of the night air on my cooling skin.

'But not you, Luna, that's what you're saying, isn't it? You're saying that you don't belong in any other version except this one.'

'Yes, I think that's probably right,' I say, steadily. 'I think that's what I am saying. And maybe that's the whole reason that the universe has given me this chance to correct what's wrong.'

'What? What reason?' Pea asks.

'That I was never meant to be born at all.'

11 JULY

'Forever – is composed of Nows –'

—Emily Dickinson

CHAPTER TWENTY-NINE

Sleep came easily, and it was dreamless, as if my mind had no images left to conjure up mere dreams. As Pea wakes me, it feels like being dragged out of a very dark, very still, river, a thick tapestry of weeds, writhing above my head.

It takes a moment for everything to come trickling back, to remember where I am, who I have lost, what I am doing, who I am not.

'I didn't want to wake you, last night after you ... you know. You looked so pale, like if you stood in front of a strong light I'd be able to see right through you.' Pea hands me a strong mug of coffee. 'But Mr Gillespie called Mrs Finkle to ask us to come down to his office.'

'Why?' I take a scalding gulp of coffee and scramble out of bed. 'We don't have to give the keys back for three more days.'

It surprises me, how calm I am. None of the bad stuff matters anymore, it's as if I have already erased it all; I feel light and happy ... peaceful. Like I don't quite exist in this painful reality where the people I love are hurt, and the people I love die too soon. And it's a good feeling.

The business of now doesn't concern me anymore. I need to get on with the business of then. I sink back into the pillows.

'I know, but it's Mum's sister. It's Stephanie.' Pea gathers her hair back from her face, pinning it into a knot. 'Apparently she flew in from Florida last night. She's with Gillespie right now. She wants to see us.'

Stephanie does not look up when we enter Gillespie's office. She's sitting in his ancient leather-backed chair, and he is standing by the window.

An unfinished conversation hangs in the warm, still air, and as we sit down they make a conscious effort to realign their body language. We heard no raised voices, but I think they were arguing as we arrived.

'Well.' Stephanie sits back in the chair, and examines us. 'You look like her. Both of you, in different ways. And you ...' She stands up slowly as she examines me, and I realise I am wearing almost the same clothes as the last time I saw her, in the workshop, right down to my lazily laced Converse. 'Luna. What it is it you do? You remind me of someone, like I've seen you before ...'

'I expect I remind you of Mum,' I say. 'And my father; you knew him after all.'

I don't say Delaney's name out loud. I don't have to; she knows who I am talking about. Somehow I know she does.

Stephanie doesn't flinch, her face remains impassive.

'Perhaps we should all sit down,' Mr Gillespie suggests with gentle authority, and takes a seat.

'I'm sorry,' she says eventually, shifting uncomfortably in her chair as Mr Gillespie watches her. 'I'm sorry that I wasn't at the funeral. You've got to understand ... letting her go, saying goodbye, that night when she ... when she left, was one of the hardest things I have ever had to do. I felt abandoned. So I didn't come to the funeral. How could I show up then, when I hadn't showed up for so long before?'

There is no movement in the room, just the sound of traffic outside the open window, and the faint tap of Lucy's fingertips on a keyboard in the next room. I'd realised it would be hard to see Stephanie as she is now – plumper and yet harder around the edges, her hair sculpted and short, her skin florid and aged by so much sunshine – but not how hard. She doesn't even seem loosely connected to the girl who danced to Donna Summer. That girl, though tough and aloof, was suffused with colour and vitality. This woman seems stiff, not with age, but with a lifetime of fighting against feelings she doesn't want to have.

'So Riss left you some packages, then?'

Hearing her use Mum's nickname jars. She knows about the packages, that must have been what brought her down, afraid that the secret she and Mum shared for so long might come to light now, implicating her in a murder. She's testing us. 'What was in them?'

'The truth,' I say. 'We know what happened that night that she left. Everything.'

Stephanie looks at Mr Gillespie, who keeps his gaze trained out of the window.

'Just a reminder,' he says quietly. 'Everything you say in this office is privileged.'

'You know everything?' Stephanie asks us.

'Not who,' Pea admits. 'But everything else, everything she went through. What she did. We know you helped her get away with Dad.'

'I truly believed that I did the right thing.' Stephanie holds Pea's gaze. 'I hoped I did, and then, for a long time, I was afraid I hadn't done enough.'

'You never thought about the police? I mean, it was self-defence ...'

'A man like him,' Stephanie places every word with great care, like pieces on a chessboard. 'Well, a man like that never pays for what he does. He was revered, respected, not because of who he was, but because of what he was, what he represented. Even now, even today, it would be very hard to make an accusation against a man like that stick, not without damaging the person making the accusation, not without consequences. What we did, the choices we made – it was for the best. It was a fresh chance. For her, for you, too.'

I think of Delaney, protected from justice by his dog collar and his church. It must have seemed like there was no way out for Mum other than the way she took.

As I watch Stephanie struggling to describe the indescribable, there is no sign of the fierce protector I met in the past. She seems meek, defeated.

'The thing is,' Pea says, 'she never recovered from that night. She never came to terms with what had happened. She couldn't, because of what she did. If she'd had her family, especially you, maybe she would have been able to face it. I know that I can face the world a thousand times over with my sister at my side.'

'Listen –' Stephanie leans forward in her seat, impressing every word onto us with surgical precision '– I realise that you girls have been through a lot, but you can't tell anyone about this. You can't go to the police now. It's very important that you don't. She's gone. He can't hurt her anymore. But if the authorities find out what we did … People round here have long memories, I could still get hurt, and maybe you think that wouldn't matter so much, but it wouldn't just be me. It would be you too. That night, while she waited, I had to …' Stephanie paused, her gaze turning inwards as she remembers. 'I had to do difficult things, ask for help from some serious people, you know what I mean? I paid the price, my price. After that night … I married the man that made it happen; that was his fee. I married him and it wasn't a good marriage; he wasn't a good man. The longer I knew him, the more cruel and twisted he became. But I was never going to leave him and he knew that; I couldn't because he knew everything. He had the power to hurt me, but not only me, her too. He's dead now, I don't miss him. But those people, the people he worked for, they never forget *anything*, they never let *any* slight go. So, you have to realise, it's done, it's over with. You don't talk about it outside this room. Not ever. Not just for me, but for yourselves.'

As Stephanie lowers her eyes, a tug of empathy pulls at my chest. These last thirty years must have been hard on her, alone, separated from the person she loved most, trapped in a marriage that made her unhappy. She felt that she didn't have any choice but to abandon my mother; she couldn't have known that cutting her free the way she did was one of the reasons that Mum always felt so adrift.

'If I'd known, if I'd known how it would stay with her, how she'd never be able to get it out of her head, if I'd known that she'd never be happy after the sacrifices we made ...' She falters, glancing up at Gillespie.

'You wouldn't have made them?' I say, and again her head snaps up and she studies me, hard, absorbing every feature. I know she sees that man in me.

'Luna.' She says my name carefully. 'I would have done it exactly the same way again. That's what you have to understand: there was no other choice where Marissa had a chance. I had to give her a chance. I had to. I loved her. I would have done – did do – anything for her, the same way that you would do anything for your sister.'

'Why haven't you asked his name?' Mr Gillespie asks as he turns back from the window to look at me. 'Don't you want to know who your father was?'

'I know who my father is,' I say, wondering if this is what Gillespie and Stephanie were arguing about before we came in, whether to tell us the truth or not. 'I know the name of the man that raped my mother.'

Stephanie sits up a little in her chair, her shoulders stiffening, and Gillespie, despite his professional calm, raises an eyebrow.

'How?' Stephanie asks, suddenly bristling with fear. 'We swore we'd never tell.'

'I was talking to Mrs Finkle about what it was like when Mum left, and she mentioned the other person who vanished on the night of the blackout. He walked right out of a party and never came back. Father Thomas Delaney. It's him, isn't it?'

'Yes.' Stephanie lowers her eyes, and any doubt I had is gone.

'When did you find out?' There's a tremor in Pea's voice as she looks at me, and tears brim in her eyes. 'Her *priest*?'

'I'm sorry, I was going to tell you. I meant to ...' I turn back to Stephanie. 'We aren't going to tell anyone anything, not even my father ... Henry, I mean. You don't need to worry, Stephanie.'

Stephanie nods, then stands and walks towards the door.

'I missed her every single day for the last thirty years, and I always will. I thought she'd live her life, be happy, be the person she could be. I only knew about you after you were born, when she sent me a letter with a photo in. Maybe I should have written back then; I wanted to, but Curtis wouldn't let me. He didn't let me see any of my old friends after we were married, and if I even mentioned Riss's name … he got real angry. Pops was sick, the neighbourhood was going to hell, and I thought, So what, you had a baby, so what? At least you've got a baby. I was jealous of her, God help me. When Curtis died a couple of years ago, it felt like it had been too long to try again.'

'I'm sorry, for what this whole mess did to your life too,' I say to my aunt, and her features soften and she almost smiles, and I almost catch a glimpse of the girl I met before.

'I just wish for both of you that she'd had the life she should have had,' Stephanie says sadly. 'Maybe you two girls can live it for her, the way she would have wanted. Selling the building will help. All these years it's stood there empty, it's felt like a mausoleum. Just sign the papers and I'll have it sold in no time, a weight off all our backs.'

'I want to wait a little longer,' I say.

Stephanie looks at me.

'I'm just not ready yet, not right now. I need a few days, that's all. We can sign the papers before we go.'

'Why?' Stephanie is curt, suddenly desperate for the nightmare of the last thirty years to be over at last. She has been just as trapped and imprisoned by her sister's tragedy as the rest of us have, and she longs to be free, as free as she can be. 'Luna, what will change in a couple of days that hasn't changed for the last thirty years?'

'Maybe everything,' I say.

CHAPTER THIRTY

The Church of the Transfiguration soars upwards, cutting purposefully into the flawless blue sky, all straight decisive lines and acute angles. Over the imposing light-oak door that seems designed for giants, the date 1925 is carved into a plain rectangle tablet. There was nothing about it I recognise from my own experience of places of worship. The village church that we had sometimes gone to with school or for weddings was so old, so familiar, it seemed almost as much part of the landscape as the hills behind it, and the woods around it. St Mary's is made of thousands of flint stones, constructed with Norman arches and a spire that has become crooked and twisted over time, although somehow it still stands. Stone effigies of long-dead nobles, their names and lives forgotten, are set into the walls and there is a sense of not only the passing of time, but timelessness. One place, that is always constant, always true.

Yet these two building thousands of miles and years apart still have one thing in common: they are both declaring to the sky, 'Look at this triumph. Look what Man has done in your name.'

Lifting my camera, I focus it upwards. From where I am standing I can't get the full extent of the architecture into frame, but somehow that seems like the point.

'It looks like that church from *The Omen*,' Pea mutters.

'This place must have been a second home to Mum,' I say. 'She must have felt safe here, especially after Rosa died. She must have felt safe with him. When we were growing up, she never went anywhere near a church if she could help it.'

A great knot of emotion has coiled in and around my gut. I'm not sure exactly what it is that I am feeling so intensely; something like grief, something like fear and fury, in a heaving tangle.

'What are we looking for here, Luna?' Pea asks, as we stand on the threshold. 'I mean, we know he's not here anymore, don't we? He's dead. She killed him.'

'Oh, he's here,' I tell her. 'I can feel him.'

As soon as the words are out of my mouth I am battling an unseen head wind, something powerful that seems to be seeking to push me away from this place. Nothing physical changes, the air doesn't even stir around me, but I feel it, this pressure, this force of some kind of will meeting my own, determined to deny me. Somehow I know that it isn't a malignance or an enemy that is barring my way, it's a warning, a foreshadowing. In this place, for the first time since the impossible became true, the universe is telling me this is my last chance to turn back.

But all of my life has been leading me towards this moment.

'Come on,' I say, grabbing Pea's hand, pushing open the heavy door and the warning aside with quite some force of effort.

I can feel, I can *hear*, a thousand single moments reflect all around me. A thousand footsteps and whispered prayers. A thousand hopes, a thousand fears, all reaching for the same thing, the same need for comfort and reassurance, and in amongst those moments I hear my mother, grieving for her own, meeting me in a perfect loop.

I don't believe in ghosts, but I don't need to. I know, somehow, that just a hair's breath away, behind one gossamer-fine sheet of fabric, every other person who has ever walked up and down these steps, and every person who ever will, is doing it forever more, in this one moment. Soon, I'll leave this moment behind and walk into the next, but that won't mean that it's gone. It's still there, echoing forever. And in one of them, he's there too, waiting for me, without knowing why. I can sense him getting near.

Inside the church it's unexpectedly bright and light. The clear-glass windows are long and high, letting in dramatic slants of sunlight that make the whitewashed walls luminous. Light-oak pews stand to attention in regimented lines either side of a central aisle, focused on the altar, where the figure of Christ on the cross presides over all. There's a vividness to it, a drama, and you can feel the thrum of faith in the air, humming like an electric charge.

A lady comes in behind us, and gives a faintly disapproving glance before dipping her finger in what must be the holy water, fixed to a wall just inside the door. She bows before the altar, making a sign of the cross, before she slips into a pew. Pea and I exchange a nervous look. There are rules, rituals, that we are not privy to. We are both outsiders here.

'What do we do?' Pea whispers to me, out of the side of her mouth.

'I don't know,' I admit. 'Wait.'

'For what?'

I'm about to tell her I don't know that either when another woman touches me on the shoulder.

'Can I help you?' she speaks softly, and as I turn I know her at once. Riss's friend Michelle, her hair still tightly curly, although peppered with silver, and while she is heavier now than she was, her face is still open, happy and peaceful. She starts when she sees me, startled by a flash of recognition that is dismissed at once, because after all I cannot possibly be that woman she met one summer, exactly thirty years ago.

'This isn't really a church for tourists,' she says pleasantly. 'If you want, I can point you in the direction of our beautiful cathedral, although you'll need to take a subway, or a cab if you can find one.'

'Oh, we're not tourists, we're from England,' I say.

She represses a smile. 'Since we won the War of Independence, that makes you a tourist.'

'Our mum used to come here,' Pea explains. 'She grew up in Bay Ridge and we ... we recently lost her, so we're just visiting the places that meant a lot to her and this was one of them.'

'I'm so sorry,' she says, her face softening. 'Do you mind me asking who your mother was? Perhaps I knew your family.'

'Marissa Lupo.' I break the news gently, predicting exactly how her face will fall, how her hands will cover her mouth in shock.

'You're Riss's girls?' Her tone raises just enough to disturb the atmosphere, making little ripples in the quiet.

'You knew her?' Pea whispers.

'Knew her? I loved her.' Michelle turns away from us for a second, the light making a halo of her profile. Shaking her head, she takes a breath. 'I'm Michelle Cavates, or at least I was then. Michelle Knight now. And Riss ... we grew up together, I must have seen her every single day of my life since grade school. Until the day she left. Oh my god, oh Riss, how?'

Neither of us answer; even now, after everything we've seen and know, it seems impossible to speak of Mum's death as if it were a real event that happened to us, and not some story that belongs to a stranger.

'I'm sorry, the shock,' she says, taking our hands and squeezing them. 'I don't mean to pry. Here, come with me. Come sit in my office and we can talk properly.'

'Coffee?' Michelle gestures to a pot she has on the go in the corner of her office. We had followed her through a side door of the church itself and through a glass-covered walkway that had been built to connect the church to an administrative ante-building in the late sixties. 'Or tea ... you Brits like tea, don't you? I have some around here, I think ...'

She starts opening and shutting the drawers of her desk.

'Water would be great, please,' I say, and Pea nods.

'There's a cooler just down the hall, I'll bring you both a cup.'

As we wait for her to return, Pea reaches her hand out to me and I take it.

'Are you OK?' she asks me. 'You look ... you don't look great.'

'I'm OK.' I smile. 'I feel good actually. Strong.'

Pea looks sceptical, but still she takes me at my word, releasing my fingers as Michelle returns to the room.

Michelle puts two plastic cups of water down in front of us, resting her chin on the heels of hand as she takes a seat. 'I'm so sorry for your loss. How long ago since she passed?'

'A few months, not long,' I say. 'It was an accident.'

I know Pea won't mind me saying what is partially true, although what's written on our mother's death certificate is accidental overdose. When I think of the woman that Michelle knew for so long, that woman had nothing to do with the one that took her own life. I don't want to take her memories away from her.

'I can't believe it, you know.' Michelle blinks in disbelief. 'It's like she wasn't really gone until just now. She was gone, sure, one minute she was here, and then the lights went out all over the city, and when they came back on she wasn't. But somehow that didn't matter, because I knew she was still out there. I used to think about her, you know? I used to think that, if ever I saw her again, it'd be just the same as it always was, we'd pick up where we left off without missing a beat, and I always used to hope I'd get that chance someday. That she'd come home for a visit or I'd go to England. And now I know I won't – well, it hurts.'

I take a sip of water, and already it feels warmed by the air. Michelle rubs her palms over her face, leaving traces of electric-blue mascara on her cheeks.

'We wrote to each other for a while,' she says. 'Then life gets in the way, and what you mean to be a couple of weeks turns into months and then it's years since you've been in touch. How are you girls doing? How's Henry?'

'We take it day by day,' Pea says.

'What else do you remember about that summer?' I ask, searching for something, a phrase or a memory that might act as a door, a way through.

If Michelle is surprised by my question she doesn't show it. 'It was hot, so hot – it felt like you only really came alive after the sun went down. Things were different that summer, the film crew were still in town right up until August. Well, you guys must know that. Even though I didn't have anything to do with it, it felt like the whole place was somehow shinier, like this little corner of nowhere we lived in was finally on the map, you know?' Michelle smiles, sitting up and straightening her shoulders as she speaks. 'I never felt proud of where I lived before then. I loved it, don't get me wrong, but to feel proud of it … I guess most of that happened in seventy-eight, though, when the movie came out …'

'And you were there when Mum and Dad met? It was in the White Castle burger joint, wasn't it, when the production was shooting there?' Pea asks, drawing Michelle back to us.

'Sure. That was a real love story, right there.' Michelle beams at us, clearly grateful to have something good to give us. 'I was sick with envy; the way it happened, it was better than in the movies. Your dad was taking pictures, of the actors, the set, the scenes. And there were kids, so many kids hanging out on the street, and then his lens stopped on Riss. She didn't notice at first, but I did. Because he just stopped, brought his camera down and just looked at her. And when she finally looked back at him, *ka-bam*, it happened just like that. It's different now, I guess, but I dreamt of my wedding day from when I was a little girl. I dreamt of meeting Mr Right. And it was obvious to all of us that Riss had gone and done it first.'

'And wasn't there someone from the church that disappeared the same night?' I frame the question as casually as I can. 'A priest?'

'Yes, that's right, Father Thomas ...' Michelle bites her lip, a crease of concern appearing between her eyebrows. 'For a little while some people thought she might of run off with him. Can you imagine? But I knew better, I knew *her*. She'd secretly gotten a passport, even before she met Henry, when the rest of us hardly ever thought of even crossing the bridge to Manhattan. Riss was born with itchy feet. She wanted to see the world; she wanted the world to see her. I always thought she'd end up doing something big, you know? Something we'd hear about one day and I wouldn't be surprised.'

'So you work here?' I ask. 'I didn't think women were allowed to work in the Catholic Church.'

'Sure they are, it's not the dark ages.' Michelle smiles. 'I'm the sacristan. It's sort of like an office manager and church historian role all in one, serving a parish of around twelve hundred souls.'

'So did anyone ever find out what happened to Father Thomas?'

Something in Michelle's face changes, and she sits back in her chair a little, her expression closing slightly.

'All I can tell you is, he was good-looking man, plenty of the wives of the parish used to flutter their lashes at him during communion. And he was a good priest; the congregation flourished under him. But still he was just a man, and men make mistakes. My guess is he probably got too close to the wrong woman; Bay Ridge could be a dangerous place if you crossed the wrong man, even for a priest. He probably had to cut town and fast. I guess we'll never know.'

Without warning, her voice seems to be coming from very far away, and when I glance at Pea, she is out of focus and, somehow, even sitting so close to me that her forearm brushes mine, I know she is out of reach.

'Excuse me, I just need the ...' It seems too difficult to finish the sentence, and I hope they will get the gist. Pea looks at me anxiously, but I shake my head, hoping that's enough to ensure she doesn't try and follow me.

Out in the hallway, I press the small of my back into the wall, drooping over, bracing my arms on my knees. I feel as if I can taste my stomach in my mouth, sour and acrid, and I focus on the toes of my shoes.

My feet push through the vinyl floor, slipping into space. I see the air thicken and solidify around me, and, as I gasp for breath, I feel it in my throat and lungs; I chew on it, and it becomes stuck between my teeth like candyfloss. I close my eyes and wait.

When I open them the corridor looks exactly the same, empty and quiet, except for the sounds of muffled voices behind closed doors. It was just a wobble, just a moment, brought on by the heat and the emotion, passed now. I am both disappointed and relieved as I open the office door.

'Sorry, about that, I was just—' I stop. An older man in his fifties is sitting at the desk. He's wearing thick, black-rimmed glasses, and his silver hair is slicked back off his forehead. He's smoking as he keys numbers into an adding machine.

'And who are you ... ?'

'I'm sorry, wrong room,' I say. Backing out and shutting the door behind me, I lean against the wall and take in deep breaths. It happened fast, faster than ever before; either I am mastering the transition or it's mastering me, shaving away layer after a layer of me, until I can walk through walls.

Venturing a little further down the corridor I hesitate outside a room that seems quiet. I knock and there is no answer. Opening the door, I walk into the empty room and close the door behind me, taking a moment to catch my breath and compose myself. I'm here, right in the heart of the place where Thomas Delaney worked and lived, back in 1977.

Chances are he's just around the corner.

CHAPTER THIRTY-ONE

It's just as I realise how close I am when my courage fails me. I'm overcome with the sudden need to get out of here and as far away from him as I can, as fast as I can. The thought of seeing him, admitting to his existence and how it is so deeply connected to mine, horrifies me. Blood crunches in my ears as I head back down the glass-covered walkway, looking for a place of safety, a calm harbour to hide in until I figure out what exactly it is that I am going to do. What was I thinking? Did I imagine that I was going to save the day by simply walking up to him and telling him to steer clear of my mother, or by telling her to stay away from him? Did I plan to push him under a passing cab and save everyone else the trouble? Perhaps I'd thought that whatever I did it wouldn't matter, I wouldn't care, or even feel it, because by then I would already be half gone, returning exactly that same amount of energy to the universe that it had taken to create me.

I thought I could be cold and heartless like him. But I am no avenging angel. At the end of all this drama, all this grand theatre playing out across decades, I'm just a lost girl. An outsider. A daughter who has never known her true father and somehow misses him just as much as he hates him.

The idea of actually coming face to face with him now makes me feel sick and scared and, yes, full of longing to know him. It's not less that I feel, as I set in motion the events that will remove me from this life. It's more – *more* love, *more* alive, more of *everything* – and it *hurts*.

Instead of finding my way barred by the coded lock that Michelle had swiftly punched an access number into, I swing open the door and head back down into the church. The pungent scent of incense stings my nostrils. A male voice sings in Latin and a meagre congregation returns each phrase as one. I hesitate, afraid to look over my shoulder; is that his voice?

Nausea sweeps through me; I struggle to keep control of my gut. I don't want to look at him, see him, hear him, and yet ... if I turned my head now I could see the face of the man that makes up half of me. Trembling, keeping my eyes focused on the door that leads to the street, I walk as quickly and as calmly as I can towards it, constantly afraid that the repetitive incantations that are crashing over me, wave after wave, will somehow trap me here, like a fly caught in amber.

My relief as I all but fall out of the church and onto the street is short lived. I feel very far from home. People are hurrying by, low slung, noisy sedan cars screech their horns at each other in the slow-moving traffic. There's the heavy stink of humanity, people, cars, industry, the sweet smell of food mingling with the decay of rotting trash, a summer of strikes leaving its mark. This is real, it's really happening, and I am much less certain, much less brave, in the daylight than I am wandering the empty streets at night. I might as well have just crash-landed on Mars. I have no idea how to exist here amongst these people, how to walk or talk. I'm afraid to move, and afraid to stay still.

Heat scorches the sidewalk, giving the smell of the street a charred and acrid edge; the midday sun burns the back of my neck at once. A drunk lies across the sidewalk, lost in his own private world, as people walk by, the flow of feet parting around him, like he is no more than a rock on a riverbed. An angry woman in a ripped, sequined skirt is sitting on the bench on the corner, arguing with thin air. Beneath her feet a newish-looking red handbag with its guts turned inside out lies on the floor, a lipstick with its lid off, crushed against the concrete in a shocking scarlet smear.

'Jesus, move it, will you, lady.' A guy shoves past me and I retreat to the safety of the church wall, trying to get my bearings, searching the street for something I recognise. It had been a little more than ten-minute walk from Mrs Finkle's place to the church. All I need to do is to find the intersection of a street and an avenue, then I'll know exactly where I am. I can find Riss, and wherever she is – even in 1977 – I feel safe.

In the exact second I formulate a plan, a door that I haven't noticed until now, set deep into the wall of the church, swings open. A girl of about fifteen, in red shorts and a little, white, camisole top edged with embroidered strawberries, comes out onto the street. Her long, bare legs and her almost womanly figure is both awkward and balletic, as if she hasn't quite learnt to inhabit herself yet. The back of her neck and shoulders are burnt bright red, except for two things: her white, spaghetti straps pushed off her shoulder, and the paler flesh beneath now revealed to the sun.

Turning on her heels, her parting smile is shy.

'Thank you, Father Thomas,' she says, blushing the same shade as her sunburnt shoulders. An electric surge of anxiety charges through to my fingertips. 'I can't talk to anyone the way I can to you, you just seem to get me.'

Her voice is full of admiration, affection and, yes, unknowing longing for something half desired but barely understood.

'I'm always here for you, Fay.' His voice. I wouldn't have had to know who was speaking to know it was him; the sound of it resonates in my chest: an accent that isn't Brooklyn, could easily come from any state, tinged with an affectation of Irish. 'Any time, you know that. Just call in and I'll make time for you. You're a very special young woman.'

The door remains open as the girl half walks, half skips away, turning back once more to offer him a cheerful little wave. I know with total certainty that he is standing in the shadow of the doorway, watching her go.

Standing motionless, I watch the door close and I hear the slide of a bolt, my breathing only slowing as I imagine him disappearing deeper into the bowels of the church.

Knowing he is still in there, and could appear at any moment, gives me the impetus to peel myself off of the wall. I can see the corner from here.

'Hey, wait a second, would you?' His voice stops me in my tracks. 'Yeah, you. I saw you from the walkway. Were you waiting to come in?'

Slowly, very slowly, I turn around and see him framed by the doorway, his face standing out from the shadowy background. Thick, red-brown hair, long sideburns. A black shirt, open at the neck, no sign of a dog collar, and blue eyes that sing out to the sky.

'Don't go now.' His voice is friendly, reassuring. 'Stay a while, won't you? Come and talk to me. All are welcome here, no matter what.'

'Even me?' I take a step closer to observe him, expecting something more than his benign smile, from him and me. Perhaps a gut reaction, a spark of some deep primal recognition, but there is nothing. I feel nothing.

'God welcomes all who are ready to repent of their sins and commit to his love,' he tells me cheerfully, stepping out of the door and onto the sidewalk, closing the space between us by a fraction more. 'You look lost.'

'I know where I am.' I point at the street sign opposite, and he laughs.

'Lost in your life, I mean. Our heavenly father can show you the way, if you'll let him.'

'You truly believe that?' I ask him. 'Even when there are drunks and addicts outside your door? Is there a way back for them too?'

He nods. 'For everyone. Even you. Come inside, talk to me.'

Instinct pushes me from the inside out. I'm glad I bought the Pentax, loaded with fresh film, and I lift it to my eye. A man who works so hard to keep his crimes invisible won't want to be seen in a way that is so permanent, so easily reproduced.

'Can I take your picture?' I ask him.

Through the eye of the lens, he simply smiles, shrugs, crossing his arms and leaning in the frame of the doorway, one leg positioned casually in front of the other. He looks like a catalogue model, not a monster. He looks like any man, not the man who is so intrinsically woven into my flesh. My finger hovers over the shutter, but it doesn't click.

'Come inside,' he repeats. 'Talk to me about what is troubling you.'

'I don't want to.'

'Well –' he shrugs '– you'll know where to find me when you're ready.'

'Yes,' I say. 'I will.'

My feet stumble over themselves in my haste to be away from him. It's not the fear or repulsion I expected the first time I saw him, and somehow that makes it worse. He has a kind face, open and trusting. If I didn't know what he was, I'd think he looked like a man you could turn to; a good man, with a church at his back. That's how Mum must have seen him, and how it must have hurt her in those first few seconds when she realised everything she thought she knew about him was a lie. How it must have frightened her.

I need to be with someone I love so badly that it hurts, so I head for Lupo's. I head for my mother, following instinct over design.

My mouth is dry, limbs trembling, my veins full of adrenalin, and the heat is pouring into me, melting me into the asphalt. Delaney was right about one thing – I am lost, a stranger in a strange land, with no place to go – and then I see a face I know. And it's Michael.

'Hey, it's you.' His smile of recognition makes my heart leap, and it's hard not to think that fate, or some grand plan, has us turning endless corners always into one another.

'Michael.' Taking a step towards him, I stop just short of flinging my arms around him, so grateful am I to see him.

'Hey, what's up? You gonna cry?' He ducks a little to peer into my face, and I shake my head, although tears are already rolling down my cheeks.

'What happened, who's upset you? Want me to talk to them, huh?' He makes a fist. 'Like Rocky would?'

I smile, not just because he makes me smile, but because he sees me. I exist.

'Where you been at?' he asks, puzzled and smiling all at once. 'I asked Riss, and she said she saw you too last night. I knocked on the door of the place you were staying and they didn't know you.'

'Ah, I ... I moved. I didn't like it there.' I pause. 'You were asking about me?'

'I was worried about you, walking around on your own. I wish you wouldn't, OK? Look, if it's money, if you can't afford anywhere to stay, well, I'm sure we can find you somewhere, with one of the girls, until you get straight.'

'That's sweet,' I say. 'It really is, but ... I'm fine on my own.'

'OK.' He nods once, deciding not to question me anymore. 'That's cool. And sure I went looking for you. I wanted to see you again. Feels like a lifetime since I last saw you. But it was only last night.'

He is so impossibly sweet that I can't help but deflect it. 'Do you practise these lines in front of the mirror?'

'You bet I do.' He grins. 'I say them over and over again to my picture of Farrah Fawcett. Judging by the look on her face, she thinks I'm pretty hot. I'm supposed to be back at work, but ...' He digs his hands deep into his pockets, lifting his shoulders, suddenly coy. 'Come spend the afternoon with me. We can sit in the sun and talk about nothing.'

My first instinct is to say no, Michael is not the reason I am here. And then somehow, almost unconsciously, my fingers gravitate towards his, and I find his hand in mine.

'Sure, why not?' I say.

'Really?' He is so surprised, so delighted, and it shows in his smile. His beautiful smile.

I let him lead me down the street, his gait confident, almost a strut, his head held high, uninterested in the curious glances and sometime naked stares we are attracting. For a minute or so, I'm sure it's me people are staring at. My faded jeans, plain white T-shirt and no make-up mean I stand out a mile among women who seem to take special care with how they look. Then I realise it's him; wherever he goes people want to look at him.

He slows as we near the end of 3rd Avenue, a block from Lupo's.

'I'd better go see Dad,' he says reluctantly. 'Wait here a sec.'

'Where the hell have you been?' A raised voice greets him as he walks through the door.

'I was on my break, Dad, you know that.' Michael's reply is quieter, respectful. 'I don't feel so good; I think maybe it's the flu.'

'The flu? The flu! I'll give you the goddam flu,' his father bellows, and I'm struck by how much he looks like that version of Michael I met in the present, only exhausted, and seemingly furious at his son. 'When are you going to grow up? You ain't no kid anymore, you got responsibilities, and you got a job, whether you like it or not. I haven't broken my back every single day of your life, just so you walk out on me, you little prick. You don't get to do that.'

'Who says I can't? Watch me.' Michael reappears, backing out of the shop, and grabs my hand. 'Let's get out of here.'

'You get back here, you little shit!' Michael's father hollers down the street after us. 'You get back here, and I'll show you, you aren't too big to feel the back of my hand.'

Michael's grip tightens on mine, but he doesn't flinch or hesitate. He doesn't look back; we just keep on walking, marching, and the further from the shop we get, the more his shoulders square, his chin lifts.

'Are you OK?' I ask him eventually, when we stop at the last road before the park. The Verrazano–Narrows Bridge soars above the treeline.

'Sure, I'm fine,' he mutters. 'Why wouldn't I be fine?'

His expression tells another story though: he suddenly looks much younger, and hurt. There are unshed tears in his eyes. I touch his cheek with my fingertips.

'I don't know why I care so much,' he says. 'It's just when I was a kid, he got me, you know? We got each other. But now I'm a man, and I'm not like him. It's like he hates me. Sometimes I hate me for not being the son he needs.'

'Maybe he thinks he wants you to be just like him,' I say. 'But one day he'll see that he's wrong.'

'Just like that.' Michael smiles.

'Just like that,' I say. 'I'm much older and wiser than you, trust me on this.'

There's a moment as we look into each other's eyes when it feels like it could end in a kiss, which isn't a surprise. What is, though, is how much I want it to.

It's Michael that pulls away.

'I got it, we should have a picnic. Wait there.' Pressing my hand to his lips, before returning it to me, he goes into a general store.

A few moments later he returns. 'Here,' he says, handing me a Coke, with a red-and-white-striped straw in it, and a Twinkie.

He leads me all the way down to the end of 3rd Avenue, past where the commercial properties become homes and apartments, trimmed with balconies that are brimming with flowers. We cross a busy road, and all but race down the shady path that leads to an expanse of grass, the only thing beyond it the bridge, silver against the skyline, an arrow dividing the otherwise seamless blue water and sky.

'It can be a little dangerous down here at night,' Michael tells me, as he finds us a bench, giving a small bow as he offers me a seat. 'But it's cool now, especially with me here to protect you.'

All of his bravado is back, and I'm happy.

I sip sweet, dark Coke, and feel the long grass around my ankles tickle and scratch. Is it wrong that I am so happy? Is it dangerous to feel so content here? This feeling, this happiness that I feel, is so rare, so precious. It's a happiness I can't keep; I can't let it be mine.

'I grew up watching them build it,' Michael says, nodding at the bridge. 'In my head, when I was a kid, I thought as soon as they finish building that bridge I'm going to run over it as fast as I can and get out of here. I sort of thought it would get me anywhere, you know? Anywhere I dreamt of.'

'Where do you dream of?' I ask him.

'Well, not fucking Staten Island, which is the only place that bridge goes to.' He chuckles. 'You can't even walk over it either, just cars.'

'Where then?'

He falters, and looks away from me, back out to the bridge, suddenly shy.

'Tell me.' I lean into him, the skin of my arm grazing his. He sighs as he looks at me, and I love the sound of his longing.

'I want to write stories,' he confesses. 'But not just for fun, like, for real. Real stories in books and shit. I know I can't, I know I don't have the right schooling to be a writer. But I want to write books like *The Shining*. Not scary shit, but stuff that's exciting, that anyone can get into. Books for people like me. But fuck it, I'm not even supposed to read books. I don't tell Dad, I don't tell the guys, I don't even tell most of the girls I date that I read books and write stories …'

'I think men that read books are the most attractive kind,' I tell him. His eyes widen, his cheeks colour beneath his tan.

'You don't think I'm a dope, some baker's kid with a high-school diploma, getting ideas above his station?'

'No, I don't,' I say. 'That's not what I think about you at all. I find you rather compelling.'

'Compelling?' He mimics my accent, throwing his head back as he laughs, suddenly carefree again. 'Well, chicks have called me a lot of things, but never compelling. It's a dumb dream, it won't never happen. Just like that bridge looks so pretty; it don't really go nowhere. That's me, my friend.'

'That isn't you,' I counter, thinking of the future I have seen for him. I couldn't know how happy or content that Michael was, what love waited for him at home. Was there a wife, children? All I know is that man I met was a man who had never gone anywhere after all. 'If came to see you in thirty years' time what would you be doing?' I ask him. 'Where would you be?'

'If I'm still alive by then?' He laughs. 'I'll be driving my hover car to work at the goddam bakery, selling space food to Martians!'

'Huh, the future sounds fun,' I say. 'I've lived a quiet life, until now. Stayed in one place, done one thing. Never really fallen in love, never really made any kind of mark on the world. I saw my mum live her whole life with this aching urge to be small and quiet and unseen, when she was meant to be big and loud and in everyone's faces. Life, circumstance, got the better of her, and I don't want that for me, or the people I care about. I want my life to have mattered, to have made a difference. What I'm trying to say is, you might as well try as hard as you can to follow your dreams, otherwise what are they for, except to remind you of everything you didn't do.'

The sun has dipped a little, and turned the afternoon golden, dappling through the tree canopy and playing over his face. When I thought he was a bit player in this drama it was easier to look at him, but now I know how important he has become, I feel suddenly a little shy.

'That beautiful bridge might not go anywhere you want to go, but there are plenty of other bridges and tunnels that do,' I tell him.

'Would you come with me, if I go?' His green eyes intensify, and I feel the world fall apart. It's not time that is shifting inside me, it's my heart. There's a rise of bubbles from my belly; this is exactly the wrong moment to fall in love for the first time in my life. And precisely the wrong man to fall in love with. There can be no future, no hope, no chance for this love. There won't even be a memory of it.

And yet.

And yet, I know this is both my first and last chance to be in love, and I know that somehow, for some reason I don't understand, it was always only ever going to be here that I found the person I could love, that I found Michael. And, dear god, I don't want to cease to live without having known what it means to feel this way.

Everything about him, about me, makes these feeling utterly impossible, and yet I feel them; longing and desire inhabit every living cell that makes me what I am. My body rings for him, like a struck bell.

So, slowly, very slowly, I let myself fall, knowing that there is no turning back.

Michael slides along the bench towards me, his eyes locked on mine. His hand finds my waist, pulling me flush against him. We lean into one another and we both feel it, this pull, this magnetism made just for us two; a desperate need to be connected.

In any decade, in any time, this is what it feels like to fall in love.

'Hey, Luna!' Riss breaks us apart with her call, crossing her arms and rocking back on her hips as she really looks at us. 'Oh, hey Michael.'

'Hello,' I say, tucking my hair primly behind my ear as I move away from him. After all my mother *has* just caught me with a boy.

'Great timing, Riss. Perfect.' Michael sits back, his arm stretching out behind me. Even in the heat I miss the warmth of his body near mine. 'Where you been? Why aren't you at your little sewing machine making me a nice shirt for Saturday night?'

'Because I'm sick,' Riss says, looking about as healthy as a girl can, her bare, brown skin seeming to glow in the sun, against a yellow, cotton sundress edged in white, a green purse slung over her shoulder, a brown, paper package under her arm. She is fully charged with love and sunlight, and for once I don't have to guess what that might be like. I know, and knowing makes it even harder to realise that, not long from now, one moment, one decision, one action, will destroy all the joy she carries with her now, smashing it into pieces. And all her life long, no matter how she will try to gather them up again, and reassemble what once was, she will never be complete again.

The more I don't want to leave this life, the more I know I must.

'Are you OK?' I ask, sensing a flush in her cheeks, a glitter in her eyes.

She crosses to the bench and sits down next to me, forcing Michael to move up to the end of the bench. She stares at me intently.

'You are a mystery, you know that?' she says, so close I can smell the scent of her hair, see the little scar on her chin.

'A mystery, me?' I say, 'I don't think so.'

'Yeah, you're like that movie, *The Man Who Fell to Earth*, except you're a girl, of course. You just drop out of the sky, out of nowhere, and the funny thing is, I feel like I know you somehow. I wish I could work out who it is you remind me of,' she says.

'I just have a face like that, I suppose ...'

'Those eyes,' she says. 'You've got the bluest eyes, just like ...'

'So tell us, what have you really been doing?' Michael cuts in, and I wonder if he could see how uncomfortable I was becoming with her questions, her closeness.

'Seeing Henry.' Riss leans back against the bench, stretching her arms out along its back; her smile is a perfect curl of joy. 'I told Pops I was sick, and Stephanie is covering for me. Henry's got to go back soon, and I need to spend as much time with him as I can, so ...'

Michael pretends to gag, and Riss cuffs him mildly around the back of his head.

'Just because you've never been in love,' she says, glancing at me. 'Or maybe that's changed recently.'

I repress a smile as Michael blushes rather sweetly.

'Listen, can you two keep a secret? I mean like a huge fucking secret?'

'Yes,' I say at once.

'Depends what you gonna give me to keep quiet,' Michael teases her, and she cuffs him again.

'Can you fucking keep a secret or not, Michael?' Riss levels a dark-eyed glare at him, and he raises his palms in surrender.

'Nice language from a lady,' he says.

'Well, we went for a picnic, down on the shore,' Riss says. 'I knew it was coming, but even so when he asked ...' Biting her lip, she stretches out her left hand for both of us to see, wriggling her fingers so that her newly acquired piece of jewellery sparkles in the sun. 'Henry asked me to marry him and, it wasn't until then, until he asked me, that I knew what the right thing to do was, and I said yes! I'm engaged, can you believe it?'

'Wow!' Reaching out, I take her hand, and as I do time tilts and disintegrates around me.

Not now, this can't happen now. I concentrate very hard on the ring, desperate to stay in this moment. Of course I know it, better than the back of my own hand. A tiny flower of diamonds, arranged like a daisy on a thin, gold band. I've gazed at it as I held Mum's hand walking to school, seen her rub and twist it, day after day, decade after decade. Watched it shine through mud as we weeded in the garden.

Buried her, with it still on her finger.

Time settles for the moment at least, leaving me be.

'Well, that's wonderful news.' I make myself stay bright. 'Congratulations. Are you going home to tell your dad? When will you be going to the UK? You should go with him right away. Go tonight, go tomorrow!'

Riss frowns and laughs at the same time.

'Are you crazy?' Riss shakes her head. 'Pops would *die* if I just ran off like that. His daughter marrying a non-Catholic? And moving to England, leaving him with Stephanie? I told you before, I got to be careful; if I tell him in the wrong way at the wrong time, then this whole thing is over. I'll lose Henry or my family or both, and I don't want to choose. We've got time; he's going back in a few days, but we have this now, to show how serious we are, and time to make it right.'

'Sometimes time is the last thing you need,' I say urgently. This moment is my chance; it might be my one chance to change things, and I can't let it slip away. If I can't get her to deviate from the path she is on, I will lose everything that I have only just found. 'Just tell your dad. What's the point in lying? You want to marry Henry, right? You're a grown woman, you don't need anyone's permission. It will be difficult, of course, but it's better than keeping it a secret. Secrets *always* makes things worse.'

'Maybe,' Riss says, drawing back from me a little. 'Why's it such a big deal to you anyways?'

'It's not,' I say carefully, trying to sound older, wiser. 'It's just, well, I've seen people drift apart in long-distance relationships. Things start out well, but if you don't see someone, and there are other people on the scene ... who knows?'

My mother's scowl can turn a bright day black as night.

'Those are the people you know, not me, not Henry. I know him, and I know us. We're forever, whatever happens.'

'I agree with Luna,' Michael says, and Riss laughs.

'No kidding, you'd agree white is black if you thought it'd get you laid.'

'That's not what it's like with me and her,' he says so seriously that even Riss is surprised.

'OK, I'm sorry.' Something shifts in her expression, something softens. 'I didn't realise. Even so, you should get why I can't just run away, Michael.'

'Maybe I do, but maybe she's right about just being straight about it now. Your pop's a decent guy, and he loves you. So Henry's not Catholic, does that really matter? He's a good man, *that's* what matters, not what God he prays to or what lies he tells himself to feel better about winding up dead one day.'

Riss hesitates and, for a moment, hope and fear combine as I wonder if it could be Michael that makes the difference, if that's why I've been so drawn to him. But then she shakes her head.

'I need time. Time to think and time to pray on what to do about it. I'm going see if I can talk to Father Thomas. Priests can't tell anyone what you tell them; they've got to keep it a secret.'

My hearts plummets into my stomach and just as fast panic rises again, and I can feel myself lose any semblance of reason.

'Don't,' I say urgently, grabbing her arms and trying to pull her towards me. 'Don't talk to him. Please, stay away from that man.'

'Are you crazy?' Riss stands up rubbing at the red finger marks I left on her arms. 'Have you even met him? I've known him since I was a kid. Of course I should ask him for guidance, he's cool. He understands what life is about. He wasn't always a priest. I respect that about him.'

'But ...' I flail around for something, anything to stop her talking to him. 'I don't like him.'

'You haven't even met him!' Riss's eyes flash with furious lightening.

'Today. Today I did,' I tell her frantically. 'I was outside the church and he was talking to a girl, and the way he was looking at her ...'

'Luna, shut up before we fall out,' she says, and I bite back any more words, afraid of pushing her away. She offers me the package. 'Here, it's your dress. I was going to drop it round to Mrs Oberman's or wherever you're staying now, but as you are here ... we're meeting at 2001 Odyssey tonight, around ten, if you want to come.'

It's a less welcoming invitation than the last one.

'Thank you,' I say as I take it. 'I'll do my best to be there.'

'You're welcome. But don't ever talk about Father Thomas that way again, do you hear me? It matters to me. God matters to me.'

I nod, carefully inching my way through the next few seconds, terrified of losing her trust altogether.

'See you around.'

I watch as she vanishes into the tunnel of shadows made by the trees.

'Shit.' I bury my face in my hands.

'You OK?' Michael touches my shoulder and I shrug him off. 'That's not like Riss to get so wound up about something, go off like that about what you said. It's like you really got under her skin. I guess this means a lot to her.'

As I try and focus on him, he seems to flicker in and out of my vision. I've failed and it feels like I'm being thrown back to the future in disgust. Every second that passes I see the park around me disintegrate and reform, a couple walking hand in hand, both listening to the same iPod, appear and disappear in an instant.

'I have to go,' I struggle to speak. 'I need to be alone right now.'

'She should never have spoken to you like that.' Michael is kind, serious. His eyes are full of concern. Oh God, I don't want to leave him and still I stand up to go, unsteady on my feet.

'Whoa, steady.' He stands up, but as he tries to touch me I flinch away.

'No, I ... no, go away,' I say again. 'I just need to be alone.'

'Luna, I thought we—'

'Go away!' I raise my voice this time, and he takes a few steps back. 'Please go away!'

'Fine.' He turns on his heel.

As soon as he is out of sight I lose the battle. I stumble down a quiet street into some stranger's backyard and I fall onto the long grass. And then it feels like I am falling through it, through the earth, through soil, through rock and heat, and molten lava, and it hurts. Being torn apart atom by atom hurts. I wait and *hope* that, when every molecule around me stops vibrating, I will survive just long enough to know I've done what I set out to do. This can't be the end, not this. I can't die not knowing if this warning is enough to save her.

CHAPTER THIRTY-TWO

'What happened?' Pea is sitting on Mrs Finkle's steps as I finally make my way back to our lodgings. Her face is tight and pinched. 'One minute you were there, the next I was alone with Michelle.'

'It happened again.' Wearily, every one of my limbs stiff and sore, I take a seat beside her, resting the package beside me on the step. It has aged thirty years in the last three minutes. The paper is faded and foxed, the string that ties it thin and unravelling.

'It happened so quickly, right there, right in the hall outside Michelle's office. It was quicker this time, more violent. I feel like the more I do it, the less of me there is to make the transition, so the faster it is, the easier it is in a way. But every time it happens, it hurts me. And I wasn't ready. I don't have enough control over it, over me.'

I turn to her. 'I saw him.'

'Shit.'

Taking a sip from the bottle of Coke she offers me, I try and recall what it felt like to be near him, but that feeling has gone, like it was a dream and it troubles me that being near him affected me so slightly. I wanted him to be a blue-eyed monster with a tail and horns, a beast that I could easily destroy. But he was just a man. Soon, I think, soon, if I'm not very careful, I won't know which place is which or where I am supposed to be.

'I had this idea that seeing him would give me this kind of power, or direction. That it might even weaken my resolve, that I'd see myself in him and hesitate. But ... there was nothing.'

'These last few hours ...' Pea slides her entwined fingers between her knees, and for the first time I realise that she has been doing more than just waiting for me. 'They've been awful for me, terrifying. Not knowing if you were coming back, not knowing what you were going through, waiting from second to second of this reality for it to shift. It's freaky.'

'I'm sorry,' I say. 'I didn't think.'

'I went to a bar.'

I start, turning to her but she shakes her head.

'The one across the street. I went in and I ordered a shot, and I sat there on the barstool and I thought, what does it matter if I drink this, and the next one and the next, because in the next five seconds everything could change forever, and nothing I do now will mean a single thing.'

'Did you ... ?' I almost can't look at her.

'No,' she says. 'No, because even if there are only five seconds of this life left, I won't throw away what I've worked so hard for. But God, I wanted to. Luna ... I thought I could do this with you, but I'm a coward. Please just stop. Let's go home. Just accept, like everyone else, how life has been, and let's live the rest of our lives the best we can. That's what she would want for us, you know. Please.'

Pea slides down one step, twisting to face me.

'Please, let's just go home.'

'I saw her,' I say instead of replying. 'I saw Riss. I tried to warn her ...'

Her head dips so that I see her dark roots and the white of her scalp beneath; she looks almost as if she might be praying.

'It's not fair that you get to see her and I don't,' she says.

'Do you know today is the day that Dad asked her to marry him?' I reach out to stroke her hair. 'I wonder if he remembers, while he's at home in the garden or shut away in his darkroom. I wonder if he remembers the way she looked on the day he took her down to the shore and gave her a ring? I think, if he did, he'd want me to stay. To see it through.'

'But why, when although the life we have isn't perfect, it is at least ours?'

I should tell her about Michael. I should tell her about how when I'm there the last twenty-nine years seem like nothing, like twenty-nine seconds, breathing that air, being with Riss and Michael. I should try to explain that it's more than just saving her, than simply paying the price for the debt the man that made me owes. It's about really living, living much more in a few minutes there than I could ever do in one whole lifetime here. I should, but I don't. I'm afraid she will try and talk some sense into me.

'Because something this miraculous has to have a purpose,' I say eventually. 'There has to be a reason for it to happen, and ... I just don't see that walking away and pretending it hasn't happened is possible. After all, Mum never managed it.'

Pea turns her back on me, and for a moment we stare at an unexpected edifice erected in the narrow strip of land alongside one of the houses over the road. A huge glass cabinet, as tall as me, framed with carved wood that would have been painted gold once, but now all rotted away, and filled with tiny models, animals, people, buildings, windmills, gnomes, populating a scale model of Crete. A whole tiny world, created with pride, designed to be seen, tucked away down this street where only the same people would see it every day.

'Today is the eleventh, right?' I ask her. She checks her watch and nods. 'The attack happens on the thirteenth, the same night as the blackout.'

Only two more days before it's too late, but if I fail, then at least I can live with knowing that I tried.

Pea is quiet for a moment. 'I just wish I could come with you.'

'I wish that too,' I say.

'You know, I was thinking. The movies, they're all the things she cut out of the films she showed at home. Her perfect Christmas edit of our "perfect life". In this box, this is all the bad stuff, the stuff we never talked about. She packed it all away and sent it back to the place where it all went wrong.'

'I think you're right,' I say.

'So shall we watch movie number three?'

'Yes, just ... I just need to see something.'

Pea follows me as I walk, breaking into a trot, beads of sweat trickling from my hairline as I run the last few yards and come to a stumbling halt across the street from where Michael's bakery was, where we bought our doughnuts.

It's gone, long gone by the looks of it. Now in its place stands a guitar store specialising in Gretsch guitars, one particularly beautiful model revolving around and around in a glass cabinet in the window. There's a banner across the window celebrating twenty-five years in business. I can see beyond the faded fliers deep into the shop, where racks of instruments are pinned to the walls.

'It's changed.' I speak softly, sadness and joy mixing sharply. 'He got out.'

'What are we looking at?'

'One of the people I met in seventy-seven,' I say, trying to sound casual. 'Michael, he used to work here. This used to be a bakery and now it's gone.'

'Does that mean something?' Pea walks into my frame of vision to make me look at her. 'Is he important?'

How wrong it feels, how disjointed, to wonder what ever happened to someone who, as far as my heart is concerned, I was so close to just minutes ago. Perhaps it was something I did or said that meant he left Bay Ridge and changed his life for the better. I hope so. And yet even as I hope, I feel how much I miss him, the very possibility of him. All I can do is brace myself against the searing hot pain of only understanding what it means to really want someone at the very moment you know they can never be yours.

CHAPTER THIRTY-THREE

The light is a pale gold, and one that I don't immediately recognise. Paint peels away from creamy wooden shutters, flung outwards to reveal a landscape made up of buttermilk-painted buildings and ancient terracotta roof tiles.

'France,' Pea says, her legs crossed as she sits at my feet. 'That amazing old house we stayed in somewhere near Bordeaux, do you remember? With bullet holes in the wall from the Nazi occupation, and you told me that after the war the locals hung all the collaborators from our balcony? Dad was working on a war film somewhere nearby, and he arranged for us to come over for a week or two. Mum hated it because we weren't at home, and we didn't see him anyway.'

'Yes,' I say. I remember spending hot afternoons in a small bright-blue pool, the dog of the house following Pea and I as we laboured from end to end, as if he were intent on keeping us from drowning. But when I think of it, I don't feel warm and sunny like my snapshot memories are. I feel cold.

Mum comes into frame, wearing a loose, turquoise kaftan. Her hair, wild with washing and sun, has silvered a little and, when she approaches the lens to refocus, I can see the first traces of lines, a little paler that her normal skin tone, etched around her eyes – she is around thirty years old and so beautiful.

'What will they say,' she speaks into the camera, her tone confidential. 'Let's see.'

'Girls!' She takes a few steps back as she calls us, mild afternoon light flowing through the silk of the kaftan to outline her legs. 'Luna! Pea? It's time!'

Pea arrives first, of course, bounding in to the room with such gusto that the camera trembles as she springs off the floorboards.

'I've arrived,' she says with a flourish, bowing towards my mother, who curtsies in return. I am second, hovering in the corner in shorts that I have almost outgrown, crossing my arms across my chest, self-conscious in the blue-and-white-striped halter-necked top that Pea had chosen for me.

'Pia Sinclair –' Mum makes a hand of her fist, pretending to hold a microphone '– please tells us what you will be when you grow up.'

'Easy,' Pea says, her hands behind her back, chin up, just as she had seen the von Trapp children do in *The Sound of Music*. 'I am going to be a singer, a dancer and an artist, mainly an artist, more famous than anyone else, and I will draw with all of the colours every time, and not care if I colour over the lines and sometimes go through the paper a bit. Also I'll be very rich and buy Mummy a house with gates that lock, and roses that grow up the wall and ivy that covers the window like *Sleeping Beauty*, so that no one can see in.' She nods emphatically, and turns to Mum. 'Can I go back in the pool now?'

Mum nods, her hand covering a smile.

'Bella Luna?' She turns to me, and I stay in the corner, half in the shadows.

'Miss Luna Sinclair.' She holds the invisible microphone again, and I am lured out into the sunlight that streaks the honey-coloured floorboards. 'Tell us what you will be when you grow up?'

As I watch myself squirm, under the camera, I am inhabiting that version of my body once more. Feeling the smooth, warm oak under my bare feet, the trickle of icy pool water, dripping from my hair and down my back, and I try to remember why it is that I don't want to be there, why it is I don't want to see Mum, but I can't. Whatever it was that gave me that sense of confusion and unease that radiates from the film, it will not reveal itself.

'What will you be?' Mum asks me softly.

'Honest,' I say so softly it's barely audible, perhaps even not audible, and I am only able hear it because I am reciting what the girl I was once said under her breath. 'Honest, happy and good.' Anger mounts as my tone rises, my small fists balling at my sides as I glare at her, as I glare at the mother I love. Still the reason why won't present itself. 'Grateful and loyal,' I add, 'and I will never, never ever, ever leave my children alone. Never, ever.'

Mum kneels down on the hard floor, the sun at her back, and reaches out to touch me. And in that moment what I remember is spent; everything else I see feels like the film of someone else's life.

'You weren't meant to see that,' she says softly. 'It wasn't real, I didn't mean it,' she adds.

Still the nine-year-old girl in the blue-and-white stripes says nothing.

'I would never, I could never, leave you, especially not like that. It was wrong, stupid, more of an accident that anything. I was cutting my hair and the scissors slipped and you happened to come in just when there was the most blood, that's all. That's all it was, an accident, but it's healing now, see?'

She holds up her arm and the long medieval sleeve of the kaftan falls back to reveal her wrist neatly bound with a bandage.

'Everything is fine, Luna,' she says, holding me close to her. 'I'll try harder, I promise. I won't ever let you down. I'll be braver, I will. I'll be brave.'

The girl trembles, suddenly freezing cold in the pool of sunlight, and Mum gathers her up in her arms, sinking to the floor as she holds her daughter, muttering something soft and safe, rocking them both gently in one lulling moment.

'It wasn't about wanting to leave you,' Mum says at last. 'It was about wanting to hurt myself. I just needed to feel something else, enough of something else to let me feel how much I love you.'

'Do you promise?' the girl asks her.

'I promise you that I will be honest, kind and good and true, always, and never leave you while you need me, ever.'

Pea and I sit transfixed, watching in silence as, for several minutes more, the girl and the woman sit on the floor, holding each other, rocking back and forth, until eventually the girl's thumb steals into her mouth and she stares out of the window at the passing white clouds.

And then, quite suddenly, the girl gets up.

'I'm going to swim, too,' she says, and for one moment I remember how the cool stone of the marble stairs felt beneath my bare feet.

Mum sits there on the floor for a few seconds more, before getting up, and glancing out of the window, pulling the kaftan off, and grabbing a pair of shorts to put on over her bikini bottoms, taking a raft of bracelets from her bag and fastening them on her wrist, one after the other, until the bandage is completely concealed.

CHAPTER THIRTY-FOUR

'The key is going to be the centre parting,' Pea says as she looks from me to an illustration of Ali McGraw on the cover of an old copy of *Time* she had found in Milo's store. 'And really, really dim lighting. Aren't you afraid they might think you're somebody's mum, come to take them home?'

'That magazine was printed in nineteen seventy-one,' I tell her. 'What if I look out of date?'

'Are you kidding me?' Pea has her brave face on, being cheerful, trying to pretend that she isn't worried about her crazy sister who is about to go and loiter around a derelict car lot, wearing a ripped-off Yves Saint Laurent gown, waiting to travel back in time to go clubbing. And I am grateful.

'And, I'm not,' I say. 'They didn't worry about sun cream or fancy face serums back then, and I've always, always looked after my skin. I don't drink much or smoke. I can't help it if I'm naturally youthful. I hold up pretty well in the nineteen seventies.'

'Well, at least you do somewhere,' Pea retorts, as she aims the spray can at my head once more.

After the film had spluttered to a stop, I had carefully wound it back, putting it away in the tin and closing the lid.

'I don't remember any of that,' I'd told Pea. 'I remember the house, the pool, how Mum cried at night because Dad came home for dinner and then left again, but I don't remember seeing what I must have seen. My mind has simply locked it away.'

'We always knew she smoked,' Pea had said, ticking words off on her finger as she talked. 'And we knew about the anti-depressants and the tranqs.'

'We knew that sometimes she'd go to bed as soon as we get home from school, and we'd be eating sandwiches for tea and breakfast,' I'd continued. 'We knew she cried and cried and cried until her skin was raw and her eyes were puffy, but never in front of us.

'But I never knew she'd tried to kill herself before,' I'd said. 'Or didn't remember it clearly enough. If we'd known ... ?

'She didn't want us to know, not until now. It's part of her way of explaining, don't you see?' Pea had insisted. 'Explaining that what she did wasn't out of the blue, and telling you that she kept her promise to you, the promise she made in this film. She didn't leave us while we needed her. She's telling us she chose her moment, and she's asking us to forgive her.'

Afterwards, I'd carefully unwrapped the fragile paper parcel, and taken out the dress. The folds were set in the cheap, false silk, and the cherry-red fabric had darkened a little along the seams, but, of course, it was in great condition; it had never been worn.

'Well, I guess this is what I'm wearing when I meet her at the disco tonight,' I'd said to Pea. 'Will you help me get ready, do my make-up the right way, and my hair?'

'You want me to do your hair?' Pea had been instantly suspicious.

'I can't very well arrive at a night club looking like this, can I?' I'd insisted, gesturing at my jeans. 'And besides, Riss made this for me; if I don't wear it, she'll be hurt.'

Now, as she does my hair, a faint smile plays around her lips. 'There's a boy. There's a boy you like in seventy-seven. Oh my God, Luna, you've got to see how wrong that is; you aren't even born yet!'

'There isn't a boy,' I say, maintaining a tradition of never talking about the men I like to my nosy little sister. 'And even if there was, I'd be older than him there, not the other way around. Older than him there and younger than him here . . .'

'The guitar shop!' Pea hits her target with precision. 'You were wondering what happened to him!'

'It doesn't matter anyway,' I say.

'Why not, we can go in, ask about the previous owner? Someone must know where he is.' Pea is excited, stepping away from me as she pictures some kind of Hollywood ending.

'Because, I won't be here, don't forget. If I do what I need to do, I won't be here. I can't have him, not for more than a few hours anyway.'

Pea stops, her shoulders falling, cloaked in her hair, her teasing smile fading away as she reads my expression.

'Well, let me make you truly beautiful then,' she says. 'And at least you can have him tonight.'

At last I am ready. Pea makes me stand up as she turns around the chair to face a mirror she has covered with a towel, because she has to create drama in whatever she does.

'Ready for the big reveal?'

'No,' I tell her. 'What happens if I go there and it doesn't work. The club closed down decades ago. What if I go there dressed like a hooker and nothing happens? One more night will be gone, one more chance. I don't have a plan, I don't know what I'm doing. What if I'm doing it all wrong?'

'Then you come home again,' Pea says, curling a stray strand of my hair around her finger and spraying it into position. 'And maybe by tomorrow you'll change your mind about all of this, and just let the present be the way it is.'

'Everything will be how it's meant to be,' I say, gesturing around the room. 'This isn't how it's meant to be. This is the wrong version.'

'How do you know that?' she asks me.

'Because I've always known it, ever since I was a child. I've always felt uncomfortable in my own skin, always felt out of sync with everything, everyone else. It's not just having a different father. There isn't a place for me here, or anywhere.'

'If you feel that way, then this is where you get help, where you look around you and see how important you are to a lot of other people. It's not the part where you ...' She can't finish the sentence.

'Pea.' I take her hand. 'Don't feel sad, don't feel frightened, because if you do, then I will too, and I don't want to. I want to feel brave and strong, and like I can do this. Have faith.'

'Faith in what?' Pea asks me.

'In me, I suppose,' I say.

'Well, I have faith you will turn heads in this ...'

She sweeps the towel covering the full-length mirror away, and I see my reflection. Except that it doesn't seem to be me that I am looking at, but rather someone I only know in passing, someone I'd like to have the guts to be like now and again. This woman in high heels, wearing a dress with a plunging neckline, her blue eyes shining brightly, intensified by expertly applied eyeshadow, cheekbones highlighted, lips glossed. Then again, perhaps it's just another version of what I feel like when I look in the mirror usually, like I am looking a stranger. This strange woman, she is just a change from the other strange woman I usually see.

'You look beautiful, sis,' Pea says. 'I mean, like a crazy person in two thousand and seven, but good for nineteen seventy-seven. I'll get the bus up there with you, OK? Can't have you wandering around looking like that on your own.'

'You don't have to,' I say.

'Yes, I bloody do.'

'Right, then,' I say, gripped with nerves. 'I'm ready.'

'No, you aren't,' Pea says. 'Here.'

She hands me a few moth-eaten-looking dollar bills.

'What this?' I ask her.

'Money from nineteen seventy-seven. Well, some is nineteen seventy-six, but anyway, Milo had some, so I bought it. It wasn't very expensive. And you might need to buy someone a drink. Hell, you'll probably need several drinks yourself. Ask for a Seven and Seven, it was all the rage back then.'

'How do you know?' I am worried. 'Have you been talking to Milo?'

'No, you idiot; like you keep telling me, I've seen *Saturday Night Fever* like a thousand times. John Travolta orders it in the club. Take it.'

'Pea, thank you.' The few crumpled notes somehow mean much more to me than anything else she has ever given me.

'Now I'm ready.'

'I'm glad you are,' she says. 'Because I'm not.'

'This feels wrong,' Pea says as we stand on the corner of 64th Street. 'It feels wrong to just leave you out here, in the arse end of nowhere, dressed to the nines. It's a really long walk home, and you won't find a cab to take you back if anything goes wrong.'

Nodding I look up and down the empty street, a commercial area of town. Maybe during the day it's pretty busy, but for now, it's silent, perfectly still.

'I'll be OK.' I don't really believe that, and it sounds in my voice, which in turn echoes loudly in the empty streets; too loud, loud enough for the shadows to overhear us talking. 'What will you do?'

I'm asking her if she will go to a bar again, although I don't need to say it out loud.

'I said I'd meet Milo,' she says. 'I like him. If you have to completely change the universe tonight, try and keep him and me somewhere in the same vicinity.'

'I'll do my best,' I promise. 'Don't worry about me, I'll be fine.'

We hug, and she squeezes me so tightly it hurts.

'Take me with you, Luna.' Pea takes my face in her hands. I know that she means it. 'Please take me with you. Let me try, please. I saw her too, Mum. I saw a little bit of her. Maybe ... maybe if you hold on to me or something I can come with you, I can see her too. I don't want to stay here on my own, take me with you.'

'I don't know if I can,' I say. 'I don't think it works that way.'

'You have no idea how it works,' Pea reminds me, and she is right about that. 'You can try, at least,' she says. 'I'm wearing my platform sandals and everything.'

'OK,' I say, 'let's try.'

I hold her hands in mine and look at her, and we stand there in the near silence.

'What happens next?' Pea whispers.

'I sang an old song once, that seemed to work . . .' I said.

Pea begins to hum 'Disco Inferno', but nothing happens, we just stand there, holding hands in the middle of nowhere, and I get this image of us, as if I was looking down at us from the moon, a couple of crazy women who think they might be able to travel through time by humming disco tracks, and I laugh.

'What?' Peas asks me, and then she laughs too. 'Oh god, we're nuts.'

'I think I have to go it alone,' I tell her, and she nods.

'It kills me that there is something you can do and I can't,' she says. 'It's like when you got the stabilisers off your bike all over again, only this time I definitely won't catch up with you.'

'At least you'll get to see Milo,' I say.

'What if it's now,' she asks, her voice barely more than a whisper in the dark.

'What if what is now?'

'The last time I ever see you,' she says. 'The last time I ever know you.'

It's a question I don't know how to answer.

CHAPTER THIRTY-FIVE

There have been moments in my life before when I have felt excruciatingly out of place: my first day at work in a room full of men, who looked at me as if I'd arrived from out of space; the time I turned up for a blind date in my habitual jeans and a T-shirt to meet a guy at a quiz night and it turned out to be a black-tie event. But I think climbing my way through the rubble and rubbish of a disused parking lot in red imitation-silk probably beats the lot.

It seems impossible to find a way in at first and I wonder if I'm in the right place at all, but I'm sure I am. Pea would never get a *Saturday Night Fever* location wrong. I just need to get close enough; at least that's what I tell myself. As if I have any idea how this works, or what triggers it, but getting close enough is all I can control, so I focus on that.

Feeling my way around an old, makeshift chipboard fence, put up around the derelict site some time ago, I presume, I keep going until I find a weakness, a board that's partially rotted away. I half tear one corner away, working it loose, and the noise of the wood splintering jars against the still night. The space it leaves is just enough for me to be able to squeeze through, although a stray needle of wood drags at my upper arm as I pass through, leaving a thin, stinging, trail of blood behind. Once inside I shove the panel of wood back as far as it will go, offering me some small amount of security from the great, vast silence that watches me from the other side of the fence.

Whatever I thought I might find on the other side, it wasn't this ... nothing. None of the building that housed the 2001 Odyssey club remains, I knew that, but I expected that there would be *something* here, something that I could focus on and draw from. Instead, all I can see in the near dark is more rubble, and weeds. Taking a hesitant step forwards, broken glass crunches under my feet, and an empty fast food wrapper snags at my toe. There I was, beginning to believe in resonance as a fact – the feelings I got inside the place where Mum used to live and work, the experience I had at the church, and at the park, the sense of thousands of moments stretching out side by side in the same space, each one existing separately, but somehow, sometimes, influencing another. But this place has none of that. It is empty and it feels it; it feels dead.

For a few years after the movie came out, this very spot that I'm standing on, which smells faintly of dust and dog shit, had been the epicentre of disco; the whole world wanted to come here, to be seen *here*. But only a few years later Bay Ridge's moment in the spotlight was over, and that's what it feels like as I stand here, alone, like this crazy adventure I have been on has come to an abrupt, pathetic end.

Dad must have taken hundreds of photos of the outside of the club and the interior, but I can't find any visual clues as to how the building might have been positioned on this corner. At a loss, I pick my way through the stiff, dead vegetation and over lumps of stone and concrete, and then I stop and close my eyes.

If I listen very carefully, I can hear the traffic from a few blocks over. On a busy night here there would have been a lot of cars, a lot of engines revving, girls laughing, guys talking. I imagine all of that until I can almost hear it, and then into that I insert my own imaginary bass beat, a distance thud, thud, thud. Once, on one of her sunshine days, Mum told us how the guys would always stand outside, no matter what the weather, in their thin, fake-silk, patterned shirts; that couples would make out – and more – in the backs of their cars; that there was a guy on the door called Sandy, who'd look you up and down when you came in, and turn you around again if he didn't like your face or the way you were dressed. I take all these details and set them loose in my imagination, like a series of spinning plates, concentrating really hard, and yet nothing happens, and all my efforts crash to the floor.

What is the use of this superpower if I can't control it? If I have to wait for it to take me when I don't expect it, when I don't have a plan or a strategy? There *has* to be something more, something more important that just wanting it to happen; there has to be a bigger mystery, a reason for every shift. A clue that's waiting for me each time I travel that is going to show me what I need to do. There's always been something that seemed important the other times I've been back: the medallion, the tree carving, hearing Delaney's voice outside the church, meeting Riss in the park. Each moment had something, a piece of the puzzle to lead me to what I have to do, but I can't see it now. I can't see any answer except that I have to stop what happens to Riss one way or another, and save my mother's life. I'm running out of time. And standing on a lump of concrete in an abandoned car lot isn't going to change that.

Closing my eyes, I try harder to visualise what it would have been like here on a typical busy club night. I picture the cars lining up on the road, the groups of friends gathering in the warm night air. The sounds of the chatter, the laughter, car horns maybe, engines revving.

The world seems to tip a little, and a swarm of luminous dots swims before my closed eyes. An unexpected rush of warm air whooshes past me, and for a moment I think I hear a voice, smell the scent of beer and perfume in the air. I can do this. Focus, listen, think, be ready.

But it's Michael I am thinking of, and a guitar shop that used to be a bakery. And then there is this thought, this sudden knowing that I won't know what to do until I am in that precise moment when something can be done, and I won't know who I truly am until I'm that person no more.

Just as that strange and disconnected thought appears, it happens, as quickly as before, and even more violently.

My head swims and it takes a moment to adjust, as I find a wall to lean against. The second I make contact with the brickwork, I feel the bass vibrate along my spine, followed closely by the noise, the smell, and finally the terror of being here, and what it means. And then I laugh, and whoop, and shout at the sky.

'I did it! I did it!' I whirl around, taking it all in, but this is perhaps a bad idea as I stumble and fall, shoulder first, back into the wall, just about staying on my feet.

'Hey, sweetheart.' An older man, who seems to be manning the door, cocks his head and looks at me. 'If you've already had that much, maybe you want to go home, huh? I can take you. Happy to help.'

'I'm fine,' I tell him. 'What I really need is a drink.'

He gives me a long, admiring glance, and I feel myself flush.

'Well, there won't be a queue at the bar. You're early, no one gets here for at least another hour. This your first time?' There's an air of innuendo that comes with the comment. I wonder if this is Sandy from my mother's stories.

'No, I'm meeting friends. I am with the movie production, sorting out some final details.'

'Yeah? You should have brought your camera. Want to get a couple of shots of me?' He grins and gives me his profile, turning one way and then the other. 'Which is my best side, huh?'

For a moment I wonder how he knows I have a camera, and then I dismiss it; I'm becoming too sensitive, imaging that everything that happens has meaning.

'That's fine, thank you,' I say, and when he slaps me on the backside I just keep walking into boogie wonderland.

It's surreal and terrifying and wonderful all at once. A live band is sound-checking somewhere, probably in the main dance hall. The crash of the high hat, the thrump of bass as they tune up, sends a thrill down my spine. Looking around for anything that might be familiar, I find a small horseshoe bar; it's the one in the movie that a stripper dances on. A crazy sense of vertigo almost sweeps me off my feet as I enter; I feel as if I'm stepping into a reel of film. Thankfully there is no exotic dancer now and it's virtually empty, apart from one man, who already looks like he's had more than enough.

'You the dancer for tonight?' the barman asks me, the look on his face clearly showing he wouldn't be impressed if I was.

'Er, no, I just want a drink please ... just a Coke.'

'Don't you got enough money?' the drunk asks me, leaning dangerously forward on his stool. 'I'll buy you a drink, baby. You can sit on my knee.'

'I'm OK, thanks,' I say.

'Whore,' he replies, mildly.

Finding some of the cash that Pea gave me crumpled in my purse, I leave it on the bar, taking my drink and hurrying down the hallway where a pair of double doors vibrate and open slightly in time to the music, the band warming up. Holding my breath, I push them open and there it is, the *Saturday Night Fever* dance floor, squares of coloured light pulsating in time to the music.

Something like joy, something like hysteria, overtakes me, and I run down onto the floor, into its centre, staring at my feet. How Pea would love this; I wish she could be with me now. I wish she could be here to feel how it jumps and fizzes under my feet, with every drum beat. The temptation to pull the same Travolta moves is amusing, but the grin on the guitarist's face as he watches me, arms outstretched, feet apart, standing like a toddler experiencing grass for the time, dissuades me. After all, I have never been the one that dances.

Clinging on to my drink, I try and find a quiet corner to wait for Riss and Henry to arrive. The cavernous room is practically empty; there is no one manning the turntables and just a handful of people sit at tables around the dance floor. Finding a table opposite the door isn't hard. Slipping into my seat, I sip my drink and I wait, my foot tapping under the table.

Clubbers start to trickle in just after the band starts in earnest, and, for a moment, I forget why I am there, as the rhythms of the music fill every corner of the room, my feet still moving, my shoulders swaying to the beat, as the band plays to an empty dance floor. Gradually the trickle becomes a flow. Young men, in pressed trousers and pattern Qiana shirts, all of them with their top buttons undone, giving off a confidence and peacockish preen as they strut down the stairs; small packs of guys, each one led by an alpha. A tall blond guy in a white suit arrives, followed by an older man who positions himself at the centre of the room as if he owns it, or the dance floor at least. Keeping my eyes trained on the door, I see a flurry of girls arrive, dressed to kill, but staying close together, careful not to look like they are looking at the guys, although they are. Before long it becomes harder to see who is making their grand entrance, as the flow and mass of young, hot bodies doubles and redoubles, eventually spilling out onto the dance floor.

My heart springs into my throat as I catch a glimpse of Riss, her dark hair swinging smoothly against the white of her dress, and, at her side, looking utterly out of place, is Henry – tall, elegant and alien amongst the seething dancers. Not far behind I spot Stephanie and Curtis, but not Michael. It's almost like he's already left. Maybe it would be for the best if I never saw him again; perhaps that would be the safest way. To do this I need to focus on Riss.

I've rehearsed and rehearsed what I'm going to say to her this time, and how I'm going to say it, again and again. But now that the moment is here, all the plans and practised words seem to have evaporated in the heat and the noise. I feel weak and scared, lonely and sad. And I wish that tonight she wasn't the girl I'm trying to save; I wish she was my mother, holding her arms out, ready to wrap me in them and keep me safe.

CHAPTER THIRTY-SIX

'You're here.' I feel him before I hear his voice, and I stand up as he approaches. 'Wow, you look knockout.'

'Oh, I ... thank you.' Glancing down at my dress, I feel suddenly ridiculously overdressed and exposed at the same time. I sit down again, glad for the coverage of the table. Michael slides into the seat next to mine.

A little time passes as we watch each other, the sound of the music and the slowly intensifying heat of the bodies all around us disintegrating into a blur. Oh, it would be easy to forget everything, to forget Riss and Pea, the past and the future, and just stay here, running these few perfect seconds on an endless loop, knowing that sometime tonight I'm going to kiss him, and knowing that makes not kissing him now all the more thrilling.

Breaking the moment is hard, but I must.

'I'm sorry I just disappeared the way that I did,' I tell him, leaning in close so that he can hear me over the music. He doesn't know how close to the truth that is. 'I just got a bit ... overwhelmed. But I've been thinking about you, thinking about what you said and, you know? I just know that you are going to be OK. I know that you aren't going to spend the rest of your life in a bakery in Bay Ridge. I don't know what your future holds, but I know it's much more than you think.'

'Will it include you?' Michael moves his lips to within millimetres of my ear.

'Tonight it will,' I say.

'Will you dance with me?' He offers me his hand, but I don't take it.

'Is Riss here? After what happened I think I need to see her. I'm worried I upset her.'

'I'll take you to her.' Michael pulls my chair out for me, and offers me his arm when I stand.

Taking it, I let him escort me through the crowd, somehow he's able to find a pathway through without having to stop, wait or even slow down.

Riss and Henry are leaning on a balcony around the dance floor, watching the band, Riss's shoulders responding to the groove of the music. Halted in my tracks, I watch her perfect profile, backlit with the ever-changing colours of the floor. She stands there, chin lifted, hair tossed her over her shoulder, as if, for tonight at least, the world and everything in it belongs to her.

'Come on,' Michael whispers in my ear, his fingers interlocking with mine. 'Come say hi to her. Show her how good you look in the dress she made for you.'

He leads me over to where Riss is and lets go of my hand, propelling me forwards a couple of steps.

'Riss,' I say her name, and she turns her head towards me, her face lighting up with a smile when she sees her handiwork.

'Spin!' she commands, and I obey, laughing to see how delighted she is with the movement of the skirt she designed.

'It suits you. Do you love it?' she asks me, her arm around my waist.

'I really love it,' I tell her, although I think what I mean is that I really love that she is still so open, so friendly, after how I upset her. 'Look, I'm sorry about before. I shouldn't have said those things; they were stupid and thoughtless. It's just that I have some bad experiences, and I just . . . All I want really is for you to be happy.'

'I get that,' she says. 'What I don't get is why? Why do you want me to me happy, when we barely know each other? Why is it so important to you? Stephanie thinks you got a crush on me. She says you look at me like you're in love with me.'

'In love with you . . . ? No, it's not like *that*!' I laugh, then she laughs. 'Could we talk, somewhere quieter?'

Riss looks longingly at the dance floor and then nods, jerking her head in the direction of the door. Following her at a slight delay, I see her as everyone around does. Flinging her arms around a couple, tossing her head back as she laughs. I see the wide sway of her hips, confident, certain. The way she inclines her head at a guy checking her out, giving him the smallest of smiles, keeping his attention tethered by a gossamer-fine thread until she snaps it, and he is reluctantly released.

Outside the air is warm, scented with a sea of combatting perfume and cigarette smoke. Riss swats away catcalls with a toss of her head, as we bisect a group of guys smoking. She leads me a little away from grappling couples, and groups of boys and girls all looking for the right person to do exactly that with.

The street is almost as busy as the club, a parade of tail lights, engines on, seats occupied, windows steamy. The purr and hiccup of engines low in the background and radios turned up loud. Out here, though, at least we can hear each other speak.

Riss must have found what seems like a good enough spot to her for talking, and looks me up and down, waiting.

'I realise it must seem weird to you,' I begin, exactly as I feel – hesitant, scared. 'I just turn up one night at your house, and then you keep seeing me around and I said that stuff I said before in the park . . .'

'I don't think you are weird, that's the weird thing.' Riss takes a pack of cigarettes from her small evening bag, pausing to light one. 'It's like, when I met you I knew you. My other girlfriends, I've known them all my life and I never felt that before. Like you and me have already been friends for a long time. I don't get why.'

She lifts her chin to blow smoke into the air in a long and practised plume.

'Maybe it's because ...' How am I going to begin this? 'You remind me of me.'

Riss doesn't speak, she only watches, waits.

'You reminded me of who I wanted to be when I was younger. I wanted to be like you are now. And ... I just want you to take care of yourself, protect yourself. Things happen, bad things that change everything, and that's why I think it's so important to just grab happiness when it comes along, just take it and grab it and don't look back, don't ask for permission to live your life, don't assume that just because someone is older and wiser than you, they know better.'

'Someone like you, you mean?' She smiles. 'What is it about Father Thomas you don't like, really?'

'I just don't see how you can let a man who has such a clear set of rules, and an agenda that has nothing to do with what you want from life, help you make such important choices. He's not going to tell you go and marry Henry, to move away from your family, is he? It's his job to talk you out of it.'

'I don't think that's true,' Riss says. 'I know him, and I don't think he's like that.'

'People change,' I tell her. 'Sometimes in an instant. You think you know what's going to happen, you think you have the future all mapped out and then something happens.

Something bad knocks you off your feet and, before you know it, everything you thought you knew about yourself is gone. All I'm saying is sometimes it good to do something unexpected.'

'To, like, trick life into not getting the chance to fuck with you?' Riss frowns and laughs at the same time as she drops the stub of her cigarette to the floor and stubs it out under the toe of her shoe.

'Will you do me a favour?' I ask her. 'Will you just not talk to him alone? There's a social at the church on the thirteenth, right? Why don't you talk to him there?'

'You're crazy.' Riss shakes her head. 'But if it makes you feel better, why not?'

That's it, isn't it? That should be it, any minute now I should be fading away into stardust. Except I don't; instead I just stand here looking at my hands, waiting for them to vanish.

'Are you high on something?' Riss wrinkles her nose as she looks at me.

I shake my head.

'Good,' Riss says, catching my wrist and tugging me after her. 'Because we are done with talking – it's time to go dancing.'

CHAPTER THIRTY-SEVEN

* *

The floor is full of dancers, the heat coming off of their bodies unifying with the relentless heat of the balmy night. There is no room for dance-floor Casanovas here, no choreographed moves, just a mass of hips and shoulders moving to the music, skin grazes skin, hips coincide, lips collide.

Unlike Pea, I was never a dancer, preferring always to stand on the sidelines or in dark corners, swaying from side to side. And yet, somehow, among this crowd of people, it doesn't seem like a choice to dance; it's more of an impulse, a reflex.

And once I start, I can't stop. For a little while I'm dancing with Riss, her smile flashing under the lights, her hair forming miraculous arcs as she tosses her head, and then the tide changes and she's caught in an invisible current, moved away in a series of spins and turns.

Elation charges through me; I feel triumphant, incredible. I've done enough, I'm sure I have, to change her path, and what's more I'm still here, here in this moment and, because I don't how long for, I fling myself into it with more gusto and joy than I've ever done anything.

I'm a dancer now, and that's all I am, filled with the grinding, skin-on-skin rhythms of disco. I am layer upon layer of sound and instruments; drum, guitars, voices all combine, speaking through my body. It doesn't matter that I'm dancing with strangers, we laugh and turn and move all at odds with each other, and yet somehow in perfect synch.

Time has become a meaningless notion, and not only am I not sure how long I've been on the floor, I don't care. All I know is that the soles of my feet are burning, my hair and skin are slicked with sweat.

Gradually I become aware of someone close behind me, and I don't have to look to know it's Michael. His hands connect with my waist, moving down to my hips, and I move myself against him, feeling the pounding of his heart between my shoulder blades.

A new tracks spins onto the floor.

'Follow me,' Michael whispers into my ear; his hips sway, matching the beat, spinning. I look at his feet, and try to match what he is doing, concentrating so hard that I am always one fraction of a second behind the beat. I shake my head.

'I was doing better before you showed up!' I laugh, and he pulls me very close, close enough to make me catch my breath.

'Just feel the music. Just let it be in you.' I feel his breath on my neck. He takes a step back and spins me several times before letting go of me, and I don't know how I keep on my feet but I do. A small space forms around him as he dances, and I love him all the more because he is not a perfect dancer. Untidy, chaotic, the shapes he makes in the air are sort of ugly, but he is smiling and his smile is beautiful.

So when he reaches for my hand I close my eyes and dance with him, next to him, letting the music into my muscles, my arms, my shoulders, my fingertips. Dancing until I can feel the smile spreading across my face. The sweat pours down my back and my throat is parched, but still I dance. Until Michael touches my wrist and I open my eyes to find him there, grinning at me.

'You got me beat,' he grins. 'I need some air, you coming?'

Nodding, I follow him outside, feeling each delicious moment of anticipation peel away, knowing that the moment when I am finally able to kiss him is now.

Michael leads me away from the bright pool of light that surrounds the club and into the soft, inky dark that is waiting, just a little way down the street.

'I think there was fresh air right outside the club,' I tease him, as we turn down a side street and are all at once completely alone.

'I like this air better,' he says, moving a little closer to me. 'It's only got you in it.'

He pulls me closer to him until I can taste the sweetness of his breath.

'Michael …' I try to think of a way to explain what I want to say, instead of what I want to feel, because the two things are so entirely different. 'I need you to know that when I leave it isn't because I don't want to be here, don't want to be with you. I've wanted to be with you more than any man I've ever met.'

He doesn't move, doesn't speak, and panic rushes my chest. What if all of this was just my fantasy after all, and nothing to him?

'Obviously I don't mean that this means anything,' I mutter turning my face away from him. Ever so slowly he places his forefinger under my chin and draws my gaze to meet his.

'No one has ever said anything like that to me before.' When he speaks I am moved by the force of emotion in his voice. 'And being here with you, it does mean something; it means everything to me, Luna. I never even kissed you, but I know I never want to let you go.'

For one delirious moment I wonder what it would be like to lose myself in this world with him, to just stay here, forever in this moment, no more time, no more years ticking by, just this one moment.

'Come for a walk with me?' He offers his hand and I take it, leaning my shoulder into his. How strange that here – on this cusp of this new day that I don't belong in, with a man that I never should have met – is the first time, in such a long time, that I have felt truly safe.

'Where are we going now? There's nothing out here is there ... ?'

'Just around the corner, away from everyone, away from the noise. This building came down a couple of months ago and that means that we can see ...'

'The moon.' I gasp as I see the waning crescent that hangs so perfectly in the air. 'Oh, it's beautiful.'

'Right?' Michael smiles, wrapping his arms around me. 'I like to look at the moon when it's like this, when it's almost completely dark, because somehow it seems more alien, more real. Because you can feel it, can't you, turning in the night.'

'Yes,' I say. 'You can.'

'Luna.' Michael's hands tighten around me as we stare up at the alien world, hanging in the suburban sky. 'I want to kiss you so much.'

The moon keeps looking down on us, its gaze constant and unchanging, and I keep perfectly still. 'The thing is, I have done since the first moment I saw you. Even as I was saying goodbye to you, I got this strange feeling in my gut, this need to see you. This *hope* to see you. When I found you in the bookstore on Third Avenue, I felt ... I felt like I'd wished you into existence.'

I let out a breath, closing my eyes so I can really feel this moment, this feeling, and capture it, just like a photograph.

'Jesus, say something will you?' He half laughs, half pleads.

'Oh God, I feel the same, I do,' I tell him, words spinning around in my head, speeding past like a carousel that seems to make it impossible to find the right one. 'And I want you, I want you so badly, but I don't know if it's real, I don't think we can do this.'

'We can.' Michael's hands travel down the bare skin of my back, grazing over the silk and georgette as he spans first my waist, my hips and buttocks, pulling me closer to him in tantalising fractions. I lean towards his kiss, hungry for it, needing it.

'This feels real, doesn't it?' he whispers. 'This feels right.'

I don't need to answer.

Long, sweet moments pass in the dark, our bodies connected by our lips, shoulders, hips and hands. His heart races against my breast, my hands find their way under his shirt, and we kiss like there has been no yesterday and as if tomorrow is a lifetime away. Nothing more, nothing less than two bodies connected by their lips; it's almost chaste, almost innocent, and the most desire I have ever felt.

It's only that when we break apart finally, breathless and uncertain of our feet, that I see there are tears on Michael's cheeks, glittering in the moonlight.

'What is it?' I ask him gently, wiping them away with the ball of my thumb.

'I don't know why,' he says, turning his face away from me. 'But I feel like the moment I have you, I'm going to lose you. It scares me.'

'Don't be scared of me,' I say, touching his cheek. 'I just wish that I could find a way to tell you ...' I trail off, finding myself unable to say the words out loud. I want to have existed for Michael, I want to be lodged right in the heart of his memory forever; every time he looks at a waning moon, I want him to think of me. 'I do have to leave soon, and I won't see you again, but please, please don't forget me, or even if you do, whenever there is a moon just like this one, just remember what a moment like this feels like, and then you'll be remembering me too.'

'I'll never forget you.'

'You may not have a choice.'

I kiss him harder, fiercer than before. We lose our footing on the sidewalk, and stumble against a wall, hands racing over and under, entwining and pressing ourselves into one being.

What I want more than anything is for him to know me, to really know the extraordinary thing that has brought me into these minutes with him.

As the thought occurs it begins to happen, against my will and relentless.

It feels as if the sun has forced its way out again for one more glorious moment as heat and light sears through me. I am bursting into flame, burning in seconds into embers and ashes. Universes shift around me and Michael is gone.

A sob tears out of my throat and I taste blood.

I am standing in a well-lit street. An MPV speeds past, the base turned up loud. Michael is gone. No, I am gone. I vanished in his arms.

When I touch my face I realise my nose is bleeding. I wipe it away the best I can with the back of my hand. I close my eyes, trying to sense him, somewhere through this thin veil of time that separates us, hoping to somehow hear him calling my name, to feel his movement in the air. But there is nothing, except the night, and the fear of tomorrow and the taste of blood on my lips.

Even if he doesn't believe it, at least now he will know the truth.

12 JULY

*'But at my back I always hear
Time's wingèd chariot hurrying near;
And yonder all before us lie
Deserts of vast eternity.'*

—Andrew Marvell

CHAPTER THIRTY-EIGHT

Dawn is threatening to break as I climb the steps to Mrs Finkle's place, exhausted and confused, past plaster Mary. I pause for a moment to take her in – her faded, benign expression of resignation, her palms opened outwards, facing towards heaven, in a gesture of what? Acceptance, supplication? Maternal tenderness? Maternal hopelessness? I hardly know what I am doing as I push her off the windowsill, watching as she hits the stones beneath with a dull thud. Her body splits in two and her head rolls off, gazing skyward at last.

I'm numb from my head to my feet, so battered and bruised by this transition, and so full of longing for the man whose arms I was ripped out of, that I think my poor mortal brain simply can't process anymore.

'Been painting the town red?' Mrs Finkle makes me start as I close her front door.

'Something like that,' I say, wearily.

'You feeling OK?' she asks me. 'You look like a stiff breeze would knock you flat.'

'Honestly, I hardly know.'

'Want some coffee? I'm always up this early these days, be nice to share it with someone for a minute or two.' Guiltily, I remember how I assassinated the Virgin Mary. Perhaps after coffee I'll have worked up the courage to confess and find out how to replace her.

'Yes, please.'

Sitting at her kitchen table in the golden light of early morning, I watch Mrs Finkle busy herself, putting cream in a little jug and sugar in a bowl just for me, and then setting it all out on the table.

She sets a cup of steaming black coffee in front of me, in which I put both sugar and milk because it seems rude not to. We sit in silence, neither one of us speaking, just enjoying the early warmth of the day and the peace and stillness of the kitchen. 'Maybe you need to see someone,' she says at last. 'Someone who can guide you. Not a doctor or a shrink, but someone who understand *mysterious ways.*'

'Mysterious ways?' I look at her.

'I'm an old woman, but I'm not a stupid one,' she says. 'You're here for more than the sale of that building. There's something else. Something haunting you, I think. I don't know what, or how. But I know you're here looking for answers, about your mother, about you. And all I'm saying is that sometimes you can find them if you're willing to open your mind.'

I laugh, scalding my mouth on the coffee that I gulp too fast.

'You know, I think it would be difficult to open my mind any further,' I say.

'Then, you think about it; I can point you in the right direction.' She nods her head once. 'I know people.'

'Thank you, Mrs Finkle,' I say. 'Thank you for the coffee, too, I needed that. And I'm so sorry, but I broke your statue. I'll replace it, of course.'

'I expect no less.' She nods, and, of course, I realise belatedly, she already knew. She had probably watched me do it.

'You know,' she says, as I reach the bottom of the stairs, 'sometimes in this life you think you're going to break, you're certain of it, you think there is no other possible outcome. And yet somehow you don't. You just remember that.'

'I will,' I say. But just as I begin to head up the stairs there's a knock at the door.

It's Stephanie.

'I had to say something,' she says, sitting uncomfortably on the edge of the sofa bed in our apartment, leaning forward, her palms pressed between her knees. Pea sits curled up in an armchair opposite her; she looks like she hasn't slept at all, and when I had come in through the door, she had grabbed me and hugged me so hard, I'd felt my ribs creak.

'I couldn't just go back to Florida pretending like none of this happened and just take the money from the building.

I couldn't, not unless I told you the truth. It's not right not to. I'm afraid to, but ... well, it's about time I did the right thing.'

'What is the truth?' I ask. A deep disquiet gnaws at my gut.

'You got to understand,' she says. 'That man – he was, he still is, protected. And there are times in life you have to understand that some people, they're untouchable. You could try and stand up to them, you could try and fight them, but it's never worth it. Because of the organisation that protects them. Nothing matters more to them than their reputation, what people think of them; you got to understand that. Whatever you do, they'll just raise up one big giant foot and squash you down under it.'

Her balled fist comes down on her knee, hard.

'What does it matter? She killed him. Not even God protected him then,' Pea says, fiercely.

'I thought ... I thought it was best for her, I truly did, knowing he was gone from the world; that's what I thought was best, for her. Because he was never going to pay, he was never going to jail, she would never have got justice, she would have only got the blame, and her life would have been even worse. You've got to believe me when I tell you that.'

'What are you saying?' I can barely speak.

Stephanie draws in a ragged breath.

'Riss, she hurt him real bad, real bad. And he could have died, but he didn't. She didn't kill him.' Stephanie hesitates, still unable to say his name out loud. 'Your father, he's still alive.'

CHAPTER THIRTY-NINE

There has never been fury like my fury, never anger like I feel as I surge to my feet, and grab her arm, pulling her up and propelling her towards the door.

'Luna, please ...' She tries to disengage my grip but what little is left of my strength is still enough to tear open the door and start half shoving, half dragging her down the stairs.

'Get out, get out, GET OUT!' I shout, dimly aware of Pea behind me, crying out my name.

Finally, I rip open the front door and return Stephanie to the steps, and not even the sight of her red-raw face, streaked with tears, or how she trembles and cowers, diminishes how I feel.

'Of all the things she couldn't live with,' I told her, 'it was knowing that she took a life. And *you* did that to her.'

'I thought it was for the best, I did. Something happened to him, when she hit his head. He was a different man after that; he swore he'd never hurt anyone else again, in front of me, and I believed him. And Curtis put the fear of God into him. And the powers that be, they said they'd keep him in check, that he was too important for them to lose. They struck a bargain. That's the kind of thing that happened then. As long as it all looked good on the outside, it didn't matter how much evil was done behind closed doors. But he never should have touched Marissa, they told him that. You don't hurt your own, that's the rule we all lived by. He knew that if he hurt another Bay Ridge girl he'd end up in the Narrows weighted down by rocks.'

'So they let him leave? You all let him get away with it,' I sob.

'I thought it was her I was letting get away,' Stephanie pleads with me. 'You got to see that? Please – I'm not supposed to say, I made a promise, it's dangerous to break it but ... if you want I'll tell, I'll tell you where you can find him.'

'I know where to find him,' I tell her. 'And as for you, I never want to see you again.' I slam the door shut behind her and stare at Pea, both of us breathing hard.

Mrs Finkle stands hesitant on the threshold of her dining room behind us. The wispy thin strands of sunlight shoot through the tiny holes in her lace curtains, cutting across us in a crisscross cathedral of light.

Neither my sister or I are able to articulate what we are feeling. Fury, yes, regret, yes, hurt, yes, fear, yes, and somewhere, buried very deep and almost hidden, something more for me, at least.

If our mother had only known she hadn't murdered a man, she would have had the strength and courage to heal, to live properly, I know she would have, I've seen it. Marissa Lupo would not have let her attacker ruin her whole life; she would have fought back and found a way back to the woman she was, despite what she had been through. It was his blood on her hands she couldn't live with, no matter how long and how hard she tried. She couldn't stand the sickening guilt that greeted her every morning.

Stephanie thought she was helping her sister, but really she had condemned her.

'I won't let her go through this,' I say, my resolve strengthening, as Mrs Finkle watches us curiously with her light grey eyes.

Pea nods. 'I know.'

'There's only one thing left I can think of to do,' I say.

'You need to talk to him, show him who you are,' Pea says.

'Yes, how do you know?'

'Because you're part of him, whether we like that or not; maybe you can reach him, scare him – maybe even change him, change what he's about to do.'

'I don't know,' I say. 'I suppose I'm going to find out, and it has to be today. Tomorrow will be too late.'

'You make it sound so final,' Pea says. 'As if the day after tomorrow the world will end.'

'Well,' I say, 'maybe it will, this version of it anyway.'

Mrs Finkle clasps her long, fine hands together. 'When are you two girls going to tell me what's going on here?' she asks.

'I don't think you'd believe us if we tried,' I say.

'So try me, won't you?' She takes a step towards us. 'I loved her too; we all of us lost something the night she left.'

I look at Pea, and she shrugs.

Between us we fill Mrs Finkle in on some of my mother's secrets – and my own. We save the impossible for last.

'Since the night I arrived in Bay Ridge, I've been able to step through time, to nineteen seventy-seven, to see Riss and, I think ... I think if I can find a way, I can stop what happened to her, change everything that happened on that night.'

'I see.' Mrs Finkle thinks for a moment, turns on her heels and disappears into the kitchen. It seems she isn't as open-minded as she'd thought.

'So where do you start?' Pea asks me.

'Church.'

'Church.' She nods. 'Seems like as good a place as any.'

'Not yet though.' Mrs Finkle returns and in her hand she is holding a dog-eared and faded business card. 'Before you go, you need as much armour, as much power, as you can get. Go and see Lydia, she'll tell you all she can, and it might help.'

'Mrs Finkle ...' I wonder how to tell her that whatever she thinks we are doing, a back-street psychic won't help us. 'I don't think you understand exactly what we're doing ...'

'Maybe I don't, exactly, but I believe you,' Mrs Finkle says, pressing the card into my hands, her grey eyes searching mine out. 'Like it or not, I've been on this earth a long time, I've seen things that men in white coats would cart me away for. I've heard them. I've talked with my darling Bill every third Thursday of the month for the last forty years, and don't try and tell me it's a scam, I know it ain't. I know what I'm looking at, Luna, when I look at you. I seen it before, in Lydia.'

She clasps my face with both her hands, her long fingers feeling for the bones under the skin.

'You've got the same look Lydia has when she's been talking to the dead, like some of you has blown away in the wind. So I know, wherever you are going, it's somewhere people made of blood and flesh ain't meant to go. And if you're intent on going, don't go without making yourself as strong as you can.'

Releasing my face from her grasp, she puts her thin arms around me, and I hug her back, feeling the frailty she hides so well, her bird-light bones and papery skin. And yet, although her body has begun to fail her, her spirit, her soul – whatever it is that makes us human – radiates from her, and I know that whether she is right or wrong about Lydia, she has chosen to love both Pea and me, and I can't help but be grateful for that.

Taking the card, I turn it over in my hands, Lydia La Castillon is only a couple of block away. 'Spirits contacted, psychic blocks cleared, futures foreseen', her card reads in spidery hot-pink print against a faded and creased, black background.

'I wonder if she knows we are coming,' I say.

CHAPTER FORTY

Lydia La Castillon is not at all what we were expecting, or not what I was expecting anyway: some mysterious old lady, perhaps with dyed, red hair and hooped earrings, sitting in a dim back room, lit only by lamps covered with tasselled shawls. In fact, she greets us with a smile and a professional handshake. She seems to be somewhere in her seventies; her crisp, white shirt worn over pale-blue jeans is something I could wear. She has silver hair cropped close to her head, and kind, soft, amber eyes.

If this was like the movies, I'd expect some kind of horrified gasp as she takes my hand and recoils in horror at my marvellous powers, but nothing like that happens; she just tilts her head slightly to one side as she looks at me, her expression remaining completely impassive.

'Come and take the weight off,' she says, showing us into a brightly lit kitchen. There are peonies in a blue jug on a freshly washed table that still glistens as it dries. The window is open, and the sounds of the street drift in, snatches of conversation, a car horn.

'Take a seat,' she says to me. 'I can only do one of you only at a time, I'm afraid, although I feel that what holds true for one of you, holds true for both.'

'Sort of a two-for-one deal, then.' I smile weakly.

The anxiety I carried with me, as Pea and I walked over here, has faded at once in this pretty but plain room. This pretty but plain woman can't hold the secrets of the universe in her hand; she can't know how to contact a realm that doesn't even exist. Mrs Finkle might know things and have seen things. And I might have known things and seen things, but there's light years between this woman's beliefs and what I know.

Lydia regards me from across the table, and as I look into her eyes I feel a kind of calm.

'I can't tell you what your future holds,' she says.

'Why, are you having an off day?' I ask her.

'You don't have a future, it seems.' She says it with a regretful smile, and so simply that it takes me a moment to understand what she means.

'You mean, I'm going to die?' I ask her, but she shakes her head.

'Not quite, no.' Her hands fall from the table to her sides. 'When I look at people, I see their colours; some people call them auras. And I can see, just by how intense or what shade their colours are, what it is that troubles them, and what it is they need to know.' Leaning forward, she reaches for my hand, and holds it loosely in hers. Her skin is cool, smooth. 'Your colour has been stripped away, and there are only a few things I know that do that. A very serious illness, a visit with the spirit world or ... for you, it's something else. You've been reaching into other universes, I think, or something like that. Seeking vengeance, and forgiveness.'

'Did Mrs Finkle call you?' I ask her, withdrawing my hand.

'No, dear.' Lydia folds her cool, white hands neatly on her lap, but her eyes don't leave me. 'It's just that you and I are a lot alike. What we do is very similar; the same really. I reach into other dimensions and make contact – although I can't travel to that dimension myself, I can hear the voices there, the voices that want to talk.'

'So when you are telling Mrs Finkle what her dead husband is up to, you are really talking to him in the time before he died?' I ask her. 'Is that how it works?'

'Oh no, he's dead,' Lydia says. 'You see, there is time, all of time before and all of time after, all at once, divided up by us into neat little packets ...'

'I get time,' I say. 'I'm a physicist.'

'I bet you don't know time as much as you thought you did.' She smiles, and I have to concede she is right.

'There's that sea of constant tidal happenings that you seem to be travelling through. And then there is the spiritual realm.'

I sigh with frustration.

'It's OK.' Lydia shrugs. 'You don't have to believe in what I do for me to be able to help you. All that matters is that I believe in you, but I would say one thing ... There's more to any one of us than just blood and bones. And when the dark times come, and they will for sure, you are going to want to hang on to the part of you that isn't flesh as hard as you possibly can, or risk losing it forever. Be careful of your soul.'

'So how can you help me?' I ask her.

'By preparing you, telling you what I know. If you choose to believe it, well, that's up to you.' She takes my hand once more. My first instinct is to pull away, but there is something there, when I'm touching her. A sense of anchoring that I haven't felt since we arrived in Brooklyn, or maybe ever. I feel fixed to this one spot, and safe.

'Like you, I didn't choose my path at first, it simply claimed me,' Lydia says. 'As yours is claiming you. But in time I was able to choose how to navigate my own way. You, though, your path reaches its end very soon. No future. Your path is very dangerous; when you reach the end, you may not find a new path.'

'I know that,' I say. 'I've accepted it.'

Lydia nods. 'You're very brave. This might not work if you aren't willing to travel a little way with me, but take my hand, and we will see what we can see together. How far I am able to travel where you go, I don't know.'

Once more I reach for her hand, and seeing her close her eyes I do the same.

The sound of traffic rushes on; a slight breeze rattles her blinds. A pigeon coos somewhere nearby, and soon a deep tiredness washes over me, trickling through my pores and into my blood. I can't remember the last time I slept, because I only know this moment and it's heavy with fatigue. Lights flicker and dim behind my closed lids, and I feel myself drifting away, snatches of dreams flashing before me as I struggle to stay awake.

'You're doing well,' Lydia whispers, and it seems like her voice is inside my head. 'You're doing really well. Now, open your eyes and what do you see?'

The kitchen is the same, but painted a different colour; at the sink a woman in a white, lace apron washes dishes; a chubby baby sits at her feet playing with a spoon. Lydia still sits opposite me, and I know that, although her eyes are closed, she sees exactly what I do.

'Again.' Her voice sounds like a bell, and between one blink and another the scene has changed; now there's a bed in the corner, and no sink. A man in a dirty shirt grabs a young woman, as thin as a whip, and kisses her as hard as he can; her lily-white arms wrap around his neck.

'Further still,' Lydia says.

And then the building is gone; there is nothing but a mottled sky above and long grass around our feet, around the legs of the kitchen table that seems to have come with us. Beyond the horizon I can see water rising to meet the sky and nothing else, perfect silence except for the wind in the grass and the chirrup of crickets.

'Thank you.' Lydia takes her hand from mine, and her kitchen is restored around us. I twist in my seat to look at Pea, who seems unmoved by what happened. For her, it doesn't seem like Lydia, the table or me disappeared into thin air.

'That was interesting. I've never seen such things before.' Lydia smiles. 'Never met another like you. Someone who can move through the living, in the same way that I can move through the dead; quite amazing.'

'So those people we saw, those versions of this room, they weren't what you'd call ghosts?' I ask, fearful for a moment that I have been talking to, falling in love, with the dead all along.

'No, no, dear girl. They were all moments, just like this moment or the one just after and before. You are bound to one moment, held to it like a kite on a piece of string. But if you were free of it, well, I think maybe you could go anywhere, any time.'

'Can I go into the future?' I ask her. 'Can I see what will happen if I change things, what the consequences will be?'

Lydia shakes her head. 'No one should know what lies beyond their own death, and, besides, right now you have no future. You can't see what doesn't exist.'

'Luna.' Pea comes to my side her hand on my shoulder. 'You can turn back. You don't have to do this, we can just go home and everything *will* be fine.'

Lydia shakes her head. 'I'm so sorry, but she can't; the time for turning back was a long time ago, right at the first. If you'd fought then, maybe, but you so wanted to see, you just wanted to know. And now too much of you remains in the past where you are visiting. There is no turning back, not now. You must finish what you started, fate will demand it. Time has you in its grip and it won't let you go until it's done with you, or you with it.'

It's a relief, somehow, to know that climbing on a plane and flying home isn't an option. At least now I know I don't have to be brave, or make a difficult choice, because there is no choice. And I don't have to fear for or mourn what I will lose, because really, in some other version of this life, it's already gone.

'There's no other way?' Pea asks Lydia urgently. 'A better way?'

'I don't know,' Lydia says honestly, that same mild smile. 'I don't know what it is you are doing. But I do know this: have faith. Faith in God, perhaps; faith in the people that matter, definitely. More than that, though, have faith in love. Love outlasts even death. It's present in every moment, even those filled with darkness; it's never exhausted, it never gives up or waivers. It's the one force of the universe that will never be captured by an equation or your science. Have faith in love, and let it guide you, and you never know. Impossible things happen all the time.'

CHAPTER FORTY-ONE

When humans believe in stories extraordinary things happen.

Sometimes, it's simply a moment of unity between strangers, seeing themselves in someone else's narrative. When a story is told and retold so many times it becomes more than just ideas, it becomes truth, and that's when wars are fought, people are martyred, lives are altered, rituals become habit, and habit becomes imbued in magic. Belief makes us who we are. Each religion is a story told so many times it has become the truth to some.

That's what I have always believed. On those rare occasions spent in church, amongst the scent of flowers and dust, sometimes with sunlight streaming through the window, I'd think all this is just a story, and it doesn't matter.

Now, though, I see exactly how important stories are.

Not just the big stories, the stories that involve everyone, but the small ones too, the ones told from mother to daughter, lover to lover, father to son, shared again and again, and each time they are retold, binding those that tell them a little closer together.

Stories are the only things that can ever really change the world. The stories that people believe in are the only ones that matter. Those are the stories that have the power to change everything we think we understand.

This is my story – my story and my mother's – and I am the only one with the power to tell it, and to change it, to change the way it ends.

I walk quietly into the church and stand at the back in the shadows, listening to the quiet, breathing in the peace. Pressing my back against the wall, I close my eyes and I listen, I listen to the minute sounds that make up the air. The murmur of prayers, the rustle of skirts, the scrape of shoes, the breeze that blows over the tops of the candles, the crackle of wax. Listening, I wait until I can see each sound dancing before me, bright and wonderful. The cool surface of the bricks at my back crumble into dust and reassemble, the floor beneath my feet churns into nothing and become solid again, and I tune into the smallness of the noises. A breath of contrition, pressed together palms peeling apart, the jangle of rosary beads, the soft inhalation of incense.

If there is one thing I seem to have brought away from Lydia's, it's this new way to understand, almost control, what's happening around me, to move the minutes, hours and years that separate me from Riss with precision and design.

As I open my eyes, my heart trembles, but I know at once that it has worked. I am back in 1977, now to make it count.

The church itself seems quiet, the pews empty, no sign of any clergy.

Walking out to the lobby, I see that the lunchtime mass is due to start in a little over an hour. Where would he be: somewhere in here, in the church or in the offices?

Sticking to the sides of the building where the light is warded off by shadow, I skirt around the edges of the building, my focus on finding him pushing away the fear I am feeling to the very pit of my stomach where it lies in waiting.

Treading as softly as I can, I walk between the front two rows of pews, crossing the aisle, heading towards the vestry door. It opens with an anguished creak, and it's so 'bad horror novel' I almost laugh, filling in the tension with the appropriate sound effect. The first room, lined with robes on hooks, is empty, but behind the inner door, I can hear movement. Nerves grip at my gut, holding me in place for a moment before I tear myself off the spot and make my way towards the door. Pushing it open I see him, his back turned to me.

'Father Delancy?' I say the words, but they are expressed as barely more than a whisper, loud enough, however, for him to turn around and look at me.

He smiles in recognition. Bright-blue eyes as vivid as the sky and just like mine, from the slanted outer corner to the fringe of thick, black lashes; my best feature, I have always been told. I see this in him for the first time, and I see myself reflected there, and the leap of recognition makes me smile. It makes him smile too, although he doesn't know why.

'I know you,' he says, pleasantly, with an air of perpetual amusement. He is very handsome. 'You're the girl with the camera. You came back, I'm glad. Come in, I have a little time to talk.'

Stepping into the room, I'm careful to leave the door ajar behind me, securing my exit route. What if Lydia was right, I wonder; what if the church itself was right, and love could be enough to save the day? If I could find it in my heart to love this man, then perhaps my love would be enough to alter his path. But no matter how deeply I search, there is no love here, not a shred. Only a deep abiding fury.

'My name is Luna Sinclair,' I say. 'I'm your daughter.'

His eyes widen, and for a moment I think I might see unease, but if do it is fleeting, because he laughs, bellows almost. His eyes sparkle when he laughs.

'My dear, you are mistaken, and I'm so sorry that you have come all this way, but you must see that's impossible. Apart from the obvious.' He gestures at his dog collar. 'I'm not old enough to be your father, I apologise is that seems ungentlemanly.'

'Ungentlemanly.' I laugh. 'What I'm going to tell you is going to sound like I'm mad, but the truth is the truth and if you really listen you will hear it. In two days you will go to the home of my mother, and you will rape her. I don't know why, I don't know if you've done it before, if that's the sort of monster you are, or if you're the kind who hardly knew it himself until the moment is upon you. But either way, that's what you do. You rape her, and nine months later I am born. I am born and her life is ruined. Not by me, you understand, but by you and what she does to you. She kills you.'

Despite what Stephanie told us, I still tell him the version in which he dies, desperate to connect to him somehow, and to appeal to his self-preservation instinct if nothing else. But he doesn't flinch, his expression doesn't waiver.

'So you're from the future, come to warn me?' he says, and his smirk makes me want to kill him myself.

'I told you it would be hard to believe.' I take a step closer to him. 'But you of all people should know that just because something is implausible, that doesn't mean it's not true.'

'Are you comparing yourself to Christ?' he says, and there his smile fades, a shadow falling across his eyes.

'Just look at me,' I tell him. 'Look at me and tell me you don't see that I am telling the truth. What you do, it changes so many lives, stunts them, deforms them away from who they should have been, not just my mother's, but the people she loves too – and yours. Yours most of all. I've been given a chance to try and change your path, and I took it. Can't you look at me and see that I am telling the truth? I am your daughter.'

Delaney shakes his head slowly. 'Luna, is it? I do believe that you think you are telling the truth, and if you'll wait here for a moment I can find you some places you can go to get a little help. But what you are saying about me is not only deeply troubling, and offensive, it's just wrong. I'm a man of God, I lead a quiet life here, despite everything – the crime, the poverty. The people of this parish are hardworking, simple people of good faith. I try to reflect that in my service to them. Before I became a priest there was a time that I loved many women, and not all of them well. If you'd come to me aged ten, with those blue eyes, then, perhaps. But what you're saying, your story just isn't possible. And I have never forced myself on a woman, not before or after I took the vow.'

I discover that I want to believe him. No, it's more than a want, it's a need, a sudden vivid yearning, an actual ache to believe that everything Mum told us is wrong, that it was her fault, she did tempt him, put sin in his way and then destroy him. It was my mother that corrupted this good kind man. He is so charming, so credible, and if I am not very careful I could easily be drawn into his web of lies and never escape.

'It's time to take your mask off and tell me how many women you've raped, Father Delaney.' I drop the bomb into the still of the air, and step back to watch it explode. Emotion floods over his face: fear, fury and shame, but not surprise. Thomas Delaney was not surprised by my question, not even in an age when priests were never questioned. The sickness returns in the pit of my stomach and I want to cry.

'Women trust you, don't they? They like you, they flatter you, but they aren't the ones you want, are they? The ones you want are the ones you can't have, am I right?' I continue, forcing the words out of my mouth, determined to make him show his true self to me. 'When was the first time you simply couldn't stop yourself?'

'Who the hell are you?!' he bellows, his composure falling away, his words crashing out of the room to echo in the very tops of the chambers that make the church. 'Get out of God's house with your filthy talk.'

'You think you're safe here,' I say, standing up as he marches towards me, holding my ground as he towers over. 'You think you're safe and that no one knows what you do, but I know. I know everything about you.'

He is standing so close to me that the air between us fluctuates, makes and remakes itself, unable to find sense in the disruption I have caused, a grown woman standing next to the man that hasn't fathered her yet. 'I know what you have done and what you're going to do, but I will make you a deal. You leave here today, right now. You pack your bags and you get as far away from here as you possibly can and I will keep your filthy secret for you. You leave Marissa Lupo alone, and I will let you be.'

He pushes me away from him and I stumble, onto the floor.

'Marissa.' He crouches down studying my face. 'The young woman from the tailors, she wants to see me.'

'Just leave her alone.' I want it to sound like an order, but its chimes more like a plea. 'Leave her alone.'

'Who are you?' he asks me again, leaning closer to me, his voice quiet this time, almost a whisper as he reaches past my shoulder, and pushes to the door shut behind me, closing his secrets in. 'Tell me what it is you want.'

'I want her to be safe, that's all,' I beg. 'Safe from you.'

Delaney stares at me, his bright eyes suddenly intensified by tears.

'Do you believe in God at all?' I ask him, despairing.

'Of course I do,' he says. 'God lives through me.'

He sits back on his heels staring at me, and I scramble to my feet, my soft soles taking a moment to gain purchase on the tiled floor.

There's a rapid knock at the door, and a younger man hurries in.

'Sorry I'm late, father,' the man, hardly more than a boy, says. 'I forgot the time.'

'Not a problem, Danny,' Father Delaney says, looking right at me. 'Thank you for visiting, my child. You can be assured that I will certainly take into consideration what you told me today.' He takes some leaflets out of a drawer. 'I hope you will consider looking at these, there are good people who can help you. May God go with you.'

I'm not sure exactly how I get out of the church, only that somehow I do. One moment I am cloistered in shadow and the next I am standing in the glaring sun and throwing up. I lean against the wall as people walk past me, a couple of people muttering insults under their breath. All I've had is one cup of coffee in the last few hours, though my body keeps convulsing long after my stomach is empty, until I'm eventually still, but even in the blazing heat I shiver, screwing up the leaflets about how to get my life back on track and throwing them in the trash.

The horror that I can't shake, that keeps rising like bile in my throat, is that he wasn't scared of me; he wasn't afraid. It's as if his bright-blue smiling eyes won't stop looking at me as I walk as fast as I can away from the church, bracing my trembling knees every time they threaten to buckle from underneath me. No, he wasn't afraid of me, and he believed me when I told him who I was, and somehow that is the most frightening thing of all.

Somehow I keep going, lowering my head, breaking into an uneven trot. I'm not even aware as I run past Sam's Bakery that it's the place where Michael works. If he hadn't been standing in the window I would have kept on running, and even when I hear him call out after me my heart stops, but my feet don't at first.

'Luna, wait,' he says. 'I got to talk to you!'

'I can't ...' I turn on my heel to look back at him. 'I feel like if I stop I'll collapse.'

'WAIT!' I hear fear in his voice, but I start walking. 'Wait, you can't just ... Goddam it, Luna, wait up!' He rips off his apron and runs to catch up with me.

'What the fuck?' he says grabbing hold of my arms. As he grips my flesh hard, his gaze runs over me, and I know he is checking if I'm real or a fragment, a ghost. 'You're here, you're real, you're a real person. What the fuck was that all about last night? Was I drunk? I didn't take anything ... It was like ... it was like the world melted around you.'

'I'm so sorry,' I say, wearily, falling into his arms and leaning against his chest. 'I'm so sorry that happened the way it did, but I didn't know how to explain ... to explain something that doesn't have any explanations.'

'That you are not from here,' Michael says. 'That you're what, a ghost? An alien?'

'I'm from another time – the future,' I say. 'I've come back to ... right a wrong. To try to, anyway.'

He doesn't say anything, but he doesn't flinch or pull away. And I wait.

'What does that mean?' he says, at last. 'Does that mean I'm going to lose you?'

'Yes, I think so,' I say and my eyes fill with tears. 'You really believe me? You don't think I'm mad?'

His fingers relax their grip as he watches me, every sweep of his gaze trying to decipher what he understands, and what he doesn't.

'Luna, last night you vanished. I mean you actually dissolved. The air seemed to ... kind of buckle and, I don't know, fall apart, and you went with it. One minute you and I were there, together, maybe more together than I have been with anyone. The next I was alone. And out of my mind. I thought maybe you were gone for good, I thought maybe you were dead ...'

'I'm sorry,' I say. 'I don't want to leave you, I don't ever want to leave you, Michael, but I must. I can't do this anymore, this thing between you and me; it's hard enough as it is. When I see you, I know you aren't mine, and I'm not yours and my heart can't take anymore. This needs to stop now. For both our sakes.'

He shakes his head, pulling me into his arms again. 'No, no, I won't believe that. I don't. I can help you, let me help you. Tell me the reason you're here, please. At least give me that?' His hooded eyes are so intense, so focused on me, as if he thinks that even if he blinks I might disappear again, and it's hard not to want to be seen the way he sees me, as if my existence were vital to his.

'I'm here to save a life, my mother's life, my sister's, my father's,' I tell him. 'I'm here to right wrongs.'

'Then let me help. Let me be the one that saves you,' he says.

'You can't be,' I say with sadness, because it seems like such a nice idea, to surrender into the arms of another, to be rescued. But I'm the one who is the rescuer here. 'And I didn't mean for this ... for us to happen, it shouldn't have. But it's OK, I'll be gone soon, and you go and write your books and you get out of here and everything you want from your life will happen. Years from now you'll forget about me, or think I was that crazy woman that got under your skin for a bit. Who knows, maybe when you are a famous writer, you'll put me in a book.'

'Do you know that?' he asks. 'Do you know that about my future?'

'No,' I say. 'I know that about you now. I know from spending some time with you, I know what you are capable of. But your story isn't mine, Michael.'

'How do you know that?' he asks me. 'How do you know that it's not me that you came back to find? Luna, think about it, every time you're here, so am I. Have you ever thought that maybe it's me? Maybe I'm your fate, and you just need to choose me.'

For a brief shining moment, I imagine what it would be like if that were true, what it would be like to surrender to this time and stay here with him always, not looking, not seeing the world that falls apart all around, my mother being torn apart by what happens to her. It's a choice I cannot make.

'I ... I have to go,' I tell him. 'I'm running out of time.'

'Why, what's going to happen?'

'Nothing bad, not to you. Not to anyone I love, if I can help it.' I smile, and allow myself to touch his cheek. 'Look, you're the man that taught me how to dance – badly – but you did, and that might have been the happiest hour of my life, so thank you.'

I take his hands from my arms and bring them to my lips.

'Thank you,' I say kissing his fingertips. 'Goodbye, Michael. When you look up at the moon, remember it's the same one that I will be seeing.'

'No.' He keeps hold of my hands. 'No fucking way am I saying goodbye to you, Luna. You *are* my story. I don't care what you say ... I can't let you go. I just ... I can't.'

'Michael ... you have to. I have to do this on my own.'

'Who fucking says so?' Michael asks. 'Luna, please, let me help you. Who says you have to do this alone?'

Slowly, tenderly, I peel his fingers away from mine, each movement full of regret.

'I do,' I say.

CHAPTER FORTY-TWO

Watkins Gillespie's offices are in the same place, only the window front is freshly painted black, and there are only four plates in the window, standing side by side, neatly displayed in wire racks. Now they aren't stacked and filmed in dust, I can see that they seem to commemorate historical scenes, one of the Brooklyn Bridge, one of the Empire State Building, printed in sepia.

Every time I've met Mr Gillespie, in the past and in the present, he has helped me, and I trust him. And he did tell me once that if I ever needed help to come to him, no appointment necessary.

The girl behind the typewriter on the front desk is skinny and very young, scowling at the typewriter she is sitting in front of as if this is the first time she has ever seen such a contraption. When she sees me, she draws herself up in her seat and looks down her nose at me.

'Got an appointment?'

'Er, no. I met Mr Gillespie the other day and he gave me his card, said I could come to him if I ever needed any help, anytime.'

'He says that a lot,' she tells me, pressing her lips together.

'Oh, it's just ... can I see him? It's sort of urgent.'

'You can see him, you'll just have to wait is all. He's seeing a client right now.' She nods at a row of three wooden chairs leaning against the store wall, and I take one and I wait.

And I wait.

The clock ticks by on the wall, the second hand seeming to decelerate with every turn of the cogs and wheels the face conceals. I pick up a dog-eared magazine and put it down again, unable to lose myself in the small matter of thirty-year-old real estate laws, when everything I know and love is at stake, and yet still I wait.

Lucy mostly ignores me, except for the occasional glance, followed by a raised eyebrow and pursed lip that silently tells me she thinks I'm an idiot.

Eventually, an explosion of male laughter comes from the other side of Mr Gillespie's office door and it opens, two very well-dressed men emerge: one fat and greasy in the heat, a heavy gold chain cutting into his neck; one tall and good-looking, dark hair slicked back to show off high cheekbones. It's the third man to exit the cramped office that surprises me, making look twice – it's definitely Curtis, in a denim jacket, his eyes on the floor. He doesn't see me before he is ushered out onto the street by the other two men, the larger of the two with his heavy hand on Curtis's shoulder.

'Now I got you out of trouble, you stay out of it,' Mr Gillespie calls after him, shaking his head.

'This here individual has been waiting to see you,' Lucy says, jerking her head in my direction.

'Really?' Mr Gillespie smiles at me enquiringly.

'We met the other day, you stopped a kid from stealing my camera?'

'Oh yes.' His smile is charming. 'Yes, come in, Miss ...'

'Sinclair,' I say, before I even think of offering a false name. If this works, nothing else will matter.

He shuts his door as I take a seat, not on a garden chair this time, but an upholstered office chair that looks brand new. Framed certificates line the wall, and I'm pretty sure his desk is still the same one, but now it's clear and smells of polish. A photo of his wife sits on the desk, facing away from him as if the last people in here were just admiring it. Gillespie himself looks like a man on the up – dark tailored suit, perhaps even stitched by Riss, manicured hands and a clean-shaven jaw.

'How can I help you?'

'I have reason to believe that Father Thomas Delaney is taking advantage of the young women in his parish. And that he could be at risk of raping them.'

I don't have time for preamble, every second counts.

Gillespie's eyes widen and he sits back in his chair, as if I have pushed him.

'That's quite some wild accusation, young lady.'

'I realise that, but I can't stand by and let him hurt people I ... know don't deserve it. Someone needs to speak up.'

'So why me?' He leans forward, across the desk. 'The precinct's just a few blocks away, why not tell the cops?'

'Because I don't have any evidence,' I say. 'And someone told me it's not the cops you go to round here, they told me that in Bay Ridge people take care of their own.'

'Is that right?' He hooks his hands behind his head. 'And you're "one of our own"?'

'Perhaps not, but the people who are at the risk ... the person is.'

'OK, so tell me, what is it you think I can do?' He spreads his hands as he talks, but he doesn't sound dismissive or disbelieving. Something about this concerns him, and I hook onto that.

'Watch him,' I say. 'Maybe even talk to him, tell him that you're watching him. People around here respect you, and you have a standing in the community that means something. That could be enough, enough to stop him, don't you think? If he thinks someone like you is keeping an eye on him.'

Gillespie regards me for a moment, his pale-blue eyes looking into mine.

'Maybe, but it's very hard to stop a man who doesn't want to be stopped, Miss Sinclair.' It isn't said as a warning or a threat; it's simply a statement of fact. 'And the Church, well, let's just say I've seen families in here who do have proof, who do have evidence of a priest interfering with a loved one, and at the end of the day no one ever hears about it, because families round here, they don't want to rock the boat. You talk about us looking after our own, that's true, but the Church? The Catholic Church? For many people it's beyond reproach. What you've said today in my office would just instantly be dismissed as lies, maybe even some kind of lunacy.'

I can't help but smile, because it seems fitting. Luna the lunatic.

'Is the name that's come up before Delaney's?' I question, leaning forward in my seat. 'Have other people made allegations against him?'

'I can't comment on that.' Watkins frowns. 'Tell me exactly whose safety it is that you are worrying about?'

I'm not sure why I hesitate, except that I can feel something bigger than me, bigger than anything, grating along the surface of reality, distant planets turning, the fabric of the universe creaking and stretching. But when I look at Gillespie I trust him; after all, I know him already.

'It's Marissa. Marissa Lupo. She's vulnerable at the moment, in love and scared about the future. And I've heard things about him. She needs someone to talk to and I'm afraid, if it's him ... I don't know how to explain it. I'm just afraid for her and what I think he will do to her.'

'Well, I know Marissa Lupo. I've known her since she was five years old. She made the pants of this suit, you know,' Mr Gillespie tells me thoughtfully, running his hand down his leg, before making a church of his fingers as he leans back in his chair. 'I know her father well. Why don't I talk to him, tell him to keep an eye on her.'

'No, no, that would be the worst thing you can do. Riss loves her dad, but he doesn't know everything about her life, not yet anyway. It's important she's able to explain things to him at the right time.'

'She's keeping secrets from Leo Lupo? She's braver than most grown men I know.'

'She thinks she's invincible,' I say. 'She isn't.'

'Well, Miss Sinclair, you can see there is really nothing I can do, but I like you, and I don't like to see you looking so worried. So, I'll tell you what'll do. I go and see Delaney, get the measure of him, and I'll keep an eye on Marissa. She's known me her whole life. If she knows she can talk to me about whatever secrets she is keeping, then maybe I can make sure she steers clear of Delaney. Does that reassure you?'

There is something about him so innately kind and strong that just the sound of his voice makes me feel better. Perhaps this could be the one thing that makes all the difference.

'It does,' I tell him.

CHAPTER FORTY-THREE

This time back it's just like walking through a door, almost exactly like it, except it feels like I left half of myself on the other side, a wraith that cannot follow me, watching me as I depart. I return in a single step to my own time, although with so much of my heart left behind, I'm not really sure what time I belong to anymore. Or even what time he belongs to, my father. And yet he is inside me, crawling through my veins. If I am part of him, then perhaps I am capable of what he is capable of, because I feel it, that rage I saw in his eyes. It's still there, outlasting the other more familiar parts of me that I can feel falling away. And if that's the only thing left at the end, then I'm afraid of what I could do with a rage that wants to tear the world apart.

Walking towards Mrs Finkle's house, the first thing I see is the plaster statue of the Virgin Mary, standing on the sill, still faded, still benevolent, and somehow still whole. Did Mrs Finkle glue her back together? The second thing I see is Pea, a laptop that I don't remember her bringing with her open on her knees, sitting on the steps.

'Hey,' I say, glad to rest, glad to see her. 'What are you doing?'

'Hey.' She glances up at me. 'I thought I'd just catch up on some work while I can. There's no Internet, of course, Mrs Finkle lives in the dark ages, but it's better than just doing nothing ... Sometimes I wish she had never told us.'

'Yes,' I say, wondering what work Pea has ever done on a computer, and where the laptop came from. I suppose I expected her to be happier to see me, more grateful that I'm home. Our last goodbye was such an emotional one, I want her to hug me like she normally would. Instead, I feel something has changed, like she is stranger to me.

'I know it's wrong to think that,' Pea says, 'but whenever I think of how long she has had to live with what that monster did to her, all alone ... only feeling like she could tell us now.' She stops. 'I'm sorry, it must be even harder for you.'

I stand back a little and look at her, taking in this woman who is my dearest friend and somehow so unfamiliar. Her hair is blonde to the roots, when did she do that? It's smooth and shiny, conditioned to the very tips. Her face is clean of any make-up, but her skin looks plumper, shiny. The whites of her eyes are white and bright. She looks like she slept really well last night. She's wearing a pair of running shoes and she looks like she's actually been for a run.

'So where have you been, Mum was wondering? She worries about how you're taking all of this.'

'What?' I ask her. 'What are you talking about?'

'Mum, she's been worried about you. I told her: Luna is an adult, let her process it in her own way.'

'Mum is ...' I cover my mouth with my hands, feeling my eyes stretch wide, a twist of pain in my chest stopping my heart for a moment. 'Mum is here, you're sure?'

'Of course I'm sure, wait, Luna ...' I am already scrambling up the steps, almost on my hands and knees, elbows and shoulders scraping and bruising against the walls as I struggle to get upstairs. And then outside the apartment door I stop, sink down onto the top step, as I try to catch my breath.

Carefully I get up, compose myself, brush my face from my hair, tucking it behind my ears the way she likes it, smooth down my rumpled T-shirt over my breasts, and I take a breath.

And when I see her I don't care what it has taken to bring her back to me. I don't care if meddling with time means that dinosaurs are walking down 5th Avenue, or Nazis are in the White House. I don't care about anything except that she is here, she is back. In this timeline she has never left us, she's here.

She is here.

Mum, my beautiful mum, is sitting at the table, newspaper spread out before her, a notepad and pen at her side. Sunlight catches the silver in her hair, and just the sight of her fingers, holding the pen, her blue-veined wrist resting against the edge of the table, makes me want to whoop and scream and cry. I'm scared to approach her, in case I reach out to touch her and she dissolves before my eyes.

'Mum?' I say, stopping short of the table, catching my breath as I look at her.

Turning around she looks at me, concern in her face, the same freckles as before, the same line between her eyebrows, but in her eyes there is something missing. I can no longer see it, that desperate unbearable sadness; it's gone.

'Darling girl, come and sit down and tell me that you are OK?'

Her arms are suddenly open to me, and I find myself falling to my knees, wrapping my arms around her waist, pressing my head against her breast, listening for the beat of her heart, rejoicing as I feel it against my cheek. Her arms encircle me, I feel the press of her lips on top my head, and I feel so much happiness, so much gratitude that she is here and I'm here and whatever it was that changed, it hasn't cost me my own life. We are all here ... almost.

'Where's Dad?' I ask her suddenly.

'In England.' Mum frowns, looking puzzled. 'Have you forgotten? He really didn't want me to come here; he wanted it left all in the past. He'll come round when he sees how important it is to me, I know he will. This hurts him too, more than he can talk about really, but I won't let it push us apart. It won't, I promise.'

As I look into her eyes, a hundred new moments of history fall into place in my head, not replacing everything that I know, but pushing it over to one side. I know that I have lived a whole other life, another dual set of memories just as real as everything I knew before. My mother is exactly as I remember her, full of life and fun, her Super 8 never far away, except every time she laughs it is true laughter, every time she dances it is without a shadow following her every step. In this set of memories there are no secret stashes of pills, no endless cigarettes, no weeks in bed or a life spent mostly in an English country garden, walled away from the rest of the world.

The rape still happened; I feel a tiny tear in my heart as I realise that is the only reason I am still here. But it's stitched by hope when I remember my mother gathering me to her, a few short week ago, and telling me that it was Pia and me who made her whole again; Pia and me who made her determined never to let anything push her down into the darkness again; and that now she has one final battle to face to know that the man who hurt her has not won a single moment of her life. Her battle to confront him.

And I hold her again, all the tighter now as the memories of this new life I have forged pour into me. My mother who carried the secret of her rape all of her life. My mother who worked in a refuge for abused women, encouraging other women to speak out, until one day she felt she had the strength to speak out herself, to tell her family – the world – what had happened to her, despite what it might cost her, because she knew the truth would help others. My beautiful, strong, tender mother who held me in her arms and told me that she loved me, and that Dad loved me, and that they had always thought I was a blessing from the very beginning.

My mother who had come back to the place where she grew up to use the money from the sale of her old home to start another refuge here for local women, a safe place to go to and begin a journey away from victimhood.

Elation sears through me; I feel like I have won some great cosmic gamble. Whatever happened, whatever I did, it was enough. It was enough; not to save her, no, but not to ruin her completely, and not to let her ruin the lives around her. Something, some small change, meant she didn't kill him, that she always knew she never killed him. It meant that in not committing that worst or sins – taking a life – she found the courage to forgive herself, the strength to help so many others.

I wait for all the new memories to reveal themselves to me, and I know that they are there, but at the moment they are fuzzy and out of focus, remaining unseen. I must be patient. Dad's not here, but at least he is somewhere. After this nightmare is over we can all be together again For the first time in a very long time I feel hope, and I realise how much I love being alive. There is no Michael here, there is no love for me in this reality, and I will miss him every moment of my life, but, even though it hurts, I accept it, because I understand; I'm not allowed perfect happiness, that was never meant for me.

This Mum, I know, is a different woman, her guilt and anger transformed into a quiet determination. But one thing is different once again.

'Where's your medal?' I ask her, and she frowns. 'Your Maria Goretti medal?'

'Oh, I threw that away a long time ago,' she says. 'I threw it away the night we left Brooklyn. I'm surprised you remember I used to have one.' She gives a shrug. 'Maria Goretti, the girl who asked to be killed rather than raped, the girl who forgave her attacker and became a saint. It used to be a symbol of how I had failed to protect my virtue, of how I wanted to live more than please God, and now … well, now I know that God wants me to live too, and do good with my life.'

Relief floods through me, releasing the building torrent of tears. My arms are still wrapped around her waist and she holds me close to her.

'Sweetheart, don't cry. I know this is hard for you, perhaps most of all, but we're together.'

'It's just I missed you so much.'

'Silly girl, you saw me a few hours ago!' Mum kisses my forehead and I hold her tight, pressing my ear against her chest to feel the beat of her heart against my cheek. 'I know it will be difficult, but I promise you we will face it together.'

'Face what together?' I ask, looking up at her, my smile fading as I see the look of grave concern on her face.

'Meeting his other victims. All those that he raped after me.'

It's nearly impossible to tear myself away from her, but I need to decompress, get my feet on solid ground and get a sense of what I've done.

These others. They aren't because of me; they can't be.

Stephanie already told us that Delaney hadn't died that night; that for the good of all of them, or at least that's what she'd thought, they'd swept the whole thing under the carpet. So wherever he disappeared to, there could always have been more victims, and that's not on me.

Stephanie said he was watched, that he was prevented from hurting anyone else, but how could she know once she went to Florida? How could anyone know? I'd heard about priests moved from parish to parish, 'transgressions' covered up and buried deep. Is that what happened to him? He was moved on to harm again.

And then a new memory flowers to me, and I realise Mum dealt with what happened all alone. Ran a scalding hot bath all alone, after it had happened. I remember her telling us every detail. How she knew she couldn't stay in Bay Ridge anymore, not knowing she would see him every day, and how she had left with Henry in the pitch black night of the 13th. The only thing she could not bear to say out loud was his name, as if it still had some power over her, an invisible brand she could never be rid of.

Closing the door on the only bedroom, I fall onto the soft, white bed, shutting my eyes, and try to shut out the clamouring and competing memories in my head. I focus instead on this life, this universe that I have created. I try to remember the last days and weeks and years as they are now.

There's Mum's stuff all around me. Her hairbrush laced with midnight-and-silver strands. Her clothes hang neatly on the clothes rail, her dresses no longer pale silvers and white, but colours all of them, a rainbow of expression. A pair of brightly woven, gold, leather, beaded sandals are set neatly by the drawers. And in the air, mingled with the particles of sunlight and dust, her scent still lingers. To be here among her things, her living things, to lay my head next to the dent in the pillow where hers lay only a few hours ago, fills me with so much peace, an ocean of it. And yet, at its centre, a tiny black pearl of fear worries itself into formation.

If it isn't me who is paying the price for this wondrous miracle, who is?

'It's time to go, Luna.' Pia pushes open the door, and I realise at once that she is Pia here; I stopped calling her Pea a long time ago.

'Where are we going?' I find it almost impossible to drag myself to my feet, out of the little oasis of peace and sanctuary I have found amongst Mum's things.

'Mum had another reply to her ad in the paper, that's five so far,' Pia tells me, as if she's reminding me, with an edge of impatience.

'She put an ad in the paper?' I realise that I hadn't known this, not even in this life. 'She's named him? What if he sees it?'

'She didn't have to. There was a phrase he used with her; she thought it was probably his thing, and she was right, the sick bastard. It's that phrase the others recognise.'

'So where are we going now?' I ask.

'To meet her, we're going to meet another victim.'

CHAPTER FORTY-FOUR

* *

The young woman that opens the door looks very young, and that troubles me more. I don't know why, perhaps because her grief and pain are more likely to be raw, but more likely because I thought time would have robbed him of the power to hurt and maim. If there is one thing I know, it's that time changes nothing if you simply let it pass by.

Perhaps she's eighteen, maybe as much as twenty, I think. It's hard to tell; her body is still soft-looking, as if it hasn't fully formed, or maybe it has and yet was somehow pulled out of shape. A basket of dead flowers hangs outside the front door, yellowing desiccated petals crumble to the floor as it sways. It reminds me of the dried blood on my mother's dress in another time. Patricia, that's what Pia said her name was. Patricia has green eyes, fair hair, and is a little heavy set in white leggings, a long T-shirt over the top. Her fingers, laden with cheap-looking dress rings, are caught in the neckline, worrying at it.

'Hello, Patricia,' my mum says. 'My name is Marissa Sinclair. These are my daughters, Pia and Luna. Thank you for agreeing to see us, it must be hard to have a load of strangers coming into your home, especially to talk about something so ... difficult. But maybe it might help just a little bit to know that you're not alone. It can be the start to finding your way back to life again.'

Patricia doesn't move, she only watches us, trapped by indecision.

'If you're not ready to talk, that's fine too,' Mum tells her gently, her voice low and tender. She searches out each second with fingertip care, testing it before she goes on. Strong, protective and gentle all at once; I see Riss in her there. The young warrior woman in the way she stands, inclines her head. Also, I see the mother I've always known, in this life and the last, brimful of feelings, not only hers, but mine, my sister's and sometimes the whole world's, always at risk of being engulfed by her empathy, but never able to close it off entirely. Everything that Patricia is feeling now, my mother feels it too, she doesn't just guess at it, she feels it in her gut, and it hurts her.

'You only have to tell us what you want, and we'll listen,' Mum speaks again. 'That's it, that's all.'

First Patricia bows her head, and then looks over her shoulder, as if she is expecting a reason for her to close the door to arrive at any moment. When it doesn't, she steps aside and gestures us in.

We follow her down a short hallway, where she stands with her back to us on the threshold of her small living room. There is a couch, a TV in the corner, a short counter at one end dividing a few feet off into a kitchen area. Uncertainty cuts through every angle of her body; large as she is, I can see she is doing all she can to minimise her impact on the space around her.

'I never thought I'd want to talk about it,' she says at last, her voice quiet, girlish. 'Then I saw the ad, and I couldn't stop thinking about it, about the fact that it hadn't been just me. I'd always thought it was just me.

'I never expected to feel so relieved. All this time I thought it was my fault, something I said or did made it happen, and ... he said I was special, that was the reason it was happening, because there something about me he couldn't resist, something special.'

'He said that to me too.' Mum doesn't wait to be invited to sit, and as soon as she does, Patricia takes her lead, taking a seat opposite her. Pia and I follow, taking stools at the makeshift breakfast counter. Mum waits until Patricia is ready to meet her gaze; there's no sense of the impatience or restlessness from her that I was once so used to. No eyes darting to the door, always looking for a way out whenever we were anywhere but at home. Marissa simply sits, and waits and, as I watch her, my heart fills with joy, knowing that in this life she has found her sense of peace again; she feels safe at last.

'He told me that I had made him do what he did.' Patricia tucks her palms between her thighs, her shoulders hunching around her ears. 'That it was my fault.' Her voice drops to a frightened whisper. 'It was like you said in the ad, he told me not to ever say his name, to never speak it. He said if I did he would know, and he'd make sure I never said it again. I believed him. I was – am – so afraid of him, it felt like he was the devil, like it didn't matter where I went he could always reach me and hurt me. I still … I don't want to say his name.'

'You don't have to,' Mum reassures her. 'I don't like to say it either. But one day soon, he – it – won't have any power anymore.'

Patricia's eyes are huge with fear; the hold this man maintains over her is so strong it half feels as if Delaney's in the room with us, poised to strike.

'This must be hard, you don't have to tell us details.' Mum leans a little towards her; not too much, just enough. 'But if you can talk a little, it really helps. And once the centre is up and running you'll have more support. Counsellors, people who can get you back to who you were meant to be.'

Patricia shakes her head.

'There's no going back to that person,' she says, with dull certainty. 'Sometimes I wonder what life would have been like if it hadn't happened …'

She cracks open a packet of cigarettes and lights up, inhaling so deeply, her body arches to meet the inward breath.

'I wonder if I would had done some of the things I dreamt of as a kid. I wanted to be a teacher, you know. But afterwards, after that, I never felt like I would ever be good enough to teach kids things. I mean how could I, when …'

She takes another long drag on her cigarette. Tipping her chin back to blow the smoke into the air above her head,

ROWAN COLEMAN

she watches it dissipate and I get the sense that a lot of time passes around here with her simply watching it go by. The heat is so intense, outside and in, because although there is an aged-looking air conditioning unit in the corner, it looks like it hasn't worked in a long time. Each time she draws strength from her addiction, the room fills with a little more smoke, pushing the air further and further away. A closed window beckons me, but I daren't move, afraid that if I do I will scare her, she will stop talking.

'Funny thing is, he was supposed to be on my side, that was the whole point. He was so kind and funny, and he said he'd help. I was in foster care, you see, had been for a long time. He said he could help find me a family.'

'Foster care?' I ask, the horrific answer dawning on me even more.

'Well, I was only eleven,' she says with a shrug.

The world drops from under my feet. I look at Mum, who closes her eyes and I know what she is thinking, because I am thinking it too. How many more lives has he ruined? How many more children?

'I'm so sorry.' Mum reaches out taking Patricia's hands. 'If I'd spoken up, then ... perhaps I could have protected you.'

'Don't be sorry,' she says, again, her voice flat and thin. 'I didn't tell anybody about it, and I wouldn't now, except ... well, you believe me, don't you? I'd just like someone to believe me.'

'I'm sorry,' I say, the heat and smoke stifling me, horror rising like bile in my throat. 'I just have to ... I won't be a moment.'

The air outside is no cooler, or fresher, but I gulp it in anyway, steadying myself against a wall, and wait for the sickness to subside. A few seconds pass before I realise that Pia is with me.

'You look like you need a stiff drink,' she says. 'I don't blame you, in fact let's go to the bar on the way home.'

In this life, my sister Pia drinks wine like other people, a little too much sometimes, but not too much. In this reality she is no longer an addict; she is healthy and strong, together and successful. There is so much here that is good, that is wonderful. So much here to be happy with and grateful for; most of all, more than anything, it's that I still exist to see it.

There is so very much that will be hard to let go of.

'I'm fine, I'm just pathetic. Everything she says, it's so hard to bear. It's not like I have the right to feel like this, it didn't happen to me.'

'Well.' Pia rubs my shoulder briskly. She doesn't hug me so much now, I remember, not since she got the design job in London and a boyfriend called Andrew. 'All of this is hard on you, you especially. The man that did that to her, he's part of you.'

Pia isn't saying anything but the truth, and yet it stings like a hard slap. Knowing he is alive somewhere, knowing I could find him and look into his eyes as his ... not his child, not even his offspring, that's too kind a word. What I am to him, I don't know. And knowing that he is alive doesn't make it any easier, because now he isn't the past turned to dust; he's a present thing, a monster, that could come around any corner any time. He frightens me.

'How many more do you think there might be?' I ask Pia.

'It's hard to know,' she says. 'But thirty years is a long time.'

And then I know. Everything I have discovered here, everyone that is so much better; it's not enough to justify one more person going through what Patricia did.

All along I believed that everything that was happening to me, around me, was to save just *her*. I was wrong, I see it now. That man is part of me, just as Pia says. And it's only me, me alone, who can save not just my mother, but all of his victims.

'Luna, you can't let every story you hear eat you up like this,' Pia tells me. 'Mum doesn't. Look at how strong she is! And, besides, all we can do is try and help these women make a life now – we can't turn the clock back.'

'You can't,' I mutter.

It doesn't take me long to find my way back to the bridge; crossing the busy road, I find the bench I sat on thirty years ago with Michael, and I look back at it, stretching out so far away into the blue, as if it could go anywhere, even to the other side of the universe.

Until this point I haven't really known what it is I have been doing. I've been a hero, on a crusade. And I committed the cardinal sin of a scientist, I let my personal hopes and expectations shade the results I was getting. I let myself believe I could save Mum and simply correct the life I had. Now it has come to it, I realise that I am not ready for the truth that there is no coming back from what I must do, and there is no more time left to get ready.

I'm going to stop. I suppose there is no other way of framing it. Not die, because if I died there'd be people to mourn me and remember me. I will have never been. Everything I've ever thought and felt will mean nothing, will be nothing. Everything I am, everything I've done, won't leave even the slightest of marks on the lives of the people I love. The idea that I can just cease to be frightens me, and I know now I have longed for some kind of salvation more that I realised. I don't want to die; I want to live. But I cannot live and let many other women suffer.

I have less than twenty-four hours to stop Delaney.

Because, yes, maybe I did enough for Mum, enough to make her life bearable in the present, and for her to have been someone capable of loving us. I did enough to make her alive. I did enough for my family.

But I didn't do enough to stop the man that fathered me from hurting so many more. So very many more.

It won't be him that will pay the price of his sins, it will be me.

Because I have to go back.

And this time I have to kill him myself.

CHAPTER FORTY-FIVE

Evening arrives very slowly, as if the sun is dawdling, and I watch it gradually sink behind the skyline, torn between wanting this day to last forever, and longing for it all to be done with, and for the quiet that will come after it is.

'Miss Sinclair?' A familiar voice speaks my name, and I turn to see Watkins Gillespie, his light, linen suit rumpled, but his tie still done up to the neck, even in this heat.

'Mr Gillespie.' I smile at him as he takes a seat next to me on the bench.

'I hope you don't mind me talking to you,' he says. 'I wasn't sure if you'd know my name. Someone pointed you out to me.'

Of course, there should be no memory of him. This is the first time I am meeting him.

'We walked past your practice, Mum told me she used to make your suits,' I tell him. He looks older, more frail, than the last time I saw him. As if this reality has used up his life force faster.

Watkins Gillespie looks at me for a long time, his watery eyes traveling over and over my face on a loop, and I know he's trying to place me. A lifetime, my lifetime, has gone by since I saw him last, but he still recognises me from somewhere.

'I'm getting old,' he tells me at last. 'Either I think I know a person, and treat them as an old friend, or I treat old friends like strangers. You seem like one or the other to me, but I am not sure which.'

'Maybe both,' I say with a smile.

'Is your mother well?' he asks me. 'I've recently come back into contact with your Aunt Stephanie, after she heard your mother was back in Bay Ridge. I thought it might be wise for me to ... contact her, but I didn't want it to come out of the blue; I thought perhaps you might broach the subject with her first.'

'I'm sure when the time is right Mum will be in touch with her sister,' I say. 'She wants to sell up, move on as soon as she can.'

'Is she well?' Watkins asks me. 'Riss, is she well?'

'Very well,' I tell him. 'Better than I've ever seen her.'

'And what brings her back to Brooklyn?' Mr Gillespie leans a little closer to me, so that I can feel the weight of him against my shoulder. 'Is she selling the old building at last, because if I can be of any assistance to her, just tell her, will you? I'd be happy to help in any way. I know a lot of people round here, lots of very well-connected people. You tell her ... just mention my name to her and tell her I can make sure she gets what she wants.'

'I'll tell her,' I say, and then a thought crosses my mind. 'How did you know I would be here?'

'Well, you've come here every day since you all arrived, sitting there staring at the bridge, looking for all the world like you are waiting for someone who never comes,' Watkins Gillespie tells me. 'Looking kind of lonely and sad, if I'm honest. So today I thought I'd come and meet you here.'

'Did you used to know a man called Michael Bellamo?' I ask him, tasting the name of my lips, savouring it.

'Ah, yes, young Michael, I knew him. He sold up after his father died, went to live in California.'

'Did he marry?' I ask him, slowly bracing myself. 'Have children? Do anything with his life?'

'Well, now, is it your mother you are asking for?' Watkins asks, and I nod.

'Be careful then how you tell her, I know they were friends.'

'Tell her what?' A tight string draws its way around my heart.

'Last I heard, Michael never married. Never had children. Went to California to try and be a writer, and he did pretty well too, had a pretty good life, travelled a lot, had a lot of friends. Not famous exactly, but he made a living from it. Had a pretty nice place near the beach.'

'He did?' I smile, and again hesitate, and again hold my breath. 'And where is he now, still in California?'

'Oh no, my dear.' Mr Gillespie shakes his head. 'I'm sorry to have to tell you Michael passed away, ten years ago now. Swimming accident.'

'No,' I say, shaking my head, over and over. 'No, that's not right. He didn't die. I mean Michael Bellamo, his father owned Sam's Bakery?'

'Yes, dear, will that upset your mother, do you think? Oh dear, you look quite pale.' Watkins Gillespie put his arm around my shoulder; I feel his hand tighten on my upper arm, and let myself fold into his shoulder, let tears flow into his suit, soaking through to his shirt, and I don't try to check them, I don't try to stop. I cry for a man that could never be mine, for a life that I lost and found, and must lose again. Mr Gillespie doesn't move, he doesn't speak, he just lets me cry until I am done.

And when I'm done the sky beyond the bridge blazes with colour, a last glorious haze of beauty before this day dies and is gone; not for good, just for now.

'I'm so sorry,' I say, sitting up, wiping my tears, and pushing my hair back from my face. 'I don't know what came over me.'

'I'm sorry,' Mr Gillespie says. 'I never like to make a young lady cry.'

'I should go,' I say. 'I've got a lot to do. I don't know what to say ... Thank you.'

Removing his arm from around my shoulder he takes my hand, between his two.

'I don't know how it's possible,' he says, 'but I do feel like I know you, somehow. There's something about you that's so familiar to me. You can come to me, anytime you want. Whatever happens, you remember that. You and your mother, you can come to me, and I'll help.'

'Thank you,' I say, squeezing his hand, and it's a moment before he will let my fingers go. 'Take care, Mr Gillespie.'

'Remember me to your mother,' Mr Gillespie calls out after me. 'Remember to tell her if she needs any help, to call me. I know a lot of people. I can make things happen.'

'I will,' I say, although I won't. There's no point; after tonight everything will be different once again.

CHAPTER FORTY-SIX

* *

The part of Mrs Finkle's house that belongs to her alone is bathed in shadows and silence when I let myself in through the door.

'Hello?' I call out, but there is no reply, and I'm sad. I would have liked to have seen her one more time, to say goodbye. I can hear movement in the apartment even before I get to the top of the stairs, and I wait for a moment, before letting myself in, reminding myself that this must be a goodbye where that one word is never used.

'There you are. Don't you answer your phone anymore?' Pia asks me the moment I shut the door behind me.

'I lost it,' I say. 'I'm sorry, I just needed to clear my head.'

'Honestly, Luna, you are such a ditz,' Pia says, and I pause. No, I'm not, I'm not the one who is a ditz, am I? I pause for a moment, struggling to recall my life apart from my family, and I remember that Brian is at home, in the flat we share, that we talked last night and he said our cat had ripped the sofa to shreds, and I remember that I found text messages from him to another girl on his phone, but I hadn't found a way to ask him about them yet, and it hurt my pride but not my heart, because I've never really been in love with him. And I remember my job with a start, because it is not my job. I am not doing what I love anymore, what I've always wanted to do. I'm in PR.

'Don't worry,' Mum greets me with an arm around my waist, pulling me to her. 'That was a tough one. She talked a lot, she wanted to talk a lot. I think she is finding life tough on her own. She's been using drugs, drinking. You know ... this is my fault, if I'd spoken up before.'

'It isn't, it isn't your fault. It's his,' Pia says. 'Mum, speak up now. It isn't too late. Name him, tell the world about him. It's not like you'd be the only one.'

'When the time is right,' Mum says. 'This isn't about vengeance, not yet. It's about lives, real people. Pulling them together, making them strong. And then ... then we'll see. I wish, I just wish I'd killed him that night. There was a moment, when maybe I could have; I've thought about it a million times since. I just wish I had.'

'No, you don't, Mum,' I tell her. 'You don't wish that at all. You're not a killer, you're not. But you are a hero, you're my hero.'

'Luna's right, Mum,' Pia says. 'And look, Patricia is still young, and everything we are doing now, supporting other women who have been victims, that's giving each and every one of them, including you, a chance to start afresh, to turn a new page; even Patricia can do that, once she knows that she's believed and that people care about her. You're doing that for her, and the others.'

'I wish I could be stronger, strong enough,' Mum says.

'Everything you've done, even just surviving this far, it's been more than enough.' I put my arms around her and hug her tight. A goodbye with no goodbyes. 'You're brave and strong and wonderful. And I just ... I want you to know, Mum, that I have always loved you. Every version of you, all you have ever been, I have loved. And I know you've loved me, despite everything you went though. I love you and Dad and Pia – you've all been the joy in my life. I've been so lucky, so blessed to have been part of it all.'

Mum's brow furrows and I know I have allowed too much of what I am really feeling to spill out.

'What's wrong, Luna?' she asks. 'What aren't you telling me?'

'Nothing's wrong,' I tell her. 'Don't worry about me.'

'Well, that's impossible for any mother,' she says. 'One day you will find that out.'

'I should cook something,' Pia says, and I almost laugh out loud; the idea of my sister as a person who cooks is a funny one. 'Mum, here's a large glass of wine. Luna, come and help me chop things.'

She hands Mum the glass, and gives me a pointed look.

'Chop things, what things?' I ask her once we are in the small kitchen.

Pia is silent as she takes out two large onions, puts them on a board and hands me a knife.

'Chop,' she tells me, with a nod of her smooth hair. 'Dice not slice, and while you are at it, you can tell me why you are saying goodbye to us.'

'I'm not saying goodbye.' My eyes sting and a tear rolls down my cheek, breaking on the back of my hand.

'You are,' Pia says. 'I don't know why, but you are. It feels like you're leaving us, for good, Luna. Why do I feel like that?'

'I'm not,' I protest, the tears still flowing. 'I just wanted to say that I love you guys, that's all.'

'I know I haven't been around so much,' Pia begins. 'That I've let my job and Andrew take over a bit, but you realise, don't you, that I still bloody love you. You get that, right? Because you seem a bit disconnected, somehow, like you're not all here.'

'I'm here right now,' I say, putting the knife down and drying my eyes. 'So, why don't we top up our glasses and drink to us, to the best two sisters the world has ever known.'

'Well, there's no need to go over the top,' she says.

13 JULY

'Love is space and time measured by the heart.'

—Marcel Proust

'Three days with you I could fill with more delight
than fifty common years could ever contain.'

—John Keats

CHAPTER FORTY-SEVEN

This is my last day on earth, my last day as Luna Sinclair, and after that, I don't know what I will be or where. Perhaps I'll be a billion different things, travelling in opposite directions, flowing from one universe to another, free of knowing what I am. Although it started twenty-nine years ago, this is where my journey truly began, and where it will end, tonight.

I've grown up all of my life with this sense of ... not foreboding; no, that isn't the right word. But with the knowledge that something was coming, something very far away at first, but with every day, hour and second that ticked by, I felt something draw slowly nearer and fractionally louder. It was so constant that I got used to it, tuned it out, choosing a life where I stay more or less within the same fifty square miles I grew up in, child, student, teacher, girlfriend, ex-girlfriend, sister, daughter. Unremarkable markers of who I am, who I was. I didn't see then what I see now, that the things that make us unremarkable are also the very things we'll fight to death to protect. Unremarkable things turn us into heroes.

We live in this world where bad people get to do terrible things, and more often than we know or want to admit they get away with it. No comeback, no justice. They do terrible things and even if they are punished, they still have that, the knowledge and the memories of it. Not him, he won't have that. Because I am going to make this one tiny corner of everything safe from him. Bad men will rise and rise again, but not this one. This one is almost done.

And God only knows that it's not that I don't want to live, because I do, more than I ever have. Only now, at the brink of the end, have I really known what it means to be alive, to dance, to love, to fear and to want. I *want* to live more than anything. But that's just what I want, not what I must do ... And somehow, wanting it is enough. It's almost enough; wanting life so badly means that I have lived it, at least.

This is when my wonderful, terrifying, tragic, beautiful and impossible journey began, and here is where it will end. As for what will become of me when I take that last step, I have no idea.

I don't sleep; sleeping would seem like a terrible waste. I wait until Mum goes to bed in the little bedroom, pressing a kiss to my forehead. Pia drifts off on her half of the sofa bed, her legs sprawling into my territory. In sleep she is the same old Pea, chaotic and haphazard, as dear to me as my own life.

As she mutters in her sleep I climb carefully out of bed, relishing every sensation, the cool floor beneath my tired feet, the water running over my fingers as I turn the tap on and fill a glass. Even the exhaustion that's deep in my bones, and crowding my peripheral vision with flash hallucination, I greet with open arms; this is what it means to be human. This is what it feels like.

Looking out at the houses across the street, I wait until the lights go out, one by one. The street becomes quiet and still, just a breath of wind as I open all of the windows as wide as they will go and lean into the night, closing my eyes to feel hot air passing over my skin. I tell the wind my story, I tell it to the universe, and to the dense, black and hidden stars. Not to be heard, not to be believed, but just so I know myself that this has all been real, that I was real, and this happened to me.

It's funny how quickly I got used to Mum being here, being real, asleep in the next room, the sound of her breathing even and steady. Then, I suppose I never really got used to her being gone, that never felt real to me. I push open the door to her room, just a crack, and, for a little while, watch her, listen to her. I try to remember everything, everything we ever did or said or felt together, the warmth of her hugs, the sound of her heartbeat, the way only her kisses could heal grazed knees, the way that she always tried to understand me, how she tried to never cry in front of me, how she always smiled whenever she saw me, even though smiling was the last thing she felt like doing, how she fought every day of her life and showed me how to fight every day of mine.

When I step in the freezing shower, letting it run cold as ice to keep me alert and awake, the rivulets of water drive into me, forcing me to stir myself for action. I stay there as long as I can, turning my back to the shower, bracing myself against the pain of the cold. Still wrapped in my towel, hot, strong, black coffee warms me from the inside out, cup after cup, until my heart races in my chest, tripping over itself as it accelerates. Everything is in perfect focus, maximum resolution. Every one of my nerve endings is calcified and brittle, like a stiff wind could blow me to pieces. I am nearly done, almost at the end.

Dressing carefully, I choose my oldest jeans, white T-shirt, dependable Converse. I don't have any sort of weapon, so I take a kitchen knife from the magnetic holder on the wall, but it is too long. I put it back and find a folding fruit knife in the drawer; it's small but sharp.

It's funny, it makes me want to laugh out loud, and I press my hands over my mouth: the idea of me overpowering a man and bringing him down with a folding fruit knife. And, anyway, even if I can overpower a man twice my size, to actually do it, to actually kill him. I know who I am; I know I'm still my mother's daughter, who would never harm another living thing. It's my father's daughter who must take charge this time. I remember Henry's penknife, the one I left behind the vent in the Lupo's kitchen. I left it there a long time ago, before the universes split and reformed. Putting the fruit knife back in the drawer, I hope it will still be there.

One last thing. I set the camera up on a pile of books, switching the flash on and setting the timer to ten seconds. I sit on a chair opposite and look into the lens. Chances are that after tonight this camera, this image, won't exist, but if I could take one photo of the past who knows, maybe I can take one now of this present? And if Pea finds an image of a strange woman in the prints if she ever gets the film developed, well, then at least she would have seen my face, even if it meant nothing to her.

Just as I am about to leave, I stop beside my sleeping sister, gently touching her hand with the tips of my fingers. Taking great care, I set my camera down on my pillow for her to find. There might be grander reasons to give up your life than your own family, but not for me. How hard, how almost impossible it is, to find the strength to turn my back on them both and to gently pull the door to a close, but I do.

Tiptoeing down the stairs, the shadows thrown by the moonlight dance on the walls of photographs, somehow bringing them to life. Moment after moment explodes into action, candles blown out, kisses shared, a thousand smiles and bursts of laughter follow me on my path, through the front door and out into the dark of a very early morning.

All is still, the heat only now just peeling away to leave the world cooling at the edges. Everywhere I look there is exquisite beauty, the wooden-fronted houses, the slumbering trees and the cars that line the sidewalk all seem to shine, even in the absence of light. Dawn is hours away yet, but I know where I want to start my last day. My feet quicken, breaking into a jog, as my need to be in one particular place balloons inside me, lifting me up, driving me on. The pain in my lungs resisting, my heart pounding, the ache in the soles of my feet and my shins reverberating are all reminders that I am flesh and blood, and it's wonderful.

When I find the bench I collapse onto it, feeling my cheeks burn and sweat prickle my scalp. The bridge reaches out of the dark, still and elegant, stretching up towards the fading stars.

With the bridge as my companion, I imagine a life, a life where I'm married to a man with green eyes; a life where we take walks on long beaches, dogs and children playing around our feet. In that life, every night we'd kiss goodnight with just as much passion as the night we first kissed, with just as much tenderness and urgency, because we'd know what it would be like to lose the love we have. And so it would never be commonplace to us, never be routine or become tired. Our love would be one that would stretch through a whole lifetime, and when the time came, a very, very long time from now, we'd part, just for a little while, knowing we could not have loved each other more.

Perhaps the story becomes a dream, or even for a little while it's somehow real; I don't know which, but do know I whisper it on to the wind as if it were a prayer, as the hours until sunrise slowly unwind, and when the day breaks, it breaks in 1977. For the first time there is no pain, no sense of loss or mismatch on my journey.

I am exactly where I am meant to me.

As the sun rises, the heat builds with slow determination, even this early. I wait until the sky is a perfect dome of blue, and the traffic has begun to build on the bridge. Standing, I stretch my arms out into the sky, until every muscle sings like a plucked string. One last time I look at the bridge, and, pressing my fingertips to my lips, I blow it a kiss, before heading down 3rd Avenue, Bay Ridge, Brooklyn – the very last place you'd think a person might be able to change the world.

CHAPTER FORTY-EIGHT

Lupo's Tailoring and Alterations is only just open.

Although I have never met him, I recognise the man behind the counter filling the cash register with change. I've seen a photograph of him; there is only one, the one that Mum managed to grab as she left her home. He is smiling awkwardly, eyes not meeting the camera, looking like he'd rather be anywhere else in the world than on the end of the lens. Trace elements of me are hard to see in a man of his age, with his tight, round belly and oiled back hair, but I am there, in the shape of his ear, the way his fingers splay out as they rest on the counter.

There's no reason I couldn't sneak around the side and knock on the workroom door – I'm almost certain Riss will be in there already – and yet I open this door and a bell jangles over my head.

'Morning,' I say.

'What can I do for you?' Leopold Lupo asks his granddaughter pleasantly enough. 'Something you need altering? Or my girls can work to any pattern, even a photo from a magazine, if it's a new look you're after. Something a bit less tomboy, maybe?'

'Thank you, but no. I was hoping to see Marissa, please?' Grandfathers always like polite children, that's what my Grandma Pat told me, when I was once too loud around Grandpa Martin.

'You know her?' he answers quickly, his accent mostly Italian, just a hint of Brooklyn flattening his vowels.

'We're friends and—'

'I never seen you around before,' he answers. 'Where are you from?'

'Well, I've been around. I just need to have a quick word with her—'

'Luna!'

Riss appears, fresh faced, wearing denim shorts and a pretty floral cotton top, her hair tied back from her face with a headscarf.

'Where you been? I don't know this girl,' Leo points out.

'Really?' Riss gasps with mock surprised. 'There are people in the world you don't know?'

'Well, what does she want?' He doesn't register that she is joking at all, which makes her smile all the more.

'Well, I guess if I ask her I'll find out,' she says, tipping the hatch in the counter, and jerking her head in the direction of the door as she steps through it. I notice her Super 8 in its neat carrying case is slung over her shoulder. 'I'm going to fetch some breakfast ... I'll be back soon.'

The bell jangles over our head as we leave.

'Are you planning to film breakfast?' I ask her, nodding at the camera.

'No, I'm gonna film everything.' She pops open the case, and carefully takes her camera out. 'The street, everyone I see, you. All these things I take for granted, all these sights and sounds I smell every single day. I've grown up with them, it's like I don't see them anymore. If I do go, I want to have a reminder. Because I love this place, Luna. Wherever I go, whatever I do, there's a part of me I will have to leave behind here, and knowing that kind of hurts.'

Her expression stills for a moment and she lifts the camera, pushing the record button.

'Smile!'

'No!' I yell, hiding my face behind my hands, afraid that capturing my image on film might somehow ruin everything; that there can't be any proof that I was ever here. 'Film the street, don't film me!'

Riss laughs. 'Anyone would think you were on the lam or something.'

Shrugging she turns the camera away from me, aiming at the shops signs, the people walking past. A young man blows her a kiss, two skinny little boys in shorts and nothing else pull faces. An older woman, in a printed cotton dress, huffs and puffs and waves Riss away with a dismissive hand, and yet she still smiles coquettishly at the camera. Everyone we meet, whether they know Riss or not, loves her. Even the street we walk on seems to adore her, I can feel it rising, preening in pleasure to meet her step. Then, laughing, she puts her arm around me and turns the camera on us both. This time, I don't shy away. This may be our last moment together so I smile and kiss her on the cheek, making her laugh, and she is so beautiful.

If I don't end him tonight this will be the last time this ever happens for her, the last time she ever feels like a duchess on 3rd Avenue or anywhere else.

'You OK?' Riss asks, dropping the camera to her side, as we head away from the store. I steal a sideways glance at her, her nut-brown skin, the hair tucked behind that headscarf; this morning her beauty is the perfectly still surface of a lake, just before a rock is tossed into its midst.

'I am, are you? Henry's due to leave first thing tomorrow, right?'

'Oh God, I know, I can't eat or sleep. I'm a nervous wreck!' Her laugh is high and tense. 'Henry's got me a ticket, my passport is in my nightstand. I could go. I mean, I could throw some stuff in a bag and just go! But somehow, I'm still here, treating today just like it is any other day. Going to work for Pops, acting like everything is just fine. Poor Pops, he acts like the tough guy, but deep down you know, he's like marshmallow. He don't deserve what I'm doing. I don't like lying to him.'

She links her arms through mine, dragging me around in a circle.

'Oh God, Luna, tell me what to do?'

'Just trust your heart, I guess?' Pathetic. How did I ever land a job in PR, even in an alternative timeline?

'The thing is, I know that I love Henry and I want to be with him. But to just disappear tomorrow, to run away, that doesn't seem real, it's doesn't seem possible. I just have to figure out a way to tell my family what I am doing and hope that they forgive me. I'll figure out what to say to Pops, and then I'll follow him in a week or two. That's not crazy, that's real mature, and Pops will see that. At least I think he will.'

'Don't do that,' I say. 'Don't tell them. This is your life, live it your way, just go, go now and find Henry, and stay with him until it's time to go. Just go before you lose your nerve. Do all the talking later.'

'Are you crazy?' Riss stares at me as if that is exactly what she thinks. 'If I don't tell them first, then they'll never forgive me. I'll never see them again. They're my family, they *are* me. Of course I have to tell them, to their faces. And, look, I know you aren't a believer, that's fine, you've got your own thing. But I know if I can get Father Delaney onside then it will make the whole thing a lot easier.'

Anguish seems to build up in me, flooding into my gut and chest. I could offer Riss up as bait for the man I am intending to make my victim, but even the thought of putting her in harm's way is unbearable, and what if I fail?

I can't fail; this is my last chance.

I have no idea how to kill a man, how to even attempt it, and the thought of it, the thought of finishing off a human life, even his, makes me sick inside, fills my mouth and nostril with black fear, and yet ... I can't let him go on to live his monstrous life. On this day, as it turns into the darkest of nights, it's Riss that I have to protect, Riss and all those other girls.

'Let me come with you when you see Delaney,' I say, with no idea what I'll do in that moment when I look into his eyes again, only that somehow I need to do it. 'I can be your chaperone.'

'Really?" Riss looks bemused. 'A chaperone? You really are English.'

'I know you think I'm crazy, and maybe I am, but I have to go soon too, and I like you, Riss, I like who you are. You're smart and funny and strong. And you'll make something wonderful of your life, I know you will. One day, years from now, when you've been married for a really long time and you have daughters of your own, you'll realise how grateful you would be to someone taking time to watch out for them. And that really is all I am trying to do for you. So would you just let me see you safely through tonight?'

'Sure,' she says, studying my face, her own full of confusion. 'If it will make you feel better then, sure, come with me. Meet me tonight, at home. He said he'd come over about nine thirty.'

Riss put her slender arms around me, drawing me into a hug. Returning it, it feels like the universe is threatening to explode in all the spaces between us, parts of what make me real and whole detonating within, that as every second passes a little less of me exists.

'Thank you,' she says. 'Thank you for caring about me. That's something nice I didn't expect, to have a friend walk into my life out of nowhere. I'm so glad to know you, Luna.'

'Me too.' I smile for her. 'I'm so glad to know you too.'

Riss nods towards the bakery, Michael's bakery. 'Want a bagel? Because I think there's a guy in there that would like to see you.'

'I ... I better not,' I say, turning, walking back towards the bridge.

'Why not?' Riss calls after me. 'Shouldn't you be listening to your heart?'

I stop, and turn around. I know what my heart wants.

CHAPTER FORTY-NINE

'Hey sweetheart,' Michael's dad greets Riss as she walks in, and he produces a bag with her name written on it marker. 'My finest bagels, still warm, just for you.'

Hanging back from the counter, I inhale deeply, almost tasting the freshly baked breads and cakes, the scent and sweetness of sugar hanging is the air. Since the sun rose with me, everywhere I go seems to be glazed in gold, everything brighter, sharper, saturated with colours, just like the films taken by the Super 8.

'I'll take a couple of coffees too,' Riss says. 'I'm just going to sit awhile with my friend here.'

'Pleased to meet you,' Michael's dad says, as if he doesn't know I'm the woman that drew Michael away from his shop twice. 'I'm Sam Bellamo.'

'Hello, Sam.' I take his hand and shake it, wishing there was a way I could avoid the look of quiet concern in his face, afraid that somehow what I know about his son's future might show in my face. But all that might change too, I remind myself; everything will change a little after tonight. And a little is all it takes to save a life.

Sam leans a little over the counter and speaks in a low voice. 'Listen, my boy and me we go at it sometimes – it don't mean we don't love each other. It don't mean I don't look out for him. He's talked about you, almost non-stop actually, you've really gotten under his skin.' He cocks his head, and smiles at me. 'And his mother's too. Though you should know, no girl will ever be good enough for her son.'

'Really, I've just come to say goodbye,' I tell him. 'I have to leave soon.'

'He's gonna be sorry about that,' he says. 'I guess, if I'd met a fine-looking woman like you, back when I was his age, I'd have gone a bit crazy for her too. You related to Riss?'

I shake my head.

'Strange, no one has ever told you that you're the spit of her?' Sam shakes his and laughs. 'Like two peas in a pod, you two. Cut from the same cloth. When you get home, you ask your mother if she ever met a Leopold Lupo on her travels.'

He grins and I laugh too, liking him all the more because of the comparison he made between me and Riss, when, all my life, in every life I've ever lived, it's usually only the differences that anyone has ever noticed. Perhaps I am more my mother than anyone, after all. What a wonderful thing that would be.

He lets go of my fingers and I sit down in the booth opposite Riss. A slight, fair-haired girl in an apron brings us two cups of black coffee, in red-and-white paper cups with fold-out handles. It's strong and bitter, and just what I need.

'He warning you off?' Riss asks me, amused.

'He's just worried about Michael, he thinks I'm dangerous,' I say, and my body tenses at his name, the thought of seeing him fizzes through me. I want to see him, but before I even have, I am afraid to miss him, afraid of how much missing him weakens me.

'Dangerous?' Riss laughs. 'You're a strange chick, Luna, but dangerous, that's the last thing you are. Anyways, Michael's like two feet taller than you and a hundred pounds heavier, what are you going to do to him, apart from teach him a few things about women and maybe break his heart. And that's OK; he's done his fair share of the breaking. Do him good to know what it feels like the other way around.'

'You're here.' Michael arrives, staring at me as if I have just fallen from space, and I stare back, dimly away that Riss is filming us. 'I didn't know if I was ever going to see you again.'

'I didn't know if you would either,' I say. 'It's good to see you.'

Good isn't the right word, there isn't a right word to describe what it means to see the only person who can quench the thirst you didn't know you had until you first tasted them.

'How long are you here for?' He seems unaware of the whirl of Riss's camera.

'Until tonight,' I say, 'and then I have to go. For good.'

'Are you leaving tomorrow too?' Riss asks me, putting her camera down. 'Why didn't you say? I bet you are on the same flight as Henry. You could travel together.'

Neither Michael and I speak, we only look at each other.

'You know what, I'm going to go.' Riss tucks the camera back in its case, and slides out from her seat. 'It's going to be a real hot day today. Wherever you two go, make sure you stay out of the sun.'

'I'll meet you at your place,' I tell her as she leaves, and she waves assent as she walks past the plate-glass window. 'At nine thirty.'

'Can you get away now?' I ask him.

Michael shakes his head. 'I'm working.'

'No, you're not,' Michael's dad, who has been listening intently, calls over. 'You can have the day off, kid. We'll manage.'

'For real?' Michael asks him.

'You only got until tonight. Go and make the most it.'

Michael grins at me and offers me his hand.

'I remember what it was like to be in love, you know,' Sam calls after us. 'And then I met your mother.'

'Where do you want to go?' Michael asks, taking my hand. 'I mean what can we do, with your incredible powers? Travel anywhere in space and time?'

'Or we could just think about now,' I say, bringing his hand to my cheek. 'Just this moment. And just ... hang out?'

'Come on,' he says, 'I know a place.'

'Where are we going?' I ask him.

'Home.'

Michael's bedroom is small and dark, with a small triangular window in the end wall that lets in only a little light. The faded blue wallpaper is printed with small pink flowers and is almost hidden behind an array of posters – Bruce Lee, Al Pacino and girls, lots of beautiful young women in revealing bikinis.

Two mismatched bookshelves stand side by side, full to the brim with well-read paperbacks, some with spines so cracked you can barely read the titles anymore. On a shelf on the wall, there are some school trophies, and a photo of him when he was younger, all awkward and angles, grinning like a loon, braces glinting in the flashlight. I look at it for a long time, pretending I haven't noticed him hastily shoving discarded clothes under the bed.

'Mom's away visiting,' he says; he's nervous. 'Normally she handles this stuff.'

'Maybe you should tidy your own room if you're thinking of bringing girls back here,' I say with a smile, as I turn to look at him.

'Well, I wasn't thinking about bringing a girl, bringing you, back here. I thought you'd gone forever, it was driving me crazy not knowing if I'd ever see you again. I just wanted to get old, old enough to be able to go and look for you, and then I realised, I had no idea where ... when ... you're from.'

He crosses the room, stopping short just inches from me.

Longing populates the air around us and, more than that, desire.

'After today I'll never see you again,' he says, leaning towards me.

'No,' I say. 'You won't see me again.'

'So tell me.' He edges closer. 'Tell me where I'll find you? In the future?'

'I can't. I can't tell you because ...' I am about to say there is no future, not for me, but instead I finish, 'I have seen the future; once I had a future but I don't know what the future will be after tonight. Every time I come here, it changes.'

A sea of goosebumps washes over me as I take his fingers in mine, and it feels as if a layer of my skin has already vanished, every touch, every sensation seems more acute; I can feel the ridges and swirls of his fingerprints, the rise and fall against my skin. Taking a step closer to him, I can almost see the heat of his body coming off of him in rainbow waves.

'I never have,' Michael says; there's a tremble in his voice. 'I've never brought a girl back here before, just you. So what do want to do, you want to listen to some music, or ... would you like a drink? We probably have something in the fridge ... Or I could read to you?'

'I never expected to meet you here,' I say, bringing his fingertips to my lips, speaking against them. 'In this place that I was never supposed to be. And I suppose that's a good thing, because if this was my life, then you and I ... would be impossible. But now everything I do is impossible, you and I seem likes the most sane thing in this world. Like a fixed point in all this madness. I didn't expect it, but I am grateful for it, for you. Being with you, it's taught me how to fall in love.'

'Jesus, Luna.' He closes the small space between us, circling his arms around my waist. 'I just, I don't know what to do with the way I feel about you. I feel like I've known you forever, since before now and always. I'm in love with you, Luna.'

When I close my eyes a tear rolls down my cheek, and, as it does, I know now that even the tears I have left to cry are numbered.

'I'll miss you every day for the rest of my life,' Michael whispers.

'Don't,' I whisper. 'Don't miss me.'

'Will you tell me one thing about the future?' he asks me. 'The time you come from, is it within my lifetime?'

I'm uncertain what to say; I hesitate, but he sees it in my face.

'It is, isn't it? It's in my lifetime?' He lowers his gaze for a moment. 'Well, then, I'll just wait until I catch up to you, Luna. I'll just wait. And then it can be me who's saying I'm too old for you, how about that? I'll wait for you.'

'Don't wait for me.' I shake my head, not wanting to tell him that I know he doesn't anyway, that there will be no me to wait for. 'Live your life. Know me now, today in this moment, but please, please, whatever you do, don't wait for me. I might never come.'

'But you don't understand.' Michael takes my hands. 'I don't have a choice but to wait for the woman I love. I'll still love you in a thousand years. Whatever happens next, I will always wait for you, because I have to. Whether you come or not.'

The hours drain away through my fingers, too quickly and too slowly, all at once. The heat builds in the air, charging the afternoon with an intense atmosphere. I sit up, brushing my hair from my shoulders. Michael sits up behind me and kisses my neck.

'What would happen if you never went back, if you just lived here forever,' he says.

'I don't think I can,' I say. 'I think my time would pull me back eventually. I think if I tried to resist it might just rip me in two.'

'Then just stay here a little longer,' he says. 'Stay with me. Another five minutes, what harm can it do?'

'Maybe all the harm in the world,' I tell him.

'So this is it?' He sits up, pulling on a T-shirt as I dress slowly. 'This time you're going for good? Shall I walk you there? We don't have to say goodbye now, we can say it on the corner or ... someplace else, but not now. I don't want it to ever be now.'

Standing up, I turn around and smile at him.

'I don't want it to be now, either. Walk me to the corner.'

'It's going to storm tonight,' he says, as we walk to the end of his street. 'You can feel the electricity in the air. Maybe that's a good thing, some rain will wash away all the heat and dirt for one night.'

'Maybe,' I say, as we reach the very end of the road. A rumble of thunder rolls across the skyline. 'Well, this is where we say goodbye.'

'Let me walk you all the way. Tell me what you're going to do? Maybe I can do something to help. Let me come with you, please Luna.'

'I can't,' I say. 'And you can't walk me any further. From this point on I have to go alone.'

'Luna, I ...'

'You know what, let's not say goodbye,' I interrupt him. 'Let's not say anything else.'

I stand on my tiptoes and kiss him on the cheek. As I walk into the darkness, I don't look back. Because if I did, all the courage, all the determination I have, would ebb away in an instant, consumed by the sharp longing to spend whatever time I have left in this world next to him.

CHAPTER FIFTY

. . . .

I am a little early, but Riss's building is almost entirely in darkness. There is no doorbell or buzzer on the shop door, so I go round the side. The green-painted door is locked away behind a rusty-looking, wrought-iron ornate grill, so I can't get to the buzzer on the other side. Even knocking on the door is something of a struggle, but I do it, trying to make my knocks as loud as I can. Marissa must have known her family would be out, or perhaps she just plans to exit through her bedroom window again, but why would the building be locked up so tightly?

Everything seems unnaturally quiet as I cross the street and look up at her window, as if I am the last person left alive in this corner of the world, and everyone else who ever lived here, or ever will, has vanished into nothing.

The only light I can see in the building is coming from Riss's room, a tug of a breeze pulls the end of her curtains out of the window – it's open.

The only way I can find to get in is via the old and rusting fire escape. Stretching, reaching, I try to grab the metal ladder and pull it down, but it remains a good foot above my grasp.

'Riss!' I call up, the sound of my voice echoes in the charged air.

'Riss!' No answer comes, not from Riss's window, or anywhere.

She said for me to be here at 9.30. I look at my watch; in the next five minutes the blackout strikes, and this is going to get a whole lot more difficult. And then a terrible thought strikes me.

What if he's up there with her already, what if she's trapped with him *now?*

I drag a garbage can overflowing with trash beneath the ladder, forcing the stinking rubbish as far into the can as I'm able, so that the dome lid sits almost level. Bracing my weight against the wall, I scramble onto the lid; it slips and shifts under my feet and I will myself not to fall, locking my knees, tensing my thighs. I don't have time to fall, to fail.

Stretching up as tall as I can, I just about reach the ladder, the lid of the unstable trash can tilting and falling over, leaving me hanging off of it. I waggle my legs until it extends enough for me to be able to put my feet on the ground. Finally, I am able to climb up, the muscles in my arms burning, my lungs bursting as I hit the first balcony level. I'm gasping, unable to take in enough oxygen, but I can't pause, not even for a second.

I scramble up the remaining two flights to Riss's room, ignoring the steadily increasing failure of my body; metal scrapes and bruises me, but I will not stop.

The lights go out across New York City just as I reach her open window, just as I knew they would.

It is 9.34 p.m., 13 July, and the great blackout of 1977 begins. There's no time to stop to look, but behind me a whole city is plunged into pitch darkness. I fall into the room, my shoulder hitting the corner of something hard, and sharp. The wardrobe.

'Riss,' I whisper, gripping the place where a bruise is forming. 'Riss?'

There is nothing, not a breath in the darkness, only the ticking of a clock on the hallway. My hands outstretched, I stumble against her bed, and feel its surface smooth and unruffled under my palms. Riss is not here, the attack happens here, just after the lights go out, but she isn't here so ... That should be a good thing, that should mean that she changed her mind, decided against meeting Delaney at all, that she is safe somewhere. Except I'm still here, and I still have this feeling of cold, hard fear in my heart.

She changed her plans because of me.

Riss doesn't think she needs a chaperone; she never has and why would she, with him? She's known him all her life. She trusts him completely. She's rearranged where she was going to meet him, because of me.

It's happening all over again – just some other location – because of me.

Where would she meet him, where?

Lightning flares, illuminating the room for a moment, followed by a deep roll of thunder, and I take my opportunity to find my way back to the window. There is nothing but darkness above and below.

It's strange to know that out there this vast city still exists, hidden in the darkness. Sirens wail in the distance, people start to wander out onto the street, standing in small shadowy groups, lit by the occasional torch or cigarette lighter, shouting to each other, perhaps to try and find comfort in the dense dark. Riss said her whole family, much of the neighbourhood, were going to the church for a fundraising social. If that where Delaney is, then that has to be where she is, she has to be meeting him there, or somewhere nearby. In any case, it's the only idea I have, and however this is all about to play out, one way or another I am running out of time.

Climbing back out of the window I make my descent as quickly as I can, down the almost-invisible fire escape. The sky rumbles and groans above me, the first few drops of rain sounding against the black metal, and I start to slip and slide as the rain becomes slick. As I near the bottom, my feet shoot out from under me, catching the sharp edge of the stair, a sharp rip of pain travels up my calf. I feel what is probably a trickle of blood running into my shoes as I slam onto the ground.

'Hey, who are you?' Some guy, probably a neighbour, sees me jumping out of his friend's home. 'What are you doing?'

'I'm sorry, I've got to go,' I call out, ducking out of his grasp and running as fast as I can down the middle of the street.

'Hey, you won't get away with this, you know!' he calls after me. 'We don't do things like that in Bay Ridge.'

Keeping my head down I run, surprised by how weightless I feel, how light and fast. The pain and weakness I felt climbing into Riss's room has evaporated, and now I'm fuelled by anger, fury so powerful it pumps blood to every corner of me.

The pavement offers no resistance to my footsteps; I am fast and I am true, flying to her, little more than a ghost now, and I wonder, just briefly, if I could run through the walls and buildings that stand in my way.

Every now and then the sky is bright with fierce flashes of electricity, slashing into the black, showing the empty streets in stark black and white. It's a ghost town, a city that seems to have suddenly arrived on the other side of the moon.

CHAPTER FIFTY-ONE

The church comes at me, out of nowhere, rising up towards the next lightning strike, fierce and angry, defiant. I can almost see its fury and anger, like sparks striking against the sky. This place that was meant for faith has been misused, and I know that Riss is in there. I know I'm in the right place. I know that this is it.

Struggling, I force open the heavy oak door, slipping in through the narrowest of gaps.

It's silent inside and dark, with just the votive candles flickering near the altar, and for a moment I am lost, I am thrown. Where is she?

Of course, she's not here. There must be a room somewhere, a place where the community meets up for events. Walking as fast as I can, I find the connecting door that will take me into the adjoining building, but it's locked. I rattle the handle, pounding on the door, but there is nothing, not a single sound on the other side, not a whisper.

Frantically, I run outside and around the side of the building. I can see a long window with flashes of light inside, maybe torches, more candles. Remembering the door the young girl stumbled out of that first day I came here, I search blindly along the wall, until I find it, my finger closing around the handle.

It opens when I try it.

The hall is full of people. A woman is sitting at a piano in the corner, and someone is passing around candles.

I scan the faces, looking for Riss, but I can't see her. I can't see Delaney either.

'Hi, is Marissa Lupo here?' I ask one person, moving on to the next before they can answer, knowing they will not have seen her. And then I see Stephanie, her face lit up as she holds her candle against the flame of another, in the process of passing light around the room.

'Stephanie,' I hiss. 'Where's Riss?'

'Here somewhere, I guess,' she says. 'What are you doing here?'

'I need to find her, it's important.'

'Who?' Michelle appears at our side.

'Riss. Have you seen her?'

'Oh yeah, she went to talk to Father Delaney, in the church.'

The door was locked.

Pushing my way through the crowds, I run back into the street, back into the dark silent church and shout his name.

'Delaney!'

'You again?' He appears like a shadow in the dark and I run into him, into his chest, so that he staggers backwards.

'Where is she? Where is she?' I shove him hard enough to make him stumble to the floor, and I fall onto him, driving my knees into his chest. The sky sets on fire and I see fear and surprise in his eyes.

'Where is she, what have you done?' I take the knife from my pocket, and there is no hesitation not a moment of regret as I hold it to his throat. This man means nothing to me. 'Tell me!'

'Please, I know it's wrong, I'm a priest, but I love her ...' he stutters, and I press hard.

'Love her, what do you know about love? Where's Riss?'

'Riss?' His eyes widen, white glowing in the candlelight. 'You're talking about Riss?'

'Don't lie to me.' I jab the blade harder against his throat. 'Where's Riss, where is she? She went to talk to you.'

'Y ... yes, but I didn't find her. I was going to meet her in the vestry, but she isn't there. P ... please ... let me go.'

'Where is she?' I ask him again.

'Last time I saw her, she was with that lawyer. Watkins Gillespie. He told her he could help out with something, that's all I know, I swear it. I'm not a bad man, just a weak one, please.'

And then I know; the reason I feel nothing for Delaney is because he is nothing.

Darkness pulls me down, down into the ground, and I see it all. A protected man, a trusted man, a man who has power and position. A lawyer who works for the mob.

And I was the one who pointed her out to him. I walked right into his office and asked him to look after her.

Watkins Gillespie is my father.

'Where did they go?' I get up, still wired with adrenalin.

'I don't know.'

There are so many places in the dark where they could go. Where would they be?

Delaney scrambles away from me against the wall.

The church; I feel her, I feel him. They are somewhere in the church.

The inside of the building yawns as I enter, gaping with secrets and shadows.

There is no sound, nothing. Delaney had said he was going to be in the vestry; perhaps they might be there. As soon as I begin to move down the aisle, I hear it. The slightest whimper, the scrape of wood against stone.

Standing perfectly still in the darkness, I wait for one more sound that will tell me where she is. I bleed into the darkness, become part of it, occupying every space it does, pressing into every corner and narrow hiding place.

A breath, fast and outward. A stifled cry. Turning round, I look up.

The choir's gallery.

Guesswork is all I have as I make it to a door to the left of the foyer and tug on it. It's locked. There is an identical door opposite and I race to that one. This one is open.

It's when I'm at the bottom of the stairs that I freeze, and what's left of the woman I used to be clamours and screams at me. What am I going to do at the top of these stairs? Every tiny particle I am screams at me to leave, to run away, but I can't.

I cannot.

This is the moment, the one moment in my life where I must be brave, where I must have courage. This is the moment, soon to be lost and forgotten forever, that will define me. This is the moment when my life will mean something. Only now, and then never again.

The void at the top of the stairs is nothing but darkness, and yet I know they are in here. Even though breaths are held tight, I can sense them, two heartbeats in the darkness. Looking around, every dark shape merges into another. Shroud-like sheets have been thrown over stacks of chairs or something. I walk a little further into what I sense is space.

'Riss?' My voice sounds unnaturally loud in the darkness. 'Are you OK?'

'Luna!' Her shriek pierces the dark. 'Run!'

I sense her breaking away, hurtling towards me in the dark, but something brings her down hard and she hits the floor, the sound of her breath being forced out of her.

Lightning strikes just as a hand, his hand, reaches out of the dark, reaching around her ankle and pulling her back into the shadows.

'You bitch,' Gillespie says, throwing Riss somewhere behind him. 'You came here to ruin my life, didn't you? You don't know who you're dealing with. You don't know what hell I will bring down on you and everyone you love.'

And I remember how I trusted him, how he was kind to me, how I wept on his shoulder. But I love Henry, my true father, and this man is nothing to me, nothing good, or kind.

'Let her go!' Screaming, I run at him, at where I think he is, with no idea what I am going to do in the seconds that follow, only that this is all I can do.

My trajectory stops when he grabs my hair and drags me to him. Pain burns through my scalp and down my neck, but there is a burning agony greater than that, of just being near him, knowing what he is. Knowing that half of the blood that is burning away to nothing in my veins right now comes from him. I kick him as hard as I can, and Riss arrives from behind leaping onto his back, pulling him away from me.

He releases his grip on me and I stumble back against the low balcony, feeling the weight of my body almost pendulum over the rail onto the stone floor below. I redress the balance just in time as I see him, the shadow of him, rise up again. Riss, wherever she is in the darkness, does not move or make a sound.

Gripping the rail, I force myself onto my feet with an almighty roar, so loud I can't believe it comes from me.

Launching myself at him, I clasp my hands around his face, refusing to relinquish my grip, even when his fingers encircle my wrists. Pain burns as he crushes my bones. But still, I fight, determined. He will look at me, my father; he will look into my blue eyes, so like his own.

'Is there no part of you left that cares?' I ask him. 'Is there no part of you left that wishes you weren't this man? You want to live the rest of life hating, and hurting and tearing people apart?'

All at once he is still, his eyes riveted to mine.

'You don't understand,' he says. 'When you've done the things I've done, seen the things I've seen, the time comes when you don't care anymore.'

He lets go of my wrists and I stumble backwards. It's now I think; now that I will grab him and pull him over the balcony. Father and daughter, we go together. I pray that it won't hurt.

Before I can move, he hurls himself at me in a rage, and for a moment I think it might be my creator who is also my destroyer, that both us are going over the railing, but I keep my grip as momentum propels him forwards, past me, above me, beyond me. There is a shout, cut short by a sickening thud. I wait for a scream of agony. But there is only silence.

My legs tremble as I pull myself into a standing position and peer into the darkness below. In the flickering light of the sea of votive candles, I can see him, sprawled broken across two rows of pews, his back twisted out of shape, his eyes open and blank, watching me. Staring at me, but seeing nothing. He's dead, I'm sure. But even so, I run down the stairs as fast as I can in the dark, and go to where he's sprawled, flung across a row of pews. His skin is already cooling as I lift his wrist and feel for a pulse. This time I wanted to be sure it was done.

'Did he hurt you?' I ask Riss as I return upstairs to find her still crouching in the corner, frozen by shock.

'Yes.' Her voice is trembling, and I almost weep when I hear it. 'Yes, my arms, my neck. He was choking me, I almost passed out ...'

'Did he ... ?'

'No, you came before he could. Oh God, Luna ...' She crawls through the darkness and into my arms, and as I hold her, this woman who was once my mother, my friend. I expect the world to set on fire around me, burning me away to embers, but it doesn't.

And I know why. I'm no longer hers, I'm no longer his. I am no longer anything.

A sense of deep peace settles in me as I hold Riss in my arms and she weeps, and talks of her fear and her shock, her certainty and her fury. I hold her and I listen.

'What are we going to say?' she asks me eventually.

'It's dark,' I say. 'There's a blackout and he fell. It was an accident. We don't have to say anything.'

'Did anyone see you come up here?'

'One person, Father Delaney. But he has just left town.'

'So, we don't have to tell anyone about what he was going to do?' she asks me.

I think for a moment. I am sure there have been others, others before Riss, but now there will be no more after, and that is the only justice I can offer those that came before. The next time they hear his name, they will hear that he is dead, and that might offer them some little comfort.

'No, we don't tell them anything. You tell them that you spoke to him, that he was going to talk to your father about Henry. That he heard a noise below, went to look and tripped and fell. And then you tell your family that you love Henry, and you want to marry him.'

'Will you be there with me?' she asks me, holding hard onto my wrist, and I want her to squeeze harder, I want to feel the pain.

'No.' I smile. 'I've got to go now. But you're safe, everything is OK. Just remember, remember to marry Henry and be happy, and one day all of this will just seem like a weird dream to you. And maybe ...' I hesitate, would it be so wrong to ask for one thing to be remembered by? 'Maybe if you have a daughter you'll call her Luna.'

Outside, as the lightning crackles on above, the heat builds all around me still, even in the night. I know it's not the summer but the fire inside me igniting in my brain, and this time burning brighter than a supernova, pulsing through my arteries, stopping and starting my heart, or what used to be my heart. The world goes dark and I feel the slam of the sidewalk against my head, and maybe that is the last thing that I will ever feel. This precious fragile vessel that has carried me so far and for so long is done, and the last thing I will see will be the silver of a waning moon, and the stars shining over Brooklyn, and the last thing I will feel is this all-abiding stillness. This peace.

CHAPTER FIFTY-TWO

I didn't expect to be able to see, but I can – or, at least, it seems like I am seeing, white. Brilliant white all around me, and it feels like I have woken up. It's unexpected.

I didn't expect to wake up to anything.

Perhaps this is heaven, perhaps some kind of limbo, where lost or decommissioned souls go to wait, maybe forever.

Except this white void smells of good coffee and bacon, and I feel hungry. Hunger is also unexpected.

Stretching out my fingers, I find that I do have fingers, which seems curious to me. Raising my hand in front of my face I look at them, long and pink. Steady and flexible, just your run-of-the-mill fingers, except to me they seem like miracles.

I sit up, my eyes adjusting to the blinding sunlight that is streaming in through the window. And I know where I am; I'm in the apartment at the top of Mrs Finkle's house. That's where I am.

How am I?

Did I fail? Did I somehow still fail, and I'm back here again?

Opening the door, there is laughter in the sitting room, Dad's and Pea's but another laugh too: my mother's laugh.

I follow the trail of their chatter, and, as I see them, I wonder if this is my exhausted, beaten-up brain's last gift to myself? This mirage of my family, my beautiful wonderful family.

'You're here,' I whisper. 'You're all here.'

'Where else would we be, numbskull,' Pea says, laughing.

'I knew we should have woken her earlier,' Mum says. 'She always gets so dumb when she has too much sleep.'

'Mum, I love you.' I run to her, falling onto my knees, wrapping my arms around her waist.

Laughing, she kisses the top of my head. 'Crazy child, I love you too.'

'Typical looney.' Pea sighs. 'Always wants to be parents' pet. Even on our first-ever family holiday to Brooklyn, she's trying to get all the attention.'

'Come and sit at the table,' Dad says. 'Eat your breakfast and then I am taking you on a day-long walking tour of movie locations.'

'We knew this day would come.' Pea laughs as I take a seat beside her. 'There can be no escape!'

'This is wonderful,' I say, sitting at the table, beaming at them each in turn. 'This is just lovely! I hope this lasts forever.'

'Maybe she's still drunk from dinner last night,' Pea says. 'Are you still drunk, Luna?'

That's when it begins, a sensation I have become familiar with. The slow process of memories dropping into me like coins into a slot machine. I remember that Mum and Dad wanted to come back to New York to celebrate the anniversary of their meeting. And for all of us to meet Aunt Stephanie and her family. I remember we went past the building which Mum and Aunt Stephanie sold for not enough money in the late 1980s and talked about how we could have been millionaires if we'd only kept it a bit longer. I remember a childhood full of sunshine and laughter, Christmases and kept promises. My sister, Pea, joyous and healthy and full of fun, a career as an illustrator that is just starting to grow. I remember I am happy; I remember I have the job of my dreams researching neutrinos in a lab in Oxford. I remember I am still me. And as each new memory blossoms, I sense an old pain or injury fading away, healed by the impossible.

The universe returned me, my soul, to my family. The universe gave me more than I could ever have hoped for; it gave me back life, not just any life, but my life. My life, but better. And then I wonder ... I can't help but wonder, a sudden sense of urgency grips me and I stand up abruptly.

'I have to go somewhere,' I say.

'In your pyjamas?' Mum's laugh is bright and beautiful.

'Oh!' I look down at myself. Running into the bedroom, I look around for anything to wear, jeans, a T-shirt. I jam my feet into a pair of Converse, and grabbing a hairbrush run it through my hair, which is when I stop and stare at my reflection.

Those strange blue eyes that never belonged have gone.

My eyes are brown now.

My beautiful brown eyes are just like my mother's. I look just like my mother, but with my father's chin – Henry's chin – and I know it is exactly how I am supposed to look.

Dropping the brush, I head out of the door, down the stairs as fast as I can, running onto 3rd Avenue, because suddenly, I have to know. I just have to know.

I stop outside the guitar shop and slowly turn to look.

A glitter-covered Gretsch turns slowly in this glass cabinet in the window, and deep sadness chimes somewhere inside my heart.

'You can't have everything,' I tell myself. 'You can have your father's chin, and your mother's eyes and still hope for ...'

As I turn around I catch my breath.

Across the street, a smartly painted shopfront catches my eye; the sign reads 'Bellamo's New Bakery and Bookstore'.

Very, very slowly, I cross the road and simply stare. He's alive. He's *here*.

Underneath the sign, a sliver of a crescent moon is painted, and the words, 'Always here for you.'

In all those years since I last saw him, it's not possible that he never met anyone else, loved someone else, is it? This, the sign, the words. They're just nostalgia, a memory. A memory of a strange girl he met one hot summer that probably has long since lost its meaning. That's all it is. Standing outside the bakery, I make myself look in through the window, and see that the front of the store area is a series of tables, and that bookshelves cover every wall. In the window are the latest bestsellers, and in the corner there's a little display of a book called *The Girl Who Came Back from the Moon*. It has Michael's name on the cover.

I smile, lit up with joy for him; he did it. He did what he wanted to do.

Then I feel it, someone looking at me, and I look past the glare of the glass and into the shop, and I see him standing perfectly still, staring back at me.

His face is weathered, his hair is silver around the temples, but he looks strong, fit and healthy. And he is still the most beautiful thing I have ever seen.

Opening the door, I step inside, and very slowly walk towards him.

He doesn't move.

'Hello,' I say. 'Do you remember me?'

'You came,' he says.

'I know,' I say. 'I'm sorry, I didn't mean to ... I mean it's been such a long time, and I know that ...' I laugh. 'You know what? I don't really know what to say. As far as I'm concerned we only said goodbye yesterday.'

'We did only say goodbye yesterday,' he says. 'In my heart we only said goodbye last night.'

'I told you not to wait for me.' I take one step closer.

'And I told you that I would because I had to,' he replies.

'So what does this mean?'

'It means the future has finally arrived,' he says.

EPILOGUE

Lazy bees drone on outside the window, and somewhere in the garden beyond I can hear Michael and Dad laughing about old times. Finally, Dad has gotten over the fact that I'm going to marry a man not much younger than him. Pea's voice is there too, high and loud, commanding attention, and I smile.

It all feels exactly right. Just as it should be.

Pushing the door of Mum's study open, I find another box, full of film. Most of them are labelled with a name, an event and a date, birthdays, weddings, holidays; there are hundreds of them, but I know the one I'm looking for.

It's when I'm about to give up, to call myself a fool, that I see it, pushed right to the back of a shelf, books stacked on top of it.

Film number four.

Glancing out of the window, I see Pea delivering a tray of drinks, and Mum returning to the kitchen; something smells wonderful.

Quickly I load the film onto the projector, and press play.

Prisms of light and colour flare and dance, before 3rd Avenue, Bay Ridge, Brooklyn, comes into focus, bright colours, intensified by the glare of the heat. A young man blows a kiss, a child pulls a face and an old woman waves the camera away with a smile. There is a cut, a moment of white, a thin, bright glare from the sun washing out the image. It adjusts and I catch my breath.

It's us, the two of us, caught together on this film, my mother and me in 1977, we're there. She laughs as I kiss her cheek. I freeze frame and stare at the image. Two women laughing, embracing, bonded by unbreakable love. Two brown-eyed women.

I start as the door opens, and Mum leans against the doorframe smiling.

'That was quite a day,' she says, coming into the room. 'A day and night I will never forget.'

She bends, her cheek meeting mine, and she kisses me once before she whispers, 'Thank you. Thank you for being brave.'

AUTHOR'S NOTE

Time is a curious thing. We all know how it seems to trickle through our fingers when all we want is a few seconds more.

A few seconds more to hold the ones we love, savour that longed-for sleep, watch the sun go down or the moon rise. And everyone has endured a lesson, a meeting or a sermon, and wondered if the clock on the wall had stopped, or even starting ticking backwards, and that perhaps they might be forced to sit there forever, time's hostage.

When I was younger, I thought I had forever to start my life for real, and it's not until half of it slips you by, in a blink of an eye, that you realise it has all been real, it's been all you will have had. All those years of waiting when you could have been doing.

It's well documented that in moments of extreme danger, your brain slows time down, or at least that's the way you perceive it, allowing you the time and space to react to what is happening around you, a chance to avoid that high-speed collision or pull back from that cliff edge. A chance to make a life or death decision that will alter the course of events.

I'm a writer. I try to capture emotions, moments, on the page, and hold on to them forever, captured in words. It's that desire to keep hold of those rare golden seconds that makes me human. Our very machinery is built to make time stand still.

Many scientists now believe that the moment of death, though physically instantaneous, unravels itself in the mind in slow motion, flooding the brain with neurochemicals that can trigger hallucinations that, to the person experiencing them, can seem to go on for hours, days – maybe even years. We can only guess at why this happens, a sort of inbuilt anaesthesia to protect us from the shock of dying, perhaps. Or, as some people believe, a glimpse into heaven. Or maybe that tunnel with the light at the end of it leads to another universe entirely.

How time works within us is something that is only partially understood; how time works across the whole of the universe is something we can only comprehend by the set of rules we impose on it. We need years, months, days, hours, minutes and seconds to make logic from entropy, the decay that began the moment both the universe and we were born; to make sense of our lives passing and to understand why we can't have back what we have lost. Time passes, flowing away from us never to return, impossible to revisit. Past, present and future – that is how we make sense of the world. But sometimes, the one thing we forget, for all of our rules, theories and ideas that we impose on this strange unfathomable place we miraculously exist in, is that we didn't make the universe.

The universe made us.

Rowan Coleman, 4 August 2016

ACKNOWLEDGEMENTS

There are so many people to thank who have come on this journey with me, and cheered me on all the way.

Thank you to my wonderful publisher and editor Gillian Green, who is always unfailingly supportive and insightful, and who never tired of having complicated time travel conversations with me. And to the amazing Ebury team, I feel very lucky to be part of, including Emily Yau, Tessa Henderson, Stephenie Naulls and everyone there who works so hard on my behalf.

I can't thank my brilliant agent and dear friend Lizzy Kremer enough. She is simply one of the best humans I know and I'm grateful every day to have her on my side; not to mention the whole fantastic David Higham team, including Harriet Moore, Laura West, Alice Howe, Emma Jamison, Emily Randle, Camilla Dubini, Margaux Vialleron and Georgina Ruffhead.

Last year an old school friend, Michelle Knight, bid on a charity auction to have her name included in this book and the acknowledgements, and it's great that I get to include someone I grew up with; thank you Michelle.

Thank you to my father-in-law John Evans, for lending me his 70s Pentax and talking me through film photography. And to Lisa J Hill who answered my questions on neuroscience. Thank you to the people of Bay Ridge, Brooklyn, where I spent several very lovely, very hot days working out the places where Riss and Michael walked and lived, and chatting to the community about their memories of the 70s.

A writer is nothing without the support of faithful readers. Thank you so much to mine. I feel very lucky to have readers who are willing to come on these journeys with me. A special mention to Tracy Fenton and The Book Club members who have been amazing over the last couple of years.

To all the brilliant bloggers who never tire of reading and championing books. You have my heartfelt thanks.

My dear friends Julie Cohen, Tamsyn Murray, Miranda Dickinson, Kate Harrison, C.L. Taylor, Kirstie Seaman, Catherine Rogers, Margie Harris, Jenny Matthews, Katy Regan and everyone who is there for me in good times and bad. I'm so lucky to have you in my life.

The writers' community is a very warm and supportive place, so thank you to all the writers I interact with every day, and who make the lonely business of book writing much more fun.

Finally, thank you to my family, who I love more than I can say: my hilarious and inspirational children, who give me something to be thankful for every day and, of course, my husband Adam, who I love very much and who probably doesn't know how much he helps me stay on the right side of sane. Of course, I mustn't forget my dogs, Blossom and Bluebell, who have accompanied me on many long walks and sat at my feet as I have worked this book out.

As I write this, I realise if I had the opportunity to go back in time, I wouldn't change a thing.

'one of my favourite writers'
Cara Delevingne

'Hauntingly beautiful,
heart-rending and unique!'
Miranda Dickinson

'magical, wonderful
and beautifully written'
Trisha Ashley

'a girls' own Back to the
future story set in New York'.
Amanda Craig

'Disco, time travel,
fierce love in all its forms...'
Katy Regan

'impossibly page-turning,
impossibly beautiful'.
Kate Harrison

'a gorgeous book.'
Milly Johnson

'truly a thing of great beauty.'
Paul Burston